I0611616

THE MAJOR

RALPH CONNOR

1st WORLD
LIBRARY
Literary Society

The Major

Ralph Connor

© 1st World Library, 2007
PO Box 2211
Fairfield, IA 52556
www.1stworldlibrary.com
First Edition

LCCN: 2007927854

Softcover ISBN: 978-1-4218-4567-8
Hardcover ISBN: 978-1-4218-4483-1
eBook ISBN: 978-1-4218-4651-4

Purchase *"The Major"*
as a traditional bound book at:
www.1stWorldLibrary.com/purchase.asp?ISBN=978-1-4218-4567-8

1st World Library is a literary, educational organization
dedicated to:

- Creating a free internet library of downloadable ebooks

- Hosting writing competitions and offering book
publishing scholarships.

Interested in more 1st World Library books?
contact: literacy@1stworldlibrary.com
Check us out at: www.1stworldlibrary.com

1ˢᵗ World Library Literary Society

Giving Back to the World

"If you want to work on the core problem, it's early school literacy."

- James Barksdale, former CEO of Netscape

"No skill is more crucial to the future of a child, or to a democratic and prosperous society, than literacy."

- Los Angeles Times

"Literacy... means far more than learning how to read and write... The aim is to transmit... knowledge and promote social participation."

- UNESCO

"Literacy is not a luxury, it is a right and a responsibility. If our world is to meet the challenges of the twenty-first century we must harness the energy and creativity of all our citizens."

- President Bill Clinton

"Parents should be encouraged to read to their children, and teachers should be equipped with all available techniques for teaching literacy, so the varying needs and capacities of individual kids can be taken into account."

- Hugh Mackay

CONTENTS

CHAPTER I

THE COWARD

Spring had come. Despite the many wet and gusty days which April had thrust in rude challenge upon reluctant May, in the glory of the triumphant sun which flooded the concave blue of heaven and the myriad shaded green of earth, the whole world knew to-day, the whole world proclaimed that spring had come. The yearly miracle had been performed. The leaves of the maple trees lining the village street unbound from their winter casings, the violets that lifted brave blue eyes from the vivid grass carpeting the roadside banks, the cherry and plum blossoms in the orchards decking the still leafless trees with their pink and white favours, the timid grain tingeing with green the brown fields that ran up to the village street on every side—all shouted in chorus that spring had come. And all the things with new blood running wild in their veins, the lambs of a few days still wobbly on ridiculous legs skipping over and upon the huge boulders in farmer Martin's meadow, the birds thronging the orchard trees, the humming insects rioting in the genial sun, all of them gave token of strange new impulses calling for something more than mere living because spring had come.

Upon the topmost tip of the taller of the twin poplars that

flanked the picket gate opening upon the Gwynnes' little garden sat a robin, his head thrown back to give full throat to the song that was like to burst his heart, monotonous, unceasing, rapturous. On the door step of the Gwynnes' house, arrested on the threshold by the robin's song, stood the Gwynne boy of ten years, his eager face uplifted, himself poised like a bird for flight.

"Law-r-ence," clear as a bird call came the voice from within.

"Mo-th-er," rang the boy's voice in reply, high, joyous and shrill.

"Ear-ly! Remember!"

"Ri-ght a-way af-ter school. Good-bye, mo-ther, dear," called the boy.

"W-a-i-t," came the clear, birdlike call again, and in a moment the mother came running, stood beside the boy, and followed his eye to the robin on the poplar tree. "A brave little bird," she said. "That is the way to meet the day, with a brave heart and a bright song. Goodbye, boy." She kissed him as she spoke, giving him a slight pat on the shoulder. "Away you go."

But the boy stood fascinated by the bird so gallantly facing his day. His mother's words awoke in him a strange feeling. "A brave heart and a bright song"—so the knights in the brave days of old, according to his Stories of the Round Table, were wont to go forth. In imitation of the bird, the boy threw back his head, and with another cheery good-bye to his mother, sprang clear of the steps and ran down the grass edged path, through the gate and out onto the village street. There he stood first looking up the country road which in the village became a street.

There was nothing to be seen except that in the Martin orchard "Ol' Martin" was working with his team under the trees which came in rows down to the road. Finding nothing to interest him there, he turned toward the village and his eyes searched the street. Opposite the Gwynnes' gate, Dr. Bush's house stood back among the trees, but there was no sign of life about it. Further down on the same side of the street, the Widow Martin's cottage, with porch vine covered and windows bright with flowers, hid itself under a great spreading maple. In front of the cottage the Widow Martin herself was busy in the garden. He liked the Widow Martin but found her not sufficiently exciting to hold him this spring morning. A vacant lot or two and still on the same side came the blacksmith's shop just at the crossroads, and across the street from it his father's store. But neither at the blacksmith's shop nor at the store across from it was there anything to awaken even a passing interest. Some farmers' teams and dogs, Pat Larkin's milk wagon with its load of great cans on its way to the cheese factory and some stray villagers here and there upon the street intent upon their business. Up the street his eye travelled beyond the crossroads where stood on the left Cheatley's butcher shop and on the right McKenny's hotel with attached sheds and outhouses. Over the bridge and up the hill the street went straight away, past the stone built Episcopal Church whose spire lifted itself above the maple trees, past the Rectory, solid, square and built of stone, past the mill standing on the right back from the street beside the dam, over the hill, and so disappeared. The whole village seemed asleep and dreaming among its maple trees in the bright sunlight.

Throwing another glance at the robin still singing on the treetop overhead, the boy took from his pocket a mouth-organ, threw back his head, squared his elbows out from his sides to give him the lung room he needed, and in obedience to a sharp word of command after a preliminary tum, tum, tum, struck up the ancient triumph hymn in memory of that hero of the underground railroad by which so many slaves of the South in bygone days made their escape "up No'th" to Canada and to freedom.

"Glory, glory, hallelujah, his soul goes marching on." By means of "double-tongueing," a recently acquired accomplishment, he was able to give a full brass band effect to his hymn of freedom. Many villagers from door or window cast a kindly and admiring eye upon the gallant little figure stepping to his own music down the street. He was brass band, conductor, brigadier general all in one, and behind him marched an army of heroes off for war and deathless glory, invisible and invincible. To the Widow Martin as he swung past the leader flung a wave of his hand. With a tender light in her old eyes the Widow Martin waved back at him. "God bless his bright face," she murmured, pausing in her work to watch the upright little figure as he passed along. At the blacksmith's shop the band paused.

Tink, tink, tink, tink,
Tink, tink-a-tink-tink-tink.
Tink tink, tink, tink,
Tink, tink-a-tink-tink-tink.

The conductor graduated the tempo so as to include the rhythmic beat of the hammer with the other instruments in his band. The blacksmith looked, smiled and let his hammer fall in consonance with the beat of the boy's hand, and for some moments there was glorious harmony between anvil and mouth organ and the band invisible. At the store door across the street the band paused long enough simply to give and receive an answering salute from the storekeeper, who smiled upon his boy as he marched past. At the crossroads the band paused, marking time. There was evidently a momentary uncertainty in the leader's mind as to direction. The road to the right led straight, direct, but treeless, dusty, uninviting, to the school. It held no lure for the leader and his knightly following. Further on a path led in a curve under shady trees and away from the street. It made the way to school longer, but the lure of the curving, shady path was irresistible. Still stepping bravely to the old abolitionist hymn, the procession moved along, swung into the path under the trees and suddenly came to a halt. With a magnificent flourish the band concluded its triumphant hymn and with the conductor and brigadier the whole brigade stood rigidly at attention. The cause of this sudden halt was to be seen at the foot of a maple tree in the person of a fat lump of good natured boy flesh supine upon the ground.

"Hello, Joe; coming to school?"

"Ugh," grunted Joe, from the repose of limitless calm.

"Come on, then, quick, march." Once more the band struck up its hymn.

"Hol' on, Larry, it's plenty tam again," said Joe. The band came to a stop. "I don' lak dat school me," he continued, still immersed in calm.

Joe's struggles with an English education were indeed tragically pathetic. His attempts with aspirates were a continual humiliation to himself and a joy to the whole school. No wonder he "no lak dat school." Besides, Joe was a creature of the open fields. His French Canadian father, Joe Gagneau, "Ol' Joe," was a survival of a bygone age, the glorious golden age of the river and the bush, of the shanty and the raft, of the axe and the gun, the age of Canadian romance, of daring deed, of wild adventure.

"An' it ees half-hour too queek," persisted Joe. "Come on hup to de dam." A little worn path invited their feet from the curving road, and following their feet, they found themselves upon a steep embankment which dammed the waters into a pond that formed the driving power for the grist mill standing near. At the farther end of the pond a cedar bush interposed a barrier to the sight and suggested mysterious things beyond. Back of the cedar barrier a woods of great trees, spruce, balsam, with tall elms and maples on the higher ground beyond, offered deeper mysteries and delights unutterable. They knew well the cedar swamp and the woods beyond. Partridges drummed there, rabbits darted along their beaten runways, and Joe had seen a woodcock, that shyest of all shy birds, disappear in glancing, shadowy flight, a ghostly, silent denizen of the ghostly, silent spaces of the forest. Even as they gazed upon that inviting line of woods, the boys could see and hear the bluejays flash in swift flight from tree to tree and scream their joy of rage and love. From the farther side of the pond two boys put out in a flat-bottomed boat.

"There's big Ben and Mop," cried Larry eagerly. "Hello, Ben," he called across the pond. "Goin' to school?"

"Yap," cried Mop, so denominated from the quantity and cut of the hair that crowned his head. Ben was at the oars which creaked and thumped between the pins, but were steadily driving the snub-nosed craft on its toilsome way past the boys.

"Hello, Ben," cried Larry. "Take us in too."

"All right," said Ben, heading the boat for the bank. "Let me take an oar, Ben," said Larry, whose experience upon the world of waters was not any too wide.

"Here, where you goin'," cried Mop, as the boat slowly but surely pointed toward the cedars. "You stop pulling, Ben. Now, Larry, pull around again. There now, she's right. Pull, Ben." But Ben sat rigid with his eyes intent upon the cedars.

"What's the matter, Ben?" said Larry. Still Ben sat with fixed gaze.

"By gum, he's in, boys," said Ben in a low voice. "I thought he had his nest in one of them stubs."

"What is it—in what stub?" inquired Larry, his voice shrill with excitement.

"That big middle stub, there," said Ben. "It's a woodpecker. Say, let's pull down and see it." Under Mop's direction the old scow gradually made its way toward the big stub.

They explored the stub, finding in it a hole and in the hole a nest, the mother and father woodpeckers meanwhile flying in wild agitation from stub to stub and protesting with shrill cries against the intruders. Then they each must climb up and feel the eggs lying soft and snug in their comfy cavity. After that they all must discuss the probable time of hatching, the likelihood of there being other nests in other stubs which they proceeded to visit. So the eager moments gaily passed into minutes all unheeded, till inevitable recollection dragged them back from the world of adventure and romance to that of stern duty and dull toil.

"Say, boys, we'll be late," cried Larry, in sudden panic, seizing his oar. "Come on, Ben, let's go."

"I guess it's pretty late now," replied Ben, slowly taking

up his oar.

"Dat bell, I hear him long tam," said Joe placidly. "Oh, Joe!" cried Larry in distress. "Why didn't you tell us?"

Joe shrugged his shoulders. He was his own master and superbly indifferent to the flight of time. With him attendance at school was a thing of more or less incidental obligation.

"We'll catch it all right," said Mop with dark foreboding. "He was awful mad last time and said he'd lick any one who came late again and keep him in for noon too."

The prospect was sufficiently gloomy.

"Aw, let's hurry up anyway," cried Larry, who during his school career had achieved a perfect record for prompt and punctual attendance.

In ever deepening dejection the discussion proceeded until at length Mop came forward with a daring suggestion.

"Say, boys, let's wait until noon. He won't notice any-thing. We can easily fool him."

This brought no comfort to Larry, however, whose previous virtues would only render this lapse the more conspicuous. A suggestion of Joe's turned the scale.

"Dat woodchuck," he said, "he's got one hole on de hill by dere. He's big feller. We dron heem out."

"Come on, let's," cried Mop. "It will be awful fun to drown the beggar out."

"Guess we can't do much this morning, anyway," said Ben, philosophically making the best of a bad job. "Let's go, Larry." And much against his will, but seeing no way out of the dilemma, Larry agreed.

They explored the woodchuck hole, failing to drown out that cunning subterranean architect who apparently had provided lines of retreat for just such emergencies as confronted him now. Wearied of the woodchuck, they ranged the bush seeking and finding the nests of bluejays and of woodpeckers, and in a gravel pit those of the sand martens. Joe led them to the haunts of the woodcock, but that shy bird they failed to glimpse. Long before the noon hour they felt the need of sustenance and found that Larry's lunch divided among the four went but a small way in satisfying their pangs of hunger. The other three, carefree and unconcerned for what the future might hold, roamed the woods during the afternoon, but to Larry what in other circumstances would have been a day of unalloyed joy, brought him only a present misery and a dread for the future. The question of school for the afternoon was only mentioned to be dismissed. They were too dirty and muddy to venture into the presence of the master. Consequently the obvious course was to wait until four o'clock when joining the other children they might slip home unnoticed.

The afternoon soon began to lag. The woods had lost their first glamour. Their games grew to be burdensome. They were weary and hungry, and becoming correspondingly brittle in temper. Already Nemesis was on their trail. Sick at heart and weighted with forebodings, Larry listened to the plans of the other boys by which they expected to elude the consequences of their truancy. In the discussion of their plans Larry took no part. They offered him no hope. He knew that if he were prepared to lie, as they had cheerfully decided, his simple word would carry him through at home. But there the difficulty arose. Was he willing to lie? He had never lied to his mother in all his life. He visualised her face as she listened to him recounting his falsified tale of the day's doings and unconsciously he groaned aloud.

"What's the matter with you, Larry?" inquired Mop, noticing his pale face.

"Oh, nothing; it's getting a little cold, I guess."

"Cold!" laughed Mop. "I guess you're getting scared all right."

To this Larry made no reply. He was too miserable, too tired to explain his state of mind. He was doubtful whether he could explain to Mop or to Joe his unwillingness to lie to his mother.

"It don't take much to scare you anyway," said Mop with an ugly grin.

The situation was not without its anxieties to Mop, for while he felt fairly confident as to his ability to meet successfully his mother's cross examination, there was always a possibility of his father's taking a hand, and that filled him with a real dismay. For Mr. Sam Cheatley, the village butcher, was a man of violent temper, hasty in his judgments and merciless in his punishment. There was a possibility of unhappy consequences for Mop in spite of his practiced ability in deception. Hence his nerves were set a-jangling, and his temper, never very certain, was rather on edge. The pale face of the little boy annoyed him, and the little whimsical smile which never quite left his face confronted him like an insult.

"You're scared," reiterated Mop with increasing contempt,

Ralph Connor

"and you know you're scared. You ain't got any spunk anyway. You ain't got the spunk of a louse." With a quick grip he caught the boy by the collar (he was almost twice Larry's size), and with a jerk landed him on his back in a brush heap. The fall brought Larry no physical hurt, but the laughter of Joe and especially of big Ben, who in his eyes was something of a hero, wounded and humiliated him. The little smile, however, did not leave his face and he picked himself up and settled his coat about his collar.

"You ain't no good anyway," continued Mop, with the native instinct of the bully to worry his victim. "You can't play nothin' and you can't lick nobody in the whole school."

Both of these charges Larry felt were true. He was not fond of games and never had he experienced a desire to win fame as a fighter.

"Aw, let him alone, can't you, Mop?" said big Ben. "He ain't hurtin' you none."

"Hurtin' me," cried Mop, who for some unaccountable reason had worked himself into a rage. "He couldn't hurt me if he tried. I could lick him on my knees with one hand behind my back. I believe Joe there could lick him with one hand tied behind his back."

"I bet he can't," said Ben, measuring Larry with his eye and desiring to defend him from this degrading accusation. "I bet he'd put up a pretty fine scrap," continued Ben, "if he had to." Larry's heart warmed to his champion.

"Yes, if he had to," replied Mop with a sneer. "But he would never have to. He wouldn't fight a flea. Joe can lick him with one hand, can't you, Joe?"

"I donno. I don' want fight me," said Joe.

"No, I know you don't want to, but you could, couldn't you?" persisted Mop. Joe shrugged his shoulders. "Ha, I told you so. Hurrah for my man," cried Mop, clapping Joe on the back and pushing him toward Larry.

Ben began to scent sport. He was also conscious of a rising resentment against Mop's exultant tone and manner.

"I bet you," he said, "if Larry wanted to, he could lick Joe even if he had both hands, but if Joe's one hand is tied behind his back, why Larry would just whale the tar out of him. But Larry does not want to fight."

"No," jeered Mop, "you bet he don't, he ain't got it in him. I bet you he daren't knock a chip off Joe's shoulder, and I will tie Joe's hand behind his back with his belt. Now there he is, bring your man on. There's a chip on his shoulder too."

Larry looked at Joe, the little smile still on his face. "I don't want to fight Joe. What would I fight Joe for?" he said.

"I told you so," cried Mop, dancing about. "He ain't got no fight in him.

> Take a dare,
> Take a dare,
> Chase a cat,
> And hunt a hare."

Ben looked critically at Larry as if appraising the quality of his soul. "Joe can't lick you with one hand tied behind his back, can he, Larry?"

"I don't want to fight Joe," persisted Larry still smiling.

"Ya, ya," persisted Mop. "Here, Joe, you knock this chip off Larry's shoulder." Mop placed the gauge of battle on Larry's shoulder. "Go ahead, Joe."

To Joe a fight with a friend or a foe was an event of common occurrence. With even a more dangerous opponent than Larry he would not have hesitated. For to decline a fight was with Joe utterly despicable. So placing himself in readiness for the blow that should have been the inevitable consequence, he knocked the chip off Larry's shoulder. Still Larry smiled at him.

"Aw, your man's no good. He won't fight," cried Mop with unspeakable disgust. "I told you he wouldn't fight. Do you know why he won't fight? His mother belongs to that people, them Quakers, that won't fight for anything. He's a coward an' his mother's a coward before him."

The smile faded from Larry's lips. His face which had been pale flamed a quick red, then as quickly became dead white. He turned from Joe and looked at the boy who was tormenting him. Mop was at least four years older, strongly and heavily built. For a moment Larry stood as though estimating Mop's fighting qualities. Then apparently making up his mind that on ordinary terms, owing to his lack in size and in strength, he was quite unequal to his foe, he looked quickly about him and his eye fell upon a stout and serviceable beechwood stake. With quiet deliberation he seized the club and began walking slowly toward Mop, his eyes glittering as if with madness, his face white as that of the dead. So terrifying was his appearance that Mop began to back away. "Here you, look out," he cried, "I will smash you." But Larry still moved steadily upon him. His white face, his burning eyes, his steady advance was more than Mop could endure. His courage broke. He turned and incontinently fled. Whirling the stick over his head, Larry flung the club with all his might after him. The club caught the fleeing Mop fairly between the shoulders. At the same time his foot caught a root. Down he went upon his face, uttering cries of deadly terror.

"Keep him off, keep him off. He will kill me, he will kill me."

But Larry having shot his bolt ignored his fallen enemy, and without a glance at him, or at either of the other boys, or without a word to any of them, he walked away through the wood, and deaf to their calling disappeared through the cedar swamp and made straight for home and to his mother. With even, passionless voice, with almost no sign of penitence, he told her the story of the day's truancy.

As her discriminating eye was quick in discerning his penitence, so her forgiveness was quick in meeting his sin. But though her forgiveness brought the boy a certain measure of relief he seemed almost to take it for granted, and there still remained on his face a look of pain and of more than pain that puzzled his mother. He seemed to be in a maze of uncertainty and doubt and fear. His mother could not understand his distress, for Larry had told her nothing of his encounter with Mop. Throughout the evening there pounded through the boy's memory the terrible words, "He is a coward and his mother is a coward before him." Through his father's prayer at evening worship those words continued to beat upon his brain. He tried to prepare his school lessons for the day following, but upon the page before his eyes the same words took shape. He could not analyse his unutterable sense of shame. He had been afraid to fight. He knew he was a coward, but there was a deeper shame in which his mother was involved. She was a Quaker, he knew, and he had a more or less vague idea that Quakers would not fight. Was she then a coward? That any reflection should be made upon his mother stabbed him to the heart. Again and again Mop's sneering, grinning face appeared before his eyes. He felt that he could have gladly killed him in the woods, but after all, the paralysing thought ever recurred that what Mop said was true. His mother was a coward! He put his head down upon his books and groaned aloud.

"What is it, dear?" inquired his mother.

"I am going to bed, mother," he said.

"Is your head bad?" she asked.

"No, no, mother. It is nothing. I am tired," he said, and went upstairs.

Before she went to sleep the mother, as was her custom, looked in upon him. The boy was lying upon his face with his arms flung over his head, and when she turned him over to an easier position, on the pillow and on his cheeks were the marks of tears. Gently she pushed back the thick, black, wavy locks from his forehead, and kissed him once and again. The boy turned his face toward her. A long sobbing sigh came from his parted lips. He opened his eyes.

"That you, mother?" he asked, the old whimsical smile at his lips. "Good-night."

He settled down into the clothes and in a moment was fast asleep. The mother stood looking down upon her boy. He had not told her his trouble, but her touch had brought him comfort, and for the rest she was content to wait.

CHAPTER II

A FIGHT FOR FREEDOM

The village schoolhouse was packed to the door. Over the crowded forms there fell a murky light from the smoky swinging lamp that left dark unexplored depths in the corners of the room. On the walls hung dilapidated maps at angles suggesting the interior of a ship's cabin during a storm, or a party of revellers, returning homeward, after the night before, gravely hilarious. Behind the platform a blackboard, cracked into irregular spaces, preserved the mental processes of the pupils during their working hours, and in sharp contrast to these the terribly depressing perfection of the teacher's exemplar in penmanship, which reminded the self-complacent slacker that "Eternal vigilance is the price of freedom."

It was an evangelistic meeting. Behind the table, his face illumined by the lamp thereon, stood a man turning over the leaves of a hymn book. His aspect suggested a soul, gentle, mild and somewhat abstracted from its material environment. The lofty forehead gave promise of an idealism capable of high courage, indeed of sacrifice—a promise, however, belied somewhat by an irresolute chin partly hidden by a straggling beard. But the face was sincere and tenderly human. At his side upon the platform sat his wife behind a little portable organ, her face equally

Ralph Connor

gentle, sincere and irresolute.

The assembly—with the extraordinary patience that characterises public assemblies—waited for the opening of the meeting, following with attentive eyes the vague and trifling movements of the man at the table. Occasionally there was a rumble of deep voices in conversation, and in the dark corners subdued laughter—while on the front benches the animated and giggling whispering of three little girls tended to relieve the hour from an almost superhuman gravity.

At length with a sudden acquisition of resolution the evangelist glanced at his watch, rose, and catching up a bundle of hymn books from the table thrust them with unnecessary energy into the hands of a boy who sat on the side bench beside his mother. The boy was Lawrence Gwynne.

"Take these," said the man, "and distribute them, please."

Lawrence taken thus by surprise paled, then flushed a quick red. He glanced up at his mother and at her slight nod took the books and distributed them among the audience on one side of the room while the evangelist took the other. As the lad passed from bench to bench with his books he was greeted with jocular and slightly jeering remarks in undertone by the younger members of the company, which had the effect of obviously increasing the ineptitude of his thin nervous fingers, but could not quite dispel the whimsical smile that lingered about the corners of his mouth and glanced from the corners of his grey-blue eyes.

The meeting opened with the singing of a popular hymn which carried a refrain catchy enough but running to doggerel. Another hymn followed and another. Then abruptly the evangelist announced,

"Now we shall have a truly GREAT hymn, a hymn you must sing in a truly great way, in what we call the grand style, number three hundred and sixty-seven."

Then in a voice, deep, thrilling, vibrant with a noble emotion, he read the words:

> "When I survey the wondrous cross
> On which the Prince of Glory died,
> My richest gain I count but loss,
> And pour contempt on all my pride."

They sang the verse, and when they had finished he stood looking at them in silence for a moment or two, then announced solemnly:

"Friends, that will not do for this hymn. Sing it with your hearts. Listen to me."

Then he sang a verse in a deep, strong baritone.

"Now try."

Timidly they obeyed him.

"No, no, not at all," he shouted at them. "Listen."

Again with exquisitely distinct articulation and in a tone rich in emotion and carrying in it the noble, penetrating pathos of the great words in which is embodied the passion of that heart subduing world tragedy. He would not let them try it again, but alone sang the hymn to the end. By the spell of his voice he had gripped them by the heart. The giggling girls in the front seat sat gazing at him with open mouths and lifted eyes. From every corner of the room faces once dull were filled with a great expectant look.

"You will never sing those words as you should," he cried, "until you know and feel the glory of that wondrous cross. Never, never, never." His voice rose in a passionate crescendo.

After he had finished singing the last great verse, he let his eyes wander over the benches until they rested upon the face of the lad on the side bench near him.

"Aha, boy," he cried. "You can sing those words. Try that last verse."

The boy stared, fascinated, at him.

"Sing the last verse, boy," commanded the evangelist, "sing."

As if impelled by another will than his own, the boy slowly, with his eyes still fastened on the man's face, threw back his head and began to sing. His voice rose, full, strong, in a quaint imitation in method of articulation and in voice production of the evangelist himself. At the third line of the verse the evangelist joined in great massive tones, beating time vigorously in a rallentando.

"Love so amazing, so divine,
Demands my soul, my life, my all."

The effect was a great emotional climax, the spiritual atmosphere was charged with fervour. The people sat rigid, fixed in their places, incapable of motion, until released by the invitation of the leader, "Let us pray." The boy seemed to wake as from a sleep, glanced at his mother, then at the faces of the people in the room, sat down, and quickly covered his face with his hands and so remained during the prayer.

The dramatic effect of the singing was gradually dispelled in the prayer and in a Scripture reading which followed. By the time the leader was about to begin his address, the people had almost relapsed into their normal mental and spiritual condition of benevolent neutrality. A second time a text was announced, when abruptly the door opened and up the aisle, with portentous impressiveness as of a stately ocean liner coming to berth, a man advanced whose presence seemed to fill the room and give it the feeling of being unpleasantly crowded. A buzz went through the seats. "The Rector! The Rector!" The evangelist gazed upon the approaching form and stood as if incapable of proceeding until this impressive personage should come to rest. Deliberately the Rector advanced to the side bench upon which Larry and his mother were seated, and slowly swinging into position calmly viewed the man upon the platform, the woman at the organ, the audience filling the room and then definitely came to anchor upon the bench.

The preacher waited until this manoeuvre had been successfully accomplished, coughed nervously, made as if to move in the direction of the important personage on the side bench, hesitated, and finally with an air of embarrassment once more announced his text. At once the Rector was upon his feet.

"Will you pardon me, sir," he began with elaborate politeness. "Do I understand you're a clergyman?"

"Oh, no, sir," replied the evangelist, "just a plain preacher."

"You are not in any Holy Orders then?"

"Oh, no, sir."

"Are you an ordained or accredited minister of any of the—ah—dissenting bodies?"

"Not exactly, sir."

"Then, sir," demanded the Rector, "may I ask by what authority you presume to exercise the functions of the holy ministry and in my parish?"

"Well—really—sir, I do not know why I—"

"Then, sir, let me tell you this will not be permitted," said the Rector sternly. "There are regularly ordained and accredited ministers of the Church and of all religious bodies represented in this neighbourhood, and your ministrations are not required."

"But surely, sir," said the evangelist hurriedly as if anxious to get in a word, "I may be permitted in this free country to preach the Gospel."

"Sir, there are regularly ordained and approved ministers of the Gospel who are quite capable of performing this duty. I won't have it, sir. I must protect these people from unlicensed, unregulated—ah—persons, of whose character and antecedents we have no knowledge. Pray, sir," cried the Rector, taking a step toward the man on the platform, "whom do you represent?"

The evangelist drew himself up quietly and said, "My Lord and Master, sir. May I ask whom do you represent?"

It was a deadly thrust. For the first time during the encounter the Rector palpably gave ground.

"Eh? Ah—sir—I—ah—ahem—my standing in this community is perfectly assured as an ordained clergyman of the Church of England in Canada. Have you any organisation or church, any organised Christian body to which you adhere and to which you are responsible?"

"Yes."

"What is that body?"

"The Church of Christ—the body of believers."

"Is that an organised body with ordained ministers and holy sacraments?"

"We do not believe in a paid ministry with special privileges and powers," said the evangelist. "We believe that every disciple has a right to preach the glorious Gospel."

"Ah, then you receive no support from any source in this ministry of yours?"

The evangelist hesitated. "I receive no salary, sir."

"No support?"

"I receive no regular salary," reiterated the evangelist.

"Do not quibble, sir," said the Rector sternly. "Do you receive any financial support from any source whatever in your mission about the country?"

"I receive—" began the evangelist.

"Do you or do you not?" thundered the Rector.

"I was about to say that my expenses are paid by my society."

"Thank you, no more need be said. These people can judge for themselves."

"I am willing that they should judge, but I remind you that there is another Judge."

"Yes, sir," replied the Rector with portentous solemnity, "there is, before whom both you and I must stand."

"And now then," said the evangelist, taking up the Bible, "we may proceed with our meeting."

"No, sir," replied the Rector, stepping upon the platform. "I will not permit it."

"You have no right to—"

"I have every right to protect this community from heretical and disingenuous, not to say dishonest, persons."

"You call me dishonest?"

"I said disingenuous."

The evangelist turned toward the audience. "I protest against this intrusion upon this meeting. I appeal to the audience for British fair play."

Murmurs were heard from the audience and subdued signs of approval. The Rector glanced upon the people.

"Fair play," he cried, "you will get as will any man who appears properly accredited and properly qualified to proclaim the Gospel, but in the name of this Christian community, I will prevent the exploitation of an unwary and trusting people."

"Liberty of speech!" called a voice from a dark corner.

"Liberty of speech," roared the Rector. "Who of you wants liberty of speech? Let him stand forth."

There followed a strained and breathless silence. The champion of free speech retreated behind his discretion.

"Ah, I thought so," said the Rector in grim contempt.

But even as he spoke a quiet voice invaded the tense silence like a bell in a quiet night. It was Mrs. Gwynne, her slight girlish figure standing quietly erect, her face glowing as with an inner light, her eyes resting in calm fearlessness upon the Rector's heated countenance.

"Sir," she said, "my conscience will not permit me to sit in silence in the presence of what I feel to be an infringement of the rights of free people. I venture very humbly to protest against this injustice, and to say that this gentleman has a right to be heard."

An even more intense silence fell upon the people. The Rector stood speechless, gazing upon the little woman who had thus broken every tradition of the community in lifting her voice in a public assembly and who had dared to challenge the authority of one who for nearly twenty years had been recognised as the autocrat of the village and of the whole countryside. But the Rector was an alert and gallant fighter. He quickly recovered his poise.

"If Mrs. Gwynne, our good friend and neighbour, desires to address this meeting," he said with a courteous and elaborate bow, "and I am sure by training and tradition she is quite capable of doing so, I am confident that all of us will be delighted to listen to her. But the question in hand is not quite so simple as she imagines. It is—"

"Liberty of speech," said the voice again from the dark corner.

The Rector wheeled fiercely in the direction from which the interruption came.

"Who speaks," he cried; "why does he shrink into the darkness? Let him come forth."

Again discretion held the interrupter silent.

"As for you—you, sir," continued the Rector, turning upon the evangelist, "if you desire—"

But at this point there was a sudden commotion from the opposite side of the room. A quaint dwarfish figure, crippled but full of vigour, stumped up to the platform.

"My son," he said, grandly waving the Rector to one side, "allow me, my son. You have done well. Now I shall deal with this gentleman."

The owner of the misshapen body had a noble head, a face marked with intellectual quality, but the glitter in the large blue eye told the same tale of mental anarchy. Startled and astonished, the evangelist backed away from the extraordinary creature that continued to advance upon him.

"Sir," cried the dwarf, "by what right do you proclaim the divine message to your fellowmen? Have you known the cross, have you felt the piercing crown, do you bear upon your body the mark of the spear?" At this with a swift upward hitch of his shirt the dwarf exposed his bare side. The evangelist continued to back away from his new assailant, who continued vigorously to follow him up. The youngsters in the crowd broke into laughter. The scene passed swiftly from tragedy to farce. At this point the Rector interposed.

"Come, come, John," he said, laying a firm, but gentle, hand upon the dwarf's shoulder. "That will do now. He is perfectly harmless, sir," he said, addressing the evangelist. Then turning to the audience, "I think we may dismiss this meeting," and, raising his hands, he pronounced the benediction, and the people dispersed in disorder.

With a strained "Good-night, sir," to the evangelist and a courteous bow to Mrs. Gwynne, the Rector followed the people, leaving the evangelist and his wife behind packing up their hymn books and organ, their faces only too clearly showing the distress which they felt. Mrs. Gwynne moved toward them.

"I am truly grieved," she said, addressing the evangelist, "that you were not given an opportunity to deliver your message."

"What a terrible creature that is," he exclaimed in a tone indicating nervous anxiety.

"Oh, you mean poor John?" said Mrs. Gwynne. "The poor man is quite harmless. He became excited with the unusual character of the meeting. He will disturb you no more."

"I fear it is useless," said the evangelist. "I cannot continue in the face of this opposition."

"It may be difficult, but not useless," replied Mrs.

Gwynne, the light of battle glowing in her grey eyes.

"Ah, I do not know. It may not be wise to stir up bad feeling in a community, to bring the name of religion into disrepute by strife. But," he continued, offering his hand, "let me thank you warmly for your sympathy. It was splendidly courageous of you. Do you—do you attend his church?"

"Yes, we worship with the Episcopal Church. I am a Friend myself."

"Ah, then it was a splendidly courageous act. I honour you for it."

"But you will continue your mission?" she replied earnestly.

"Alas, I can hardly see how the mission can be continued. There seems to be no opening."

Mrs. Gwynne apparently lost interest. "Good-bye," she said simply, shaking hands with them both, and without further words left the room with her boy. For some distance they walked together along the dark road in silence. Then in an awed voice the boy said:

"How could you do it, mother? You were not a bit afraid."

"Afraid of what, the Rector?"

"No, not the Rector—but to speak up that way before all the people."

"It was hard to speak," said his mother, "very hard, but it was harder to keep silent. It did not seem right."

The boy's heart swelled with a new pride in his mother. "Oh, mother," he said, "you were splendid. You were like a soldier standing there. You were like the martyrs in my book."

"Oh, no, no, my boy."

"I tell you yes, mother, I was proud of you."

The thrilling passion in the little boy's voice went to his mother's heart. "Were you, my boy?" she said, her voice faltering. "I am glad you were."

Hand in hand they walked along, the boy exulting in his restored pride in his mother and in her courage. But a new feeling soon stirred within him. He remembered with a pain intolerable that he had allowed the word of so despicable a creature as Mop Cheatley to shake his faith in his mother's courage. Indignation at the wretched creature who had maligned her, but chiefly a passionate self-contempt that he had allowed himself to doubt her, raged tumultuously in his heart and drove him in a silent fury through the dark until they reached their own gate. Then as his mother's hand reached toward the latch, the boy abruptly caught her arm in a fierce grip.

"Mother," he burst forth in a passionate declaration of faith, "you're not a coward."

"A coward?" replied his mother, astonished.

The boy's arms went around her, his head pressed into her bosom. In a voice broken with passionate sobs he poured forth his tale of shame and self-contempt.

"He said you were a Quaker, that the Quakers were cowards, and would never fight, and that you were a coward, and that you would never fight. But you would, mother, wouldn't you? And you're not a real Quaker, are you, mother?"

"A Quaker," said his mother. "Yes, dear, I belong to the Friends, as we call them."

"And they, won't they ever fight?" demanded the boy anxiously.

"They do not believe that fighting with fists, or sticks, or like wild beasts," said his mother, "ever wins anything worth while."

"Never, mother?" cried the boy, anxiety and fear in his tones. "You would fight, you would fight to-night, you would fight the Rector."

"Yes, my boy," said his mother quietly, "that kind of fighting we believe in. Our people have never been afraid to stand up for the right, and to suffer for it too. Remember that, my boy," a certain pride rang out in the mother's voice. She continued, "We must never be afraid to suffer for what we believe to be right. You must never forget that through all your life, Larry." Her voice grew solemn. "You must never, never go back from what you know to be right, even if you have to suffer for it."

"Oh, mother," whispered the boy through his sobs, "I wish I were brave like you."

"No, no, not like me," whispered his mother, putting her face down to his. "You will be much braver than your mother, my boy, oh, very much braver than your mother."

The boy still clung to her as if he feared to let her go. "Oh, mother," he whispered, "do you think I can be brave?"

"Yes, my boy," her voice rang out again confident and clear. "It always makes us brave to know that He bore the cross for us and died rather than betray us."

There were no more words between them, but the memory of that night never faded from the boy's mind. A new standard of heroism was set up within his soul which he might fail to reach but which he could never lower.

CHAPTER III

THE ESCUTCHEON CLEARED

Mr. Michael Gwynne, the Mapleton storekeeper, was undoubtedly the most popular man not in the village only but in the whole township. To begin with he was a man of high character, which was sufficiently guaranteed by the fact that he was chosen as Rector's Warden in All Saints Episcopal Church. He was moreover the Rector's right-hand man, ready to back up any good cause with personal effort, with a purse always open but not often full, and with a tongue that was irresistible, for he had to an extraordinary degree the gift of persuasive speech. Therefore, the Rector's first move in launching any new scheme was to secure the approval and co-operation of his Warden.

By the whole community too Mr. Gwynne was recognised as a gentleman, a gentleman not in appearance and bearing only, a type calculated to repel plain folk, but a gentleman in heart, with a charm of manner which proceeded from a real interest in and consideration for the welfare of others. This charm of manner proved a valuable asset to him in his business, for behind his counter Mr. Gwynne had a rare gift of investing the very calicoes and muslins which he displayed before the dazzled eyes of the ladies who came to buy with a glamour that never failed to make them appear altogether desirable; and even the hard-headed farmers fell under this spell of his whether he described to them the superexcellent qualities of a newly patented cream separator or the virtues of a new patent medicine for ailing horses whose real complaint was overwork or underfeeding. With all this, moreover, Mr. Gwynne was rigidly honest. No one ever thought of disputing an account whether he paid it or not, and truth demands that with Mr. Gwynne's customers the latter course was more frequently adopted.

It was at this point that Mr. Gwynne failed of success as a business man. He could buy with discrimination, he had a rare gift of salesmanship, but as a collector, in the words of Sam Cheatley, the village butcher, himself a conspicuous star in that department of business activity, "He was not worth a tinker's curse." His accounts were sent out punctually twice a year. His wife saw to that. At times of desperation when pressure from the wholesale houses became urgent, special statements were sent out by Mr. Gwynne himself. But in such cases the apology accompanying these statements was frequently such as to make immediate payment seem almost an insult. His customers held him in high esteem, respected his intellectual ability—for he was a Trinity man—were fascinated by his charm of manner, loved him for his kindly qualities, but would not pay their bills.

Many years ago, having failed to work harmoniously with his business partner, a shrewd, hard-headed, Belfast draper—hard-hearted Mr. Gwynne considered him—Mr. Gwynne had decided to emigrate to Canada with the remnant of a small fortune which was found to be just sufficient to purchase the Mapleton general store, and with it a small farm of fifty acres on the corner of which the store stood. It was the farm that decided the investment; for Mr. Gwynne was possessed of the town man's infatuation for farm life and of the optimistic conviction that on the farm a living at least for himself and his small family would be assured.

But his years of business in Mapleton had gradually exhausted his fortune and accumulated a staggering load of debt which was the occasion of moments of anxiety, even of fear, to the storekeeper. There was always the thought in his mind that against his indebtedness on the credit side there were his book accounts which ran up into big figures. There was always, if the worst came to the worst, the farm. But if Mr. Gwynne was no business man still less was he a farmer. Tied to his store by reason of his inability to afford a competent assistant, the farming operations were carried on in haphazard fashion by neighbours who were willing to liquidate their store debts with odd days' work at times most convenient to themselves, but not always most seasonable for the crops. Hence in good years, none too good with such haphazard farming, the farm was called upon to make up the deficiency in the financial returns of the store. In bad years notes had to be renewed with formidable accumulations of interest. But such was Mr. Gwynne's invincible optimism that he met every new embarrass-ment with some new project giving new promise of success.

Meanwhile during these painful years his brave little wife by her garden and her poultry materially helped to keep the family in food and to meet in some degree the household expenses. She was her own servant except that the Widow Martin came to her aid twice a week. Her skill with needle and sewing machine and a certain creative genius which she possessed enabled her to evolve from her husband's old clothes new clothes for her boy, and from her own clothing, when not too utterly worn, dresses for her two little girls. And throughout these years with all their toil and anxiety she met each day with a spirit undaunted and with a face that remained serene as far at least as her husband and her children ever saw. Nor did she allow the whole weight of trials to taint the sweetness of her spirit or to dim her faith in God. Devoted to her husband, she refused to allow herself to criticise his business ability or methods. The failure, which she could not but admit, was not his fault; it was the fault of those debtors who declined to pay their just dues.

In an hour of desperation she ventured to point out to her husband that these farmers were extending their holdings and buying machinery with notes that bore interest. "And besides, Michael," she said, "Lawrence must go to High School next year. He will pass the Entrance examination this summer, and he must go."

"He shall go," said her husband. "I am resolved to make a change in my method of business. I shall go after these men. They shall no longer use my money for their business and for their families while my business and my family suffer. You need not look that way, I have made up my mind and I shall begin at once."

Unfortunately the season was not suitable for collections. The farmers were engrossed with their harvesting, and after that with the fall ploughing, and later with the marketing of their grain. And as the weeks passed Mr. Gwynne's indignant resolve that his customers should not do business on his money gradually cooled down. The accounts were sent out as usual, and with the usual disappointing result.

Meantime Mr. Gwynne's attention was diverted from his delinquent debtors by an enterprise which to an unusual degree awakened his sympathy and kindled his imagination. The Reverend Heber Harding, ever since his unfortunate encounter with the travelling evangelist, was haunted with the uneasy feeling that he and his church were not completely fulfilling their functions in the community and justifying their existence. The impression had been the more painfully deepened in him by the sudden eruption of a spirit of recklessness and a certain tendency to general lawlessness in some of the young men of the village. As a result of a conference with the leading men of his congregation, he had decided to organise a young men's club. The business of setting this club in active operation was handed over to Mr. Gwynne, than whom no one in the village was better fitted for the work. The project appealed to Mr. Gwynne's imagination. A room was secured in the disused Orange Hall. Subscriptions were received to make purchase of apparatus and equipment necessary for games of various sorts. With vivid remembrance of his college days, Mr. Gwynne saw to it that as part of the equipment a place should be found for a number of sets of boxing gloves.

There were those who were not too sure of the uplifting influence of the boxing gloves. But after Mr. Gwynne had given an exhibition of the superior advantages of science over brute force in a bout with Mack Morrison before a crowded hall, whatever doubt might exist as to the ethical value of the boxing gloves, there was no doubt at all as to their value as an attractive force in the building up of the membership of the Young Men's Club. The boxing class became immensely popular, and being conducted under Mr. Gwynne's most rigid supervision, it gradually came to exert a most salutary influence upon its members. They learned, for one thing, to take hard knocks without losing their tempers.

In the boxing class thus established, none showed a greater eagerness to learn than did Larry. Every moment of his father's spare time he utilised to add to his knowledge of the various feints and guards and cuts and punches and hooks that appeared necessary to a scientific acquaintance with the manly art. He developed an amazing capacity to accept punishment. Indeed, he appeared almost to welcome rough handling, especially from the young men and boys bigger than himself. Light in weight and not very muscular, he was wiry and quick in eye and in action, and under his father's teaching he learned how to "make his heels save his head." He was always ready for a go with any one who might offer, and when all others had wearied of the sport Larry would put in an extra half hour with the punching bag. With one boy only he refused to spar. No persuasion, no taunts, no challenge could entice him to put on the gloves with Mop Cheatley. He could never look steadily at Mop for any length of time without seeing again on his face the sneering grin and hearing again the terrible words spoken two years ago in the cedar woods behind the mill pond: "You're a coward and your mother's a coward before you." He refused to spar with Mop for he knew that once face to face with him he could not spar, he must fight. But circumstances made the contest inevitable. In the working out of a tournament, it chanced that Mop was drawn to face Larry, and although the disparity both in age and weight seemed to handicap the smaller boy to an excessive degree, Larry's friends who were arranging the schedule, among them Mack Morrison with big Ben Hopper and Joe Gagneau as chorus, and who knew something of Larry's skill with his hands and speed on his feet, were not unwilling to allow the draw to stand.

The days preceding the tournament were days of misery for Larry. The decision in the contest would of course be on points and he knew that he could outpoint without much difficulty his antagonist who was clumsy and slow. For the decision Larry cared nothing at all. At the most he had little to lose for it would be but small disgrace to be beaten by a boy so much bigger. The cause of his distress was something quite other than this. He knew that from the first moment of the bout he would be fighting. That this undoubtedly would make Mop fight back, and he was haunted by the fear that in the stress of battle he might play the coward. Would he be able to stand up to Mop when the fight began to go against him? And suppose he should run away, should show himself a coward? How could he ever live after that, how look any of the boys in the face? Worst of all, how could he face his father, whose approval in this boxing game since he had revealed himself as a "fighting man" the boy coveted more than anything else. But his father was not present when the boy stepped into the ring. Impelled by the dread of showing himself a coward and running away, Larry flung to the winds his father's favourite maxim, "Let your heels save your head," a maxim which ought if ever to be observed in such a bout as this in which he was so out-classed in weight.

At the word "Time" Larry leaped for his opponent and almost before Mop was aware that the battle had begun he was being blinded, staggered and beaten all around the ring, and only a lucky blow, flung wildly into space and landing heavily upon Larry's face, saved him from complete defeat in the first round. That single heavy blow was sufficient to give temporary pause to Larry's impetuosity, but as soon as he got back his wind he once more ran in, feinting, ducking, plunging, but ever pressing hard upon his antagonist, who, having recovered from his first surprise, began to plant heavy blows upon Larry's ribs, until at the end of the round the boy was glad enough to sink back into his corner gasping for breath.

Ben Hopper, who was acting as Larry's second, was filled with surprise and indignation at his principal's fighting tactics. "You blame fool," he said to Larry as he ministered to his all too apparent necessities. "What do you think you're doing? Do you think he's a sausage machine and you a bloody porker? Keep away from him. You know he's too heavy for you. If he were not so clumsy he would have had you out before this. One good punch from him would do it. Why don't you do your foot work?"

"Corec," said Joe. "Larree, you fight all the same Mack Morrison's ram. Head down, jump in—head down, jump in. Why you run so queek on dat Mop feller? Why you not make him run after you?"

"He's right, Larry," said Ben. "Use your feet; make him come after you. You will sure get his wind."

But Larry stood recovering his breath, glowering meanwhile at his enemy across the ring. He neither heeded nor heard the entreaties of his friends. In his ears one phrase only rang with insistent reiteration. "He's a coward, an' his mother's a coward before him." Only one obsession possessed him, he must keep hard at his enemy.

"Time!" The second round was on. Like a tiger upon his prey, Larry was upon his foe, driving fast and furious blows upon his head and face. But this time Mop was ready for him, and bearing in, head down, he took on his left guard the driving blows with no apparent injury, and sent back some half a dozen heavy swings that broke down Larry's guard, drove him across the ring and finally brought him gasping to his knees.

"Stay where you are," yelled Ben. "Take your count, Larry, and keep away from him. Do you hear me? Keep away, always away."

At the ninth count Larry sprang to his feet, easily eluded Mop's swinging blow, and slipping lightly around the ring, escaped further attack until he had picked up his wind.

"That's the game," yelled Ben. "Keep it up, old boy, keep it up."

"C'est bon stuff, Larree," yelled Joe, dancing wildly in Ben's corner. "C'est bon stuff, Larree, for sure."

But once more master of his wind, Larry renewed his battering assault upon Mop's head, inflicting some damage indeed, but receiving heavy punishment in return. The close of the round found him exhausted and bleeding. In spite of the adjurations and entreaties of his friends, Larry pursued the same tactics in the third round, which ended even more disastrously than the second. His condition was serious enough to bring Mack Morrison to his side.

"What's up with you, Larry?" said Mack. "Where's your science gone? Why don't you play the game as you know it?"

"Mack, Mack," panted Larry. "It ain't a game. I'm—I'm fighting, and, Mack, I'm not afraid of him."

Mack whistled. "Who said you are afraid of him, youngster?"

"He did, Mack, he called me a coward—you remember, Ben, up in the cedar bush that day we played hookey—you remember, Ben?" Ben nodded. "He called me a coward and"—grinding the words between his teeth—"he called my mother a coward. But I am not afraid of him, Mack—he can't make me afraid; he can't make me run away." What with his rage and his secret fear, the boy had quite lost control of himself.

"So that's it," said Mack, reading both rage and fear in his eyes. "Listen to me, Larry," he continued in a voice low and stern. "You quit this monkey work right now or, by the jumping Jehoshaphat, I will lick the tar out of you myself when this is over. You're not afraid of him; I know that—we all know that. But you don't want to kill him, eh? No. What you want is to make him look like a fool. Well, then, fight, if you want to fight, but remember your rules. Play with him, make him follow you round until you get his wind; there's your chance. Then get him hard and get away."

But the boy spoke no word in reply. He was staring gloomily, desperately, before him into space.

Mack seized him, and shaking him impatiently, said, "Larry boy, listen to me. Don't you care for anybody but yourself? Don't you care for me at all?"

At that Larry appeared to wake up as from a sleep.

"What did you say, Mack?" he answered. "Of course I care, you know that, Mack."

"Then," said Mack, "for God's sake, get a smile on your face. Smile, confound you, smile."

The boy passed his gloved hand over his face, looked for a moment into Mack's eyes, and the old smile came back to his lips.

"Now you're all right," cried Mack in triumph. "Remember your father's rule, 'Keep your head with your heels.'" And Larry did remember! For on the call of "Time" he slipped from Ben's knees and began to circle lightly about Mop, smiling upon him and waiting his chance. His chance soon came, for Mop, thinking that his enemy had had about enough and was ready to quit, adopted aggressive tactics, and, feinting with his right, swung heavily with his left at the smiling face. But the face proved elusive, and upon Mop's undefended head a series of blows dealt with savage fury took all the heart out of him. So he cried to the referee as he ducked into his corner:

"He's fightin'. He's fightin'. I'm not fightin'."

"You'd better get busy then," called Ben derisively from his corner. "Now, Larry, sail into him," and Larry sailed in with such vehemence that Mop fairly turned tail and ran around the ring, Larry pursuing him amid the delighted shouts of the spectators.

This ended the contest, the judges giving the decision to Mop, who, though obviously beaten at the finish, had showed a distinct superiority on points. As for Larry, the decision grieved him not at all. He carried home a face slightly disfigured but triumphant, his sole comment to his mother upon the contest being, "I was not afraid of him anyway, mother; he could not make me run."

"I am not so sure of this boxing, Lawrence," she said, but the boy caught the glint in her eyes and was well enough content.

In the late evening Ben, with Larry and Joe following him, took occasion to look in upon Mop at the butcher shop.

"Say, Mop," said Ben pleasantly, "what do you think of Larry now? Would you say he was a coward?"

"What do you mean?" asked Mop, suspecting trouble.

"Just what I say," said Ben, while Larry moved up within range, his face white, his eyes gleaming.

"I ain't saying nothing about nobody," replied Mop sullenly, with the tail of his eye upon Larry's white face and gleaming eyes.

"You say him one tam—in de cedar swamp," said Joe.

"Would you say Larry was a coward?" repeated Ben.

"No, I wouldn't say nothing of the sort," replied Mop promptly.

"Do you think he is a coward?" persisted Ben.

"No," said Mop, "I know he ain't no coward. He don't fight like no coward."

This appeared to satisfy Ben, but Larry, moving slightly nearer, took up the word for himself.

"And would you say my mother was a coward?" he asked in a tense voice, his body gathered as if for a spring.

"Larry, I wouldn't say nothing about your mother," replied Mop earnestly. "I think your mother's a bully good woman. She was awfully good to my mother last winter, I know."

The spring went out of Larry's body. He backed away from Mop and the boys.

"Who said your mother was a coward?" inquired Mop indignantly. "If anybody says so, you bring him to me, and I'll punch his head good, I will."

Larry looked foolishly at Ben, who looked foolishly back at him.

"Say, Mop," said Larry, a smile like a warm light passing over his face, "come on up and see my new rabbits."

CHAPTER IV

SALVAGE

Another and greater enterprise was diverting Mr. Gwynne's attention from the delinquencies of his debtors, namely: the entrance of the National Machine Company into the remote and placid life of Mapleton and its district. The manager of this company, having spent an afternoon with Mr. Gwynne in his store and having been impressed by his charm and power of persuasive talk, made him a proposition that he should act as agent of the National Machine Company. The arrangement suggested was one that appealed to Mr. Gwynne's highly optimistic temperament. He was not to work for a mere salary, but was to purchase outright the various productions of the National Machine Company and receive a commission upon all his sales. The figures placed before Mr. Gwynne by the manager of the company were sufficiently impressive, indeed so impressive that Mr. Gwynne at once accepted the proposition, and the Mapleton branch of the National Machine Company became an established fact.

There was no longer any question as to the education of his family. In another year when his boy had passed his entrance examinations he would be able to send him to the high school in the neighbouring town of Easton, properly equipped and relieved of those handicaps with which poverty can so easily wash all the colour out of young life. A brilliant picture the father drew before the eyes of his wife of the educational career of their boy, who had already given promise of exceptional ability. But while she listened, charmed, delighted and filled with proud anticipation, the mother with none the less painful care saved her garden and poultry money, cut to bare necessity her household expenses, skimped herself and her children in the matter of dress, and by every device which she had learned in the bitter school of experience during the ten years of her Canadian life, made such preparation for the expenses of her boy's education as would render it unnecessary to call upon the wealth realised from the National Machine Company's business.

In the matter of providing for the expense of his education Larry himself began to take a not unimportant part. During the past two years he had gained not only in size but in the vigour of his health, and in almost every kind of work on the farm he could now take a man's place. His mother would not permit him to give his time and strength to their own farming operations for the sufficient reason that from these there would be no return in ready money, and ready money was absolutely essential to the success of her plans. The boy was quick, eager and well-mannered, and in consequence had no difficulty in finding employment with the neighbouring farmers. So much was this the case that long before the closing of school in the early summer Larry was offered work for the whole summer by their neighbour, Mr. Martin, at one dollar a day. He could hardly believe his good fortune inasmuch as he had never in all his life been paid at a rate exceeding half that amount.

"I shall have a lot of money, mother," he said, "for my high school now. I wonder how much it will cost me for the term."

Thereupon his mother seized the opportunity to discuss the problem with him which she knew they must face together.

"Let us see," said his mother.

Then each with pencil and paper they drew up to the table, but after the most careful paring down of expenses and the most optimistic estimate of their resources consistent with fact, they made the rather discouraging discovery that they were still fifty dollars short.

"I can't do it, mother," said Larry, in bitter disappointment.

"We shall not give up yet," said his mother. "Indeed, I think with what we can make out of the farm and garden and poultry, we ought to be able to manage."

But a new and chilling thought had come to the lad. He pondered silently, and as he pondered his face became heavily shadowed.

"Say, mother," he said suddenly, "we can't do it. How much are you going to spend on your clothes?"

"All I need," said his mother brightly.

"But how much?"

"I don't know."

"How much did you spend last year?"

"Oh, never mind, Lawrence; that really does not matter."

But the boy insisted. "Did you spend thirty-one dollars?"

Ralph Connor

His mother laughed at him.

"Did you spend twenty?"

"No."

"Did you spend fifteen?"

"I do not know," said his mother, "and I am not going to talk about it. My clothes and the girls' clothes will be all right for this year."

"Mother," said Larry, "I am not going to school this year. I am not going to spend thirty-one dollars for clothes while you and the girls spend nothing. I am going to work first, and then go to school. I am not going to school this year." The boy rose from his chair and stood and faced his mother with quivering lips, fighting to keep back the tears.

Mother reached out her hand and drew him toward her. "My darling boy," she said in a low voice, "I love to hear you, but listen to me. Are you listening? You must be educated. Nothing must interfere with that. No suffering is too great to be endured by all of us. The time for education is youth; first because your mind works more quickly and retains better what it acquires, and second because it is a better investment, and you will sooner be able to pay us all back what we spend now. So you will go to school this year, boy, if we can manage it, and I think we can. Some day," she added, patting him on the shoulder, and holding him off from her, "when you are rich you will give me a silk dress."

"Won't I just," cried the boy passionately, "and the girls too, and everything you want, and I will give you a good time yet, mother. You deserve the best a woman ever had and I will give it to you."

The mother turned her face away from him and looked out of the window. She saw not the fields of growing grain but a long vista of happy days ever growing in beauty and in glory until she could see no more for the tears that quietly fell. The boy dropped on his knees beside her.

"Oh, mother, mother," he said. "You have been wonderful to us all, and you have had an awfully hard time. A fellow never knows, does he?"

"A hard time? A hard time?" said his mother, a great surprise in her voice and in her face. "No, my boy, no hard time for me. A dear, dear, lovely time with you all, every day, every day. Never do I want a better time than I have had with you."

The event proved the wisdom of Mrs. Gwynne's determination to put little faith in the optimistic confidence of her husband in regard to the profits to be expected from the operations of the National Machine Company. A year's business was sufficient to demonstrate that the Mapleton branch of the National Machine Company was bankrupt. By every law of life it ought to be bankrupt. With all his many excellent qualities Mr. Gwynne possessed certain fatal defects as a business man. With him the supreme consideration was simply the getting rid of the machines purchased by him as rapidly and in such large numbers as possible. He cheerfully ignored the laws that governed the elemental item of profit. Hence the relentless Nemesis that sooner or later overtakes those who, whether ignorantly or maliciously, break laws, fell upon the National Machine Company and upon those who had the misfortune to be associated with it.

In the wreck of the business Mr. Gwynne's store, upon which the National Machine Company had taken the precaution to secure a mortgage, was also involved. The business went into the hands of a receiver and was bought up at about fifty cents on the dollar by a man recently from western Canada whose specialty was the handling of business wreckage. No one after even a cursory glance at his face would suspect Mr. H. P. Sleighter of deficiency in business qualities. The snap in the cold grey eye, the firm lines in the long jaw, the thin lips pressed hard together, all proclaimed the hard-headed, cold-hearted, iron-willed man of business. Mr. Sleighter, moreover, had a remarkable instinct for values, more especially for salvage values. It was this instinct that led him to the purchase of the National Machine Company wreckage, which included as well the Mapleton general store, with its assets in stock and book debts.

Mr. Sleighter's methods with the easy-going debtors of the company in Mapleton and the surrounding district were of such galvanic vigour that even so practiced a procrastinator as Farmer Martin found himself actually drawing money from his hoarded bank account to pay his store debts—a thing unheard of in that community—and to meet overdue payments upon the various implements which he had purchased from the National Machine Company. It was not until after the money had been drawn and actually paid that Mr. Martin came fully to realise the extraordinary nature of his act.

"That there feller," he said, looking from the receipt in his hand to the store door through which the form of Mr. Sleighter had just vanished, "that there feller, he's too swift fer me. He ain't got any innards to speak of; he'd steal the pants off a dog, he would."

The application of these same galvanically vigorous

methods to Mr. Gwynne's debtors produced surprising results. Mr. Sleighter made the astounding discovery that Mr. Gwynne's business instead of being bankrupt would produce not only one hundred cents on the dollar, but a slight profit as well. This discovery annoyed Mr. Sleighter. He hated to confess a mistake in business judgment, and he frankly confessed he "hated to see good money roll past him." Hence with something of a grudge he prepared to hand over to Mr. Gwynne some twelve hundred and fifty dollars of salvage money.

"I suppose he will be selling out his farm," said Mr. Sleighter in conversation with Mr. Martin. "What's land worth about here?"

"Oh, somewhere about a hundred."

"A hundred dollars an acre!" exclaimed Mr. Sleighter. "Don't try to put anything over on me. Personally I admire your generous, kindly nature, but as a financial adviser you don't shine. I guess I won't bother about that farm anyway."

Mr. Sleighter's question awakened earnest thought in Mr. Martin, and the next morning he approached Mr. Gwynne with a proposition to purchase his farm with its attached buildings. Mr. Martin made it clear that he was chiefly anxious to do a neighbourly turn.

"The house and the stable ain't worth much," he said, "but the farm bein' handy to my property, I own up is worth more to me than to other folks, perhaps. So bein' old neighbours, I am willin' to give four thousand dollars, half cash down, for the hull business."

"Surely that is a low figure," said Mr. Gwynne.

"Low figure!" exclaimed Mr. Martin. "All right, I ain't pressin' it on you; but if you could get any one in this neighbourhood to offer four thousand dollars for your farm, I will give you five hundred extra. But," he continued, "I ain't pressin' you. Don't much matter to me."

The offer came at a psychologically critical moment, when Mr. Gwynne was desperately seeking escape from an intolerable environment.

"I shall consult Mrs. Gwynne," he said, "and let you know in a few days."

"Don't know as I can wait that long," said Mr. Martin. "I made the offer to oblige you, and besides I got a chance at the Monroe fifty."

"Call to-morrow night," said Mr. Gwynne, and carried the proposal home to his wife.

The suggestion to break up her home to a woman of Mrs. Gwynne's type is almost shattering. In the big world full of nameless terrors the one spot offering shelter and safety for herself and her family was her home. But after all, her husband was her great concern, and she could see he was eager for the change. She made up her mind to the sacrifice and decided that she would break up the home in Mapleton and with her husband try again their fortune.

"But four thousand dollars," she said, "is surely a small price."

"Small? I know it is small, but Martin knows I am in a corner. He is a highway robber."

It was a bitter experience for him to be forced to confess himself a business failure, and with this bitterness there mingled a feeling of hostility toward all successful business men. To him it seemed that in order to win success in business a man must become, like Mr. Martin, a highway robber. In this mood of bitterness and hostility toward successful men, Mr. Sleighter found him the next day.

"Couldn't find you at the store," said that gentleman, walking in with his hat on his head. "I wanted to get this business straightened up, so I just came in. Won't take more than five minutes. I guess you won't mind taking a little check from me. Your business turned out better than that fool of an assignee thought. Don't hurt me any, of course. I got all that was comin' to me out of it, but here's this check. Perhaps you'll sign the receipt. I guess they been puttin' it over you all right. You're a little too soft with 'em."

Mr. Gwynne was an even-tempered man, but Mr. Sleighter's patronising manner and his criticism of his business ability wrought in him a rage that he could with difficulty control. He remembered he was in his own house, however, and that the man before him was a stranger. While he was searching for pen and ink the door opened and his wife entered the room. Mr. Sleighter, with his hat still upon his head, was intently gazing out of the window, easily rocking on the two hind legs of the chair. The door opened behind him.

"My dear," said Mr. Gwynne, "will you excuse me? I am engaged."

"Oh, I beg your pardon, I didn't know any one was here. I merely wanted—"

Mr. Sleighter glanced over his shoulder.

"Mr. Sleighter," said Mr. Gwynne. "My wife."

It was not his tone, however, that brought Mr. Sleighter hurriedly to his feet with his hat in his hand. It was something in the bearing of the little lady standing behind him.

"Pleased to meet you, ma'am. I hope you are well," he said, bowing elaborately before her.

"Thank you very much, I am quite well. I have heard a great deal about you, Mr. Sleighter. I am glad to meet you."

Mr. Sleighter held her hand a moment while her eyes rested quietly and kindly, if searchingly, upon his face. This was the man who had profited by her husband's loss. Was he too a highway robber? Mr. Sleighter somehow felt as if his soul were being exposed to a searchlight. It made him uncomfortable.

"It's a fine day, ma'am," he remarked, seeking cover for his soul in conversation. "A little warm for the time," he continued, wiping his forehead with a highly coloured silk handkerchief.

"Won't you sit down, Mr. Sleighter? Do you find it warm? I thought there was quite a chilly wind to-day. But then you are more accustomed to the wind than I."

The searching eyes were holding him steadily, but the face was kindly and full of genuine interest.

"I guess so," he said with a little laugh. He would have scorned to acknowledge that his laugh was nervous and thin. "I come from the windy side of the earth."

"Oh!"

"Yes, I am from out West—Alberta. We have got all the winds there is and the Chinook besides for a change."

"Alberta? The Chinook?" The eyes became less searching.

"Yes, that's the wind that comes down from the mountains and licks up the snow at ten miles an hour."

"Oh!"

"It was an Alberta man, you know, who invented a rig with runners in front and wheels behind." The lady was bewildered. "To catch up with the Chinook, you see. One of my kid's jokes. Not much of a joke I guess, but he's always ringin' 'em in."

"You have a son, Mr. Sleighter? He's in Alberta now?"

"No, the missis and the kids, three of them, are in Winnipeg. She got tired of it out there; she was always wantin' the city, so I gave in."

"I hear it's a beautiful country out there."

"Now you're talkin', ma'am." She had touched Mr. Sleighter's favourite theme. Indeed, the absorbing passion of his life, next to the picking up of good salvage bargains, was his home in the Foothill country of the West.

While he was engaged in an enthusiastic description of the glories of that wonderland the children came in and were presented. Mr. Gwynne handed his visitor his receipt and stood suggestively awaiting his departure. But Mr.

Sleighter was fairly started on his subject and was not to be denied. The little girls drew shyly near him with eyes aglow while Mr. Sleighter's words roiled forth like a mountain flood. Eloquently he described the beauty of the rolling lands, the splendour of the mountains, the richness of the soil, the health-giving qualities of the climate, the warm-hearted hospitality of the settlers.

"None of your pin-head two-by-four shysters that you see here in the East," exclaimed Mr. Sleighter. "I mean some folks, of course," he explained in some confusion.

"And the children, did they like it?" inquired Mrs. Gwynne.

"You bet they did. Why, they was all over the hull prairie, all day and all night, too, mostly—on ponies you know."

"Ponies!" exclaimed Larry. "Did they have ponies? Could they ride? How big are they?"

"How big? Blamed if I know. Let's see. There's Tom. He's just about a man, or thinks he is. He's sixteen or seventeen. Just now he's in the high school at Winnipeg. He don't like it though." Here a shadow fell on Mr. Sleighter's face. "And the girls—there's Hazel, she's fifteen, and Ethel Mary, she's eleven or somewhere thereabouts. I never can keep track of them. They keep againin' on me all the time."

"Yes," said Mrs. Gwynne. "It is hard to realise that they are growing up and will soon be away from us."

"That's so," said Mr. Sleighter.

"And the schools," continued Mrs. Gwynne, "are there good schools?"

"Schools?" exclaimed Mr. Sleighter. "There's a real good school not more than a couple of miles away."

"Two miles," exclaimed the mother aghast.

"Oh, that's nothin'. They ride, of course. But we ain't got much of a master now. He's rather—you know." Mr. Sleighter significantly tipped up with his little finger and winked toward Mr. Gwynne.

"But you love that country," she said.

"Yes, I love it and I hated to leave it. But the missis never liked it. She was city born and bred. She wanted the lights, I guess, and the shows. I don't blame her, though," he continued rapidly. "It's kind of lonely for women, you know. They've got to have amusements and things. But it's God's own country, believe me, and I would go back to-morrow, if I could."

"You still own your ranch?"

"Yes; can't sell easily. You see there's not much broke on it—only a hundred acres or so."

"Why, how big is the ranch?"

"Five hundred acres and a wood lot. I did not farm much, though—mostly cattle and horses. I was away a good deal on the trail."

"The trail?"

"Yes, buying cattle and selling again. That was the worst of it. I am not much of a farmer, though farming's all right there, and I was away almost all of the time. I guess that made it pretty hard for the missis and the kids."

At this point the Widow Martin came in to lay the table for tea. Mr. Sleighter took the hint and rose to go.

"You will do us the pleasure of staying for tea, Mr. Sleighter?" said Mrs. Gwynne earnestly.

"Oh, do," said the youngest little girl, Nora, whose snapping black eyes gleamed with eager desire to hear more of the wonderful western land.

"Yes, do, and tell us more," said the boy.

"I hope you will be able to stay," continued Mrs. Gwynne.

Mr. Sleighter glanced at her husband. "Why, certainly," said Mr. Gwynne, "we would be glad to have you."

Still Mr. Sleighter hesitated. "Say, I don't know what's come over me. I feel as if I had been on the stump," he said in an embarrassed voice. "I ain't talked to a soul about that country since I left. I guess I got pretty full, and when you pulled the cork, out she come."

During the tea hour Mrs. Gwynne tried to draw her visitor out to talk about his family, but here she failed. Indeed a restraint appeared to fall upon him that nothing could dispel. Immediately after tea Mrs. Gwynne placed the Bible and Book of Prayers on the table, saying, "We follow the custom of reading prayers every evening after tea, Mr. Sleighter. We shall be glad to have you join us."

"Sure thing, ma'am," said Mr. Sleighter, pushing back his chair and beginning to rock on its hind legs, picking his teeth with his pen knife, to the staring horror of the little girls.

The reading was from the Scripture to which throughout

the centuries the Christian Church has gone for authority and guidance in the exercise of charity and in the performance of social service, the story of the Samaritan gentleman to whom the unhappy traveller whose misfortune it was to be sorely mishandled by thieves owed his rescue and his life.

Throughout the reading Mr. Sleighter paid the strictest attention and joined in the prayers with every sign of reverence. At the close he stood awkwardly shifting from one foot to another.

"Well, I'll be goin'," he said. "Don't know how you roped me in for this here visit, ma'am. I ain't et in any one's house since I left home, and I ain't heard any family prayers since my old dad had 'em—a regular old Methodist exhorter he was. He used to pray until all was blue, though most times, specially at night, I used to fall asleep. He was great on religion."

"I don't suppose he was any the worse for that," said Mrs. Gwynne.

"Not a mite, not a mite, ma'am. A little strict, but straight as a string, ma'am. No one could say anythin' against Hiram Sleighter—H. P. Sleighter. I was named for him. He used to pray to beat creation, and then some, but he was a straight man all right. And to-night your kids and your family prayers made me think of them old days. Well, good-night and thank you for the good time you gave me. Best I've had in a dog's age."

"You will come again, Mr. Sleighter," said Mrs. Gwynne, giving him her hand.

"Yes, and tell us more about that new country," added her son. "My, I'd like to go out there!"

"It's a wonderful country all right and you might do a hull lot worse."

CHAPTER V

WESTWARD HO!

Mr. Gwynne accompanied Mr. Sleighter to the door. "Will you walk down to the store?" said Mr. Sleighter.

"Very well," said Mr. Gwynne, setting off with him.

Mr. Sleighter evidently had something on his mind. The usual fountain of his speech seemed to be dried up. As they drew near to the store, he seized Mr. Gwynne by the arm, arrested him, and said:

"Say, Mr. Gwynne, you ain't got any right to be in business. You ain't got the parts, and that Machine Company and the rest of 'em put it all over you."

"We needn't go into that now, I suppose," said Mr. Gwynne.

"No, I guess I am buttin' in—a thing I don't often do—but I am off my stride to-night anyway, and I am doin' what I never did in all my life before. I guess it was them kids of yours and your missis. I know it ain't my business, but what are you goin' to do with yourself?"

"I don't know yet," replied Mr. Gwynne, declining to

be confidential.

"Not goin' into business, I hope. You ain't got the parts. Some people ain't got 'em, and you ain't. Goin' to farm?"

"No, I think not. The fact is I'm about selling my farm."

"Selling it?"

"Yes, I had an offer to-day which I am thinking of accepting."

"An offer, eh, from a feller named Martin, I suppose?"

"How did you know?"

"I don't know. I just figgered. Offered you about a hundred dollars, eh?"

"No; I wish he had. It's worth a hundred with the house and buildings—they are good buildings."

"Say, I don't like to butt in on any man's business, but is the price a secret?"

"Oh, no; he offers four thousand, half cash."

"And how much for the buildings?"

"Four thousand for everything, it's not enough but there are not many buyers in this neighbourhood."

"Say, there's nothing rash about that feller. When do you close?"

"Must close to-morrow night. He has a chance of another place."

"Oh, he has, eh? Big rush on, eh? Well, don't you close until I see you some time to-morrow, partner."

Mr. Sleighter scented another salvage deal, his keen eyes gleamed a bit, the firm lips were pressed a little more closely together.

"And say," he said, turning back, "I don't wonder you can't do business. I couldn't do anything myself with a missis like yours. I couldn't get any smooth work over with her lookin' at me like that, durned if I could. Well, good-night; see you to-morrow."

Mr. Sleighter spent the early hours of the following day among the farmers with whom his salvage deal had brought him into contact. The wrecker's instinct was strong in him, and besides he regarded with abhorrence the tactics of Mr. Martin and welcomed an opportunity to beat that gentleman at his own game. He could easily outbid the Martin offer and still buy the farm at a low price. As a result of his inquiries he had made up his mind that the land was worth at the very least eighty dollars an acre and the buildings at least two thousand more. Five thousand would be a ridiculously low figure and six thousand not extravagantly high for both buildings and farm. The farm with the store and machine business attached might offer a fair opening to his son, who was already weary of school and anxious to engage in business for himself.

"Guess I'll take a whirl out of the old boy," he said to himself. "He's a durn fool anyway and if I don't get his money some one else will."

In the afternoon he made his way to the store. "Boss ain't in?" he inquired of the clerk.

"No, he's at the house, I guess."

"Back soon?"

"Don't know. Guess he's busy over there."

"Seen Mr. Martin around?"

"Yes, he was here a while ago. Said he would be in again later."

Mr. Sleighter greatly disliked the idea of doing business with Mr. Gwynne at his own house. "Can't do no business with his missis and kids around," he said to himself. "Can't get no action with that woman lookin' on seemingly. But that there old Martin geyser is on the job and he might close things up. I guess I will wander over."

To his great relief he found Mr. Gwynne alone and without preliminaries, and with the design of getting "quick action" before the disturbing element of Mrs. Gwynne's presence should be introduced, he made his offer. He explained his purpose in purchasing, and with something of a flourish offered five thousand for "the hull plant, lock, stock and barrel," cash down if specially desired, but he would prefer to pay half in six months. He must have his answer immediately; was not anxious to buy, but if Mr. Gwynne wanted to close up, he only had to say so. He was not going to monkey with the thing.

"You have made me a much better offer than the one I received from Mr. Martin, and I am inclined to accept it, but inasmuch as I have promised to give him an answer to-day, I feel that it's due to him that I should meet him with the bargain still unclosed."

"Why?" enquired Mr. Sleighter in surprise.

"Well, you see I asked him to hold the offer open until this afternoon. I feel I ought to go to him with the matter still open."

"Want to screw him up, eh?" said Mr. Sleighter, his lips drawing close together.

"No, sir." Mr. Gwynne's voice had a little ring in it. "I consider it fairer to Mr. Martin."

"Don't see as how he has much claim on you," replied Mr. Sleighter. "But that's your own business. Say, there he comes now. Look here, my offer is open until six o'clock. After that it's a new deal. Take it or leave it. I will be at your store."

"Very well," said Mr. Gwynne stiffly.

Mr. Sleighter was distinctly annoyed and disappointed. A few minutes' longer pressure, he was convinced, would have practically closed a deal which would have netted him a considerable profit. "Durn old fool," he muttered to himself as he passed out of the room.

In the hallway Mrs. Gwynne's kindly welcome halted him. She greeted him as she would a friend. Would he not sit down for a few moments. No, he was busy. Mr. Sleighter was quite determined to get away from her presence.

"The children were delighted with your description of your western home," she said. "The free life, the beautiful hills, the mountains in the distance—it must indeed be a lovely country."

Mr. Sleighter was taken off his guard. "Yes, ma'am, that's lovely country all right. They'd like it fine out there, and healthy too. It would make a man of that little kid of yours. He looks a little on the weak side to me. A few months in the open and you wouldn't know him. The girls too—"

"Come in here and sit down, won't you, Mr. Sleighter?" said Mrs. Gwynne.

Mr. Sleighter reluctantly passed into the room and sat down. He knew he was taking a risk. However, his offer was already made and the deal he believed would be closed in the store by six o'clock.

"I suppose the land is all taken up out there?" said Mrs. Gwynne.

"Oh, yes, mostly, unless away back. Folks are comin' in all the time, but there's still lots of cheap land around."

"Cheap land, is there?" inquired Mrs. Gwynne with a certain eagerness in her voice. "Indeed I should have thought that that beautiful land would be very dear."

"Why, bless your heart, no. I know good land going for six—seven—eight—ten dollars an acre. Ten dollars is high for good farm lands; for cattle runs four dollars is good. No, there's lots of good land lying around out of doors there. If these people around here could get their heads up long enough from grubbing in the muck they wouldn't stay here over night. They'd be hittin' the trail for the west, you bet."

Mrs. Gwynne turned her honest eyes upon him. "Mr. Sleighter, I want to ask your advice. I feel I can rely upon you ["Durn it all, she's gettin' her work in all right," thought Mr. Sleighter to himself], and I am getting quite anxious in the matter. You see, my husband is determined to leave this place. He wishes to try something else. Indeed, he must try something else. We must make a living, Mr. Sleighter." Mrs. Gwynne's voice became hurried and anxious. "We were delighted last night by your description of that wonderful country in the West, and the children especially. I have been wondering if we might venture to try a small farm in that country—quite a small farm. We have a little money to invest. I thought I might be bold enough to ask you. I know your judgment would be good and I felt somehow that we could trust you. I hope I am not taking a liberty, but somehow I feel that you are not a stranger."

"No, ma'am, certainly not," said Mr. Sleighter in a loud voice, his hope of securing "quick action on that deal" growing dim.

"Do you happen to know any farm—a small farm—which we might be able to buy? We hope to receive four thousand dollars for this place. I feel that it is worth a good deal more, but there are not many buyers about here. Then, of course, perhaps we value our place too highly. Then by your kind help we have got something out of the business—twelve hundred and fifty dollars I think Mr. Gwynne said. We are most grateful to you for that, Mr. Sleighter." Her eyes beamed on him in a most disconcerting way. "And so after our obligations here are met we might have about forty-five hundred dollars clear. Could we do anything with that?"

"I donno, I donno," said Mr. Sleighter quickly and rising from his chair, "I will think it over. I have got to go now."

At this moment Mr. Gwynne came into the room. "Oh, I am glad you are not gone, Mr. Sleighter. I have just told Mr. Martin that I cannot accept his offer."

"Cannot accept, Michael!" said Mrs. Gwynne, dismay in her voice and in her eyes.

"I believe you said your offer was good until six, Mr. Sleighter?"

"Oh, I say, Gwynne, let's get out, let's get over to the store. It's kind of hot here, and I've got to go. Come on over and we'll clean up." Without a farewell word to either of them Mr. Sleighter passed rapidly from the room.

"I do hope there's nothing wrong, Michael," said his wife. "I fear I have made a mistake. I spoke to Mr. Sleighter about the possibility of getting a small farm in the West. You were so eager about it, Michael dear, and I spoke to Mr. Sleighter about it. I hope there is nothing wrong."

"Don't worry, mother. I have his offer for five thousand dollars. Of course he is rather peculiar, I confess, but I believe—" The door opened abruptly upon them, admitting Mr. Sleighter.

"See here, Mr. Gwynne, I can't do no business with you."

"Sir, you made me an offer for my farm," said Mr. Gwynne indignantly, "and I have just refused an offer from Mr. Martin on account of yours."

"Oh, we'll cut that all out," said Mr. Sleighter, whose voice and manner indicated strong excitement. "Now don't talk. Listen to me, my son. You ain't got any right to be playing around with business men anyhow. Now I am going to do a little business for you, if you will allow me, ma'am. I take it you want to get away from here." Mr. Gwynne nodded, gazing at him in astonishment. "You want to go West." Again Mr. Gwynne nodded. "Well, there's only one spot in the West—Alberta. You want a farm."

"Yes," said Mr. Gwynne.

"Yes, certainly," said Mrs. Gwynne.

"There's just one farm that will suit you, an' that's Lakeside Farm, Wolf Willow, Alberta, owned by H. P. Sleighter, Esq., who's going to stump you to a trade. Five hundred acres, one hundred broke an' a timber lot; a granary; stables and corral, no good; house, fair to middlin'. Two hundred an' fifty acres worth ten dollars at least, best out of doors; cattle run, two hundred acres worth five; swamp and sleugh, fifty acres, only good to look at but mighty pretty in the mornin' at sun-up. Not much money in scenery though. Building worth between two and three thousand. Your plant here is worth about six thousand. I know I offered you five thousand, but I was buyin' then and now I am buyin' and sellin'. Anyway, I guess it's about even, an' we'll save you a lot of trouble an' time an' money. An' so, if you really want a western farm, you might just as well have mine. I did not think to sell. Of course I knew I must sell in the long run, but couldn't just see my place in anybody else's hands. Somehow it seems different though to see you folks on it. You seem to fit. Anyway, there's the offer. What do you say?"

"Sit down, Mr. Sleighter," said Mr. Gwynne. "This is a rather surprising proposition."

Mrs. Gwynne's eyes grew soft. "Michael, I think it is wonderful."

But Mr. Gwynne would not look at his wife. "Let me see, Mr. Sleighter, your farm, you say, with buildings, is worth about six thousand to sixty-five hundred. Mine is worth from fifty-five hundred to six thousand. I will take your offer and pay the difference."

"Oh, come off your perch," said Mr. Sleighter. "You're doin' the highfalutin' Vere de Vere act now. Listen to me. The deal is as level as I can figger it. Your farm and store with the machine business suit me all right. I feel I can place my boy right here for a while anyway. My farm, I believe, would suit you better than anythin' else you can get. There's my offer. Take it or leave it."

"I think we will take it, Mr. Sleighter," said Mrs. Gwynne. "Michael dear, I feel Mr. Sleighter is right, and besides I know he is doing us a great kindness."

"Kindness, ma'am, not at all. Business is business, and that's all there is to it. Well, I'll be goin'. Think it over, get the papers fixed up by to-morrow. No, don't thank me. Good-bye."

Mrs. Gwynne followed him to the door, her face flushed, her eyes aglow, a smile hovering uncertainly about her lips. "Mr. Sleighter," she said, "the Lord sent you to us because He knew we were in need of guiding."

"Ho, ho!" laughed Mr. Sleighter. "Like that Samaritan chap in the reading, eh? I guess you had got among thieves all right, more of 'em perhaps than you recognised too."

"He sent you to us," repeated Mrs. Gwynne, offering him her hand.

"Well, I donno but that He steered me to you. But all the same I guess the advantage is to me all right." Mr. Sleighter looked hard down the street, then turned and faced her squarely. "I want to say that it's done me a pile of good to have seen you, ma'am. It's made things look different."

"You are a good man, Mr. Sleighter," she said, looking at him with misty eyes.

"A good man!" Mr. Sleighter was seized with a cough. "A good man! Good Lord, ma'am! nobody never found it out but you—durn that cough anyway." And still troubled by his cough, Mr. Sleighter hurried down the path to the gate and out on to the road.

Once resolved to break up their home in Eastern Canada, the Gwynnes lost no time in completing their arrangements for the transportation of themselves and their household gods and such of their household goods as Mr. Sleighter advised, to the new western country.

Mr. Sleighter appeared to regard the migration of the Gwynne family to the western country as an enterprise in which he had made an investment from which he was bound to secure the greatest possible return. The principle of exchange which had been the basis of the deal as far as the farms were concerned was made to apply as far as possible to farm implements and equipment, household goods and chattels.

"What's the use of your packin' a hull bunch of stuff West an' my packin' a hull bunch of stuff East. We'll just tote up the stock an' stuff we have got and make a deal on it. I know all my stuff an' yours is here. We'll make a trade."

To this Mr. Gwynne gladly agreed. The arrangement would save trouble and useless expenditure. Hence the car was packed with such goods as Mr. Sleighter considered especially useful in the new home, and with such household furniture as the new home lacked and such articles as were precious from family or personal associations.

"What about the pictures and curtains?" inquired Mr. Gwynne. "We don't need them."

"Take 'em all," said Mr. Sleighter. "Pictures are like folks. They got faces an' looks. And curtains—my missis got hers all packed. Curtains are like clothes—they only fit them that owns them."

"And the piano?"

"Sure thing. Say, a piano in that country is like the village pump—the hull country gets about it. Take things to eat an' things to wear an' things to make the shack look pretty an' interestin' and comfortable. They don't take much room and they take the bareness off. That's what kills the women folk in the West, the bareness inside and outside. Nothin' but chairs, table an' stove inside; nothin' but grass an' sand outside. That's what makes 'em go crazy."

So the car was filled with things to eat and to wear, and things "to take the bareness off." Somewhere in the car was found a place for Rosie, the cow, a remarkable milker and "worth her weight in butter," as Mr. Sleighter said, and for Rover, Larry's collie dog, who stood to him as comrade almost as a brother. A place in the car too was found for Joe Gagneau who from the first moment of the announced departure had expressed his determination to accompany Larry no matter at what cost or against whose opposition.

"A'm goin' be in dat car' me, by gar!" was his ultimatum, and the various authorities interested recognised the inevitable and accepted it, to the great delight of both boys. Joe had a mouth organ and so had Larry, and they were both in the same key. Joe too had an old fiddle of his father's on which he could scrape with joy to himself, and with more or less agony to others, the dance tunes of local celebrity, the "Red River Jig," picked up from his father, "Money Musk" and "The Deil Amang the Tailors," the two latter from Dan Monroe at the country dances.

In due time the car, packed with the Gwynne household goods and treasures and in charge of the two superlatively happy boys, with Rosie and Rover to aid in providing them with sustenance and protection, set forth, Westward Ho! Mr. Gwynne rode in the caboose of the train to which his car was attached. Mrs. Gwynne and the girls were to follow by passenger train and would doubtless be found awaiting them on their arrival at Winnipeg.

The journey westward was to the boys full of interest and adventure. At Toronto they picked up a stowaway, who, taking advantage of their absence, boarded the car and made himself a bed behind some bales of hay. Upon discovery by Rover, he made so piteous an appeal for refuge from some pursuing terror which he declined to specify, that the boys agreed to conceal him a night and a day till they were well on their way along the north shore of Lake Superior. When Larry's conscience made further concealment a burden greater than could be borne, Mr. Gwynne was taken into the boys' confidence and, after protest, agreed to make arrangement with the railroad authorities whereby Sam—for that was the stowaway's name—might retain his place in the car.

He was a poor, wretched creature, reminding Larry of the scarecrow which he had put up in their garden the summer before. He was thin beyond anything the boys had ever seen. His face was worn and old and came to a peak at the nose, which gave him the appearance of a monster rat, a resemblance emphasised by the little blinking, red-rimmed eyes. His hair was closely cropped and of brilliant carrotty colour.

But he had seen life in a great city and had gathered a store of worldly wisdom, not all of which was for his good, and a repertoire of accomplishments that won him admiration and wonder from the simple country boys. He had all the new ragtime songs and dances, which he rendered to his own accompaniment on an old battered banjo. He was a contortionist of quite unusual cleverness, while his fund of stories never ran dry throughout the seven days' journey to Winnipeg. He set himself with the greatest assiduity to impart his accomplishments to the boys, and by the time the party had reached the end of the first stage in their westward journey, Sam had the satisfaction of observing that his pupils had made very satisfactory progress, both with the clog dancing and with the ragtime songs. Besides this, he had made for himself an assured place in their affection, and even Mr. Gwynne had come to feel such an interest in the bit of human driftwood flung up against him, that he decided to offer the waif a chance to try his fortune in the West.

CHAPTER VI

JANE BROWN

Mr. Brown was a busy man, but he never failed to be in his place at the foot of the table every day punctually at half past twelve, solely because at that hour his little daughter, Jane, would show her grave and earnest and dark brown, almost swarthy, face at the head. Eight years ago another face used to appear there, also grave, earnest, but very fair and very lovely to look upon, to the doctor the fairest of all faces on the earth. The little, plain, swarthy-faced child the next day after that lovely face had been forever shut away from the doctor's eyes was placed in her high chair at the head of the table, at first only at the lunch hour, but later at all meal times before the doctor to look at. And it was an ever-recurring joy to the lonely man to discover in the little grave face before him fleeting glimpses of the other face so tenderly loved and so long vanished. These glimpses were to be discovered now in the deep blue eyes, deep in colour and in setting, now in the smile that lit up the dark, irregular features like the sudden break of sunlight upon the rough landscape, transforming it into loveliness, now in the knitting of the heavy eyebrows, and in the firm pressing of the lips in moments of puzzled thought. In all the moods and tenses of the little maid the doctor looked for and found reminiscences of her mother.

Ralph Connor

Through those eight lonely years the little girl had divided with his profession the doctor's days. Every morning after breakfast he stood to watch the trim, sturdy, round little figure dance down the steps, step primly down the walk, turn at the gate to throw a kiss, and then march away along the street to the corner where another kiss would greet him before the final vanishing. Every day they met at noon to exchange on equal terms the experiences of the morning. Every night they closed the day with dinner and family prayers, the little girl gravely taking her part in the reading during the last year from her mother's Bible. And so it came that with the years their friendship grew in depth, in frankness and in tenderness. The doctor was widely read beyond the literature of his profession, and every day for a half hour it was his custom to share with the little girl the treasures of his library. The little maid repaid him with a passionate love and a quaint mothering care tender and infinitely comforting to the lonely man.

The forenoon had been hot and trying, and Dr. Brown, having been detained in his office beyond his regular hour, had been more than usually hurried in his round of morning calls, and hence was more than ordinarily tired with his morning's work. At his door the little girl met him.

"Come in, Papa, I know you're hot," she said, love and reproach in her face, "because I was hot myself, and you will need a nice, cool drink. I had one and yours is in here." She led him into the study, hovering about him with little touches and pushes. "You ought not to have taken so long a round this morning," she said with gentle severity. "I know you went out to St. James to see Mrs. Kale, and you know quite well she doesn't need you. It would do in the afternoon. And it was awful hot in school."

"Awful?" said the doctor.

"Well, very exceedingly then—and the kids were very tired and Miss Mutton was as cross as anything."

"It was no wonder. How many kids were there for her to watch?"

"Oh, Papa, you said 'kids!'"

"I was just quoting my young daughter."

"And she said we were to get out this afternoon an hour earlier," continued Jane, ignoring his criticism, "and so I am going to take my bicycle and go with Nora and the girls down to the freight sheds."

"The freight sheds?"

"Yes, Larry and Joe have come in, and Rover and Rosie —she's the cow, and they milked her every day twice and drank the milk and they used to have their meals together in the car."

"Rosie, too? Very interesting indeed."

"Now, Papa, you must not laugh at me. It is very interesting. They all came for days and days together in the car from somewhere down East, Ontario, I think. And Mr. Gwynne says they are just like a circus. And they play instiments and dance."

"What, Rosie too? How clever of her!"

The child's laugh rang out joyously. "Oh, Papa, that's awfully funny. And we're going down on our wheels. Nora can ride now, you know, and she's going to take

Ethel May's wheel. It's awfully hard to ride, but Nora's as strong as Kathleen."

"Well, well," said her father, greatly interested in this exciting but somewhat confused tale. "Just wait until I wash my hands and then you shall tell me what it all means. Thank you for this deliciously cool lemonade. It is very refreshing. You will tell me all about it at lunch."

The lunch hour was devoted first of all to disentangling from the mass the individual members of the car party, which after an adventurous journey across half a continent had apparently made camp at the Winnipeg freight sheds. Then followed the elucidation of the details of the plan by which this camp was to be attacked and raided during the afternoon.

"Now that I have a fairly clear conception of whom Larry, Joe, Sam, Rosie and Rover are—I think I have them right—"

"Exactly, Papa."

"I wish to find out just who are to form the advance party, the scouting party."

"The scouting party? I don't know what you mean. But Nora—you know Nora?"

"Certainly, the little black-eyed Irish Terrier—terror, I mean."

"Oh, Papa, she's just lovely and she's my friend."

"Is she, dear, then I apologise, but indeed I meant nothing derogatory to her. I greatly like her, she is so spunky."

"Yes, there's Nora, and Kathleen, Nora's sister."

"Oh, Kathleen, the tall beautiful girl with the wonderful hair?"

The little girl sighed. "Oh, such lovely long yellow hair." The little maid's hair was none of these. "And she is not a bit proud—just nice, you know—just as if she were not so lovely, but like—only like me."

"Like you, indeed!" exclaimed the doctor indignantly. "Like my little girl? I don't see any one quite like my little girl. There is not one of them with all their yellow hair and things that is to be compared with my own little girl."

"Oh, Papa. I know you think so, and I wish it was so. And I am awfully glad you think so, but of course you are prejuist, you know."

"Prejudiced? Not a bit, not a bit."

"Well, that's Kathleen and Nora, and—and perhaps Hazel—you know Hazel, Papa, Hazel Sleighter?"

"The western girl—not at all wild and woolly though. A very modern and very advanced young lady, isn't she?"

"Oh, I don't know what you mean, Papa. She says she may go down, but I don't think she likes going with a lot of kids. You know she has her hair up. She has to have it up in the store. She says the man would not have her behind the counter if she had not her hair up."

"Oh, that's it. I thought perhaps the maturity of her age made it necessary."

"I don't know what maturevy means, but she is awfully

old. She is going on sixteen."

"Dear me, as old as that?" inquired her father.

"Yes, but she said she wanted to see that circus car. That's what she calls Mr. Gwynne's car. And she says she wants to see the elephunts perform. There are not any elephunts. There's only Rosie and Rover. But she may get off. She can get off if she can fool her boss, she says. So we're all going down and we may bring Larry home with us, Mrs. Sleighter says. Though Mrs. Gwynne says there's not any room, they're so filled up now. And I said Larry could come here and Joe, too. But I am not so sure about Sam. I think he must be awfully queer. Mr. Gwynne thinks he's queer."

"It is quite possible, indeed probable, my dear," assented her father.

"Yes, Mr. Gwynne said he looked like a third-rate how-do-you-feel performer."

"A what, exactly?"

"A how-do-you-feel performer."

"Oh, a vaudeville performer."

"Yes, a fodefeel performer. I don't know what that means, but he must be queer. But I think Larry would be all right, and Joe. You see, we know THEM."

"Oh, do we?"

"Yes, certainly, Papa. Larry is Nora's brother. He's awfully clever. He's only fifteen and he passed the Entrance in Ontario and that's ever so much harder than here. He passed it before he was fourteen."

"Before he was fourteen!" replied her father. "Amazing!"

"Yes, and he plays the mouth organ and the tin whistle and the fiddle, and Mr. Gwynne says he has learned some stunts from Sam. I think he must be awfully nice. So I said he could come here. And Mrs. Gwynne thanked me so nicely, and she's just lovely, Papa."

"I have not seen her," said her father, "but I have heard her voice, and I quite agree with you. The voice always tells. Have you noticed that? The voice gives the keynote of the soul."

"I don't know, Papa. There's Mrs. Sleighter's voice. I don't like it very much, but I think she's nice inside."

"Ah, you are right, my dear. Perhaps I should have said that a certain kind of voice always goes with a beautiful soul."

"I know," replied his daughter. "That's like Mrs. Gwynne's voice. And so we'll go down to the car and bring Larry home with us, and perhaps his mother will let him come here. She did not say she would and you can't tell. She's quiet, you know, but somehow she isn't like Mrs. Sleighter. I don't think you could coax her to do what she didn't want."

"And Mrs. Sleighter—can you coax Mrs. Sleighter?"

"Oh, yes, the girls just coax her and coax her, and though she doesn't want to a bit, she just gives in."

"That's nice of her. That must be very nice for the girls, eh?"

Ralph Connor

"Oh, I don't know, Papa."

"What? don't you think it is nice to be able to coax people to do what you want?"

"It is nice to get what you want, but I think REALLY, REALLY, you'd rather you could not coax them to do it just because you coax them."

"Ah, I see."

"Yes; you see, you're never really quite sure after you get it whether you ought to get it after all."

"I see," said her father; "that rather spoils it."

"Yes, but you never do that, Papa."

"Oh, you can't coax me, eh? I am glad to know that. I was afraid, rather."

"Well, of course, I can coax you, Papa, but you usually find some other way, and then I know it is quite right."

"I wish I was quite as sure of that, Jane. But you are going to bring Larry home with you?"

"Yes, if Mrs. Gwynne will let him come. I told her we had four rooms and we were only using two, and they are all crowded up in Mrs. Sleighter's, two girls in each room, and Tom's room is so tiny, and I don't think Larry would like to go in Tom's room. And we have two empty rooms, so we might just as well."

"Yes, certainly, we might just as well. You might perhaps mention it to Anna."

"Oh, I did, Papa, and she said she would have it all ready."

"So it is all arranged. I was thinking—but never mind."

"I know you were thinking, that I ought to have asked you, Papa; and I ought to have. But I knew that when a little boy had no home to go to you would of course—"

"Of course," replied her father hurriedly. "You were quite right, Jane. And with those two rooms, why not bring them all, Joe and Pete—Pete, is it?"

"Sam, Papa. I am not so sure. I think we should leave Joe and Sam. You see Joe won't mind staying in the car. Nora says he lives in just a shack at home, and Sam—I am a little afraid of Sam. We don't know him very well, you see."

"I see. We are quite safe in your hands, little woman. You can do just as you and Mrs. Gwynne arrange."

As the father watched the little, trim, sturdy figure stepping down the street he muttered to himself, "That child grows more like her mother every day." He heaved a great sigh from the depths of his heart. "Well, God keep her, wise little woman that she is! I wish I were a wiser man. I must be firm with her; it would be a shame to spoil her. Yes, I must be firm." But he shrugged his shoulders and smiled at himself. "The worst of it is, or the best of it is," he continued, "the little witch is almost always right, God bless her, just like her mother, just like her mother." He hastily wiped his eyes, and went off to his office where Mrs. Dean awaited him and her little girl with the burned hand. And the mother wondered at the gentleness of him as he dressed the little girl's wounded hand.

It followed that the scouting party included not only Miss Hazel Sleighter, but also her big brother Tom, who, being temporarily in the high school, more perhaps because of his size and the maturity of his bearing than by virtue of his educational qualifications, was at the present moment most chiefly concerned in getting into form his baseball team for the match the following Saturday in which the High School was to meet All Comers under eighteen. The freight shed being on his way to the practice ground, Tom deigned to join the party and to take in the circus car as he passed. The car dwellers were discovered on the open prairie not far from the freight shed, keeping guard over Rosie, who was stretching her legs after her railway journey. The boys were tossing a baseball to each other as Tom pedalled up on his wheel.

"Hello, there, here you are," he shouted to Sam, holding up his hands for a catch.

The ball came with such impact that Tom was distinctly jarred, and dropped the ball. With all his force he threw the ball back to Sam, who caught it with the ease of a professional and returned it with such vigour that again Tom dropped it.

"Let's have a knock-up," he said, hitting a long fly.

Sam flew after the ball with amazing swiftness, his scarecrow garments fluttering and flapping in the air, and caught it with an upward leap that landed him on his back breathless but triumphant.

"Say, you're a crackerjack," said Tom; "here's another."

Meanwhile Larry was in the hands of his sisters, who had delightedly kissed him to his shamefaced chagrin, and introduced him to their new-found friends.

"So this is Larry." said Miss Hazel Sleighter, greeting him with a dazzling smile. "We have heard a lot about you. I think you must be quite wonderful. Come here, Tom, and meet your friends."

Poor Larry! In the presence of this radiant creature and of her well-dressed brother, he felt terribly conscious of the shabbiness of the second best suit which his mother had thought good enough for the journey in the car. Tom glanced at the slight, poorly dressed, pale-faced lad who stood before him with an embarrassed, almost a beseeching look in his eyes.

"Can you play ball?" asked Tom.

"Not much," replied Larry; "not like Sam. Come here, Sam," he called, remembering that he had not introduced his friend. Sam shuffled over with an air of complete nonchalance.

"This is Sam," said Larry. "Sam—I have forgotten your name."

"Nolan," said Sam shortly.

"Miss Hazel Sleighter," said Larry.

"How do you do, Miss Hazel," said Sam, sweeping her an elaborate bow, and then gazing boldly into her eyes. "I hope you're well. If you're as smart as you look, I guess you're way up in G."

"I am quite well, thank you," returned Miss Hazel, the angle of her chin indicating her most haughty air.

"Say, young lady, pass up the chilly stuff," replied Sam with a laugh. "It don't go with that mighty fine complexion of yours. Say, did you ever see the leading lady in 'The Spider's Web'? Well, you make me think of her, and she was a peacherino. Never seen her? No? Well, you ought to see her some day and think of me."

Hazel turned a disgusted shoulder on Sam's impudent face and engaged Larry in vivacious conversation.

"Well, I am off to the ball practice," said Tom. "Got a match on Saturday—High School against the world. Guess they would like to have you, Sam, only I wouldn't care to have you play against us. You don't play baseball, eh?" continued Tom, addressing Larry. "What do you play—football?"

"Not much; never tried much," said Larry, flushing over his lack of sporting qualifications.

"He plays the fiddle," said a quiet little voice.

Larry, flushing violently, turned around and saw a little, brown-faced maid gazing thoughtfully at him.

"Oh, he does, eh? Ha, ha, ha. Good game, eh? Ha, ha, ha." They all joined in the laugh.

"And he plays the mouth organ, too, and does funny stunts," sturdily continued the little girl, disdaining Tom's scornful laughter.

"Good for you, Jane."

"Yes, and he passed his entrance to the High School a year ago when he was fourteen, in Ontario, anyway." This appeared to check Tom's hilarity.

"My, what a wonder he is! And did he tell you all

this himself?"

"No, indeed," said Jane indignantly.

"Oh, I am glad to hear that," said Tom with a grin. "Won't you come along, Sam? It's only a little way down."

"All right," said Sam cheerfully. "So long, folks. See you later, Larry. Au reservoir, young lady, as the camel said to the elephant when he asked what he'd have. Hope I see you later if not sooner—ta-ta; tinga-ling; honk honk." Again he swept Miss Hazel an elaborate bow.

"Thinks he's smart," said that young lady, lifting her nose. "He's a regular scarecrow. Who in the world is he and where did he come from?" she demanded of Larry, who proceeded to account for Sam's presence with their party.

The visitors peered into the car and poked into its recesses, discovered the food supplies for boy and beast, and inspected the dormitories under Larry's guidance, while the boy, who had recovered from his embarrassment, discoursed upon the wonderful experience of the journey. Miss Hazel flashed her great blue eyes and her white teeth upon him, shook all her frizzes in his face, smiled at him, chattered to him, jeered at him, flattered him with all the arts and graces of the practiced flirt she was, until Larry, swept from his bearings, walked the clouds in a wonder world of rosy lights and ravishing airs. His face, his eyes, his eager words, his tremulous lips, were all eloquent of this new passion that possessed him.

As for Miss Hazel, accustomed as she was to the discriminating admiration of her fellow clerks, the sincerity and abandonment of this devotion was as incense to her flirtatious soul. Avid of admiration and experienced in most of the arts and wiles necessary to secure this from contiguous males, small wonder that the unsophisticated Larry became her easy prey long before she had brought to bear the full complement of her enginery of war.

It was a happy afternoon for the boy, but when informed by his sisters of his mother's desire that he should return with them, he was resolute in his refusal, urging many reasons why it was impossible that he should leave the car and his comrades. There was nothing for it but to leave him there and report to his mother their failure.

"I might have known," she said. "He would never come to a stranger's house in his old clothes. I will just bring down his best suit after tea."

The dinner hour at Dr. Brown's was fully occupied with an animated recital of the adventures of the afternoon. Each member of the car party was described with an accuracy and fulness of detail that would have surprised him.

"And you know, Papa," said the little maid, "Tom just laughed at Larry because he could not play baseball and things, and I just told him that Larry could play the mouth organ lovely and the fiddle, and they laughed and laughed. I think they were laughing at me. Tom laughed loudest of all, and he's not so smart himself, and anyway Larry passed the entrance a year ago and I just told him so."

"Oh, did you," said her father, "and how did Master Tom take that?"

"He didn't laugh quite as much. I don't think I like him very much."

"Ah?"

"But Hazel, she was just lovely to Larry. I think she's nice, Papa, and such lovely cheeks and hair." Here Jane sighed.

"Oh, has she? She is quite a grown-up young lady, is she not?"

"She has her hair up, Papa. She's sixteen, you know."

"I remember you told me that she had reached that mature age."

"And I think Larry liked her, too."

"Ah? And why do you think so?"

"He just looked at her, and looked, and looked."

"Well, that seems fairly good evidence."

"And he is coming up here to-night when we bring him his good clothes."

"Oh, you are to bring him his good clothes, are you?"

"Yes, Mrs. Gwynne and I are taking them down in the carriage."

"Oh, in the carriage—Mrs. Gwynne—"

"Yes, you know—Oh, here's Nora at the door. Excuse me, Papa. I am sure it is important."

She ran to the door and in a moment or two returned with a note. "It's for you, Papa, and I know it's about the carriage." She watched her father somewhat anxiously as he read the note.

"Umm-um. Very good, very nice and proper. Certainly. Just say to Mrs. Gwynne that we are very pleased to be able to serve her with the carriage, and that we hope Larry will do us the honour of coming to us."

Jane nodded delightedly. "I know, Papa. I told her that already. But I'll tell her this is the answer to the note."

Under Jane's direction and care they made their visit to the car, but on their return no Larry was with them. He would come after the picnic and baseball game tomorrow, perhaps, but not to-night. His mother was plainly disappointed, and indeed a little hurt. She could not understand her son. It was not his clothes after all as she had thought. She pondered over his last words spoken as he bade her farewell at the car door, and was even more mystified.

"I'll be glad when we get to our own place again," he said. "I hate to be beholden to anybody. We're as good as any of them anyway." The bitterness in his tone mystified her still more.

It was little Jane who supplied the key to the mystery. "I don't think he likes Tom very much," said the little girl. "He likes Hazel, though. But he might have come to our house; I did not laugh." And then the mother thought she understood.

That sudden intensity of bitterness in her boy's voice startled her a little, but deep down in her heart she was conscious of a queer feeling of satisfaction, almost of pride. "He's just like his father," she said to herself. "He likes to be independent." Strict honesty in thought made her add, "And like me, too, I fear."

The picnic day was one of those intensely hot June days

when the whole world seems to stand quivering and breathlessly attent while Nature works out one of her miracles over fields of grain, over prairie flowers, over umbrageous trees and all things borne upon the bosom of Mother Earth, checking the succulence of precocious overgrowths, hardening fibre, turning plant energy away from selfish exuberance in mere stalk building into the altruistic sacrament of ripening fruit and hardening grain. A wise old alchemist is Mother Earth, working in time but ever for eternity.

The picnickers who went out to the park early in the day were driven for refuge from the blazing sun to the trees and bushes, where prostrated by the heat they lay limp and flaccid upon the grass. Miss Hazel Sleighter, who for some reason which she could not explain to herself had joined the first contingent of picnickers, was cross, distinctly and obviously cross. The heat was trying to her nerves, but worse, it made her face red—red all over. Her pink parasol intensified the glow upon her face.

"What a fool I was to come, in this awful heat," she said to herself. "They won't be here for hours, and I will be just like a wash-rag."

Nor was Larry enjoying the picnic. The material comforts in the form of sandwiches, cakes and pies, gloriously culminating in lemonade and ice cream, while contributing a temporary pleasure, could not obliterate a sense of misery wrought in him by Miss Hazel's chilly indifference. That young lady, whose smiles so lavishly bestowed only yesterday had made for him a new heaven and a new earth, had to-day merely thrown him a passing glance and a careless "Hello," as she floated by intent on bigger game.

In addition, the boy was conscious of an overpowering

lassitude that increased as the day wore on. His misery and its chief cause had not escaped the observing eyes of the little maid, Jane Brown, whose clear and incisive voice was distinctly audible as she confided to her friend Nora her disappointment in Miss Hazel.

"She won't look at him to-day," she said. "She's just waiting for the boys to come. She'll be nicer then."

There was no animus in the voice, only surprise and disappointment. To Larry, however, the fact that the secret tragedy of his soul was thus laid bare, filled him with a sudden rage. He cast a wrathful eye upon the little maid. She met his glance with a placid smile, volunteering the cheerful remark, "They won't be long now."

A fury possessed the boy. "Oh shut your mouth, will you?" he said, glaring at her.

For a moment little Jane looked at him, surprise, dismay, finally pity succeeding each other in the deep blue eyes. Hastily she glanced about to see if the others had heard the awful outburst. She was relieved to note that only Joe and Nora were near enough to hear. She settled herself down in a position of greater comfort and confided to her friend Nora with an air of almost maternal solicitude, "I believe he has a pain. I am sure he has a pain."

Larry sprang to his feet, and without a glance at his anxious tormentor said, "Come on, Joe, let's go for a hunt in the woods."

Jane looked wistfully after the departing boys. "I wish they would ask us, Nora. Don't you? I think he is nice when he isn't mad," she said. To which Nora firmly assented.

A breeze from the west and the arrival of the High School team, resplendent in their new baseball uniforms, brought to the limp loiterers under the trees a reviving life and interest in the day's doings.

It was due to Jane that Sam got into the game, for when young Frank Smart was searching for a suitable left fielder to complete the All Comers team, he spied seated among the boys the little girl.

"Hello, Jane; in your usual place, I see!" he called out to her as he passed.

"Hello, Frank!" she called to him brightly. "Frank! Frank!" she cried, after the young man had passed, springing up and running after him.

"I am in a hurry, Jane; I must get a man for left field."

"But, Frank," she said, catching his arm, for young Smart was a great friend of hers and of her father's. "I want to tell you. You see that funny boy under the tree," she continued, lowering her voice. "Well, he's a splendid player. Tom doesn't want him to play, and I don't either, because I want the High School to beat. But it would not be fair not to tell you, would it?"

Young Smart looked at her curiously. "Say, little girl, you're a sport. And is he a good player?"

"Oh, he's splendid, but he's queer—I mean he looks queer. He's awfully funny. But that doesn't matter, does it?"

"Not a hair, if he can play ball. What's his name?"

"Sam—something."

Ralph Connor

"Sam Something? That is a funny name."

"Oh, you know, Sam. I don't know his other name."

"Well, I'll try him, Jane," said young Smart, moving toward the boy and followed by the eager eyes of the little girl.

"I say, Sam," said Smart, "we want a man for left field. Will you take a go at it?"

"Too hot," grunted Sam.

"Oh, you won't find it too hot when you get started. Rip off your coat and get into the game. You can play, can't you?"

"Aw, what yer givin' us. I guess I can give them ginks a few pointers."

"Well, come on."

"Too hot," said Sam.

Jane pulled young Smart by the sleeve. "Tell him you will give him a jersey," she said in a low voice. "His shirt is torn."

Again young Smart looked at Jane with scrutinising eyes. "You're a wonder," he said.

"Come along, Sam. You haven't got your sweater with you, but I will get one for you. Get into the bush there and change."

With apparent reluctance, but with a gleam in his little red eyes, Sam slouched into the woods to make the change, and in a few moments came forth and ran to take his position at left field.

The baseball match turned out to be a mere setting for the display of the eccentricities and superior baseball qualities of Sam, which apparently quite outclassed those of his teammates in the match. After three disastrous innings, Sam caused himself to be moved first to the position of short stop, and later to the pitcher's box, to the immense advantage of his side. But although, owing to the lead obtained by the enemy, his prowess was unable to ward off defeat from All Comers, yet under his inspiration and skilful generalship, the team made such a brilliant recovery of form and came so near victory that Sam was carried from the field in triumph shoulder high and departed with his new and enthusiastically grateful comrades to a celebration.

Larry, however, was much too miserable and much too unhappy for anything like a celebration. The boy was oppressed with a feeling of loneliness, and was conscious chiefly of a desire to reach his car and crawl into his bed there among the straw. Stumbling blindly along the dusty road; a cheery voice hailed him.

"Hello, Larry!" It was Jane seated beside her father in his car.

"Hello!" he answered faintly and just glanced at her as the car passed.

But soon the car pulled up. "Come on, Larry, we'll take you home," said Jane.

"Oh, I'm all right," said Larry, forcing his lips into his old smile and resolutely plodding on.

"Better come up, my boy," said the doctor.

"I don't mind walking, sir," replied Larry, stubbornly determined to go his lonely way.

"Come here, boy," said the doctor, regarding him keenly. Larry came over to the wheel. "Why, boy, what is the matter?" The doctor took hold of his hand.

Larry gripped the wheel hard. He was feeling desperately ill and unsteady on his legs, but still his lips twisted themselves into a smile. "I'm all right, sir," he said; "I've got a headache and it was pretty hot out there."

But even as he spoke his face grew white and he swayed on his feet. In an instant the doctor was out of his car. "Get in, lad," he said briefly, and Larry, surrendering, climbed into the back seat, fighting fiercely meanwhile to prevent the tears from showing in his eyes. Keeping up a brisk and cheerful conversation with Jane in regard to the game, the doctor drove rapidly toward his home.

"You will come in with us, my boy," said the doctor as they reached his door.

By this time Larry was past all power of resistance and yielded himself to the authority of the doctor, who had him upstairs and into bed within a few minutes of his arrival. A single word Larry uttered during this process, "Tell my mother," and then sank into a long nightmare, through which there mingled dim shapes and quiet voices, followed by dreamless sleep, and an awakening to weakness that made the lifting of his eyelids an effort and the movement of his hand a weariness. The first object that loomed intelligible through the fog in which he seemed to move was a little plain face with great blue eyes carrying in them a cloud of maternal anxiety.

Suddenly the cloud broke and the sun burst through in a joyous riot, for in a voice that seemed to him unfamiliar and remote Larry uttered the single word, "Jane."

"Oh!" cried the little girl rapturously. "Oh, Larry, wait." She slipped from the room and returned in a moment with his mother, who quickly came to his side.

"You are rested, dear," she said, putting her hand under his head. "Drink this. No, don't lift your head. Now then, go to sleep again, darling," and, stooping down, she kissed him softly.

"Why—are—you—crying?" he asked faintly. "What's the—matter?"

"Nothing, darling; you are better. Just sleep."

"Better?—Have—I—been—sick?"

"Yes, you have been sick," said his mother.

"Awfully sick," said Jane solemnly. "A whole week sick. But you are all right now," she added brightly, "and so is Joe, and Sam, and Rover and Rosie. I saw them all this morning and you know we have been praying and praying and—"

"Now he will sleep, Jane," said his mother, gently touching the little girl's brown tangle of hair.

"Yes, he will sleep; oh, I'm just awful thankful," said Jane, suddenly rushing out of the room.

"Dear little girl," said the mother. "She has been so anxious and so helpful—a wonderful little nurse."

But Larry was fast asleep, and before he was interested enough to make inquiry about his comrades in travel the car in charge of Joe and Sam, with Mr. Gwynne in the caboose, was far on its way to Alberta. After some days Jane was allowed to entertain the sick boy, as was her custom with her father, by giving an account of her day's doings. These were happy days for them both. Between the boy and the girl the beginnings of a great friendship sprang up.

"Larry, I think you are queer," said Jane to him gravely one day. "You are not a bit like you were in the car."

A quick flush appeared on the boy's face. "I guess I was queer that day, Jane," he said. "I know I felt queer."

"Yes, that's it," said Jane, delighted by some sudden recollection. "You were queer then, and now you're just ornary. My, you were sick and you were cross, too, awful cross that day. I guess it was the headick. I get awfully cross, too, when I have the headick. I don't think you will be cross again ever, will you, Larry?"

Larry, smiling at her, replied, "I'll never be cross with you, Jane, anyway, never again."

CHAPTER VII

THE GIRL OF THE WOOD LOT

June, and the sun flooding with a golden shimmer a land of tawny prairie, billowy hills, wooded valleys and mountain peaks white with eternal snows, touching with silver a stream which, glacier-born, hurled itself down mountain sides in fairy films of mist, rushed through canyons in a mad torrent, hurried between hills in a swollen flood, meandered along wide valleys in a full-lipped tide, lingered in a placid lake in a bit of lowland banked with poplar bluffs, and so onward past ranch-stead and homestead to the great Saskatchewan and Father Ocean, prairie and hills, valleys and mountains, river and lake, making a wonder world of light and warmth and colour and joyous life.

Two riders on rangey bronchos, followed by two Russian boarhounds, climbed the trail that went winding up among the hills towards a height which broke abruptly into a ridge of bare rock. Upon the ridge they paused.

"There! Can you beat that? If so, where?" The lady swept her gauntletted hand toward the scene below. Mrs. Waring-Gaunt was tall, strongly made, handsome with that comeliness which perfect health and out-of-doors life combine to give, her dark hair, dark flashing eyes, straight

Ralph Connor

nose, wide, full-lipped curving mouth, and a chin whose chiselled firmness was softened but not weakened by a dimple, making a picture good to look upon.

"There!" she cried again, "tell me, can you beat it?"

"Glorious! Sybil, utterly and splendidly glorious!" said her brother, his eyes sweeping the picture below. "And you too, Sybil," he said, turning his eyes upon her. "This country has done you well. By jove, what a trans-formation from the white-faced, willowy—"

"Weedy," said she.

"Well, as it's no longer true, weedy—woman that faded out of London, how many—eight years ago!"

"Ten years, ten long, glorious, splendid years."

"Ten years! Surely not ten!"

"Yes, ten beautiful years."

"I wish to God I had come with you then. I might have been—well, I should have been saved some bumps and a ghastly cropper at last."

"'Cut it out,' Jack, as the boys say here. En avant! We never look back in this land, but ever forward. Oh, now isn't this worth while?" Again she swept her hand toward the scene below her. "Look at that waving line in the east, that broad sweep; and here at our left, those great, majestic things. I love them. I love every scar in their old grey faces. They have been good friends to me. But for them some days might have been hard to live through, but they were always there like friends, watching, under-standing. They kept me steady."

"You must have had some difficult days, old girl, in this awful land. Yes, yes, I know it's glorious, especially on a day like this and in a light like this; but after all, you are away from the world, away from everybody, and shut off from everything, from life, art—how could you stick it?"

"Jack are you sympathising with me? Let me tell you your sympathy is wasted. I have had lonely days in this land, of course. When Tom was off on business—Oh! that man has been perfectly splendid. Jack! He's been—well, I can't tell you all he has been to me—father, mother, husband, chum, he's been to me, and more. And he's made good in the country, too. Now look again at this view. We always stop to look at it, Tom and I, from this point. Tell me if you have ever seen anything quite as wonderful!"

"Yes, it's glorious, a little like the veldt, with, of course, the mountains extra, and they do rather finish the thing in the grand style."

"Grand style, well, rather! A great traveller who has seen most of the world's beautiful spots told me he had never looked on anything quite so splendid as the view from here—so spacious, so varied, so majestic. Ah, I love it, and the country has been good to me!

"I don't mean physically only, but in every way—in body, soul and mind. And for Tom, too, the country has done much. In England, you know, he was just loafing, filling in time with one useless thing after another, and on the way to get fat and lazy. Here he is doing things, things worth while. His ranch is quite a success. Then he is always busy organising various sorts of industries in the country—dairying, lumbering and that sort of thing. He has introduced thoroughbred stock. He helps with the schools, the churches, the Agricultural Institutes. In short, he is doing his part to bring this country to its best. And this, you know, is the finest bit of all Canada!"

Her brother laughed. "Pardon me," he said, "there are so many of these 'finest bits.' In Nova Scotia, in Quebec, I have found them. The people of Ontario are certain that the 'finest bit' is in their province, while in British Columbia they are ready to fight if one suggests anything to the contrary."

"I know. I know. It is perfectly splendid of them. You know we Canadians are quite foolish about our country."

"WE Canadians!"

"Yes. WE Canadians. What else? We are quite mad about the future of our country. And that is why I wanted you to come out here, Jack. There is so much a man like you might do with your brains and training. Yes. Your Oxford training is none too good for this country, and your brain none too clever for this big work of laying the foundations of a great Empire. This is big enough for the biggest of you. Bigger, even, than the thing you were doing at home, Jack. Oh, I heard all about it!"

"You heard all about it? I hope not. I hope you have not heard of the awful mess I made of things."

"Nonsense, Jack! 'Forward' is the word here. Here is an Empire in the making, another Britain, greater, finer, and without the hideous inequalities, injustices and foolish class distinctions of the old."

"My God! Sybil, you sound like Lloyd George himself! Please don't recall that ghastly radicalism to me."

"Never mind what it sounds like. You will get it too. We all catch it here, especially Old Country folk. For instance, look away to the left there. See that little clump of buildings beside the lake just through the poplars. There is a family of Canadians typical of the best, the Gwynnes, our closest neighbours. Good Irish stock, they are. They came two years after we came. Lost their little bit of money. Suffered, my! how they must have suffered! though they were too proud to tell any of us. The father is a gentleman, finely educated, but with no business ability. The mother all gold and grit, heroic little woman who kept the family together. The eldest boy of fifteen or sixteen, rather delicate when he came, but fearfully plucky, has helped amazingly. He taught the school, putting his money into the farm year after year. While teaching the school he somehow managed to grip hold of the social life of this community in a wonderful way, preached for Mr. Rhye, taught a Bible Class for him, quite unique in its way; organised a kind of Literary-Social-Choral-Minstrel Club and has added tremendously to the life and gaiety of the neighbourhood. What we shall do when he leaves, I know not. You will like them, I am sure. We shall drop in there on our way, if you like."

"Ah, well, perhaps sometime later. They all sound rather terribly industrious and efficient for a mere slacker like myself."

Along the trail they galloped, following the dogs for a mile or so until checked by a full flowing stream.

"I say, Willow Creek is really quite in flood," said his sister. "The hot sun has brought down the snows, you know. The logs are running, too. We will have to go a bit carefully. Hold well up to the stream and watch the logs. Keep your eye on the bank opposite. No, no, keep up, follow me. Look out, or you will get into deep water. Keep to the right. There, that's better."

"I say," said her brother, as his horse clambered out of the swollen stream. "That's rather a close thing to a ducking. Awfully like the veldt streams, you know. Ice cold, too, I fancy."

"Ice cold, indeed, glacier water, you know, and these logs make it very awkward. The Gwynnes must be running down their timber and firewood. We might just run up and look in on them. It's only a mile or so. Nora will be there. She will be 'bossing the job,' as she says. It will be rather interesting."

"Well, I hope it is not too far, for I assure you I am getting quite ravenous."

"No, come along, there's a good trail here."

A smart canter brought them to a rather pretentious homestead with considerable barns and outbuildings attached. "This is the Switzers' place," said Mrs. Waring-Gaunt. "German-Americans, old settlers and quite well off. The father owned the land on which Wolf Willow village stands. He made quite a lot of money in real estate—village lots and farm lands, you know. He is an excellent farmer and ambitious for his family—one son and one daughter. They are quite plain people. They live like—well, like Germans, you know. The mother is a regular hausfrau; the daughter, quite nice, plays the violin beautifully. It was from her young Gwynne got his violining. The son went to college in the States, then to Germany for a couple of years. He came back here a year ago, terribly German and terribly military, heel clicking, ram-rod back, and all that sort of thing. Musical, too, awfully clever; rather think he has political ambitions. We'll not go in to-day. Some day, perhaps. Indecd, we must be neighbourly in this country. But the Switzers are a little trying."

"Why know them at all?"

"There you are!" cried his sister. "Fancy living beside people in this country and not knowing them. Can't you see that we must not let things get awry that way? We must all pull together. Tom is fearfully strong on that, and he is right, too, I suppose, although it is trying at times. Now we begin to climb a bit here. Then there are good stretches further along where we can hurry."

But it seemed to her brother that the good stretches were rather fewer and shorter than the others, for the sun was overhead when they pulled up their horses, steaming and ready enough to halt, in a small clearing in the midst of a thick bit of forest. The timber was for the main part of soft woods, poplar, yellow and black, cottonwood, and further up among hills spruce and red pine. In the centre of the clearing stood a rough log cabin with a wide porch running around two sides. Upon this porch a young girl was to be seen busy over a cook stove. At the noise of the approaching horses the girl turned from her work and looked across the clearing at them.

"Heavens above! who is that, Sybil?" gasped her brother.

Mrs. Waring-Gaunt gave a delighted little cry. "Oh, my dear, you are really back." In a moment she was off her horse and rushing toward the girl with her arms outstretched. "Kathleen, darling! Is it you? And you have really grown, I believe! Or is it your hair? Come let me introduce you to my brother."

Jack Romayne was a young man with thirty years of experience of the normal life of the well-born Englishman, during which time he had often known what it was to have his senses stirred and his pulses quickened by the sight of one of England's fair women, than whom none of fresher and fairer beauty are to be found in all the world; yet never had he found himself anything but master of his speech and behaviour. But to-day, when, in obedience to his sister's call, he moved across the little clearing toward the girl standing at her side, he seemed to lose consciousness of himself and control of his powers of action. He was instead faintly conscious that a girl of tall and slender grace, with an aura of golden hair about a face lovelier than he had ever known, was looking at him out of eyes as blue as the prairie crocus and as shy and sweet, that she laid her hand in his as if giving him something of herself, that holding her hand how long he knew not, he found himself gazing through those eyes of translucent blue into a soul of unstained purity as one might gaze into a shrine, and that he continued gazing until the blue eyes clouded and the fair face flushed crimson, that then, without a word, he turned from her, thrilling with a new gladness which seemed to fill not only his soul but the whole world as well. When he came to himself he found his trembling fingers fumbling with the bridle of his horse. For a few moments he became aware of a blind rage possessing him and he cursed deeply his stupidity and the gaucherie of his manner. But soon he forgot his rage for thinking of her eyes and of what he had seen behind their translucent blue.

"My dear child," again exclaimed Mrs. Waring-Gaunt, "I declare you have actually grown taller and grown—a great many other things that I may not tell you. What have they done to you at that wonderful school? Did you love it?"

The girl flushed with a quick emotion. "Oh, Mrs. Waring-Gaunt, it was really wonderful. I had such a good time and every one was lovely to me. I did not know people could be so kind. But it is good to get back home again to them all, and to you, and to all this." She waved her hand to the forest about her.

"And who are up here to-day, and what are you doing?" inquired Mrs. Waring-Gaunt.

"In the meantime I am preparing dinner," said the girl with a laugh.

"Dinner!" exclaimed Jack Romayne, who had meantime drawn near, determined to rehabilitate himself in the eyes of this girl as a man familiar with the decencies of polite society. "Dinner! It smells so good and we are desperately hungry."

"Yes," cried Mrs. Waring-Gaunt. "My brother declared he was quite faint more than an hour ago, and now I am sure he is."

"Fairly ravenous."

"But I don't know," said the girl with serious anxiety on her face. "You see, we have only pork and fried potatoes, and Nora just shot a chicken—only one—and they are always so hungry. But we have plenty of bread and tea. Would you stay?"

"It sounds really very nice," said Mrs. Waring-Gaunt.

"It would be awfully jolly of you, and I promise not to eat too much," said the young man. "I am actually faint with hunger, and a cup of tea appears necessary to revive me."

"Of course, stay," said the girl with quick sympathy. "We can't give you much, but we can give you something."

"Oh—ho!"

"O-h-o-o-o-h! O-h-o-o-o-h!" A loud call came from the woods.

"There's Nora," said Kathleen. "O-o-o-o-o-h! O-o-o-o-o-h!" The girl's answering call was like the winding of a silver horn. "Here she is."

Out from the woods, striding into the clearing, came a young girl dressed in workmanlike garb in short skirt, leggings and jersey, with a soft black hat on the black tumbled locks. "Hello, Kathleen, dinner ready? I'm famished. Oh, Mrs. Waring-Gaunt, glad to see you."

"And my brother, Nora, Mr. Jack Romayne, just come from England, and hungry as a bear."

"Just from England? And hungry? Well, we are glad to see you, Mr. Romayne." The girl came forward with a quick step and frankly offered her brown, strong hand. "We're awfully glad to see you, Mr. Romayne," she repeated. "I ought to be embarrassed, I know, only I am so hungry."

"Just my fix, Miss Nora," said the young man. "I am really anxious to be polite. I feel we should decline the invitation to dinner which your sister has pressed upon us; we know it is a shame to drop in on you like this all unprepared, but I am so hungry, and really that smell is so irresistible that I feel I simply cannot be polite."

"Don't!" cried the girl, "or rather, do, and stay. There's enough of something, and Joe will look after the horses." She put her hands to her lips and called, "J-o-o-e!"

A voice from the woods answered her, followed by Joe himself. "Here, Joe, take the horses and unsaddle them and tether them out somewhere."

Despite Kathleen's fears there was dinner enough for all.

"This is perfectly stunning!" said Romayne, glancing round the little clearing and up at the trees waving overhead, through the interstices of whose leafy canopy showed patches of blue sky. "Gorgeous, by Jove! Words are futile things for really great moments."

"Ripping," said Nora, smiling impudently into his face. "Awfully jolly! A-1! Top hole! That's the lot, I think, according to the best authorities. Do you know any others?"

"I beg pardon, what?" said Romayne, looking up from his fried pork and potatoes.

"Those are all I have learned in English at least," said Nora. "I am keen for some more. They are Oxford, I believe. Have you any others?"

Mr. Romayne diverted his attention from his dinner. "What is she talking about, Miss Gwynne? I confess to be entirely absorbed in these fried potatoes."

"Words, words, Mr. Romayne, vocabulary, adjectives," replied Nora.

"Ah," said Romayne, "but why should one worry about words, especially adjectives, when one has such divine realities as these to deal with?"

"Have some muffles, Mr. Romayne," said Nora.

"Muffles? Now what may muffles be?"

"Muffles are a cross between muffins and waffles."

"Please elucidate their nature and origin," said Mr. Romayne.

"Let me show you," said Kathleen. She sprang up, dived into the cabin and returned with a large, round, hard biscuit in her hand. "This is Hudson Bay hard tack, the stand-by of all western people—Hudson Bay freighters and cowboys, old timers and tenderfeet alike swear by it. See, you moisten it slightly in water, fry it in boiling fat, sugar it and keep hot till served. Thus Hudson Bay hard tack becomes muffles."

"Marvellous!" exclaimed Mr. Romayne, "and truly delicious! And to think that the Savoy chef knows nothing about muffles! But now that my first faintness is removed and the mystery of muffles is solved, may I inquire just what you are doing up here to-day, Miss Gwynne? What is the business on hand, I mean?"

"Oh, Nora is getting out some logs for building and firewood for next winter. The logs, you see, are cut during the winter and hauled to the dump there."

"Dump!" exclaimed Mr. Romayne faintly.

"Yes. The bank there where you dump the logs into the creek below."

"But what exactly has Miss Nora to do with all this?"

"I?" enquired Nora, "I only boss the job."

"Don't you believe her," said Mrs. Waring-Gaunt. "I happen to remember one winter day coming upon this young lady in these very woods driving her team and hauling logs to the dump while Sam and Joe did the cutting. Ask the boys there? And why shouldn't she?"

continued Mrs. Waring-Gaunt. "She can run a farm, with garden, pigs and poultry thrown in; open a coal mine and—"

"Nonsense!" exclaimed Nora, "the boys here do it all. Mother furnishes the head work."

"Oh, Nora!" protested Kathleen, "you know you manage everything. Isn't that true, boys?"

"She's the hull works herself," said Sam. "Ain't she, Joe?"

"You bet yeh," said Joe, husky with the muffles.

"She's a corker," continued Sam, "double compressed, compensating, forty horsepower, ain't she, Joe?"

"You bet yeh!" adding, for purpose of emphasis, "By gar!"

"Six cylinder, self-starter," continued Sam with increasing enthusiasm.

"Self-starter," echoed Joe, going off into a series of choking chuckles. "Sure t'ing, by gar!" Joe, having safely disposed of the muffles, gave himself up to unrestrained laughter, throwing back his head, slapping his knees and repeating at intervals, "Self-starter, by gar!"

So infectious was his laughter that the whole company joined in.

"Cut it out, boys," said Nora. "You are all talking rot, you know; and what about you," she added, turning swiftly upon her sister. "Who runs the house, I'd like to know, and looks after everything inside, and does the sewing? This outfit of mine, for instance? And her own outfit?"

Ralph Connor

"Oh, Nora," protested Kathleen, the colour rising in her face.

"Did you make your own costume?" inquired Mr. Romayne.

"She did that," said Nora, "and mine and mother's, and she makes father's working shirts."

"Oh, Nora, stop, please. You know I do very little."

"She makes the butter as well."

"They're a pair," said Sam in a low growl, but perfectly audible to the company, "a regular pair, eh, Joe?"

"Sure t'ing," replied Joe, threatening to go off again into laughter, but held in check by a glance from Nora.

For an hour they lingered over the meal. Then Nora, jumping up quickly, took Mrs. Waring-Gaunt with her to superintend the work at the dump, leaving Mr. Romayne reclining on the grass smoking his pipe in abandoned content, while Kathleen busied herself clearing away and washing up the dishes.

"May I help?" inquired Mr. Romayne, when the others had gone.

"Oh, no," replied Kathleen. "Just rest where you are, please; just take it easy; I'd really rather you would, and there's nothing to do."

"I am not an expert at this sort of thing," said Mr. Romayne, "but at least I can dry dishes. I learned that much on the veldt."

"In South Africa? You were in the war?" replied Kathleen, giving him a towel.

"Yes, I had a go at it."

"It must have been terrible—to think of actually killing men."

"It is not pleasant," replied Romayne, shrugging his shoulders, "but it has to be done sometimes."

"Oh, do you think so? It does not seem as if it should be necessary at any time," said the girl with great earnestness. "I can't believe it is either right or necessary ever to kill men; and as for the Boer War, don't you think everybody agrees now that it was unnecessary?"

Mr. Romayne was always prepared to defend with the ardour of a British soldier the righteousness of every war in which the British Army has ever been engaged. But somehow he found it difficult to conduct an argument in favour of war against this girl who stood fronting him with a look of horror in her face.

"Well," said Mr. Romayne, "I believe there is something to be said on both sides. No doubt there were blunders in the early part of the trouble, but eventually war had to come."

"But that's just it," cried the girl. "Isn't that the way it is always? In the early stages of a quarrel it is so easy to come to an understanding and to make peace; but after the quarrel has gone on, then war becomes inevitable. If only every dispute could be submitted to the judgment of some independent tribunal. Nations are just like people. They see things solely from their own point of view. Do you know, Mr. Romayne, there is no subject upon which I feel so keenly as upon the subject of war. I just loathe and hate and dread the thought of war. I think perhaps I inherit this. My mother, you know, belongs to the Friends, and she sees so clearly the wickedness and the folly of war. And don't you think that all the world is seeing this more clearly to-day than ever before?"

There was nothing new in this argument or in this position to Mr. Romayne, but somehow, as he looked at the girl's eager, enthusiastic face, and heard her passionate denunciation of war, he found it difficult to defend the justice of war under any circumstances whatever.

"I entirely agree with you, Miss Gwynne, that war is utterly horrible, that it is silly, that it is wicked. I would rather not discuss it with you, but I can't help feeling that there are circumstances that make it necessary and right for men to fight."

"You don't wish to discuss this with me?" said Kathleen. "I am sorry, for I have always wished to hear a soldier who is also"—the girl hesitated for a moment—"a gentleman and a Christian—"

"Thank you, Miss Gwynne," said Romayne, with quiet earnestness.

"Discuss the reasons why war is ever necessary."

"It is a very big subject," said Mr. Romayne, "and some day I should like to give you my point of view. There are multitudes of people in Britain to-day, Miss Gwynne, who would agree with you. Lots of books have been written on both sides. I have listened to hours and hours of discussion, so that you can easily see that there is much to be said on both sides. I always come back, however, to the point that among nations of similar ethical standards and who are equally anxious to preserve the peace of the world, arbitration as a method of settling disputes ought to be perfectly simple and easy. It is only when you have to deal with nations whose standards of ethics are widely dissimilar or who are possessed with another ambition than that of preserving the peace of the world that you get into difficulty."

"I see your point," replied Kathleen, "but I also see that just there you allow for all sorts of prejudice to enter and for the indulgence in unfair argument and special pleading. But there, we are finished," she said, "and you do not wish to discuss this just now."

"Some time, Miss Gwynne, we shall have this out, and I have some literature on the subject that I should like to give you."

"And so have I," cried the girl, with a smile that rendered Mr. Romayne for some moments quite incapable of consecutive thought. "And now shall we look up the others?"

At the dump they found Joe and Sam rolling the logs, which during the winter had been piled high upon the bank, down the steep declivity or "dump" into the stream below. Mrs. Waring-Gaunt and Nora were seated on a log beside them engaged in talk.

"May I inquire if you are bossing the job as usual?" said Mr. Romayne, after he had watched the operation for a few moments.

"Oh, no, there's no bossing going on to-day. But," said the girl, "I rather think the boys like to have me around."

"I don't wonder," said Mr. Romayne, enthusiastically.

"Are you making fun of me, Mr. Romayne?" said the girl, her face indicating that she was prepared for battle.

"God forbid," replied Mr. Romayne, fervently.

"Not a bit of it, Nora dear," said his sister. "He is simply consumed with envy. He has just come from a country, you know, where only the men do things; I mean things that really count. And it makes him furiously jealous to see a young woman calmly doing things that he knows quite well he could not attempt to do."

"Quite true," replied her brother. "I am humbled to the ground at my own all to obvious ineptitude, and am lost in admiration of the marvellous efficiency of the young ladies of Canada whom it has been my good fortune to meet."

Nora glanced at him suspiciously. "You talk well," she said. "I half believe you're just making fun of us."

"Not a bit, Nora, not a bit," said his sister. "It is as I have said before. The man is as jealous as he can be, and, like all men, he hates to discover himself inferior in any particular to a woman. But we must be going. I am so glad you are home again, dear," she said, turning to Kathleen. "We shall hope to see a great deal of you. Thank you for the delightful lunch. It was so good of you to have us."

"Yes, indeed," added the young man. "You saved my life. I had just about reached the final stage of exhaustion. I, too, hope to see you again very soon and often, for you know we must finish that discussion and settle that question."

"What question is that," inquired his sister, "if I

may ask?"

"Oh, the old question," said her brother, "the eternal question—war."

"I suppose," said Nora, "Kathleen has been giving you some of her peace talk. I want you to know, Mr. Romayne, that I don't agree with her in the least, and I am quite sure you don't either."

"I am not so sure of that," replied the young man. "We have not finished it out yet. I feel confident, however, that we shall come to an agreement on it."

"I hope not," replied Nora, "for in that case you would become a pacifist, for Kathleen, just like mother, you know, is a terrible peace person. Indeed, our family is divided on that question—Daddy and I opposed to the rest. And you know pacifists have this characteristic, that they are always ready to fight."

"Yes," said her sister. "We are always ready to fight for peace. But do not let us get into that discussion now. I shall walk with you a little way."

Arm in arm she and Mrs. Waring-Gaunt walked down the steep trail, Mr. Romayne following behind, leading the horses. As they walked together, Mrs. Waring-Gaunt talked to the girl of her brother.

"You know he was in the Diplomatic Service, went in after the South African War, and did awfully well there in the reconstruction work, was very popular with the Boers, though he had fought them in the war. He got to know their big men, and some of them are really big men. As a matter of fact, he became very fond of them and helped the Government at Home to see things from their point of view. After that he went to the Continent, was in Italy for a while and then in Germany, where, I believe, he did very good work. He saw a good deal of the men about the Kaiser. He loathed the Crown Prince, I believe, as most of our people there do. Suddenly he was recalled. He refused, of course, to talk about it, but I understand there was some sort of a row. I believe he lost his temper with some exalted personage. At any rate, he was recalled, chucked the whole service, and came out here. He felt awfully cut up about it. And now he has no faith in the German Government, says they mean war. He's awfully keen on preparation and that sort of thing. I thought I would just tell you, especially since I heard you had been discussing war with him."

As they neared the Switzer place they saw a young man standing on the little pier which jutted out into the stream with a pike-pole in his hand, keeping the logs from jambing at the turn.

"It's Ernest Switzer," cried Kathleen. "I have not seen him for ever so long. How splendidly he is looking! Hello, Ernest!" she cried, waving her hand and running forward to meet him, followed by the critical eyes of Jack Romayne.

The young man came hurrying toward her. "Kathleen!" he cried. "Is it really you?" He threw down his pole as he spoke and took her hand in both of his, the flush on his fair face spreading to the roots of his hair.

"You know Mrs. Waring-Gaunt," said Kathleen to him, for he paid no attention at all to the others. Mrs. Waring-Gaunt acknowledged Switzer's heel clicks, as also did her brother when introduced.

"You have been keeping the logs running, Ernest, I see.

That is very good of you," said Kathleen.

"Yes, there was the beginning of a nice little jamb here," said Switzer. "They are running right enough now. But when did you return?" he continued, dropping into a confidential tone and turning his back upon the others. "Do you know I have not seen you for nine months?"

"Nine months?" said Kathleen. "I was away seven months."

"Yes, but I was away two months before you went. You forget that," he added reproachfully. "But I do not forget. Nine months—nine long months. And are you glad to be back, Kathleen, glad to see all your friends again, glad to see me?"

"I am glad to be at home, Ernest, glad to see all of my friends, of course, glad to get to the West again, to the woods here and the mountains and all."

"And you did not come in to see us as you passed," gazing at her with reproachful eyes and edging her still further away from the others.

"Oh, we intended to come in on our way back."

"Let's move on," said Romayne to his sister.

"We must be going, Kathleen dear," said Mrs. Waring-Gaunt. "You will soon be coming to see us?"

"Yes, indeed, you may be sure. It is so good to see you," replied the girl warmly, as Mrs. Waring-Gaunt kissed her good-bye. "Good-bye, Mr. Romayne; we must finish our discussion another time."

"Always at your service," replied Mr. Romayne, "although I am rather afraid of you. Thank you again for your hospitality. Good-bye." He held her hand, looking down into the blue depths of her eyes until as before the crimson in her face recalled him. "Good-bye. This has been a wonderful day to me." He mounted his horse, lifted his hat, and rode off after his sister.

"What sort of a chap is the Johnnie?" said Jack to his sister as they rode away.

"Not a bad sort at all; very bright fellow, quite popular in this community with the young fellows. He has lots of money, you know, and spends it. Of course, he is fearfully German, military style and all that."

"Seems to own that girl, eh?" said Jack, glancing back over his shoulder at the pair.

"Oh, the two families are quite intimate. Ernest and his sister were in Larry's musical organisations and they are quite good friends."

"By Jove, Sybil, she is wonderful! Why didn't you give me a hint?"

"I did. But really, she has come on amazingly. That college in Winnipeg—"

"Oh, college! It is not a question of college!" said her brother impatiently. "It's herself. Why, Sybil, think of that girl in London in a Worth frock. But no! That would spoil her. She is better just as she is. Jove, she completely knocked me out! I made a fool of myself."

"She has changed indeed," said his sister. "She is a lovely girl and so simple and unaffected. I have come really to love her. We must see a lot of her."

"But where did she get that perfectly charming manner? Do you realise what a perfectly stunning girl she is? Where did she get that style of hers?"

"You must see her mother, Jack. She is a charming woman, simple, quiet, a Quaker, I believe, but quite beautiful manners. Her father, too, is a gentleman, a Trinity man, I understand."

"Well," said her brother with a laugh, "I foresee myself falling in love with that girl in the most approved style."

"You might do worse," replied his sister, "though I doubt if you are not too late."

"Why? That German Johnnie?"

"Well, it is never wise to despise the enemy. He really is a fine chap, his prospects are very good; he has known her for a long while, and he is quite mad about her."

"But, good Lord, Sybil, he's a German!"

"A German," said his sister, "yes. But what difference does that make? He is a German, but he is also a Canadian. We are all Canadians here whatever else we may be or have ever been. We are all sorts and classes, high and low, rich and poor, and of all nationalities— Germans, French, Swedes, Galicians, Russians—but we all shake down into good Canadian citizens. We are just Canadians, and that is good enough for me. We are loyal to Canada first."

"You may be right as far as other nationalities are concerned, but, Sybil, believe me, you do not know the

German. I know him and there is no such thing as a German loyal to Canada first."

"But, Jack, you are so terribly insular. You must really get rid of all that. I used to think like you, but here we have got to the place where we can laugh at all that sort of thing."

"I know, Sybil. I know. They are laughing in England to-day at Roberts and Charlie Beresford. But I know Germany and the German mind and the German aim and purpose, and I confess to you that I am in a horrible funk at the state of things in our country. And this chap Switzer—you say he has been in Germany for two years? Well, he has every mark characteristic of the German. He reproduces the young German that I have seen the world over—in Germany, in the Crown Prince's coterie (don't I know them?), in South Africa, in West Africa, in China. He has every mark, the same military style, the same arrogant self-assertion, the same brutal disregard of the ordinary decencies."

"Why, Jack, how you talk! You are actually excited."

"Did you not notice his manner with that girl? He calmly took possession of her and ignored us who were of her party, actually isolated her from us."

"But, Jack, this seems to me quite outrageous."

"Yes, Sybil, and there are more like you. But I happen to know from experience what I am talking about. The elementary governing principle of life for the young German of to-day is very simple and is easily recognised, and it is this: when you see anything you want, go for it and take it, no matter if all the decencies of life are outraged."

"Jack, I cannot, frankly, I cannot agree with you in regard to young Switzer. I know him fairly well and—"

"Let's not talk about it, Sybil," said her brother, quietly.

"Oh, all right, Jack."

They rode on in silence, Romayne gloomily keeping his eye on the trail before him until they neared the Gwynne gate, when the young man exclaimed abruptly:

"My God, it would be a crime!"

"Whatever do you mean, Jack?"

"To allow that brute to get possession of that lovely girl."

"But, Jack," persisted his sister. "Brute?"

"Sybil, I have seen them with women, their own and other women; and, now listen to me, I have yet to see the German who regards or treats his frau as an English gentleman treats his wife. That is putting it mildly."

"Oh, Jack!"

"It ought to be stopped."

"Well, stop it then."

"I wish to God I could," said her brother.

CHAPTER VIII

YOU FORGOT ME

The Lakeside House, substantially built of logs, with "frame" kitchen attached, stood cosily among the clump of trees, poplar and spruce, locally described as a bluff. The bluff ran down to the little lake a hundred yards away, itself an expansion of Wolf Willow Creek. The whitewashed walls gleaming through its festoons of Virginia creeper, a little lawn bordered with beds filled with hollyhocks, larkspur, sweet-william and other old-fashioned flowers and flanked by a heavy border of gorgeous towering sunflowers, gave a general air, not only of comfort and thrift, but of refinement as well, too seldom found in connection with the raw homesteads of the new western country.

At a little distance from the house, at the end of a lane leading through the bluff, were visible the stables, granary and other outhouses, with corral attached.

Within, the house fulfilled the promise of its external appearance and surroundings. There was dignity without stiffness, comfort without luxury, simplicity without any suggestion of the poverty that painfully obtrudes itself.

At the open window whose vine shade at once softened

the light and invited the summer airs, sat Mrs. Gwynne, with her basket of mending at her side. Eight years of life on an Alberta ranch had set their mark upon her. The summers' suns and winters' frosts and the eternal summer and winter winds had burned and browned the soft, fair skin of her earlier days. The anxieties inevitable to the struggle with poverty had lined her face and whitened her hair. But her eyes shone still with the serene light of a soul that carries within it the secret of triumph over the carking cares of life.

Seated beside her was her eldest daughter Kathleen, sewing; and stretched upon the floor lay Nora, frankly idle and half asleep, listening to the talk of the other two. Their talk turned upon the theme never long absent from their thought—that of ways and means.

"Tell you what, Mummie," droned Nora, lazily extending her lithe young body to its utmost limits, "there is a simple way out of our never ending worries, namely, a man, a rich man, if handsome, so much the better, but rich he must be, for Kathleen. They say they are hanging round the Gateway City of the West in bunches. How about it, Kate?"

"My dear Nora," gently chided her mother, "I wish you would not talk in that way. It is not quite nice. In my young days—"

"In your young days I know just exactly what happened, Mother. There was always a long queue of eligible young men dangling after the awfully lovely young Miss Meredith, and before she was well out of her teens the gallant young Gwynne carried her off."

"We never talked about those things, my dear," said her mother, shaking her head at her.

Ralph Connor

"You didn't need to, Mother."

"Well, if it comes to that, Nora," said her sister, "I don't think you need to, very much, either. You have only got to look at—"

"Halt!" cried Nora, springing to her feet. "But seriously, Mother dear, I think we can weather this winter right enough. Our food supply is practically visible. We have oats enough for man and beast, a couple of pigs to kill, a steer also, not to speak of chickens and ducks. We shall have some cattle to sell, and if our crops are good we ought to be able to pay off those notes. Oh, why will Dad buy machinery?"

"My dear," said her mother with gentle reproach, "your father says machinery is cheaper than men and we really cannot do without machines."

"That's all right, Mother. I'm not criticising father. He is a perfect dear and I am awfully glad he has got that Inspectorship."

"Yes," replied her mother, "your father is suited to his new work and likes it. And Larry will be finishing his college this year, I think. And he has earned it too," continued the mother. "When I think of all he has done and how generously he has turned his salary into the family fund, and how often he has been disappointed—" Here her voice trembled a little.

Nora dropped quickly to her knees, taking her mother in her arms. "Don't we all know, Mother, what he has done? Shall I ever forget those first two awful years, the winter mornings when he had to get up before daylight to get the house warm, and that awful school. Every day he had to face it, rain, sleet, or forty below. How often I have watched him in the school, always so white and tired. But he never gave up. He just would not give up. And when those big boys were unruly—I could have killed those boys—he would always keep his temper and joke and jolly them into good order. And all the time I knew how terribly his head was aching. What are you sniffling about, Kate?"

"I think it was splendid, just splendid, Nora," cried Kathleen, swiftly wiping away her tears. "But I can't help crying, it was all so terrible. He never thought of himself, and year after year he gave up his money—"

"Hello!" cried a voice at the door. "Who gave up his money and to whom and is there any more around?" His eye glanced around the group. "What's up, people? Mummie, are these girls behaving badly? Let me catch them at it!" The youth stood smiling down upon them. His years in the West had done much for him. He was still slight, but though his face was pale and his body thin, his movements suggested muscular strength and sound health. He had not grown handsome. His features were irregular, mouth wide, cheek bones prominent, ears large; yet withal there was a singular attractiveness about his appearance and manner. His eyes were good; grey-blue, humorous, straight-looking eyes they were, deep set under overhanging brows, and with a whimsical humour ever lingering about them; over the eyes a fore-head, broad, suggesting intellect, and set off by heavy, waving, dark hair.

"Who gave his money? I insist upon knowing. No reply, eh? I have evidently come upon a deep and deadly plot. Mother?—no use asking you. Kathleen, out with it."

"You gave your money," burst forth Nora in a kind of passion as she flew at him, "and everything else. But now that's all over. You are going to finish your college course this year, that's what."

"Oh, that's it, eh? I knew there was some women's scheme afloat. Well, children," said the youth, waving his hand over them in paternal benediction, "since this thing is up we might as well settle it 'right here and n-a-o-w,' as our American friend, Mr. Ralph Waldo Farwell, would say, and a decent sort he is too. I have thought this all out. Why should not a man gifted with a truly great brain replete with grey matter (again in the style of the aforesaid Farwell) do the thinking for his wimmin folk? Why not? Hence the problem is already solved. The result is hereby submitted, not for discussion but for acceptance, for acceptance you understand, to-wit and namely, as Dad's J. P. law books have it: I shall continue the school another year."

"You shan't," shouted Nora, seizing him by the arm and shaking him with all the strength of her vigorous young body.

"Larry, dear!" said his mother.

"Oh, Larry!" exclaimed Kathleen.

"We shall then be able to pay off all our indebtedness," continued Larry, ignoring their protests, "and that is a most important achievement. This new job of Dad's means an addition to our income. The farm management will remain in the present capable hands. No, Miss Nora, I am not thinking of the boss, but of the head, the general manager." He waved his hand toward his mother. "The only change will be in the foreman. A new appointment will be made, one who will bring to her task not only experience and with it a practical knowledge, but the advantage of intellectual discipline recently acquired at a famous educational centre; and the whole concern will go on with its usual verve, swing, snap, toward another year's success. Then next year me for the giddy lights of the metropolitan city and the sacred halls of learning."

"And me," said Nora, "what does your high mightiness plan for me this winter, pray?"

"Not quite so much truculence, young lady," replied her brother. "For you, the wide, wide world, a visit to the seat of light and learning already referred to, namely, Winnipeg."

For one single moment Nora looked at him. Then, throwing back her head, she said with unsteady voice: "Not this time, old boy. One man can lead a horse to water but ten cannot make him drink, and you may as well understand now as later that this continual post-ponement of your college career is about to cease. We have settled it otherwise. Kathleen will take your school—an awful drop for the kids, but what joy for the big boys. She and I will read together in the evenings. The farm will go on. Sam and Joe are really very good and steady; Joe at least, and Sam most of the time. Dad's new work will not take him from home so much, he says. And next year me for the fine arts and the white lights of Winnipeg. That's all that needs to be said."

"I think, dear," said the mother, looking at her son, "Nora is right."

"Now, Mother," exclaimed Larry, "I don't like to hear your foot come down just yet. I know that tone of finality, but listen—"

"We have listened," said Kathleen, "and we know we are right. I shall take the school, Mr. Farwell—"

"Mr. Farwell, eh?—" exclaimed Nora significantly.

"Mr. Farwell has promised me," continued Kathleen, "indeed has offered me, the school. Nora and I can study together. I shall keep up my music. Nora will keep things going outside, mother will look after every thing as usual, Dad will help us outside and in. So that's settled."

"Settled!" cried her brother. "You are all terribly settling. It seems to me that you apparently forget—"

Once more the mother interposed. "Larry, dear, Kathleen has put it very well. Your father and I have talked it over"—the young people glanced at each other and smiled at this ancient and well-worn phrase—"we have agreed that it is better that you should finish your college this winter. Of course we know you would suggest delay, but we are anxious that you should complete your course."

"But, Mother, listen—" began Larry.

"Nonsense, Larry, 'children, obey your parents' is still valid," said Nora. "What are you but a child after all, though with your teaching and your choral society conducting, and your nigger show business, and your preaching in the church, and your popularity, you are getting so uplifted that there's no holding you. Just make up your mind to do your duty, do you hear? Your duty. Give up this selfish determination to have your own way, this selfish pleasing of yourself." Abruptly she paused, rushed at him, threw her arms around his neck, and kissed him. "You darling old humbug," she said with a very unsteady voice. "There, I will be blubbering in a minute. I am off for the timber lot. What do you say, Katty? It's cooler now. We'll go up the cool road. Are you coming?"

"Yes; wait until I change."

"All right, I will saddle up. You coming, Larry?"

"No, I'll catch up later."

"Now, Mother," warned Nora, "I know his ways and wiles. Remember your duty to your children. You are also inclined to be horribly selfish. Be firm. Hurry up, Kate."

Left alone with his mother, Larry went deliberately to work with her. Well he knew the immovable quality of her resolution when once her mind was made up. Patiently, quietly, steadily, he argued with her, urging Nora's claims for a year at college.

"She needs a change after her years of hard work."

Her education was incomplete; the ground work was sound enough, but she had come to the age when she must have those finishing touches that girls require to fit them for their place in life. "She is a splendid girl, but in some ways still a child needing discipline; in other ways mature, too mature. She ought to have her chance and ought to have it now." One never knew what would happen in the case of girls.

His mother sighed. "Poor Nora, she has had discipline enough of a kind, and hard discipline it has been indeed for you all."

"Nonsense, Mother, we have had a perfectly fine time together, all of us. God knows if any one has had a hard time it is not the children in this home. I do not like to think of those awful winters, Mother, and of the hard time you had with us all."

"A hard time!" exclaimed his mother. "I, a hard time, and with you all here beside me, and all so well and strong?

What more could I want?" The amazed surprise in her face stirred in her son a quick rush of emotion.

"Oh, Mother, Mother, Mother," he whispered in her ear. "There is no one like you. Did you ever in all your life seek one thing for yourself, one thing, one little thing? Away back there in Ontario you slaved and slaved and went without things yourself that all the rest of us might get them. Here it has been just the same. Haven't I seen your face and your hands, your poor hands,"—here the boy's voice broke with an indignant passion—"blue with the cold when you could not get furs to protect them? Never, never shall I forget those days." The boy stopped abruptly, unable to go on.

Quickly the mother drew her son toward her. "Larry, my son, my son, you must never think that a hard time. Did ever a woman have such joy as I? When I think of other mothers and of other children, and then think of you all here, I thank God every day and many times a day that he has given us each other. And, Larry, my son, let me say this, and you will remember it afterwards. You have been a continual joy to me, always, always. You have never given me a moment's anxiety or pain. Remember that. I continually thank God for you. You have made my life very happy."

The boy put his face down on her lap with his arms tight around her waist. Never in their life together had they been able to open these deep, sacred chambers in their souls to each other's gaze. For some moments he remained thus, then lifting up his face, he kissed her again and again, her forehead, her eyes, her lips. Then rising to his feet, he stood with his usual smile about his lips. "You always beat me. But will you not think this all over again carefully, and we will do what you say? But will you promise, Mother, to think it over again and look at my side of it too?"

"Yes, Larry, I promise," said his mother. "Now run after the girls, and I shall have tea ready for you."

As Larry rode down the lane he saw the young German, Ernest Switzer, and his sister riding down the trail and gave them a call. They pulled up and waited.

"Hello, Ernest; whither bound? How are you, Dorothea?"

"Home," said the young man, "and you?"

"Going up by the timber lot, around by the cool road. The girls are on before."

"Ah, so?" said the young man, evidently waiting for an invitation.

"Do you care to come? It's not much longer that way," said Larry.

"I might," said the young man. Then looking doubtfully at his sister, "You cannot come very well, Dorothea, can you?"

"No, that is, I'm afraid not," she replied. She was a pretty girl with masses of yellow hair, light blue eyes, a plump, kindly face and a timid manner. As she spoke she, true to her German training, evidently waited for an indication of her brother's desire.

"There are the cows, you know," continued her brother.

"Yes, there are the cows," her face clouding as she spoke.

"Oh, rot!" said Larry, "you don't milk until evening, and

we get back before tea. Come along."

Still the girl hesitated. "Well," said her brother brusquely, "do you want to come?"

She glanced timidly at his rather set face and then at Larry. "I don't know. I am afraid that—"

"Oh, come along, Dorothea, do you hear me telling you? You will be in plenty of time and your brother will help you with the milking."

"Ernest help! Oh, no!"

"Not on your life!" said that young man. "I never milk. I haven't for years. Well, come along then," he added in a grudging voice.

"That is fine," said Larry. "But, Dorothea, you ought to make him learn to milk. Why shouldn't he? The lazy beggar. Do you mean to say that he never helps with the milking?"

"Oh, never," said Dorothea.

"Our men don't do women's work," said Ernest. "It is not the German way. It is not fitting."

"And what about women doing men's work?" said Larry. "It seems to me I have seen German women at work in the fields up in the Settlement."

"I have no doubt you have," replied Ernest stiffly. "It is the German custom."

"You make me tired," said Larry, "the German custom indeed! Does that make it right?"

"For us, yes," replied Ernest calmly.

"But you are Canadians, are you not? Are there to be different standards in Canada for different nationalities?"

"Oh, the Germans will follow the German way. Because it is German, and demonstrated through experience to be the best. Look at our people. Look at our prosperity at home, at our growth in population, at our wealth, at our expansion in industry and commerce abroad. Look at our social conditions and compare them with those in this country or in any other country in the world. Who will dare to say that German methods and German customs are not best, at least for Germans? But let us move a little faster, otherwise we shall never catch up with them." He touched his splendid broncho into a sharp gallop, the other horses following more slowly behind.

"He is very German, my brother," said Dorothea. "He thinks he is Canadian, but he is not the same since he went over Home. He is talking all the time about Germany, Germany, Germany. I hate it." Her blue eyes flashed fire and her usually timid voice vibrated with an intense feeling. Larry gazed at her in astonishment.

"You may look at me, Larry," she cried. "I am German but I do not like the German ways. I like the Canadian ways. The Germans treat their women like their cows. They feed them well, they keep them warm because—because—they have calves—I mean the cows—and the women have kids. I hate the German ways. Look at my mother. What is she in that house? Day and night she has worked, day and night, saving money—and what for? For Ernest. Running to wait on him and on Father and they never know it. It's women's work with us to wait on men, and that is the way in the Settlement up there. Look at your mother and you. Mein Gott! I could kill them, those men!"

"Why, Dorothea, you amaze me. What's up with you? I never heard you talk like this. I never knew that you felt like this."

"No, how could you know? Who would tell you? Not Ernest," she replied bitterly.

"But, Dorothea, you are happy, are you not?"

"Happy, I was until I knew better, till two years ago when I saw your mother and you with her. Then Ernest came back thinking himself a German officer—he is an officer, you know—and the way he treated our mother and me!"

"Treated your mother! Surely he is not unkind to your mother?" Larry had a vision of a meek, round-faced, kindly, contented woman, who was obviously proud of her only son.

"Kind, kind," cried Dorothea, "he is kind as German sons are kind. But you cannot understand. Why did I speak to you of this? Yes, I will tell you why," she added, apparently taking a sudden resolve. "Let's go slowly. Ernest is gone anyway. I will tell you why. Before Ernest went away he was more like a Canadian boy. He was good to his mother. He is good enough still but—oh, it is so hard to show you. I have seen you and your mother. You would not let your mother brush your boots for you, you would not sit smoking and let her carry in wood in the winter time, you would not stand leaning over the fence and watch your mother milk the cow. Mein Gott! Ernest, since he came back—the women are only good for waiting on him, for working in the house or on the farm. His wife, she will not work in the fields; Ernest is too rich for that. But she will not be like"—here the girl paused abruptly, a vivid colour dyeing her fair skin—"like your wife. I would die sooner than marry a German man."

"But Ernest is not like that, Dorothea. He is not like that with my sisters. Why, he is rather the other way, awfully polite and all that sort of thing, you know."

"Yes, that's the way with young German gentlemen to young ladies, that is, other people's ladies. But to their own, no. And I must tell you. Oh, I am afraid to tell you," she added breathlessly. "But I will tell you, you have been so kind, so good to me. You are my friend, and you will not tell. Promise me you will never tell." The girl's usually red face was pale, her voice was hoarse and trembling.

"What is the matter, Dorothea? Of course I won't tell."

"Ernest wants to marry your sister, Kathleen. He is just mad to get her, and he always gets his way too. I would not like to see your sister his wife. He would break her heart and," she added in a lower voice, "yours too. But remember you are not to tell. You are not to let him know I told you." A real terror shone in her eyes. "Do you hear me?" she cried. "He would beat me with his whip. He would, he would."

"Beat you, beat you?" Larry pulled up his horse short. "Beat you in this country—oh, Dorothea!"

"They do. Our men do beat their women, and Ernest would too. The women do not think the same way about it as your women. You will not tell?" she urged.

"What do you think I am, Dorothea? And as for beating you, let me catch him. By George, I'd, I'd—"

"What?" said Dorothea, turning her eyes full upon him, her pale face flushing.

Larry laughed. "Well, he's a big chap, but I'd try to knock his block off. But it's nonsense. Ernest is not that kind. He's an awfully good sort."

"He is, he is a good sort, but he is also a German officer and, ah, you cannot understand, but do not let him have your sister. I have told you. Come, let us go quickly."

They rode on in silence, but did not overtake the others until they reached the timber lot where they found the party waiting. With what Dorothea had just told him in his mind, Larry could not help a keen searching of Kathleen's face. She was quietly chatting with the young German, with face serene and quite untouched with anything but the slightest animation. "She is not worrying over anything," said Larry to himself. Then he turned and looked upon the face of the young man at her side. A shock of surprise, of consternation, thrilled him. The young man's face was alight with an intensity of eagerness, of desire, that startled Larry and filled him with a new feeling of anxiety, indeed of dismay.

"Oh, you people are slow," cried Nora. "What is keeping you? Come along or we shall be late. Shall we go through the woods straight to the dump, or shall we go around?"

"Let's go around," cried Kathleen. "Do you know I have not been around for ever so long?"

"Yes," said Larry, "let's go around by Nora's mine."

"Nora's mine!" exclaimed Ernest. "Do you know I've heard about that mine a great deal but I have never seen Nora's mine?"

"Come along, then," said Nora, "but there's almost no trail and we shall have to hurry while we can. There's only a cow track."

"Move along then," said her brother; "show us the way and we will follow. Go on, Ernest."

But Ernest apparently had difficulty with his broncho so that he was found at the rear of the line with Kathleen immediately in front of him. The cow trail led out of the coolee over a shoulder of a wooded hill and down into a ravine whose sharp sides made the riding even to those experienced westerners a matter of difficulty, in places of danger. At the bottom of the ravine a little torrent boiled and foamed on its way to join Wolf Willow Creek a mile further down. After an hour's struggle with the brushwood and fallen timber the party was halted by a huge spruce tree which had fallen fair across the trail.

"Where now, boss?" cried Larry to Nora, who from her superior knowledge of the ground, had been leading the party.

"This is something new," answered Nora. "I think we should cross the water and try to break through to the left around the top of the tree."

"No," said Ernest, "the right looks better to me, around the root here. It is something of a scramble, but it is better than the left."

"Come along," said Nora; "this is the way of the trail, and we can get through the brush of that top all right."

"I am for the right. Come, let's try it, Kathleen, shall we?" said Ernest.

Kathleen hesitated. "Come, we'll beat them out. Right turn, march."

The commanding tones of the young man appeared to dominate the girl. She set her horse to the steep hillside, following her companion to the right. A steep climb through a tangle of underbrush brought them into the cleared woods, where they paused to breathe their animals.

"Ah, that was splendidly done. You are a good horse-woman," said Ernest. "If you only had a horse as good as mine we could go anywhere together. You deserve a better horse, too. I wonder if you know how fine you look."

"My dear old Kitty is not very quick nor very beautiful, but she is very faithful, and so kind," said Kathleen, reaching down and patting her mare on the nose. "Shall we go on?"

"We need not hurry," replied her companion. "We have beaten them already. I love the woods here, and, Kathleen, I have not seen you for ever so long, for nine long months. And since your return fifteen days ago I have seen you only once, only once."

"I am sorry," said Kathleen, hurrying her horse a little. "We happened to be out every time you called."

"Other people have seen you," continued the young man with a note almost of anger in his voice. "Everywhere I hear of you, but I cannot see you. At church—I go to church to see you—but that, that Englishman is with you. He walks with you, you go in his motor car, he is in your house every day."

"What are you talking about, Ernest? Mr. Romayne? Of course. Mother likes him so much, and we all like him."

"Your mother, ah!" Ernest's tone was full of scorn.

"Yes, my mother—we all like him, and his sister, Mrs. Waring-Gaunt, you know. They are our nearest neighbours, and we have come to know them very well. Shall we go on?"

"Kathleen, listen to me," said the young man.

At this point a long call came across the ravine.

"Ah, there they are," cried the girl. "Let's hurry, please do." She brought her whip down unexpectedly on Kitty's shoulders. The mare, surprised at such unusual treatment from her mistress, sprang forward, slipped on the moss-covered sloping rock, plunged, recovered herself, slipped again, and fell over on her side. At her first slip, the young man was off his horse, and before the mare finally pitched forward was at her head, and had caught the girl from the saddle into his arms. For a moment she lay there white and breathing hard.

"My God, Kathleen!" he cried. "You are hurt? You might have been killed." His eyes burned like two blazing lights, his voice was husky, his face white. Suddenly crushing her to him, he kissed her on the cheek and again on her lips. The girl struggled to get free.

"Oh, let me go, let me go," she cried. "How can you, how can you?"

But his arms were like steel about her, and again and again he continued to kiss her, until, suddenly relaxing, she lay white and shuddering in his arms.

"Kathleen," he said, his voice hoarse with passion, "I love you, I love you. I want you. Gott in Himmel, I want you. Open your eyes, Kathleen, my darling. Speak to me. Open your eyes. Look at me. Tell me you love me." But still she lay white and shuddering. Suddenly he released her and set her on her feet. She stood looking at him with quiet, searching eyes.

"You love me," she said, her voice low and quivering with a passionate scorn, "and you treat me so? Let us go." She moved toward her horse.

"Kathleen, hear me," he entreated. "You must hear me. You shall hear me." He caught her once more by the arm. "I forgot myself. I saw you lying there so white. How could I help it? I meant no harm. I have loved you since you were a little girl, since that day I saw you first herding the cattle. You had a blue dress and long braids. I loved you then. I have loved you every day since. I think of you and I dream of you. The world is full of you. I am offering you marriage. I want you to be my wife." The hands that clutched her arm were shaking, his voice was thick and broken. But still she stood with her face turned from him, quietly trying to break from his grasp. But no word did she speak.

"Kathleen, I forgot myself," he said, letting go of her arm. "I was wrong, but, my God, Kathleen, I am not stone, and when I felt your heart beat against mine—"

"Oh," she cried, shuddering and drawing further away from him.

"—and your face so white, your dear face so near mine, I forgot myself."

"No," said the girl, turning her face toward him and

searching him with her quiet, steady, but contemptuous eyes, "you forgot me."

CHAPTER IX

EXCEPT HE STRIVE LAWFULLY

The Wolf Willow Dominion Day Celebration Committee were in session in the schoolhouse with the Reverend Evans Rhye in the chair, and all of the fifteen members in attendance. The reports from the various sub-committees had been presented and approved.

The programme for the day was in the parson's hand. "A fine programme, ladies and gentlemen, thanks to you all, and especially to our friend here," said Mr. Rhye, placing his hand on Larry's shoulder.

A chorus of approval greeted his remark, but Larry protested. "Not at all. Every one was keen to help. We are all tremendous Canadians and eager to celebrate Dominion Day."

"Well, let us go over it again," said Mr. Rhye. "The football match with the Eagle Hill boys is all right. How about the polo match with the High River men, Larry?"

"The captain of the High River team wrote to express regret that two of his seniors would not be available, but that he hoped to give us a decent game."

"There will only be one fault with the dinner and the tea, Mrs. Kemp."

"And what will that be, sir?" enquired Mrs. Kemp, who happened to be Convener of the Refreshment Committee.

"They will receive far too much for their money," said Mr. Rhye. "How about the evening entertainment, Larry?" he continued.

"Everything is all right, I think, sir," said Larry.

"Are the minstrels in good form?" enquired Mrs. Waring-Gaunt. "This is your last appearance, you know, and you must go out in a blaze of glory."

"We hope to get through somehow," said Larry.

"And the speakers?" enquired Mr. Rhye.

"Both will be on hand. Mr. Gilchrist promises a patriotic address. Mr. Alvin P. Jones will represent Wolf Willow in a kind of local glorification stunt."

"This is all perfectly splendid," said Mr. Rhye, "and I cannot tell you how grateful I am to you all. We ought to have a memorable day to-morrow."

And a memorable day it was. The weather proved worthy of Alberta's best traditions, for it was sunny, with a fine sweeping breeze to temper the heat and to quicken the pulses with its life-bringing ozone fresh from the glacier gorges and the pine forests of the Rockies.

The captain of the Wolf Willow football team was awake and afoot soon after break of day that he might be in readiness for the Eagle Hill team when they arrived. Sam

Ralph Connor

was in his most optimistic mood. His team, he knew, were in the finest condition and fit for their finest effort. Everything promised victory. But alas! for Sam's hopes. At nine o'clock a staggering blow fell when Vial, his partner on the right wing of the forward line, rode over with the news that Coleman, their star goal-keeper, their ultimate reliance on the defence line, had been stepped on by a horse and rendered useless for the day. It was, indeed, a crushing calamity. Sam spent an hour trying to dig up a substitute. The only possible substitutes were Hepworth and Biggs, neither of them first class men but passable, and Fatty Rose. The two former, however, had gone for the day to Calgary, and Fatty Rose was hopelessly slow. Sam discussed the distressing situation with such members of the team as could be hastily got together.

"Dere's dat new feller," suggested Joe.

"That's so," said Vial, familiarly known as Bottles. "That chap Sykes, Farwell's friend. He's a dandy dribbler. He could take Cassap's place on left wing and let Cassap take goal."

With immense relief the team accepted this solution of the difficulty. But gloom still covered Sam's face. "He's only been here two weeks," he said, "and you know darn well the rule calls for four."

"Oh, hang it!" said Bottles, "he's going to be a resident all right. He's a real resident right now, and anyway, they won't know anything about it."

"Oh, cut it out," said Sam, suddenly flaring into wrath. "You know we can't do that sort of thing. It ain't the game and we ain't goin' to do it."

"What ain't the game?" enquired Larry, who had come upon the anxious and downcast group.

Farwell told him the calamitous news and explained the problem under discussion. "We'd play Sykes, only he hasn't been here a month yet, and Sam won't stand for it," he said.

"Of course Sam won't stand for it, and the Captain is right," said Larry. "Is there nobody else, Sam?" Sam shook his head despondently. "Would I be any good, Sam? I am not keen about it, but if you think I could take Cassap's place on left wing, he could take goal."

Sam brightened up a little. "Guess we can't do no better," he said doubtfully. "I mean," he added in answer to the shout of laughter from the team—"Aw, shut up, can that cackle. We know the Master hates football an' this is goin' to be a real fightin' game. He'll get all knocked about an' I don't want that. You know he'll be takin' all kinds of chances."

"Oh, quit, Sam. I am in pretty good shape," said Larry. "They can't kill me. That's the best I can do anyway, so let's get to them."

The situation was sufficiently gloomy to stir Joe to his supremest efforts and to kindle Sam's spirit to a blazing flame. "We don't need Sykes nor nobody else," he shouted to his men as they moved on to the field. "They can wear their boots out on that defence line of ours an' be derned to 'em. An', Bottles, you got to play the game of your life to-day. None of your fancy embroidery, just plain knittin'. Every feller on the ball an' every feller play to his man. There'll be a lot of females hangin' around, but we don't want any frills for the girls to admire. But all at it an' all the time." Sam's little red eyes glowed with even a more fiery hue than usual; his rat-like face assumed its most belligerent aspect.

Before the match Larry took the Eagle Hill captain, a young Englishman who had been trying for ten years to make a living on a ranch far up among the foothills and was only beginning to succeed, to his mother, who had been persuaded to witness the game. They found her in Kathleen's care and under instruction from young Farwell as to the fundamental principles of the game. Near them a group of men were standing, among whom were Switzer, Waring-Gaunt, and Jack Romayne, listening to Farwell's dissertation.

"You see, Mrs. Gwynne," he said, "no one may handle the ball—head, feet, body, may be used, but not the hands."

"But I understand they sometimes hurt each other, Mr. Farwell."

"Oh, accidents will happen even on the farm, Mrs. Gwynne. For instance, Coleman this morning had a horse step on his foot, necessitating Larry's going on."

"Is Lawrence going to play?" said Mrs. Gwynne. "Ah, here he is. Lawrence, are you in good condition? You have not been playing."

"I am not really very fit, Mother, not very hard, but I have been running a good deal. I don't expect I shall be much use. Sam is quite dubious about it."

"He will be all right, Mrs. Gwynne," said Farwell confidently. "He is the fastest runner in the team. If he were only twenty pounds heavier and if he were a bit more keen about the game he would be a star."

"Why don't they play Sykes?" inquired Kathleen. "I heard some of the boys say this morning that Sykes was going to play. He is quite wonderful, I believe."

"He is," replied Larry, "quite wonderful, but unfortunately he is not eligible. But let me introduce Mr. Duckworth, Captain of our enemy."

Mrs. Gwynne received the young man with a bright smile. "I am sorry I cannot wish you victory, and all the more now that my own son is to be engaged. But I don't understand, Larry," she continued, "why Mr. Sykes cannot play."

"Why, because there's a League regulation, Mother, that makes a month's residence in the district necessary to a place on the team. Unfortunately Sykes has been here only two weeks, and so we are unwilling to put one over on our gallant foe. Got to play the game, eh, Duckworth?"

Duckworth's face grew fiery red. "Yes, certainly," he said. "Rather an awkward rule but—"

"You see, Mother, we want to eliminate every sign of professionalism," said Larry, "and emphasise the principle of local material for clubs."

"Ah, I see, and a very good idea, I should say," said his mother. "The Eagle Hill team, for instance, will be made up of Eagle Hill men only. That is really much better for the game because you get behind your team all the local pride and enthusiasm."

"A foolish rule, I call it," said Switzer abruptly to Kathleen, "and you can't enforce it anyway. Who can tell the personality of a team ten, twenty or fifty miles away?"

"I fancy they can tell themselves," said Jack Romayne. "Their Captain can certify to his men."

"Aha!" laughed Switzer. "That's good. The Captain, I suppose, is keen to win. Do you think he would keep a man off his team who is his best player, and who may bring him the game?" Switzer's face was full of scorn.

"I take it they are gentlemen," was Romayne's quiet rejoinder.

"Of course, Mr. Romayne," said Mrs. Gwynne. "That gets rid of all the difficulty. Otherwise it seems to me that all the pleasure would be gone from the contest, the essential condition of which is keeping to the rules."

"Good for you, Mother. You're a real sport," said Larry.

"Besides," replied his mother, "we have Scripture for it. You remember what it says? 'If a man strive for masteries yet is he not crowned except he strive lawfully.' 'Except he strive lawfully,' you see. The crown he might otherwise win would bring neither honour nor pleasure."

"Good again, Mother. You ought to have a place on the League committee. We shall have that Scripture entered on the rules. But I must run and dress. Farwell, you can take charge of Duckworth."

But Duckworth was uneasy to be gone. "If you will excuse me, Mrs. Gwynne, I must get my men together."

"Well, Mr. Duckworth," said Mrs. Gwynne, smiling on him as she gave him her hand, "I am sorry we cannot wish you a victory, but we can wish you your very best game and an honourable defeat."

"Thank you," said Duckworth. "I feel you have done your best."

"Come and see us afterward, Mr. Duckworth. What a splendid young man," she continued, as Duckworth left the party and set off to get his men together with the words "except he strive lawfully" ringing in his ears.

"She's a wonder," he said to himself. "I wonder how it is she got to me as she has. I know. She makes me think—" But Duckworth refused even to himself to say of whom she made him think. "Except he strive lawfully" the crown would bring "neither honour nor pleasure." Those words, and the face which had suddenly been recalled to Duckworth's memory reconstructed his whole scheme of football diplomacy. "By George, we cannot play Liebold; we can't do it. The boys will kick like steers, but how can we? I'm up against a fierce proposition, all right."

And so he found when he called his men together and put to them the problem before him. "It seems a rotten time to bring this matter up just when we are going on to the ground, but I never really thought much about it till that little lady put it to me as I told you. And, fellows, I have felt as if it were really up to me to put it before you. They have lost their goal man, Coleman—there's no better in the League—and because of this infernal rule they decline to put on a cracking good player. They are playing the game on honour, and they are expecting us to do the same, and as that English chap says, they expect us to be gentlemen. I apologise to you all, and if you say go on as we are, I will go on because I feel I ought to have kicked before. But I do so under protest and feeling like a thief. I suggest that Harremann take Liebold's place. Awfully sorry about it, Liebold, and I apologise to you. I can't tell you how sorry I am, boys, but that's how it is with me."

There was no time for discussion, and strangely enough there was little desire for it, the Captain's personality and the action of the Wolf Willow team carrying the proposition through. Harremann took his place on the team, and Liebold made his contribution that day from the side lines. But the team went on to the field with a sense that whatever might be the outcome of the match they had begun the day with victory.

The match was contested with the utmost vigour, not to say violence; but there was a absence of the rancour which had too often characterised the clashing of these teams on previous occasions, the Eagle Hill team carrying on to the field a new respect for their opponents as men who had shown a true sporting spirit. And by the time the first quarter was over their action in substituting an inferior player for Liebold for honour's sake was known to all the members of the Wolf Willow team, and awakened in them and in their friends among the spectators a new respect for their enemy. The match resulted in a victory for the home team, but the generous applause which followed the Eagle Hill team from the field and which greeted them afterward at the dinner where they occupied an honoured place at the table set apart for distinguished guests, and the excellent dinner provided by the thrifty Ladies' Aid of All Saints Church went far to soothe their wounded spirits and to atone for their defeat.

"Awfully fine of you, Duckworth," said Larry, as they left the table together. "That's the sort of thing that makes for clean sport."

"I promised to see your mother after the match," said Duckworth. "Can we find her now?"

"Sure thing," said Larry.

Mrs. Gwynne received the young man with hand stretched far out to meet him.

"You made us lose the game, Mrs. Gwynne," said Duckworth in a half-shamed manner, "and that is one reason why I came to see you again."

"I?" exclaimed Mrs. Gwynne.

"Well, you quoted Scripture against us, and you know you can't stand up against Scripture and hope to win, can you?" said Duckworth with a laugh.

"Sit down here beside me, Mr. Duckworth," she said, her eyes shining. "I won't pretend not to understand you;" she continued when he had taken his place beside her. "I can't tell you how proud I am of you."

"Thank you," said Duckworth. "I like to hear that. You see I never thought about it very much. I am not excusing myself."

"No, I know you are not, but I heard about it, Mr. Duckworth. We all think so much of you. I am sure your mother is proud of you."

Young Duckworth sat silent, his eyes fastened upon the ground.

"Please forgive me. Perhaps she is—no longer with you," said Mrs. Gwynne softly, laying her hand upon his. Duckworth nodded, refusing to look at her and keeping his lips firmly pressed together. "I was wrong in what I said just now," she continued. "She is with you still; she knows and follows all your doings, and I believe she is proud of you."

Duckworth cleared his throat and said with an evident effort, "You made me think of her to-day, and I simply had to play up. I must go now. I must see the fellows." He rose quickly to his feet.

"Come and see us, won't you?" said Mrs. Gwynne.

"Won't I just," replied Duckworth, holding her hand a moment or two. "I can't tell you how glad I am that I met you to-day."

"Oh, wait, Mr. Duckworth. Nora, come here. I want you to meet my second daughter. Nora, this is Mr. Duckworth, the Captain."

"Oh, I know him, the Captain of the enemy," cried Nora.

"Of our friends, Nora," said her mother.

"All right, of our friends, now that we have beaten you, but I want to tell you, Mr. Duckworth, that I could gladly have slain you many times to-day."

"And why, pray?"

"Oh, you were so terribly dangerous, and as for Larry, why you just played with him. It was perfectly maddening to me."

"All the same your brother got away from me and shot the winning goal. He's fearfully fast."

"A mere fluke, I tell him."

"Don't you think it for one little minute. It was a neat bit of work."

CHAPTER X

THE SPIRIT Of CANADA

Whatever it was that rendered it necessary for Duckworth to "see the fellows," that necessity vanished in the presence of Nora.

"Are you going to take in the polo?" he asked.

"Am I? Am I going to continue breathing?" cried Nora. "Come along, Mother, we must go if we are to get a good place."

"May I find one for you," said Mr. Duckworth, quite forgetting that he "must see the fellows," and thinking only of his good luck in falling in with such a "stunning-looking girl." He himself had changed into flannels, and with his athletic figure, his brown, healthy face, brown eyes and hair, was a thoroughly presentable young man. He found a place with ease for his party, a dozen people offering to make room for them. As Mr. Duckworth let his eyes rest upon the young lady at his side his sense of good-fortune grew upon him, for Nora in white pique skirt and batiste blouse smartly girdled with a scarlet patent leather belt, in white canvas shoes and sailor hat, made a picture good to look at. Her dark olive brown skin, with rich warm colour showing through the sunburn of her cheeks, her dark eyes, and her hair for once "done up in style" under Kathleen's supervision, against the white of her costume made her indeed what her escort thought, "a stunning-looking girl." Usually careless as to her appearance, she had yielded to Kathleen's persuasion and had "gotten herself up to kill." No wonder her friends of both sexes followed her with eyes of admiration, for no one envied Nora, her frank manner, her generous nature, her open scorn at all attempts to win admiration, made her only friends.

"Bring your mother over here," cried Mrs. Waring-Gaunt, who rejoiced exceedingly in the girl's beauty. "Why, how splendidly you are looking to-day," she continued in a more confidential tone as the party grouped themselves about her. "What have you been doing to yourself? You are looking awfully fine."

"Am I?" said Nora, exceedingly pleased with herself. "I am awfully glad. It is all Kathleen's doing. I got me the belt and the hat new for this show."

"Very smart, that belt, my dear," said her friend.

"I rather fancy it myself, and Kathleen would do up my hair in this new way," said Nora, removing her hat that the full glory of her coiffure might appear. "Do you like it?"

"Perfectly spiffing!" ejaculated Mr. Duckworth, who had taken a seat just behind her chair.

Nora threw him a challenging glance that made that young man's heart skip a beat or two as all the excitements of the match had not.

"Are you a judge?" said the girl, tipping her saucy chin

at him.

"Am I? With four sisters and dozens of cousins to practise on, I fancy I might claim to be a regular bench show expert."

"Then," cried Nora with sudden animation, "you are the very man I want."

"Thank you so much," replied Mr. Duckworth fervently.

"I mean, perhaps you can advise me. Now as you look at me—" The young man's eyes burned into hers so that with all her audacity Nora felt the colour rising in her face. "Which would you suggest as the most suitable style for me, the psyche knot or the neck roll?"

"I beg your pardon? I rather—"

"Or would you say the French twist?"

"Ah, the French twist—"

"Or simply marcelled and pomped?"

"I am afraid—"

"Or perhaps the pancake or the coronet?"

"Well," said the young man, desperately plunging, "the coronet I should say would certainly not be inappropriate. It goes with princesses, duchesses and that sort of thing. Don't you think so, Mrs. Waring-Gaunt?" said Duckworth, hoping to be extricated. That lady, however, gave him no assistance but continued to smile affectionately at the girl beside her. "What style is this that you have now adopted, may I ask?" inquired Mr. Duckworth cautiously.

"Oh, that's a combination of several. It's a creation of Kathleen's which as yet has received no name."

"Then it should be named at once," said Duckworth with great emphasis. "May I suggest the Thunderbolt? You see, of course—so stunning."

"They are coming on," cried Nora, turning her shoulder in disdain upon the young man. "Look, there's your brother, Mrs. Waring-Gaunt. I think he is perfectly splendid."

"Which is he?" said Mr. Duckworth, acutely interested.

"That tall, fine-looking man on the brown pony."

"Oh, yes, I see. Met him this morning. By Jove, he is some looker too," replied Mr. Duckworth with reluctant enthusiasm.

"And there is the High River Captain," said Mrs. Waring-Gaunt, "on the grey."

"Oh, yes, Monteith, he played for All Canada last year, didn't he?" said Nora with immense enthusiasm. "He is perfectly splendid."

"I hear the High River club has really sent only its second team, or at least two of them," said Mrs. Waring-Gaunt. "Certainly Tremaine is not with them."

"I hope they get properly trimmed for it," said Nora, indignantly. "Such cheek!"

The result of the match quite exceeded Nora's fondest hopes, for the High River team, having made the fatal error of despising the enemy, suffered the penalty of their mistake in a crushing defeat. It was certainly a memorable day for Wolf Willow, whose inhabitants were exalted to a height of glory as they never experienced in all their history.

"Serves us right," said Monteith, the High River Captain, apologising for his team's poor display to his friend, Hec Ross, who had commanded the Wolf Willow team. "We deserved to be jolly well licked, and we got what was coming to us."

"Oh, we're not worrying," replied the Wolf Willow Captain, himself a sturdy horseman and one of the most famous stick handlers in the West. "Of course, we know that if Murray and Knight had been with you the result would have been different."

"I am not at all sure about that," replied Monteith. "That new man of yours, Romayne, is a wonder. Army man, isn't he?"

"Yes, played in India, I believe."

"Oh, no wonder he's such a don at it. You ought to get together a great team here, Ross, and I should like to bring our team down again to give you a real game."

"When?"

"Say two weeks. No. That throws it a little late for the harvest. Say a week from to-day."

"I shall let you know to-night," said Ross. "You are staying for the spellbinding fest and entertainment, are you not?"

"Sure thing; we are out for the whole day. Who are on for the speaking?"

"Gilchrist for one, our Member for the Dominion, you know."

"Oh, yes, strong man, I believe. He's a Liberal, of Course."

"Yes," replied Ross, "he's a Grit all right, hide-bound too—"

"Which you are not, I take it," replied Monteith with a laugh.

"Traditionally I am a Conservative," said Ross, "but last election I voted Liberal. I don't know how you were but I was keen on Reciprocity."

"The contrary with me," replied Monteith. "Traditionally I am a Liberal, but I voted Conservative."

"You voted against Reciprocity, you a western man voted against a better market for our wheat and stuff, and against cheaper machinery?"

"Yes, I knew quite well it would give us a better market for our grain here, and it would give us cheaper machinery too, but—do you really care to know why I switched?"

"Sure thing; I'd like awfully to hear if you don't mind. We are not discussing politics, you understand."

"No. Well," said Monteith, "two things made me change my party. In the first place, to be quite frank, I was afraid of American domination. We are a small people yet. Their immense wealth would overwhelm our manufacturers and flood our markets with cheap stuff, and with trade dominance there would more easily go political dominance.

You remember Taft's speech? That settled it for me. That was one thing. The other was the Navy question. I didn't like Laurier's attitude. I am a Canadian, born right here in Alberta, but I am an Imperialist. I am keen about the Empire and that sort of thing. I believe that our destiny is with the Empire and that with the Empire we shall attain to our best. And since the Empire has protected us through all of our history, I believe the time has come when we should make our contribution to its defence. We ought to have a fleet, and that fleet in time of war should automatically be merged with the Imperial Navy. That's how I felt at the last election. This autonomy stuff of Laurier's is all right, but it should not interfere with Imperial unity."

"It's a funny thing," replied Ross. "I take the opposite side on both these points. I was born in the Old Country and like most Old Country people believe in Free Trade. So I was keen to wipe out all barriers between the United States and ourselves in trade. I believe in trading wherever you can get the best terms. As for American domination, I have not the slightest fear in the world of the Yankees. They might flood our markets at first, probably would, but they would certainly bring in capital. We need capital badly, you know that. And why should not factories be established on this side of the line with American money? Pennsylvania does not hurt New York, nor Illinois Dakota. Why then, with all trade barriers thrown down, should the United States hurt Canada? And then on the other side, we get a market for everything we grow at our doors. Reciprocity looked good to me. As for imperilling our Imperial connections—I do not mean to be offensive at all—of course you see what your position amounts to—that our financial interests would swamp our loyalty, that our loyalty is a thing of dollars and cents. My idea is that nothing in the world from the outside can ever break the bonds that hold Canada to the Empire, and after

Ralph Connor

all, heart bonds are the strong bonds. Then in regard to the Navy, I take the other view from you also. I believe I am a better Canadian than you, although I am not Canadian born. I think there's something awfully fine in Canada's splendid independence. She wants to run her own ranch, and by George she will, and everything on it. She is going to boss her own job and will allow no one else to butt in. I agree with what you say about the Empire. Canada ought to have a Navy and quick. She ought to take her share of the burden of defence. But I agree here with Laurier. I believe her ships should be under her own control. For after all only the Canadian Government has the right to speak the word that sends them out to war. Of course, when once Canada hands them over to the Imperial Navy, they will fall into line and take their orders from the Admiral that commands the fleet. Do you know I believe that Laurier is right in sticking out for autonomy."

"I am awfully interested in what you say, and I don't believe we are so far apart. It's a thousand pities they did not keep together in the Commons. They could easily have worked it out."

"Yes, it was a beastly shame," replied Ross.

"But isn't it rather queer," said Monteith, "and isn't it significant, too? Here I am, born in Canada, sticking out against reciprocity and anxious to guard our Imperial connection and ready to hand our Navy clean over to the Imperial authorities, and on the other hand, there you are, born in the Old Country, you don't appear to care a darn about Imperial connections. You let that take care of itself, and you stick up for Canadian autonomy to the limit."

"Well, for one thing," replied Ross, "we ought to get together on the Navy business. On the trade question we represent, of course, two schools of economics, but we ought not to mix up the flag with our freight. This flag-flapping business makes me sick."

"There you are again," said Monteith. "Here I am, born right here in the West, and yet I believe in all the flag-flapping you can bring about and right here in this country too. Why, you know how it is with these foreigners, Ruthenians, Russians, Germans, Poles. Do you know that in large sections of this western country the foreign vote controls the election? I believe we ought to take every means to teach them to love the flag and shout for it too. Oh, I know you Old Country chaps. You take the flag for granted, and despise this flag-raising business. Let me tell you something. I went across to Oregon a little while ago and saw something that opened my eyes. In a little school in the ranching country in a settlement of mixed foreigners—Swedes, Italians, Germans, Jews—they had a great show they called 'saluting the flag.' Being Scotch you despise the whole thing as a lot of rotten slushy sentimentality, and a lot of Canadians agree with you. But let me tell you how they got me. I watched those kids with their foreign faces, foreign speech—you ought to hear them read—Great Scott, you'd have to guess at the language. Then came this flag-saluting business. A kid with Yiddish written all over his face was chosen to carry in the flag, attended by a bodyguard for the colours, and believe me they appeared as proud as Punch of the honour. They placed the flag in position, sang a hymn, had a prayer, then every kid at a signal shot out his right hand toward the flag held aloft by the Yiddish colour bearer and pledged himself, heart, and soul, and body, to his flag and to his country. The ceremony closed with the singing of the national hymn, mighty poor poetry and mighty hard to sing, but do you know listening to those kids and watching their foreign faces I found myself with tears in my eyes and swallowing like a darn fool. Ever since that day I believe in flag-flapping."

"Maybe you are right," replied Ross. "You know we British folk are so fearfully afraid of showing our feelings. We go along like graven images; the more really stirred up, the more graven we appear. But suppose we move over to the platform where the speechifying is to be done."

In front of the school building a platform had been erected, and before the stage, preparations had been made for seating the spectators as far as the school benches and chairs from neighbours' houses would go. The programme consisted of patriotic songs and choruses with contributions from the minstrel company. The main events of the evening, however, were to be the addresses, the principal speech being by the local member for the Dominion Parliament, Mr. J. H. Gilchrist, who was to be followed by a local orator, Mr. Alvin P. Jones, a former resident of the United States, but now an enthusiastic, energetic and most successful farmer and business man, possessing one of the best appointed ranches in Alberta. The chairman was, of course, Reverend Evans Rhye. The parson was a little Welshman, fat and fussy and fiery of temper, but his heart was warmly human, and in his ministry he manifested a religion of such simplicity and devotion, of such complete unselfishness as drew to him the loyal affection of the whole community. Even such sturdy Presbyterians as McTavish, the Rosses, Angus Frazer and his mother, while holding tenaciously and without compromise to their own particular form of doctrine and worship, yielded Mr. Rhye, in the absence of a church and minister of their own denomination, a support and esteem unsurpassed even among his own folk. Their attitude was considered to be stated with sufficient clearness by Angus Frazer in McTavish's store one day. "I am not that sure about the doctrine, but he has the right kind of religion for me." And McTavish's reply was characteristic: "Doctrine! He has as gude as you can expec' frae thae Episcopawlian buddies. But he's a Godly man and he aye pays his debts whatever," which from McTavish was as high praise as could reasonably be expected.

The audience comprised the total population of Wolf Willow and its vicinity, as well as visitors from the country within a radius of ten or fifteen miles.

Mr. J. H. Gilchrist, M. P., possessed the initial advantages of Scotch parentage and of early Scotch training, and besides these he was a farmer and knew the farmer's mind. To these advantages he added those of a course of training in Toronto University in the departments of metaphysics and economics, and an additional advantage of five years' pedagogical experience. He possessed, moreover, the gift of lucid and forceful speech. With such equipment small wonder that he was in demand for just such occasions as a Dominion Day celebration and in just such a community as Wolf Willow. The theme of his address was Canadian Citizenship, Its Duties and Its Responsibilities, a theme somewhat worn but possessing the special advantage of being removed from the scope of party politics while at the same time affording opportunity for the elucidation of the political principles of that party which Mr. Gilchrist represented, and above all for a fervid patriotic appeal. With Scotch disdain of all that savoured of flattery or idle compliment, Mr. Gilchrist plunged at once into the heart of his subject.

"First, the area of Canada. Forty-six years ago, when Canada became a nation, the Dominion possessed an area of 662,148 square miles; to-day her area covers 3,729,665 square miles, one-third the total size of the British

Empire, as large as the continent of Europe without Russia, larger by over one hundred thousand square miles than the United States."

"Hear, hear," cried an enthusiastic voice from the rear.

"Aye, water and snow," in a rasping voice from old McTavish.

"Water and snow," replied Mr. Gilchrist. "Yes, plenty of water, 125,000 square miles of it, and a good thing it is too for Canada. Some people sniff at water," continued the speaker with a humorous glance at McTavish, "but even a Scotchman may with advantage acknowledge the value of a little water." The crowd went off into a roar of laughter at the little Scotchman who was supposed to be averse to the custom of mixing too much water with his drink.

"My friend, Mr. McTavish," continued the speaker, "has all a Scotchman's hatred of bounce and brag. I am not indulging in foolish brag, but I maintain that no Canadian can rightly prize the worth of his citizenship who does not know something of his country, something of the wealth of meaning lying behind that word 'Canada,' and I purpose to tell you this evening something of some of Canada's big things. I shall speak of them with gratitude and with pride, but chiefly with a solemnising sense of responsibility.

"As for the 'water and the snow' question: Let me settle that now. Water for a great inland continental country like ours is one of its most valuable assets for it means three things. First, cheap transportation. We have the longest continuous waterway in the world, and with two small cuttings Canada can bring ocean-going ships into the very heart of the continent. Second, water means climate rainfall, and there need be no fear of snow and frost while great bodies of open water lie about. And third, water power. Do you know that Canada stands first in the world in its water power? It possesses twice the water power of the United States (we like to get something in which we can excel our American cousins), and lying near the great centres of population too. Let me give you three examples. Within easy reach of Vancouver on the west coast there is at least 350,000 horse power, of which 75,000 is now in use. Winnipeg, the metropolitan centre of Canada, where more than in any place else can be heard the heart beat of the Dominion, has 400,000 horse power available, of which she now uses 50,000. Toronto lies within reach of the great Niagara, whose power no one can estimate, while along the course of the mighty St. Lawrence towns and cities lie within touch of water power that is beyond all calculation as yet. And do you Alberta people realise that right here in your own province the big Bassano Dam made possible by a tiny stream taken from the Bow River furnishes irrigation power for over a million acres? Perhaps that will do about the water."

"Oo aye," said McTavish, with profound resignation in his voice. "Ye'll dae wi' that."

"And snow," cried the speaker. "We would not willingly be without our snow in Canada. Snow means winter transport, better business, lumbering, and above all, wheat. Where you have no snow and frost you cannot get the No. 1 hard wheat. Don't quarrel with the snow. It is Canada's snow and frost that gives her the first place in the world in wheat production. So much for the water and the snow."

McTavish hitched about uneasily. He wanted to have the speaker get done with this part of his theme.

From Canada's area Mr. Gilchrist passed on to deal with Canada's resources, warning his audience that the greater part of these resources was as yet undeveloped and that he should have to indulge in loud-sounding phrases, but he promised them that whatever words he might employ he would still be unable to adequately picture to their imagination the magnitude of Canada's undeveloped wealth. Then in a perfect torrent he poured forth upon the people statistics setting forth Canada's possessions in mines and forests, in fisheries, in furs, in agricultural products, and especially in wheat. At the word "wheat" he pulled up abruptly.

"Wheat," he exclaimed, "the world's great food for men. And Canada holds the greatest wheat farm in all the world. Not long ago Jim Hill told the Minneapolis millers that three-fourths of the wheat lands on the American continent were north of the boundary line and that Canada could feed every mouth in Europe. Our wheat crop this year will go nearly 250,000,000 bushels, and this, remember, without fertilisation and with very poor farming, for we Western Canadians are poor farmers. We owe something to our American settlers who are teaching us something of the science and art of agriculture. Remember, too, that our crop comes from only one-seventh of our wheat lands. Had the other six-sevenths been cropped, our wheat yield would be over three and a half billion bushels—just about the world's supply. We should never be content till Canada does her full duty to the world, till Canada gives to the world all that is in her power to give. I make no apology for dwelling at such length upon Canada's extent and resources.

"Now let me speak to you about our privileges and responsibilities as citizens of this Dominion. Our possessions and material things will be our destruction unless we use them not only for our own good, but for the good of the world. And these possessions we can never properly use till we learn to prize those other possessions of heart and mind and soul."

With a light touch upon the activities of Canadians, in the development of their country in such matters as transportation and manufactures, he passed to a consideration of the educational, social, industrial, political and religious privileges which Canadian citizens enjoyed.

"These are the things," he cried, "that have to do with the nation's soul. These are the things that determine the quality of a people and their place among the nations, their influence in the world. In the matter of education it is the privilege of every child in Canada to receive a sound training, not only in the elementary branches of study, but even in higher branches as well. In Canada social distinctions are based more upon worth than upon wealth, more upon industry and ability than upon blue blood. Nowhere in the world is it more profoundly true that

> "'A man's a man for a' that;
> The rank is but the guinea's stamp;
> The man's the gowd for a' that.'"

At this old McTavish surprised the audience and himself by crying out, "Hear-r-r, hear-r-r," glancing round defiantly as if daring anyone to take up his challenge.

"In matters of religion," continued the speaker, "the churches of Canada hold a position of commanding influence, not because of any privileges accorded them by the State, nor because of any adventitious or meretricious aids, but solely because of their ability to minister to the social and spiritual needs of the people."

Briefly the speaker proceeded to touch upon some characteristic features of Canadian political institutions.

"Nowhere in the world," he said, "do the people of a country enjoy a greater measure of freedom. We belong to a great world Empire. This connection we value and mean to cherish, but our Imperial relations do not in the slightest degree infringe upon our liberties. The Government of Canada is autonomous. Forty-six years ago the four provinces of Canada were united into a single Dominion with representative Government of the most complete kind. Canada is a Democracy, and in no Democracy in the world does the will of the people find more immediate and more complete expression than in our Dominion. With us political liberty is both a heritage and an achievement, a heritage from our forefathers who made this Empire what it is, and an achievement of our own people led by great and wise statesmen. This priceless possession of liberty we shall never surrender, for the nation that surrenders its liberty, no matter what other possessions it may retain, has lost its soul."

The address concluded with an appeal to the people for loyal devotion to the daily duties of life in their various relations as members of families, members of the community, citizens of the Province and of the Dominion. In the applause that followed the conclusion of this address, even old McTavish was observed to contribute his share with something amounting almost to enthusiasm.

CHAPTER XI

THE SHADOW OF WAR

It was finally agreed that a part at least of the responsibility for the disturbance which marred the harmony of
the Dominion Day celebration at Wolf Willow upon this
occasion must rest on the shoulders of Mr. Alvin P. Jones.
The impressive presentation by Mr. Gilchrist of Canada's
greatness and the splendour of her future appeared to
stimulate Mr. Jones to unusual flights of oratory. Under
ordinary circumstances Mr. Jones' oratory was characterised by such extraordinary physical vigour, if not
violence, and by such a fluency of orotund and
picturesque speech, that with the multitude sound passed
for eloquence and platitudes on his lips achieved the
dignity of profound wisdom. Building upon the
foundation laid by the previous speaker, Mr. Jones
proceeded to extol the grandeur of the Dominion, the
wonders of her possessions, the nobility of her people, the
splendour of her institutions, the glory of her future. He
himself was not by birth a Canadian, but so powerful a
spell had the Dominion cast over him that he had become
a Canadian by adoption. Proud of his American birth and
citizenship, he was even more proud of his Canadian
citizenship. He saw before him a large number of
American citizens who had come to throw in their lot with
the Dominion of Canada. He believed they had done a

wise thing, and that among the most loyal citizens of this Dominion none would be found more devoted to the material welfare and the spiritual well-being of Canada than those who came from the other side of the line. He saw a number of those who were sometimes improperly called foreigners. He said "improperly" because whatever their origin, whether Ruthenian, Swede, French, German, or whatever their race might be, here they were simply Canadians with all the rights of Canadian citizenship assured to them. He was glad to see so many of his German friends present. They represent a great nation whose achievements in every department of human activity, in learning, in industrial enterprise, in commerce, were the envy and admiration of the world (excursus here in glorification of the great German people): To these, his German fellow citizens, he would say that no matter how deep their devotion to the Vaterland (Mr. Jones pronounced it with a "v") he knew they would be loyal citizens of Canada. The German Empire had its differences and disagreements with Great Britain, the American Republic has had the same, and indeed it was possible that there were a number present who might not cherish any very passionate regard for the wealthy, complaisant, self-contained somewhat slow-going old gentleman, John Bull. But here in Canada, we were all Canadians! First, last and all the time, Canadians (great applause). Whatever might be said of other countries, their wealth, their power, their glory, Canada was good enough for him (more applause, followed by a further elaboration of Canada's vast resources, etc., etc.). Canada's future was unclouded by the political compli-cations and entanglements of the older countries in Europe. For one hundred years they had been at peace with the Republic south of that imaginary line which delimited the boundaries, but which did not divide the hearts of these two peoples (great applause). For his part, while he rejoiced in the greatness of the British Empire he believed that Canada's first duty was to herself, to the developing here of a strong and sturdy national spirit. Canada for Canadians, Canada first, these were the motives that had guided his life both in public service and as a private citizen (loud applause). In this country there was a place for all, no matter from what country they came, a place for the Ruthenian (enumeration of the various European and Asiatic states from which potential citizens of Canada had come). Let us join hands and hearts in building up a great empire where our children, free from old-world entanglements, free to develop in our own way our own institutions (eloquent passages on freedom) in obedience to laws of our own making, defended by the strong arms and brave hearts of our own sons, aided (here the speaker permitted himself a smile of gentle humour) by the mighty wing of the American eagle (references to the Monroe Doctrine and its protection of Canada's shores) we shall abide in peace and security from all aggression and all alarm. (Thunderous and continued applause, during which the speaker resumed his seat.)

It was old McTavish who precipitated the trouble. The old Highlander belonged to a family that boasted a long line of fighting forbears. Ever since The Forty-five when the German king for the time occupying the English throne astutely diverted the martial spirit of the Scottish clans from the business of waging war against his own armies, their chief occupation, to that of fighting his continental foes, The McTavish was to be found ever in the foremost ranks of British men-of-war, joyously doing battle for his clan and for his king, who, if the truth were told, he regarded with scant loyalty. Like so many of the old timers in western Canada, this particular McTavish had been at one time a servant of the Hudson Bay Company and as such had done his part in the occupation, peaceful and otherwise, of the vast territories administered by that great trading company. In his fiery fighting soul there burned a passionate loyalty to the name and fame of the land of his birth, and a passionate pride in the Empire under whose flag the Company's ships had safely sailed the northern seas and had safely traded in these vast wild lands for nearly three hundred years. Deep as this loyalty and pride in the soul of him there lay a cold suspicion of the Yankee. He had met him in those old days of trade war, had suffered and had seen his Company suffer from his wiles, and finally had been compelled to witness with bitter but unavailing hate the steady encroachment of those rival traders upon the ancient prerogatives and preserves of his own Company, once the sole and undisputed lords of the northern half of the American continent. In the person of Mr. Alvin P. Jones, McTavish saw the representative of those ancient enemies of his, and in the oration to which he had just listened he fancied he detected a note of disloyalty to the flag, a suggestion of a break in the allegiance of Canada to the Empire, and worst of all, a hint that Canada might safely depend for protection upon something other than the naval power which had guarded the shores of his country these many years from enemy invasion. These things wrought in old McTavish an uncontrollable anger, and no sooner had the tumultuous applause died away than he was on his feet and in a high, rasping voice demanding audience.

"Will ye per-r-rmit me, Mr. Chair-r-rman, a few words in regar-r-d to the remarkable address to which we haf listened?" Permission was graciously granted by the chairman, surprise and complaisant delight mantling the steaming face of Mr. Alvin P. Jones, albeit at his heart there lurked a certain uneasiness, for on more than one occasion had he suffered under the merciless heckling of the little Scotchman.

"'Tis a wonderful address we haf been hearing, an

eloquent address. Some of it iss true an' some of it iss lies [commotion in the audience—the smile on Mr. Alvin P. Jones's face slightly less expansive]. The speaker has told us about Canada, its great extent, its vast r-r-resources. Some of us haf known about these things while yet his mother was still sucking him [snickers of delight from the younger members of the audience and cries of, 'Go to it, Mack]. 'Tis a great Dominion whatefer and will be a gr-r-reater Dominion yet so lang as it keeps to right ways. He has told us of the mighty achievements of Cher-r-rmany. I will jist be askin' him what has Cher-r-rmany done for this country or for any country but her ainsel? She has cluttered us up wi' pot-metal, cutlery an' such things, an' cheap cloth that ye can put yer finger through, an' that will be done in a month's wear-r-ring. Musick, ye'll be sayin'! Musick! I was in Calgary not long since. They took me to what they will be callin' a music-kale [delighted roars of laughter from the audience]. A music-kale indeed! I haf hear-r-rd of cauld kale an' het kale, of kale porridge an' kale brose, but nefer haf I hear-r-rd before of a music-kale. Bless me, man, I cud make neither head nor tail o' it, and they wer-r-re no better themsel's. They had printed notes about it an' a bit man makin' a speech about it, but not one of them knew a thing about the hale hypotheck. Musick, quare musick I call it! If it is musick yer wantin', gif me Angus there wi' the pipes [wild cheers testifying to Angus's popularity] or the master-r-r himsel' an' the young lady here [this with a courteous bow to Miss Switzer] wi' their feeddles. That's what I will be callin' musick. An' lairnin'! Lairnin' that will lay sacraleegious hands upon the Sacred Word, an' tear-r-r it to bits. That like thing the Cher-r-rman lairnin' is doin', and ye can ask Mr. Rhye yonder. An' other things the Cher-r-rmans are doin' that keep us all from restin' quiet in our beds. Let them come her-r-re to us if they will. Let them come from all the countries of the ear-r-rth. We will share wi' them what we haf, provided they will be behavin' themsel's and mindin' their peeziness. But this man is sayin' somethin' more. He is tellin' us how safe we are, an' that the great Republic south o' us will be guar-r-rdin' us frae our enemies. I doubt it will be the fox guar-r-rdin' the chicken frae the weasel. Now I'll ask this gentleman what it is that has guar-r-rded these shores for the past two hundred and fifty year-r-rs? I will tell him—the Br-r-ritish Navy. What has kept the peace of Europe once an' again? The Br-r-ritish Navy. Aye, what has protected America not once or twice frae her enemies? The Br-r-ritish Navy, an' that same Br-r-ritish Navy is gude enough fer me."

The tumultuous din that followed the conclusion of the cantankerous little Highlander's speech was beyond all words, but before the chairman could get to his feet, through the uproar a voice strident with passion was demanding a hearing. "Mr. Ernest Switzer has the floor," said the chairman.

The young man's face was white and his voice shaking when he began. "Mr. Chairman, Ladies and Gentlemen: I stand here to claim the fair play that you say is British for myself and for my race. I am a Canadian citizen. I was born in America, but my blood is German. As a Canadian citizen, as an American by birth, as a German by blood, I have been insulted to-night, and I demand the right to reply to the man who has insulted me. There are Canadians here to guard their own honour; the Americans can be trusted to protect themselves. Germany is not here to refute the slanders uttered against her, but I claim the honour to speak for that great nation, for she is a great nation. There is none greater. There is none so great in the world to-day." The young man's voice rang out with passionate conviction, his pale set face, his blue eyes flaming with rage proclaimed the intensity of his emotion. Before his flaming passion the audience was subdued into a silence tense and profound. "What has Germany done for the world? this man asks. I would like to ask in reply where he has lived for the last twenty-five years, and if during those years he has read anything beyond his local newspaper? What has Germany done for the world? Germany has shown the way to the world, even to America, in every activity of life, in industrial organisation, in scientific inquiry in the laboratory and in the practical application of science to every-day life. Where do your philosophers go for their training? To German universities where they seek to understand the philosophy of the immortal Emanuel Kant. Where in the world has social reform reached its highest achievement? In Germany. Where do you go for your models for municipal government? To Germany. Mention any department of human enterprise to-day and in that department Germany stands easily in the lead. This man asks what has kept Europe at peace all these years, and suggests the British Navy, the one constant menace to the peace of Europe and to the freedom of the seas. No, if you ask who has kept the peace of Europe I will tell you. The German Kaiser, Wilhelm II. To him and to the Empire of which he is the glorious head Europe owes its peace and the world its greatest blessings to-day."

When Switzer sat down a half a dozen men were on their feet demanding to be heard. Above the din a quiet, but penetrating voice was distinguished. "Mr. Romayne has the floor," said the Reverend Mr. Rhye, who himself was tingling with desire for utterance. Mr. Romayne's appearance and voice suggested the boredom of one who felt the whole thing to be rather a nuisance.

"Ladies and Gentlemen," he began, "I must apologise for venturing to speak at all, having so recently come to this country, though I am glad to say that I have been received with such cordial kindness that I do not feel myself a stranger."

"You're all right, Jack," cried a voice. "You're right at home."

"I am at home," said Jack, "and that is one thing that makes me able to speak. Few of you can understand the feeling that comes to one who, travelling six thousand miles away from the heart of the Empire, finds himself still among his own folk and under the same old flag. Nor can I express the immense satisfaction and pride that come to me when I find here in this new world a virile young nation offering a welcome to men of all nationalities, an equal opportunity to make home and fortune for themselves, and find also these various nationalities uniting in the one purpose of building solid and secure an outpost of the Empire to which we all belong. I rise chiefly to say two things. The first is that if Germany continues in her present mind she will be at war with our country within a very short time. The young man who has just sat down assures us that Germany is a great country. Let us at once frankly grant this fact, for indeed it is a fact. Whether she is as wonderful or as great as she thinks herself to be may be doubted. But it is of importance to know that the opinion stated here to-night is the opinion held by the whole body of the German people from the Kaiser to the lowest peasant in the Empire. The universal conviction throughout that Empire is that not only is Germany the greatest nation on earth, but that it has a divine mission to confer her own peculiar quality of civilisation upon the other nations of Europe, and indeed upon the whole world. We might not quarrel with Germany for cherishing this pleasing opinion in regard to herself, but when this opinion is wrought into a purpose to dominate the whole world in order that this mission might be accomplished the thing takes on a somewhat serious aspect. Let me repeat, Germany is a great nation, marvellously organised in every department of her life, agricultural, manufacturing, educational, commercial. But to what intent? What is the purpose dominating this marvellous organisation? The purpose, Ladies and Gentlemen, is war. The supreme industry of the German nation is the manufacturing of a mighty war machine. I challenge the gentleman who has just spoken to deny either of these statements, that Germany believes that she has a definite mission to lift up the other nations of Europe to her own high level and that to fulfil this mission it is necessary that she be in a position of control." The speaker paused for a moment or two. "He cannot deny these because he knows they are true. The second thing I wish to say is that the Kaiser means war and is waiting only for the favourable moment. I believe it is correct to say that for many years after his accession to the throne he used his influence on the side of peace, but I have every reason to believe that for some years past he has cherished another purpose, the purpose of war."

At this point Switzer sprang to his feet and cried, "I challenge the truth of that statement. Modern European history proves it to be false, and again and again the Kaiser has prevented war. So much is this the case that the trustees of the only European fund that recognises distinguished service in the interests of peace bestowed upon the Kaiser the Nobel Prize."

"That is quite true," replied Mr. Romayne. "But let me recall to this young man's mind a few facts. In 1875 Bismarck was determined to make war upon France. He was prevented by the united action of England and Russia. Germany made the same attempt in '87 and '91. In 1905 so definite was the threat of war that France avoided it only by dismissing her war minister, Delcasse. Perhaps my young friend remembers the Casablanca incident in 1908 where again the Kaiser threatened France with war. Indeed, for the last twenty years, even while he was doubtless anxious to maintain peace, he has been rattling

Ralph Connor

his sword in his scabbard and threatening war against the various nations of Europe. In most of these cases even when he wanted peace he bluffed with threats of war. Then came the Agadir incident in 1911 when once more the Kaiser bluffed. But Great Britain called his bluff that time and the great War Lord had to back down with great loss of prestige not only with his own people but with the whole of Europe. It hurt the Kaiser to think that any nation in Europe should move in any direction without his consent. Agadir taught him that he must quit bluffing or make up his mind to fight."

Again Switzer was upon his feet. "This is a slanderous falsehood," he cried. "How does this man know?"

"I happened to be there," was the quiet reply.

"How do we know?" again cried Switzer.

"Will you kindly repeat that remark?" said Mr. Romayne quietly.

"I believe this statement," shouted Switzer, "to be a slanderous falsehood."

"If you accuse me of falsehood," said Romayne even more quietly, "that is a matter of which we shall not discuss here, but later. But these statements that I have made are history. All Germany knows, all Europe knows, that at Agadir the Kaiser backed down. He was not ready to fight, and he lost prestige by it. When Italy, one of the Triple Alliance, went to war against Turkey without consulting him, this lowered still further German prestige. In the late Balkan War Germany was again humiliated. She backed the wrong horse. Her protege and pupil in war, Turkey, was absolutely beaten. These things convince me that Germany knows that her hope of dominating Europe is rapidly waning, and she believes that this hope can only be realised by war and, therefore, I repeat that the Kaiser and his people are only waiting a favourable moment to launch war upon Europe and more particularly upon the British Empire, which, along with the great American democracy, stands between her and the realisation of her dream."

"The British Empire!" cried Switzer scornfully as Romayne took his seat, "the British Empire! at the first stern blow this ramshackle empire will fall to pieces. Then Great Britain will be forced to surrender her robber hold upon these great free states which she has stolen and which she now keeps in chains." (Cries of "Never!" "Rot!" "Shut your trap!") Switzer sprang to his feet and, shaking his fist in their faces, cried: "I know what I am saying. This you will see before many months have passed."

Again Romayne rose to his feet and waited till a silence fell upon the audience. "Ladies and Gentlemen," he said solemnly, "this German officer knows what he is talking about. That Germany within a few months will make her supreme attempt to smash the British Empire I believe is certain. I am equally certain that the result of that attempt will not be what this gentleman anticipates and desires."

For some moments the silence remained unbroken. Then young Monteith sprang to his feet and led the audience in a succession of mad cheers that indicated the depth of passion to which they were stirred. After the cheering had subsided Larry rose and in a slightly querulous tone and with a humorous smile upon his face he said:

"Mr. Chairman, don't you think we are becoming unnecessarily serious? And are there not certain things on which we all agree? First that we are all Canadians, first, last and all the time. Secondly, that we greatly respect and admire our American cousins and we desire only better mutual acquaintance for our mutual good. Third, that we are loyal to and immensely proud of our Empire, and we mean to stick to it. And fourth, that Germany is a great country and has done great things for the world. As to the historical questions raised, these are not settled by discussion but by reliable historic documents. As to the prophecies made, we can accept or reject them as we choose. Personally I confess that I am unable to get up any real interest in this German war menace. I believe Germany has more sense, not to say proper Christian feeling, than to plunge herself and the world into war. I move, Mr. Chairman, that we pass to the next order of business."

"Hear! Hear!" cried some. "Go on with the programme."

"No! No!" said others. "Let's have it out."

"Mr. Chairman," said Hec Ross, rising to his feet, "this thing is better than any silly old programme, let's have it out."

But the chairman, much against his inclination, for he was a fighter, ruled otherwise. "The differences that separate us from one another here to-night are not differences that can be settled by argument. They are differences that are due partly to our history and partly to the ideals which we cherish. We shall go on with the programme."

At first the people were in no mood for mere amusement. They had been made to face for a brief moment the great and stern reality of war. The words and more the manner of Jack Romayne had produced a deep sense in their minds of the danger of a European conflagration, and the ominous words of the young German spoken as from intimate knowledge only served to deepen the impression made by Romayne. But the feeling was transitory, and speedily the possibility of war was dismissed as unthinkable. The bogey of a German war was familiar and therefore losing its power to disturb them. So after two or three musical numbers had been given the audience had settled back into its normal state of mind which accepted peace as the natural and permanent condition for the world.

The entertainment would have come to a perfectly proper and harmonious close had it not been for the unrestrained exuberance of Sam's humorous qualities on the one hand and the complete absence of sense of humour in Ernest Switzer on the other. The final number on the programme, which was to be a series of humorous character sketches, had been left entirely in Sam's hands and consisted of a trilogy representing the characteristics as popularly conceived of the French Canadian habitant, the humorous Irishman and the obese Teuton. Sam's early association with the vaudeville stage had given him a certain facility in the use of stage properties and theatrical paraphernalia generally, and this combined with a decided gift of mimicry enabled him to produce a really humorous if somewhat broadly burlesqued reproduction of these characters. In the presentation of his sketch Sam had reserved to the close his representation of the obese Teuton. The doings of this Teuton, while sending the audience into roars of laughter, had quite a different effect upon Switzer, who after a few moments of wrathful endurance made toward the rear of the audience.

Meantime the obese Teuton has appeared upon the stage in a famished condition demanding vociferously and plaintively from the world at large sausage. But no sausage is available. At this point a stray dog wanders upon the stage. With a cry of delight the famished Teuton seizes the unfortunate cur and joyously announcing that now sausage he will have, forthwith disappears. Immediately from the wings arise agonised canine howlings with which mingles the crashing of machinery. Gradually the howlings die into choking silence while the crash of the machinery proceeds for a few moments longer. Thereupon reappears the Teuton, ecstatic and triumphant, bearing with him a huge sausage, which he proceeds to devour with mingled lamentations over his departed "hund" and raptures over its metamorphosed condition. In the midst of this mingled lamentation and rapture is heard in the distance upon a mouth organ band the sound of the German national air. The Teuton is startled, drops his sausage upon the stage and exclaiming "Der Kronprinz," hastily beats a retreat.

At the mention of this august name Switzer disappears from the rear of the audience and makes his way to the back of the stage. In the meantime, to the accompaniment of organs and drums, appears upon the stage no less a personage than "der Kronprinz," to the reproduction of whose features Sam's peculiar facial appearance admirably lends itself. From this point the action proceeds with increased rapidity. No sooner had "der Kronprinz," who is also in a famished condition, appeared upon the stage than his eyes light upon the sausage. With a cry of delight he seizes it and proceeds ravenously to devour it. But at the first mouthful renewed howlings arise. "Der Kronprinz," in a state of intense excitement, drops his sausage and begins a wild search in the corners of the stage and in the wings for the source of the uproar. The sausage thus abandoned, aided by an invisible cord, wabbles off the stage before the eyes of the wondering and delighted audience. Thereafter "der Kronprinz" reappears with his "hund" under his arm and begins an active and distracted search for his precious sausage. Disappointed in his search for the sausage and rendered desperate by his famished condition, he seizes the wretched cur and begins gnawing at the tail and retires from the scene, accompanied by the howls of the unhappy canine and the applauding shouts of the audience.

Meantime while Sam is engaged in executing a lightning change from the role of "der Kronprinz" to that of the original obese Teuton, Switzer beside himself with rage comes upon him at the precise moment when he is engaged in tying up his shoe preparatory to making his final entry upon the stage. The posture is irresistibly inviting. The next instant the astonished audience beholds the extraordinary spectacle of the obese Teuton under the impulse of the irate Switzer's boot in rapid flight across the stage upon all fours, bearing down with terrific speed upon the rear of the unsuspecting chairman who, facing the audience and with a genial smile upon his countenance, is engaged in applauding Sam's previous performance. Making frantic but futile efforts to recover himself, Sam plunges head on with resistless impact full upon the exact spot where the legs of the parson effect a junction with the rest of his person and carries that gentleman with him clear off the stage and fairly upon the top of old McTavish, who at that moment is engaged in conversation with little Miss Haight immediately behind him. Immediately there is a terrific uproar, in which through the delighted yells of the crowd, the crashing of the overturned chairs, and the general confusion could be heard the shrieks of the little spinster and weird Scotch oaths from McTavish. After the noise had somewhat subsided and when the confusion had been reduced to a semblance of order, McTavish was discovered with his hand upon the collar of the dazed parson who in turn held the obese Teuton in a firm and wrathful grip, at which once more the whole crowd rocked with an unholy but uncontrollable joy.

It was Larry who saved the situation by appearing upon the stage and gravely announcing that this unfortunate catastrophe was due to a sudden international upheaval which as usual in such cases had come about in an absolutely unexpected manner and as a result of misunderstandings and mistakes for which no one could be held responsible. He proposed in the name of the audience votes of thanks to those who had laboured so diligently to make the Dominion Day celebration so great a success, especially to the ladies and gentlemen who had served upon the various committees, to the speakers of the evening, to those who had provided the entertainment, and last but not least to the chairman who had presided with such grace and dignity over the proceedings of the evening. The motion was carried with tumultuous applause, and after the singing of "The Maple Leaf" and the national anthem, the meeting came to a close.

After the entertainment was over Larry and his mother slowly took the trail homewards, declining many offers of a lift from their friends in cars and carriages. It was the Harvest Moon. Upon the folds of the rolling prairie, upon the round tops of the hills, upon the broad valleys, and upon the far-away peaks in the west the white light lay thick and soft like a mantle. Above the white-mantled world the concave of the sky hung blue and deep and pricked out with pale star points. About the world the night had thrown her mystic jewelled robes of white and blue, making a holy shrine, a very temple of peace for God and man. For some minutes they walked together in silence, after they had bidden good-night to the last of their friends.

"What a world it is, Mother!" said Larry, gazing about him at the beauty of the night.

"Yes, but alas, alas, that God's own children should spoil

all this glory with hatred and strife! This very night in the unhappy Balkan States men are killing each other. It is too sad and too terrible to think of. Oh, if men would be content only to do justly by each other."

"Those people of the Balkan States are semi-barbarians," said Larry, "and therefore war between them is to be expected; but I cannot get myself to believe in the possibility of war between Christians, civilised nations to-day. But, Mother, for the first time in my life, listening to those two men, Romayne and Switzer, I had a feeling that war might be possible. Switzer seemed so eager for it, and so sure about it, didn't he? And Romayne, too, seemed ready to fight. But then I always remember that military men and military nations are for ever talking war."

"That is quite true, my dear," said his mother. "I too find it difficult to believe that war is possible in spite of what we have heard to-night. Our Friends at Home do not believe that war is imminent. They tell me that the feeling between Germany and Britain is steadily improving."

"And yet two years ago, Mother, in connection with the Agadir incident war might have happened any minute."

"That is true," replied his mother, "but every year of peace makes war less likely. The Friends are working and praying for a better understanding between these nations, and they are very confident that these peace delegations that are exchanging visits are doing a great deal for peace. Your Uncle Matthew, who has had a great deal to do with them, is very hopeful that a few years of peace will carry us past the danger point."

"Well, I hope so, Mother. I loathe the very thought of war," said Larry. "I think I am like you in this. I never did fight, you know; as a boy I always got out of it. Do you know, Mother, I think I would be afraid to fight."

"I hope so," replied his mother. "Fighting is no work for man, but for brute."

"But you would not be afraid, Mother. I know you would stand up to anything."

"Oh, no, no," cried his mother. "I could stand up to very little. After all, it is only God that makes strong to endure."

"But it is not quite the question of enduring, it is not the suffering, Mother. It is the killing. I don't believe I could kill a man, and yet in the Bible they were told to kill."

"But surely, Larry, we read our Bible somewhat differently these days. Surely we have advanced since the days of Abraham. We do not find our Lord and master commanding men to kill."

"But, Mother, in these present wars should not men defend their women and children from such outrages as we read about?"

"When it comes to the question of defending women and children it seems to me that the question is changed," said his mother. "As to that I can never quite make up my mind, but generally speaking we hold that it is the Cross, not the sword, that will save the world from oppression and break the tyrant's power."

"But after all, Mother," replied Larry, "it was not Smithfield that saved England's freedom, but Naseby."

"Perhaps both Naseby and Smithfield," said his mother. "I am not very wise in these things."

At the door of their house they came upon Nora sitting in the moonlight. "Did you meet Ernest and Mr. Romayne?" she inquired. "They've only gone five minutes or so. They walked down with us."

"No, we did not meet them."

"You must be tired after the wild excitement of the day, Mother," said Nora. "I think you had better go at once to bed. As for me, I am going for a swim."

"That's bully; I'm with you," said Larry.

In a few minutes they were dressed in their bathing suits, and, wrapped up in their mackintosh coats, they strolled toward the little lake.

"Let's sit a few moments and take in this wonderful night," said Nora. "Larry, I want to talk to you about what we heard to-night from those two men. They made me feel that war was not only possible but near."

"It did not impress me in the very least," said Larry. "They talked as military men always talk. They've got the war bug. These men have both held commissions in their respective armies. Romayne, of course, has seen war, and they look at everything from the military point of view."

As he was speaking there came across the end of the lake the sound of voices. Over the water the still air carried the words distinctly to their ears.

"Explain what?" It was Switzer's voice they heard, loud and truculent.

"Just what you meant by the words 'slanderous falsehood' which you used to-night," replied a voice which they recognised to be Jack Romayne's.

"I meant just what I said."

"Did you mean to impugn my veracity, because—"

"Because what?"

"Because if you did I should have to slap your face just now."

"Mein Gott! You—!"

"Not so loud," said Romayne quietly, "unless you prefer an audience."

"You schlap my face!" cried the German, in his rage losing perfect control of his accent. "Ach, if you were only in my country, we could settle this in the only way."

"Perhaps you will answer my question." Romayne's voice was low and clear and very hard. "Did you mean to call me a liar? Yes or no."

"A liar," replied the German, speaking more quietly. "No, it is not a question of veracity. It is a question of historical accuracy."

"Oh, very well. That's all."

"No, it is not all," exclaimed the German. "My God, that I should have to take insult from you! In this country of barbarians there is no way of satisfaction except by the beastly, the savage method of fists, but some day we will show you schwein of England—"

"Stop!" Romayne's voice came across the water with a

sharp ring like the tap of a hammer on steel. "You cannot use your hands, I suppose? That saves you, but if you say any such words again in regard to England or Englishmen, I shall have to punish you."

"Punish me!" shouted the German. "Gott in Himmel, that I must bear this!"

"They are going to fight," said Nora in an awed and horrified voice. "Oh, Larry, do go over."

"He-l-l-o," cried Larry across the water. "That you, Switzer? Who is that with you? Come along around here, won't you?"

There was a silence of some moments and then Romayne's voice came quietly across the water. "That you, Gwynne? Rather late to come around, I think. I am off for home. Well, Switzer, that's all, I think, just now. I'll say good-night." There was no reply from Switzer.

"You won't come then?" called Larry. "Well, goodnight, both of you."

"Good-night, good-night," came from both men.

"Do you think they will fight?" said Nora.

"No, I think not. There's Switzer riding off now. What fools they are."

"And Jack Romayne is so quiet and gentlemanly," said Nora.

"Quiet, yes, and gentlemanly, yes too. But I guess he'd be what Sam calls a 'bad actor' in a fight. Oh, these men make me tired who can't have a difference of opinion but they must think of fighting."

"Oh, Larry, I don't understand you a bit," cried Nora. "Of course they want to fight when they get full of rage. I would myself."

"I believe you," said Larry. "You are a real Irish terrier. You are like father. I am a Quaker, or perhaps there's another word for it. I only hope I shall never be called on to prove just what I am. Come on, let's go in."

For a half hour they swam leisurely to and fro in the moonlit water. But before they parted for the night Nora returned to the subject which they had been discussing.

"Larry, I don't believe you are a coward. I could not believe that of you," she said passionately; "I think I would rather die."

"Well, don't believe it then. I hope to God I am not, but then one can never tell. I cannot see myself hitting a man on the bare face, and as for killing a fellow being, I would much rather die myself. Is that being a coward?"

"But if that man," breathed Nora hurriedly, for the household were asleep, "if that man mad with lust and rage were about to injure your mother or your sisters—"

"Ah," said Larry, drawing in his breath quickly, "that would be different, eh?"

"Good-night, you dear goose," said his sister, kissing him quickly. "I am not afraid for you."

CHAPTER XII

MEN AND A MINE

It was early in July that Mr. Gwynne met his family with a proposition which had been elaborated by Ernest Switzer to form a company for the working of Nora's mine. With characteristic energy and thoroughness Switzer had studied the proposition from every point of view, and the results of his study he had set down in a document which Mr. Gwynne laid before his wife and children for consideration. It appeared that the mine itself had been investigated by expert friends of Switzer's from the Lethbridge and Crows' Nest mines. The reports of these experts were favourable to a degree unusual with practical mining men, both as to the quality and quantity of coal and as to the cost of operation. The quality was assured by the fact that the ranchers in the neighbourhood for years had been using the coal in their own homes. In addition to this Switzer had secured a report from the Canadian Pacific Railway engineers showing that the coal possessed high steaming qualities. And as to quantity, the seam could be measured where the creek cut through, showing enough coal in sight to promise a sufficient supply to warrant operation for years to come. In brief, the report submitted by the young German was that there was every ground for believing that a paying mine, possibly a great mine, could be developed from the

Ralph Connor

property on Mr. Gwynne's land. In regard to the market, there was of course no doubt. Every ton of coal produced could be sold at the mine mouth without difficulty. There remained only the question of finance to face. This also Switzer had considered, and the result of his consideration was before them in a detailed scheme. By this scheme a local company was to be organised with a capitalisation of $500,000, which would be sufficient to begin with. Of this amount $200,000 should be assigned to the treasury, the remaining $300,000 disposed of as follows: to Mr. Gwynne, as owner of the mine, should be allotted $151,000 stock, thus giving him control; the remaining $149,000 stock should be placed locally. The proposition contained an offer from Switzer to organise the company and to place the stock, in consideration for which service he asked a block of stock such as the directors should agree upon, and further that he should be secretary of the company for a term of five years at a salary of $2,000 per annum, which should be a first charge upon the returns from the mine.

"Ernest insists on being secretary?" said Nora.

"Yes, naturally. His interests are all here. He insists also that I be president."

"And why, Dad?" enquired Nora.

"Well," said Mr. Gwynne, with a slight laugh, "he frankly says he would like to be associated with me in this business. Of course, he said some nice things about me which I need not repeat."

"Oh pshaw!" exclaimed Nora, patting him on the shoulder, "I thought you were a lot smarter man than that. Can't you see why he wants to be associated with you? Surely you don't need me to tell you."

"Nora dear, hush," said her mother.

With an imploring look at her sister, Kathleen left the room.

"Indeed, Mother, I think it is no time to hush. I will tell you, Dad, why he wants to be associated with you in this coal mine business. Ernest Switzer wants our Kathleen. Mother knows it. We all know it."

Her father gazed at her in astonishment.

"Surely this is quite unwarranted, Nora," he said. "I cannot allow a matter of this kind to be dragged into a matter of business."

"How would it do to take a few days to turn it over in our minds?" said his wife. "We must not forget, dear," she continued, a note of grave anxiety in her voice, "that if we accept this proposition it will mean a complete change in our family life."

"Family life, Mother," said Mr. Gwynne with some impatience. "You don't mean—"

"I mean, my dear," replied the mother, "that we shall no longer be ranchers, but shall become coal miners. Let us think it over and perhaps you might consult with some of our neighbours, say with Mr. Waring-Gaunt."

"Surely, surely," replied her husband. "Your advice is wise, as always. I shall just step over to Mr. Waring-Gaunt's immediately."

After Mr. Gwynne's departure, the others sat silent for some moments, their minds occupied with the question raised so abruptly by Nora.

"You may as well face it, Mother," said the girl. "Indeed, you must face it, and right now. If this Company goes on with Ernest as secretary, it means that he will necessarily be thrown into closer relationship with our family. This will help his business with Kathleen. This is what he means. Do you wish to help it on?"

The mother sat silent, her face showing deep distress. "Nora dear," at length she said, "this matter is really not in our hands. Surely you can see that. I can't discuss it with you." And so saying she left the room.

"Now, Nora," said Larry severely, "you are not to worry Mother. And besides you can't play Providence in this way. You must confess that you have a dreadful habit of trying to run things. I believe you would have a go at running the universe."

"Run things?" cried Nora. "Why not? There is altogether too much of letting things slide in this family. It is all very well to trust to Providence. Providence made the trees grow in the woods, but this house never would have been here if Mr. Sleighter had not got on to the job. Now I am going to ask you a straight question. Do you want Ernest Switzer to have Kathleen?"

"Well, he's a decent sort and a clever fellow," began Larry.

"Now, Larry, you may as well cut that 'decent sort,' 'clever fellow' stuff right out. I want to know your mind. Would you like to see Ernest Switzer have Kathleen, or not?"

"Would you?" retorted her brother.

"No. I would not," emphatically said Nora.

"Why not?"

"To tell the truth, ever since that concert night I feel I can't trust him. He is different from us. He is no real Canadian. He is a German."

"Well, Nora, you amaze me," said Larry. "What supreme nonsense you are talking! You have got that stuff of Romayne's into your mind. The war bug has bitten you too. For Heaven's sake be reasonable. If you object to Ernest because of his race, I am ashamed of you and have no sympathy with you."

"Not because of his race," said Nora, "though, Larry, let me tell you he hates Britain. I was close to him that night, and hate looked out of his eyes. But let that pass. I have seen Ernest with 'his women' as he calls them, and, Larry, I can't bear to think of our Kathleen being treated as he treats his mother and sister."

"Now, Nora, let us be reasonable. Let us look at this fairly," began Larry.

"Oh, Larry! stop or I shall be biting the furniture next. When you assume that judicial air of yours I want to swear. Answer me. Do you want him to marry Kathleen? Yes or no."

"Well, as I was about to say—"

"Larry, will you answer yes or no?"

"Well, no, then," said Larry.

"Thank God!" cried Nora, rushing at him and shaking him vigorously. "You wretch! Why did you keep me in suspense? How I wish that English stick would get a move on!"

"English stick? Whom do you mean?"

"You're as stupid as the rest, Larry. Whom should I mean? Jack Romayne, of course. There's a man for you. I just wish he'd waggle his finger at me! But he won't do things. He just 'glowers' at her, as old McTavish would say, with those deep eyes of his, and sets his jaw like a wolf trap, and waits. Oh, men are so stupid with women!"

"Indeed?" said Larry. "And how exactly?"

"Why doesn't he just make her love him, master her, swing her off her feet?" said Nora.

"Like Switzer, eh? The cave man idea?"

"No, no. Surely you see the difference?"

"Pity my ignorance and elucidate the mystery."

"Mystery? Nonsense. It is quite simple. It is a mere matter of emphasis."

"Oh, I see," said Larry, "or at least I don't see. But credit me with the earnest and humble desire to understand."

"Well," said his sister, "the one—"

"Which one?"

"Switzer. He is mad to possess her for his very own. He would carry her off against her will. He'd bully her to death."

"Ah, you would like that?"

"Not I. Let him try it on. The other, Romayne, is mad to have her too. He would give her his very soul. But he sticks there waiting till she comes and flings herself into his arms."

"You prefer that, eh?"

"Oh, that makes me tired!" said Nora in a tone of disgust.

"Well, I give it up," said Larry hopelessly. "What do you want?"

"I want both. My man must want me more than he wants Heaven itself, and he must give me all he has but honour. Such a man would be my slave! And such a man—oh, I'd just love to be bullied by him."

For some moments Larry stood looking into the glowing black eyes, then said quietly, "May God send you such a man, little sister, or none at all."

In a few weeks the Alberta Coal Mining and Development Company was an established fact. Mr. Waring-Gaunt approved of it and showed his confidence in the scheme by offering to take a large block of stock and persuade his friends to invest as well. He also agreed that it was important to the success of the scheme both that Mr. Gwynne should be the president of the company and that young Switzer should be its secretary. Mr. Gwynne's earnest request that he should become the treasurer of the company Mr. Waring-Gaunt felt constrained in the meantime to decline. He already had too many irons in the fire. But he was willing to become a director and to aid the scheme in any way possible. Before the end of the month such was the energy displayed by the new secretary of the company in the disposing of the stock it was announced that only a small block of about $25,000 remained unsold. A part of this Mr. Waring-Gaunt urged his brother-in-law to secure.

"Got twenty thousand myself, you know—looks to me like a sound proposition—think you ought to go in—what do you say, eh, what?"

"Very well; get ten or fifteen thousand for me," said his brother-in-law.

Within two days Mr. Waring-Gaunt found that the stock had all been disposed of. "Energetic chap, that young Switzer,—got all the stock placed—none left, so he told me."

"Did you tell him the stock was for me?" enquired Romayne.

"Of course, why not?"

"Probably that accounts for it. He would not be especially anxious to have me in."

"What do you say? Nothing in that, I fancy. But I must see about that, what?"

"Oh, let it go," said Romayne.

"Gwynne was after me again to take the treasurership," said Waring-Gaunt, "but I am busy with so many things—treasurership very hampering—demands close attention—that sort of thing, eh, what?"

"Personally I wish you would take it," said Romayne. "You would be able to protect your own money and the investments of your friends. Besides, I understand the manager is to be a German, which, with a German secretary, is too much German for my idea."

"Oh, you don't like Switzer, eh? Natural, I suppose. Don't like him myself; bounder sort of chap—but avoid prejudice, my boy, eh, what? German—that sort of thing —don't do in this country, eh? English, Scotch, Irish, French, Galician, Swede, German—all sound Canadians —melting pot idea, eh, what?"

"I am getting that idea, too," said his brother-in-law. "Sybil has been rubbing it into me. I believe it is right enough. But apart altogether from that, frankly I do not like that chap; I don't trust him. I fancy I know a gentleman when I see him."

"All right, all right, my boy, gentleman idea quite right too—but new country, new standards—'Old Family' idea played out, don't you know. Burke's Peerage not known here—every mug on its own bottom—rather touchy Canadians are about that sort of thing—democracy stuff and all that you know. Not too bad either, eh, what? for a chap who has got the stuff in him—architect of his fortune—founder of his own family and that sort of thing, don't you know. Not too bad, eh, what?"

"I quite agree," cried Jack, "at least with most of it. But all the same I hope you will take the treasurership. Not only will you protect your own and your friends' investments, but you will protect the interests of the Gwynnes. The father apparently is no business man, the son is to be away; anything might happen. I would hate to see them lose out. You understand?"

His brother-in-law turned his eyes upon him, gazed at him steadily for a few moments, then taking his hand, shook it warmly, exclaiming, "Perfectly, old chap, per-fectly—good sort, Gwynne—good family. Girl of the finest—hope you put it off, old boy. Madame has put me on, you know, eh, what? Jolly good thing."

"Now what the deuce do you mean?" said Romayne angrily.

"All right—don't wish to intrude, don't you know. Fine girl though—quite the finest thing I've seen—could go anywhere."

His brother-in-law's face flushed fiery red. "Now look here, Tom," he said angrily, "don't be an ass. Of course I know what you mean but as the boys say here, 'Nothing doing!'"

"What? You mean it? Nothing doing? A fine girl like that—sweet girl—good clean stock—wonderful mother—would make a wife any man would be proud of—the real thing, you know, the real thing—I have known her these eight years—watched her grow up—rare courage—pure soul. Nothing doing? My God, man, have you eyes?" It was not often that Tom Waring-Gaunt allowed himself the luxury of passion, but this seemed to him to be an occasion in which he might indulge himself. Romayne stood listening to him with his face turned away, looking out of the window. "Don't you hear me, Jack?" said Waring-Gaunt. "Do you mean there's nothing in it, or have you burned out your heart with those fool women of London and Paris?"

Swiftly his brother-in-law turned to him. "No, Tom, but I almost wish to God I had. No, I won't say that; rather do I thank God that I know now what it is to love a woman. I am not going to lie to you any longer, old chap. To love a sweet, pure woman, sweet and pure as the flowers out there, to love her with every bit of my heart, with every fibre of my soul, that is the finest thing that can come to a man. I have treated women lightly in my time, Tom. I have made them love me, taken what they have had to give, and left them without a thought. But if any of them have suffered through me, and if they could know what I am getting now, they would pity me and say I had got enough to pay me out. To think that I should ever hear myself saying that to another man, I who have made love to women and laughed at them and laughed at the poor weak devils who fell in love with women. Do you get me? I am telling you this and yet I feel no shame, no humiliation! Humiliation, great heaven! I am proud to say that I love this girl. From the minute I saw her up there in the woods I have loved her. I have cursed myself for loving her. I have called myself fool, idiot, but I cannot help it. I love her. It is hell to me or heaven, which you like. It's both." He was actually trembling, his voice hoarse and shaking.

Amazement, then pity, finally delight, succeeded each other in rapid succession across the face of his brother-in-law as he listened. "My dear chap, my dear chap," he said when Romayne had finished. "Awfully glad, you know—delighted. But why the howl? The girl is there—go in and get her, by Jove. Why not, eh, what?"

"It's no use, I tell you," said Romayne. "That damned German has got her. I have seen them together too often. I have seen in her eyes the look that women get when they are ready to give themselves body and soul to a man. She loves that man. She loves him, I tell you. She has known him for years. I have come too late to have a chance. Too late, my God, too late!" He pulled himself up with an effort, then with a laugh said, "Do you recognise me, Tom? I confess I do not recognise myself. Well, that's out. Let it go. That's the last you will get from me. But, Tom, this is more than I can stand. I must quit this country, and I want you to make it easy for me to go. We'll get up some yarn for Sibyl. You'll help me out, old man? God knows I need help in this."

"Rot, beastly rot. Give her up to that German heel-clicking bounder—rather not. Buck up, old man—give the girl a chance anyway—play the game out, eh, what? Oh, by the way, I have made up my mind to take that treasurership—beastly nuisance, eh? Goin'? Where?"

"Off with the dogs for a run somewhere."

"No, take the car—too beastly hot for riding, don't you know. Take my car. Or, I say, let's go up to the mine. Must get to know more about the beastly old thing, eh, what? We'll take the guns and Sweeper—we'll be sure to see some birds and get the evening shoot coming back. But, last word, my boy, give the girl a chance to say no. Think of it, a German, good Lord! You go and get the car ready. We'll get Sybil to drive while we shoot."

Tom Waring-Gaunt found his great, warm, simple heart overflowing with delight at the tremendous news that had come to him. It was more than his nature could bear that he should keep this from his wife. He found her immersed in her domestic duties and adamant against his persuasion to drive them to the mine.

"A shoot," she cried, "I'd love to. But, Tom, you forget I am a rancher's wife, and you know, or at least you don't know, what that means. Run along and play with Jack. Some one must work. No, don't tempt me. I have my programme all laid out. I especially prayed this morning for grace to resist the lure of the outside this day. 'Get thee behind me—' What? I am listening, but I shouldn't be. What do you say? Tom, it cannot be!" She sat down weakly in a convenient chair and listened to her husband while he retailed her brother's great secret.

"And so, my dear, we are going to begin a big campaign —begin to-day—take the girls off with us for a shoot— what do you say, eh?"

"Why, certainly, Tom. Give me half an hour to get Martha fairly on the rails, and I am with you. We'll take those dear girls along. Oh, it is perfectly splendid. Now let me go; that will do, you foolish boy. Oh, yes, how lovely. Trust me to back you up. What? Don't spoil things. Well, I like that. Didn't I land you? That was 'some job,' as dear Nora would say. You listen to me, Tom. You had better keep in the background. Finesse is not your forte. Better leave these things to me. Hurry up now. Oh, I am so excited."

Few women can resist an appeal for help from a husband. The acknowledgment of the need of help on the part of the dominating partner is in itself the most subtle flattery and almost always irresistible. No woman can resist the opportunity to join in that most fascinating of all sport— man-hunting. And when the man runs clear into the open wildly seeking not escape from but an opening into the net, this only adds a hazard and a consequent zest to the sport. Her husband's disclosures had aroused in Sybil Waring-Gaunt not so much her sporting instincts, the affair went deeper far than that with her. Beyond anything else in life she desired at that time to bring together the two beings whom, next to her husband, she loved best in the world. From the day that her brother had arrived in the country she had desired this, and more or less aggressively had tried to assist Providence in the ordering of events. But in Kathleen, with all her affection and all her sweet simplicity, there was a certain shy reserve that prevented confidences in the matter of her heart affairs.

"How far has the German got with her? That is what I would like to know," said Mrs. Waring-Gaunt to herself as she hastily prepared for the motor ride. "There's no doubt about him. Every one can see how he stands, and he has such a masterful way with him that it makes one think that everything is settled. If it is there is no chance for Jack, for she is not the changing kind." Meantime she would hope for the best and play the game as best she could.

"Would you mind running into the Gwynnes' as we pass, Tom?" said his wife as they settled themselves in the car. "I have a message for Nora."

"Righto!" said her husband, throwing his wife a look which she refused utterly to notice. "But remember you must not be long. We cannot lose the evening shoot, eh, what?"

"Oh, just a moment will do," said his wife.

At the door Nora greeted them. "Oh, you lucky people— guns and a dog, and a day like this," she cried.

"Come along—lots of room—take my gun," said Mr. Waring-Gaunt.

"Don't tempt me, or I shall come."

"Tell us what is your weakness, Miss Nora," said Jack. "How can we get you to come?"

"My weakness?" cried the girl eagerly, "you all are, and especially your dear Sweeper dog there." She put her arms around the neck of the beautiful setter, who was frantically struggling to get out to her.

"Sweeper, lucky dog, eh, Jack, what?" said Mr. Waring-Gaunt, with a warm smile of admiration at the wholesome, sun-browned face. "Come along, Miss Nora—back in a short time, eh, what?"

"Short time?" said Nora. "Not if I go. Not till we can't see the birds."

"Can't you come, Nora?" said Mrs. Waring-Gaunt, "I want to talk to you, and we'll drive to-day and let the men shoot. Where is Kathleen? Is she busy?"

"Busy? We are all positively overwhelmed with work. But, oh, do go away, or I shall certainly run from it all."

"I am going in to get your mother to send you both out. Have you had a gun this fall? I don't believe you have," said Mrs. Waring-Gaunt.

"Not once. Yes, once. I had a chance at a hawk that was paying too much attention to our chickens. No, don't go in, Mrs. Waring-Gaunt, I beg of you. Well, go, then; I have fallen shamelessly. If you can get Kathleen, I am on too."

In a few moments Mrs. Waring-Gaunt returned with Kathleen and her mother. "Your mother says, Nora, that she does not need you a bit, and she insists on your coming, both of you. So be quick."

"Oh, Mother," cried the girl in great excitement. "You cannot possibly get along without us. There's the tea for all those men."

"Nonsense, Nora, run along. I can do quite well without you. Larry is coming in early and he will help. Run along, both of you."

"But there isn't room for us all," said Kathleen.

"Room? Heaps," said Mr. Waring-Gaunt. "Climb in here beside me, Miss Nora."

"Oh, it will be great," said Nora. "Can you really get along, Mother?"

"Nonsense," said the mother. "You think far too much of yourself. Get your hat."

"Hat; who wants a hat?" cried the girl, getting in beside Mr. Waring-Gaunt. "Oh, this is more than I had ever dreamed, and I feel so wicked!"

"All the better, eh, what?"

"Here, Kathleen," said Mrs. Waring-Gaunt, "here between us."

"I am so afraid I shall crowd you," said the girl, her face showing a slight flush.

"Not a bit, my dear; the seat is quite roomy. There, are you comfortable? All right, Tom. Good-bye, Mrs. Gwynne. So good of you to let the girls come."

In high spirits they set off, waving their farewell to the mother who stood watching till they had swung out of the lane and on to the main trail.

CHAPTER XIII

A DAY IN SEPTEMBER

A September day in Alberta. There is no other day to be compared to it in any other month or in any other land. Other lands have their September days, and Alberta has days in other months, but the combination of September day in Alberta is sui generis. The foothill country with plain, and hill, and valley, and mighty mountain, laced with stream, and river, and lake; the over-arching sheet of blue with cloud shapes wandering and wistful, the kindly sun pouring its genial sheen of yellow and gold over the face of the earth below, purple in the mountains and gold and pearly grey, and all swimming in air blown through the mountain gorges and over forests of pine, tingling with ozone and reaching the heart and going to the head like new wine—these things go with a September day in Alberta.

And like new wine the air seemed to Jack Romayne as the Packard like a swallow skimmed along the undulating prairie trail, smooth, resilient, of all the roads in the world for motor cars the best. For that day at least and in that motor car life seemed good to Jack Romayne. Not many such days would be his, and he meant to take all it gave regardless of cost. His sister's proposal to call at the Gwynnes' house he would have rejected could he have found a reasonable excuse. The invitation to the Gwynne girls to accompany them on their shoot he resented also, and still more deeply he resented the arrangement of the party that set Kathleen next to him, a close fit in the back seat of the car. But at the first feeling of her warm soft body wedged closely against him, all emotions fled except one of pulsating joy. And this, with the air rushing at them from the western mountains, wrought in him the reckless resolve to take what the gods offered no matter what might follow. As he listened to the chatter about him he yielded to the intoxication of his love for this fair slim girl pressing soft against his arm and shoulder. He allowed his fancy to play with surmises as to what would happen should he turn to her and say, "Dear girl, do you know how fair you are, how entrancingly lovely? Do you know I am madly in love with you, and that I can hardly refrain from putting this arm, against which you so quietly lean your warm soft body, about you?" He looked boldly at the red curves of her lips and allowed himself to riot in the imagination of how deliciously they would yield to his pressed against them. "My God!" he cried aloud, "to think of it."

The two ladies turned their astonished eyes upon him. "What is it, Jack? Wait, Tom. Have you lost something?"

"Yes, that is, I never had it. No, go on, Tom, it cannot be helped now. Go on, please do. What a day it is!" he continued. "'What a time we are having,' as Miss Nora would say."

"Yes, what a time!" exclaimed Nora, turning her face toward them. "Mrs. Waring-Gaunt, I think I must tell you that your husband is making love to me so that I am quite losing my head."

"Poor things," said Mrs. Waring-Gaunt. "How could

either of you help it?"

"Why is it that all the nice men are married?" inquired Nora.

"I beg your pardon, Miss Nora," said Jack in a pained voice.

"I mean—why—I'm afraid I can't fix that up, can I?" she said, appealing to Mrs. Waring-Gaunt.

"Certainly you can. What you really mean is, why do all married men become so nice?" said Mrs. Waring-Gaunt.

"Oh, thank you, the answer is so obvious. Do you know, I feel wild to-day."

"And so do I," replied Kathleen, suddenly waking to life. "It is the wonderful air, or the motor, perhaps."

"Me, too," exclaimed Jack Romayne, looking straight at her, "only with me it is not the air, nor the motor."

"What then!" said Kathleen with a swift, shy look at him.

"'The heart knoweth its own bitterness and a stranger intermeddleth not with its joy.'"

"That's the Bible, I know," said Kathleen, "and it really means 'mind your own business.'"

"No, no, not that exactly," protested Jack, "rather that there are things in the heart too deep if not for tears most certainly for words. You can guess what I mean, Miss Kathleen," said Jack, trying to get her eyes.

"Oh, yes," said the girl, "there are things that we cannot

trust to words, no, not for all the world."

"I know what you are thinking of," replied Jack. "Let me guess."

"No, no, you must not, indeed," she replied quickly. "Look, isn't that the mine? What a crowd of people! Do look."

Out in the valley before them they could see a procession of teams and men weaving rhythmic figures about what was discovered to be upon a nearer view a roadway which was being constructed to cross a little coolee so as to give access to the black hole on the hillside beyond which was the coal mine. In the noise and bustle of the work the motor came to a stop unobserved behind a long wooden structure which Nora diagnosed as the "grub shack."

"In your English speech, Mr. Romayne, the dining room of the camp. He is certainly a hustler," exclaimed Nora, gazing upon the scene before them.

"Who?" inquired Mrs. Waring-Gaunt.

"Ernest Switzer," said Nora, unable to keep the grudge out of her voice. "It is only a week since I was up here and during that time he has actually made this village, the streets, the sidewalks—and if that is not actually a system of water pipes."

"Some hustler, as you say, Miss Nora, eh, what?" said Tom.

"Wonderful," replied Nora; "he is wonderful."

Jack glanced at the girl beside him. It seemed to him that it needed no mind-reader to interpret the look of pride, yes and of love, in the wonderful blue-grey eyes. Sick as from a heavy blow he turned away from her; the flicker of hope that his brother-in-law's words had kindled in his heart died out and left him cold. He was too late; why try to deceive himself any longer? The only thing to do was to pull out and leave this place where every day brought him intolerable pain. But today he would get all he could, to-day he would love her and win such poor scraps as he could from her eyes, her smiles, her words.

"Glorious view that," he said, touching her arm and sweeping his hand toward the mountains.

She started at his touch, a faint colour coming into her face. "How wonderful!" she breathed. "I love them. They bring me my best thoughts."

Before he could reply there came from behind the grub shack a torrent of abusive speech florid with profane language and other adornment and in a voice thick with rage.

"That's him," said Nora. "Some one is getting it." The satisfaction in her voice and look were in sharp contrast to the look of dismay and shame that covered the burning face of her sister. From English the voice passed into German, apparently no less vigorous or threatening. "That's better," said Nora with a wicked glance at Romayne. "You see he is talking to some one of his own people. They understand that. There are a lot of Germans from the Settlement, Freiberg, you know."

As she spoke Switzer emerged from behind the shack, driving before him a cringing creature evidently in abject terror of him. "Get back to your gang and carry out your orders, or you will get your time." He caught sight of the car and stopped abruptly, and, waving his hand imperiously to the workman, strode up to the party, followed by a mild-looking man in spectacles.

"Came to see how you are getting on, Switzer, eh, what?" said Tom.

"Getting on," he replied in a loud voice, raising his hat in salutation. "How can one get on with a lot of stupid fools who cannot carry out instructions and dare to substitute their own ideas for commands. They need discipline. If I had my way they would get it, too. But in this country there is no such thing as discipline." He made no attempt to apologise for his outrageous outburst, was probably conscious of no need of apology.

"This is your foreman, I think?" said Nora, who alone of the party seemed to be able to deal with the situation.

"Oh, yes, Mr. Steinberg," said Switzer, presenting the spectacled man.

"You are too busy to show us anything this afternoon?" said Nora sweetly.

"Yes, much too busy," said Switzer, gruffly. "I have no time for anything but work these days."

"You cannot come along for a little shoot?" she said, innocently. Nora was evidently enjoying herself.

"Shoot!" cried Switzer in a kind of contemptuous fury. "Shoot, with these dogs, these cattle, tramping around here when they need some one every minute to drive them. Shoot! No, no. I am not a gentleman of leisure."

The distress upon Kathleen's face was painfully apparent. Jack was in no hurry to bring relief. Like Nora he was enjoying himself as well. It was Tom who brought about the diversion.

"Well, we must go on, Switzer. Coming over to see you one of these days and go over the plant. Treasurer's got to know something about it, eh, what?"

Switzer started and looked at him in surprise. "Treasurer, who? Are you to be treasurer of the company? Who says so? Mr. Gwynne did not ask—did not tell me about it."

"Ah, sorry—premature announcement, eh?" said Tom. "Well, good-bye. All set."

The Packard gave forth sundry growls and snorts and glided away down the trail.

Nora was much excited. "What's this about the treasurership?" she demanded. "Are you really to be treasurer, Mr. Waring-Gaunt? I am awfully glad. You know this whole mine was getting terribly Switzery. Isn't he awful? He just terrifies me. I know he will undertake to run me one of these days."

"Then trouble, eh, what?" said Waring-Gaunt, pleasantly.

After a short run the motor pulled up at a wheat field in which the shocks were still standing and which lay contiguous to a poplar bluff.

"Good chicken country, eh?" said Tom, slipping out of the car quietly. "Nora, you come with me. Quiet now. Off to the left, eh, what? You handle Sweeper, Jack."

"I'll drive the car," said Mrs. Waring-Gaunt. "Go on with Jack, Kathleen."

Ralph Connor

"Come on, Miss Kathleen, you take the gun, and I'll look after the dog. Let me have the whistle, Tom."

They had not gone ten yards from the car when the setter stood rigid on point. "Steady, old boy," said Jack. "Move up quickly, Miss Kathleen. Is your gun ready? Sure it's off safe?"

"All right," said the girl, walking steadily on the dog.

Bang! Bang! went Nora's gun. Two birds soared safely aloft. Bang! Bang! went Kathleen's gun. "Double, by jove! Steady, Sweeper!" Again the dog stood on point. Swiftly Jack loaded the gun. "Here you are, Miss Kathleen. You will get another," he said. "There are more here." As he spoke a bird flew up at his right. Bang! went Kathleen's gun. "Another, good work." Bang! went Nora's gun to the left. "Look out, here he comes," cried Jack, as Nora's bird came careening across their front. It was a long shot. Once more Kathleen fired. The bird tumbled in the air and fell with a thump right at their feet.

Sweeper, released from his point, went bounding joyfully over the stubble. Jack rushed up toward the girl, and taking her hand in both of his, shook it warmly. "Oh, splendid, partner, splendid, great shooting!"

"Oh, it was easy. Sweeper had them fast," said Kathleen. "And that last shot was just awfully good luck."

"Good luck! Good Lord! it was anything but luck. It was great shooting. Well, come along. Oh, we're going to have a glorious day, aren't we, partner?" And catching hold of her arm, he gave her a friendly little shake.

"Yes," she cried, responding frankly to his mood, "we will. Let's have a good day."

"Where did you learn to shoot?" inquired Jack.

"Nora and I have always carried guns in the season," replied Kathleen, "even when we were going to school. You see, Larry hates shooting. We loved it and at times were glad to get them—the birds, I mean. We did not do it just for sport."

"Can your sister shoot as well as you?"

"Hardly, I think. She pulls too quickly, you see, but when she steadies down she will shoot better than I."

"You are a wonder," said Jack enthusiastically.

"Oh, not a wonder," said the girl.

"Wait till I get the birds back to the car," he cried.

"He-l-l-o," cried his sister as he came running. "What, four of them?"

"Four," he answered. "By jove, she's a wonder, isn't she. She really bowls me over."

"Nonsense," said his sister in a low voice. "She's just a fine girl with a steady hand and a quick eye, and," she added as Jack turned away from her, "a true heart."

"A true heart," Jack muttered to himself, "and given to that confounded bully of a German. If it had been any other man—but we have got one day at least." Resolutely he brushed away the thoughts that maddened him as he ran to Kathleen's side. Meantime, Tom and Nora had gone circling around toward the left with Sweeper ranging widely before them.

"Let's beat round this bluff," suggested Kathleen. "They may not have left the trees yet."

Together they strolled away through the stubble, the girl moving with an easy grace that spoke of balanced physical strength, and with an eagerness that indicated the keen hunter's spirit. The bluff brought no result.

"That bluff promised chickens if ever a bluff did," said Kathleen in a disappointed voice. "We'll get them further down, and then again in the stubble."

"Cheer-o," cried Jack. "The day is fine and we are having a ripping time, at least I am."

"And I, too," cried the girl. "I love this, the open fields,—and the sport, too."

"And good company," said Jack boldly.

"Yes, good company, of course," she said with a quick, friendly glance. "And you ARE good company to-day."

"To-day?"

"Yes. Sometimes, you know, you are rather—I don't know what to say—but queer, as if you did not like—people, or were carrying some terrible secret," she added with a little laugh.

"Secret? I am, but not for long. I am going to tell you the secret. Do you want to hear it now?"

The note of desperation in his voice startled the girl. "Oh, no," she cried hurriedly. "Where have we got to? There are no birds in this open prairie here. We must get back to the stubble."

"You are not interested in my secret, then?" said Jack. "But I am going to tell you all the same, Kathleen."

"Oh, please don't," she replied in a distressed voice. "We are having such a splendid time, and besides we are after birds, aren't we? And there are the others," she added, pointing across the stubble field, "and Sweeper is on point again. Oh, let's run." She started forward quickly, her foot caught in a tangle of vetch vine and she pitched heavily forward. Jack sprang to catch her. A shot crashed at their ears. The girl lay prone.

"My God, Kathleen, are you hurt?" said Jack.

"No, no, not a bit, but awfully scared," she panted. Then she shrieked, "Oh, oh, oh, Jack, you are wounded, you are bleeding!"

He looked down at his hand. It was dripping blood. "Oh, oh," she moaned, covering her face with her hands. Then springing to her feet, she caught up his hand in hers.

"It is nothing at all," he said. "I feel nothing. Only a bit of skin. See," he cried, lifting his arm up. "There's nothing to it. No broken bones."

"Let me see, Jack—Mr. Romayne," she said with white lips.

"Say 'Jack,'" he begged.

"Let me take off your coat—Jack, then. I know a little about this. I have done something at it in Winnipeg."

Together they removed the coat. The shirt sleeve was hanging in a tangled, bloody mass from the arm.

Ralph Connor

"Awful!" groaned Kathleen. "Sit down."

"Oh, nonsense, it is not serious."

"Sit down, Jack, dear," she entreated, clasping her hands about his sound arm.

"Say it again," said Jack.

"Oh, Jack, won't you sit down, please?"

"Say it again," he commanded sternly.

"Oh, Jack, dear, please sit down," she cried in a pitiful voice.

He sat down, then lay back reclining on his arm. "Now your knife, Jack," she said, feeling hurriedly through his pockets.

"Here you are," he said, handing her the knife, biting his lips the while and fighting back a feeling of faintness.

Quickly slipping behind him, she whipped off her white petticoat and tore it into strips. Then cutting the bloody shirt sleeve, she laid bare the arm. The wound was superficial. The shot had torn a wide gash little deeper than the skin from wrist to shoulder, with here and there a bite into the flesh. Swiftly, deftly, with fingers that never fumbled, she bandaged the arm, putting in little pads where the blood seemed to be pumping freely.

"That's fine," said Jack. "You are a brick, Kathleen. I think—I will—just lie down—a bit. I feel—rather rotten." As he spoke he caught hold of her arm to steady himself. She caught him in her arms and eased him down upon the stubble. With eyes closed and a face that looked like death he lay quite still.

"Jack," she cried aloud in her terror. "Don't faint. You must not faint."

But white and ghastly he lay unconscious, the blood still welling right through the bandages on his wounded arm. She knew that in some way she must stop the bleeding. Swiftly she undid the bandages and found a pumping artery in the forearm. "What is it that they do?" she said to herself. Then she remembered. Making a tourniquet, she applied it to the upper arm. Then rolling up a bloody bandage into a pad, she laid it upon the pumping artery and bound it firmly down into place. Then flexing the forearm hard upon it, she bandaged all securely again. Still the wounded man lay unconscious. The girl was terrified. She placed her hand over his heart. It was beating but very faintly. In the agony and terror of the moment as in a flash of light her heart stood suddenly wide open to her, and the thing that for the past months had lain hidden within her deeper than her consciousness, a secret joy and pain, leaped strong and full into the open, and she knew that this man who lay bleeding and ghastly before her was dearer to her than her own life. The sudden rush of this consciousness sweeping like a flood over her soul broke down and carried away the barrier of her maidenly reserve. Leaning over him in a passion of self-abandonment, she breathed, "Oh, Jack, dear, dear Jack." As he lay there white and still, into her love there came a maternal tender yearning of pity. She lifted his head in her arm, and murmured brokenly, "Oh, my love, my dear love." She kissed him on his white lips.

At the touch of her lips Jack opened his eyes, gazed at her for a moment, then with dawning recognition, he said with a faint smile, "Do—it—again."

"Oh, you heard," she cried, the red blood flooding face and neck, "but I don't care, only don't go off again. You will not, Jack, you must not."

"No—I won't," he said. "It's rotten—of me—to act—like this and—scare you—to death. Give me—a little—time. I will be—all right."

"If they would only come! If I could only do something!"

"You're all right—Kathleen. Just be—patient with me—a bit. I am feeling—better every minute."

For a few moments he lay quiet. Then with a little smile he looked up at her again and said, "I would go off again just to hear you say those words once more."

"Oh, please don't," she entreated, hiding her face.

"Forgive me, Kathleen, I am a beast. Forget it. I am feeling all right. I believe I could sit up."

"No, no, no," she cried. "Lie a little longer."

She laid his head down, ran a hundred yards to the wheat field, returning with two sheeves, and made a support for his head and shoulders. "That is better," she said.

"Good work," he said. "Now I am going to be fit for anything in a few moments. But," he added, "you look rather badly, as if you might faint yourself."

"I? What difference does it make how I look? I am quite right. If they would only come! I know what I will do," she cried. "Where are your cartridges?" She loaded the gun and fired in quick succession half a dozen shots. "I think I see them," she exclaimed, "but I am not sure that they heard me." Again she fired several shots.

"Don't worry about it," said Jack, into whose face the colour was beginning to come back. "They are sure to look us up. Just sit down, won't you please, beside me here? There, that's good," he continued, taking her hand. "Kathleen," he cried, "I think you know my secret."

"Oh, no, no, please don't," she implored, withdrawing her hand and hiding her face from him. "Please don't be hard on me. I really do not know what I am doing and I am feeling dreadfully."

"You have reason to feel so, Kathleen. You have been splendidly brave, and I give you my word I am not going to worry you."

"Oh, thank you; you are so good, and I love you for it," she cried in a passion of gratitude. "You understand, don't you?"

"I think I do," he said. "By the way, do you know I think I could smoke."

"Oh, splendid!" she cried, and, springing up, she searched through his coat pockets, found pipe, pouch, matches, and soon he had his pipe going. "There, that looks more like living," said Kathleen, laughing somewhat hysterically. "Oh, you did frighten me!" Again the red flush came into her face and she turned away from him.

"There they are coming. Sure enough, they are coming," she cried with a sob in her voice.

"Steady, Kathleen," said Jack quietly. "You won't blow up now, will you? You have been so splendid! Can you hold on?"

She drew a deep breath, stood for a minute or two in perfect silence, and then she said, "I can and I will. I am quite right now."

Of course they exclaimed and stared and even wept a bit—at least the ladies did—but Jack's pipe helped out amazingly, and, indeed, he had recovered sufficient strength to walk unhelped to the car. And while Tom sent the Packard humming along the smooth, resilient road he kept up with Nora and his sister a rapid fire of breezy conversation till they reached their own door. It was half an hour before Tom could bring the doctor, during which time they discussed the accident in all its bearings and from every point of view.

"I am glad it was not I who was with you," declared Nora. "I cannot stand blood, and I certainly should have fainted, and what would you have done then?"

"Not you," declared Jack. "That sort of thing does not go with your stock. God knows what would have happened to me if I had had a silly fool with me, for the blood was pumping out all over me. But, thank God, I had a woman with a brave heart and clever hands."

When the doctor came, Mrs. Waring-Gaunt went in to assist him, but when the ghastly bloody spectacle lay bare to her eyes she found herself grow weak and hurried to the kitchen where the others were.

"Oh, I am so silly," she said, "but I am afraid I cannot stand the sight of it."

Kathleen sprang at once to her feet. "Is there no one there?" she demanded with a touch of impatience in her voice, and passed quickly into the room, where she stayed while the doctor snipped off the frayed patches of skin and flesh and tied up the broken arteries, giving aid with quick fingers and steady hands till all was over.

"You have done this sort of thing before, Miss Gwynne?" said the doctor.

"No, never," she replied.

"Well, you certainly are a brick," he said, turning admiring eyes upon her. He was a young man and unmarried. "But this is a little too much for you." From a decanter which stood on a side table he poured out a little spirits. "Drink this," he said.

"No, thank you, Doctor, I am quite right," said Kathleen, quietly picking up the bloody debris and dropping them into a basin which she carried into the other room. "He is all right now," she said to Mrs. Waring-Gaunt, who took the basin from her, exclaiming,

"My poor dear, you are awfully white. I am ashamed of myself. Now you must lie down at once."

"No, please, I shall go home, I think. Where is Nora?"

"Nora has gone home. You won't lie down a little? Then Tom shall take you in the car. You are perfectly splendid. I did not think you had it in you."

"Oh, don't, don't," cried the girl, a quick rush of tears coming to her eyes. "I must go, I must go. Oh, I feel terrible. I don't know what I have done. Let me go home." She almost pushed Mrs. Waring-Gaunt from her and went out of the house and found Tom standing by the car smoking.

"Take her home, Tom," said his wife. "She needs rest."

"Come along, Kathleen; rest—well, rather. Get in beside me here. Feel rather rotten, eh, what? Fine bit of work, good soldier—no, don't talk—monologue indicated." And monologue it was till he delivered her, pale, weary and spent, to her mother.

CHAPTER XIV

AN EXTRAORDINARY NURSE

"A letter for you, Nora," said Larry, coming just in from the post office.

"From Jane!" cried Nora, tearing open the letter. "Oh, glory," she continued. "They are coming. Let's see, written on the ninth, leaving to-morrow and arrive at Melville Station on the twelfth. Why, that's tomorrow."

"Who, Nora?" said Larry. "Jane?"

"Yes, Jane and her father. She says, 'We mean to stay two or three days, if you can have us, on our way to Banff.'"

"Hurrah! Good old Jane! What train did you say?" cried Larry.

"Sixteen-forty-five to-morrow at Melville Station."

"'We'll have one trunk and two boxes, so you will need some sort of rig, I am afraid. I hope this will not be too much trouble.'"

"Isn't that just like Jane?" said Larry. "I bet you she gives the size of the trunk, doesn't she, Nora?"

Ralph Connor

"A steamer trunk and pretty heavy, she says."

"Same old girl. Does she give you the colour?" inquired Larry. "Like an old maid, she is."

"Nonsense," said Nora, closing up her letter. "Oh, it's splendid. Let's see, it is eight years since we saw her."

"Just about fifteen months since I saw her," said Larry.

"And about four months for me," said Kathleen.

"But eight years for me," cried Nora, "and she has never missed writing me every week, except once when she had the mumps, and she made her father write that week. Now we shall have to take our old democrat to meet her, the awful old thing," said Nora in a tone of disgust.

"Jane won't mind if it is a hayrack," said Larry.

"No, but her father. He's such a swell. I hate meeting him with that old bone cart. But we can't help it. Oh, I am just nutty over her coming. I wonder what she's like?"

"Why, she's the same old Jane," said Larry. "That's one immense satisfaction about her. She is always the same, no matter when, how or where you meet her. There's never a change in Jane."

"I wonder if she has improved—got any prettier, I mean."

"Prettier! What the deuce are you talking about?" said Larry indignantly. "Prettier! Like a girl that is! You never think of looks when you see Jane. All you see is just Jane and her big blue eyes and her smile. Prettier! Who wants her prettier?"

"Oh, all right, Larry. Don't fuss. She IS plain-looking, you know. But she is such a good sort. I must tell Mrs. Waring-Gaunt."

"Do," said Larry, "and be sure to ask her for her car."

Nora made a face at him, but ran to the 'phone and in an ecstatic jumble of words conveyed the tremendous news to the lady at the other end of the wire and to all the ears that might be open along the party line.

"Is that Mrs. Waring-Gaunt?—it's Nora speaking. I have the most glorious news for you. Jane is coming!—You don't know Jane? My friend, you know, in Winnipeg. You must have often heard me speak of her.—What?—Brown. —No, Brown, B-r-o-w-n. And she's coming to-morrow.— No, her father is with her.—Yes, Dr. Brown of Winnipeg. —Oh, yes. Isn't it splendid?—Three days only, far too short. And we meet her to-morrow.—I beg your pardon? —Sixteen-forty-five, she says, and she is always right. Oh, a change in the time table is there?—Yes, I will hold on.—Sixteen-forty-five, I might have known.—What do you say?—Oh, could you? Oh, dear Mrs. Waring-Gaunt, how perfectly splendid of you! But are you sure you can? —Oh, you are just lovely.—Yes, she has one trunk, but that can come in the democrat. Oh, that is perfectly lovely! Thank you so much. Good-bye.—What? Yes, oh, yes, certainly I must go.—Will there be room for him? I am sure he will love to go. That will make five, you know, and they have two bags. Oh, lovely; you are awfully good.—We shall need to start about fifteen o'clock. Good-bye. Oh, how is Mr. Romayne?—Oh, I am so sorry, it is too bad. But, Mrs. Waring-Gaunt, you know Dr. Brown is a splendid doctor, the best in Winnipeg, one of the best in Canada. He will tell you exactly what to do. —I beg your pardon?—Yes, she's here. Kathleen, you are wanted. Hurry up, don't keep her waiting. Oh, isn't she a dear?"

"What does she want of me?" said Kathleen, a flush coming to her cheek.

"Come and see," said Nora, covering the transmitter with her hand, "and don't keep her waiting. What is the matter with you?"

Reluctantly Kathleen placed the receiver to her ear. "Yes, Mrs. Waring-Gaunt, it is Kathleen speaking.—Yes, thank you, quite well.—Oh, I have been quite all right, a little shaken perhaps.—Yes, isn't it splendid? Nora is quite wild, you know. Jane is her dearest friend and she has not seen her since we were children, but they have kept up a most active correspondence. Of course, I saw a great deal of her last year. She is a splendid girl and they were so kind; their house was like a home to me. I am sure it is very kind of you to offer to meet them.—I beg your pardon?—Oh, I am so sorry to hear that. We thought he was doing so well. What brought that on?—Blood-poisoning!—Oh, Mrs. Waring-Gaunt, you don't say so? How terrible! Isn't it good that Dr. Brown is coming? He will know exactly what is wrong.—Oh, I am so sorry to hear that. Sleeplessness is so trying.—Yes—Yes—Oh, Mrs. Waring-Gaunt, I am afraid I couldn't do that." Kathleen's face had flushed bright crimson. "But I am sure Mother would be so glad to go, and she is a perfectly wonderful nurse. She knows just what to do.—Oh, I am afraid not. Wait, please, a moment."

"What does she want?" asked Nora.

Kathleen covered the transmitter with her hand. "She wants me to go and sit with Mr. Romayne while she drives you to the station. I cannot, I cannot do that. Where is Mother? Oh, Mother, I cannot go to Mrs. Waring-Gaunt's. I really cannot."

"What nonsense, Kathleen!" cried Nora impatiently. "Why can't you go, pray? Let me speak to her." She took the receiver from her sister's hand. "Yes, Mrs. Waring-Gaunt, it is Nora.—I beg your pardon?—Oh, yes, certainly, one of us will be glad to go.—No, no, certainly not. I would not have Mr. Waring-Gaunt leave his work for the world.—I know, I know, awfully slow for him. We had not heard of the change. It is too bad.—Yes, surely one of us will be glad to come. We will fix it up some way. Good-bye."

Nora hung up the receiver and turned fiercely upon her sister. "Now, what nonsense is this," she said, "and she being so nice about the car, and that poor man suffering there, and we never even heard that he was worse? He was doing so splendidly, getting about all right. Blood-poisoning is so awful. Why, you remember the Mills boy? He almost lost his arm."

"Oh, my dear Nora," said her mother. "There is no need of imagining such terrible things, but I am glad Dr. Brown is to be here. It is quite providential. I am sure he will put poor Mr. Romayne right. Kathleen, dear," continued the mother, turning to her elder daughter, "I think it would be very nice if you would run over to-morrow while Mrs. Waring-Gaunt drives to the station. I am sure it is very kind of her."

"I know it is, Mother dear," said Kathleen. "But don't you think you would be so much better?"

"Oh, rubbish!" cried Nora. "If it were not Jane that is coming, I would go myself; I would only be too glad to go. He is perfectly splendid, so patient, and so jolly too, and Kathleen, you ought to go."

"Nora, dear, we won't discuss it," said the mother in the tone that the family knew meant the end of all conversation. Kathleen hurried away from them and took refuge in her own room. Then shutting the door, she began pacing the floor, fighting once more the battle which during that last ten days she had often fought with herself and of which she was thoroughly weary. "Oh," she groaned, wringing her hands, "I cannot do it. I cannot look at him." She thought of that calm, impassive face which for the past three months this English gentleman had carried in all of his intercourse with her, and over against that reserve of his she contrasted her own passionate abandonment of herself in that dreadful moment of self-revelation. The contrast caused her to writhe in an agony of self-loathing. She knew little of men, but instinctively she felt that in his sight she had cheapened herself and never could she bear to look at him again. She tried to recall those glances of his and those broken, passionate words uttered during the moments of his physical suffering that seemed to mean something more than friendliness. Against these, however, was the constantly recurring picture of a calm cold face and of intercourse marked with cool indifference. "Oh, he cannot love me," she cried to herself. "I am sure he does not love me, and I just threw myself at him." In her march up and down the room she paused before her mirror and looked at the face that stared so wildly back at her. Her eyes rested on the red line of her mouth. "Oh," she groaned, rubbing vigorously those full red lips. "I just kissed him." She paused in the rubbing operation, gazed abstractedly into the glass; a tender glow drove the glare from her eyes, a delicious softness as from some inner well overflowed her countenance, the red blood surged up into her white face; she fled from her accusing mirror, buried her burning face in the pillow in an exultation of rapture.

She dared not put into words the thoughts that rioted in her heart. "But I loved it, I loved it; I am glad I did." Lying there, she strove to recall in shameless abandon the sensation of those ecstatic moments, whispering in passionate self-defiance, "I don't care what he thinks. I don't care if I was horrid. I am NOT sorry. Besides, he looked so dreadful." But she was too honest not to acknowledge to herself that not for pity's sake but for love's she had kissed him, and without even his invitation. Then once again she recalled the look in his eyes of surprise in the moment of his returning consciousness, and the little smile that played around his lips. Again wave upon wave of sickening self-loathing flooded from her soul every memory of the bliss of that supreme moment. Even now she could feel the bite of the cold, half humorous scorn in the eyes that had opened upon her as she withdrew her lips from his. On the back of this came another memory, sharp and stabbing, that this man was ill, perhaps terribly ill. "We are a little anxious about him," his sister had said, and she had mentioned the word "blood-poisoning." Of the full meaning of that dread word Kathleen had little knowledge, but it held for her a horror of something unspeakably dangerous. He had been restless, sleepless, suffering for the last two days and two nights. That very night and that very hour he was perhaps tossing in fever. An uncontrollable longing came over her to go to him. Perhaps she might give him a few hours' rest, might indeed help to give him the turn to health again. After all, what mattered her feelings. What difference if he should despise her, provided she brought him help in an hour of crisis. Physically weary with the long struggle through which she had been passing during the last ten days, sick at heart, and torn with anxiety for the man she loved, she threw herself upon her bed and abandoned herself to a storm of tears. Her mother came announcing tea, but this she declined, pleading headache and a desire to sleep. But no sooner had her mother withdrawn than she rose from her bed and with deliberate purpose sat herself down in front of her mirror again. She would have this out with herself now. "Well, you are a beauty, sure enough," she said, addressing her swollen and disfigured countenance. "Why can't you behave naturally? You are acting like a fool and you are not honest with yourself. Come now, tell the truth for a few minutes if you can. Do you want to go and see this man or not? Answer truly." "Well, I do then." The blue eyes looked back defiantly at her. "Why? to help him? for his sake? Come, the truth." "Yes, for his sake, at least partly." "And for your own sake, too? Come now, none of that. Never mind the blushing." "Yes, for my own sake, too." "Chiefly for your own sake?" "No, I do not think so. Chiefly I wish to help him." "Then why not go?" Ah, this is a poser. She looks herself fairly in the eye, distinctly puzzled. Why should she not simply go to him and help him through a bad hour? With searching, deliberate persistence she demanded an answer. She will have the truth out of herself. "Why not go to him if you so desire to help him?" "Because I am ashamed, because I have made myself cheap, and I cannot bear his eyes upon me. Because if I have made a mistake and he does not care for me—oh, then I never want to see him again, for he would pity me, and that I cannot bear." "What? Not even to bring him rest and relief from his pain? Not to help him in a critical hour? He has been asking for you, remember." Steadily they face each other, eye to eye, and all at once she is conscious that the struggle is over, and, looking at the face in the glass, she says, "Yes, I think I would be willing to do that for him, no matter how it would shame me." Another heart-searching pause, and the eyes answer her again, "I will go to-morrow." At once she reads a new peace in the face that gazes at her so weary and wan, and she knows that for the sake of the man she loves she is willing to endure even the shame of his pity. The battle was over and some sort of victory at least she had won.

An eager impatience possessed her to go to him at once. "I wish it were to-morrow now, this very minute."

She rose and looked out into the night. There was neither moon nor stars and a storm was brewing, but she knew she could find her way in the dark. Quietly and with a great peace in her heart she bathed her swollen face, changed her dress to one fresh from the ironing board— pale blue it was with a dainty vine running through it— threw a wrap about her and went out to her mother.

"I am going up to the Waring-Gaunts', Mother. They might need me," she said in a voice of such serene control that her mother only answered,

"Yes, dear, Larry will go with you. He will soon be in."

"There is no need, Mother, I am not afraid."

Her mother made no answer but came to her and with a display of tenderness unusual between them put her arms about her and kissed her. "Good-night, then, darling; I am sure you will do them good."

The night was gusty and black, but Kathleen had no fear. The road was known to her, and under the impulse of the purpose that possessed her she made nothing of the darkness nor of the approaching storm. She hurried down the lane toward the main trail, refusing to discuss with herself the possible consequence of what she was doing. Nor did she know just what situation she might find at the Waring-Gaunts'. They would doubtless be surprised to see her. They might not need her help at all. She might be going upon a fool's errand, but all these suppositions and forebodings she brushed aside. She was bent upon an errand of simple kindness and help. If she found she was not needed she could return home and no harm done.

Receiving no response to her knock, she went quietly into the living room. A lamp burned low upon the table. There was no one to be seen. Upstairs a child was wailing and the mother's voice could be heard soothing the little one to sleep. From a bedroom, of which the door stood open, a voice called. The girl's heart stood still. It was Jack's voice, and he was calling for his sister. She ran upstairs to the children's room.

"He is calling for you," she said to Mrs. Waring-Gaunt without preliminary greeting. "Let me take Doris."

But Doris set up a wail of such acute dismay that the distracted mother said, "Could you just step in and see what is wanted? Jack has been in bed for two days. We have been unable to get a nurse anywhere, and tonight both little girls are ill. I am so thankful you came over. Indeed, I was about to send for one of you. Just run down and see what Jack wants. I hope you don't mind. I shall be down presently when Doris goes to sleep."

"I am not going to sleep, Mamma," answered Doris emphatically. "I am going to keep awake, for if I go to sleep I know you will go away."

"All right, darling, Mother is going to stay with you," and she took the little one in her arms, adding, "Now we are all right, aren't we."

Kathleen ran downstairs, turned up the light in the living room and passed quietly into the bedroom.

"Sorry to trouble you, Sybil, but there's something wrong with this infernal bandage."

Kathleen went and brought in the lamp. "Your sister cannot leave Doris, Mr. Romayne," she said quietly.

"Perhaps I can be of use."

For a few moments the sick man gazed at her as at a vision. "Is this another of them?" he said wearily. "I have been having hallucinations of various sorts for the last two days, but you do look real. It is you, Kathleen, isn't it?"

"Really me, Mr. Romayne," said the girl cheerfully. "Let me look at your arm."

"Oh, hang it, say 'Jack,' won't you, and be decent to a fellow. My God, I have wanted you for these ten days. Why didn't you come to me? What did I do? I hurt you somehow, but you know I wouldn't willingly. Why have you stayed away from me?" He raised himself upon his elbow, his voice was high, thin, weak, his eyes glittering, his cheeks ghastly with the high lights of fever upon them.

Shocked, startled and filled with a poignant mothering pity, Kathleen struggled with a longing to take him in her arms and comfort him as the mother was the little wailing child upstairs.

"Excuse me just a moment," she cried, and ran out into the living room and then outside the door and stood for a moment in the dark, drawing deep breaths and struggling to get control of the pity and of the joy that surged through her heart. "Oh, God," she cried, lifting her hands high above her head in appeal, "help me to be strong and steady. He needs me and he wants me too."

From the darkness in answer to her appeal there came a sudden quietness of nerve and a sense of strength and fitness for her work. Quickly she entered the house and went again to the sick room.

"Thank God," cried Jack. "I thought I was fooled again. You won't go away, Kathleen, for a little while, will you? I feel just like a kiddie in the dark, do you know? Like a fool rather. You won't go again?" He raised himself upon his arm, the weak voice raised to a pitiful appeal.

It took all her own fortitude to keep her own voice steady. "No, Jack, I am going to stay. I am your nurse, you know, and I am your boss too. You must do just as I say. Remember that. You must behave yourself as a sick man should."

He sank back quietly upon the pillow. "Thank God. Anything under heaven I promise if only you stay, Kathleen. You will stay, won't you?"

"Didn't you hear me promise?"

"Yes, yes," he said, a great relief in his tired face. "All right, I am good. But you have made me suffer, Kathleen."

"Now, then, no talk," said Kathleen. "We will look at that arm."

She loosened the bandages. The inflamed and swollen appearance of the arm sickened and alarmed her. There was nothing she could do there. She replaced the bandages. "You are awfully hot. I am going to sponge your face a bit if you will let me."

"Go on," he said gratefully, "do anything you like if only you don't go away again."

"Now, none of that. A nurse doesn't run away from her job, does she?" She had gotten control of herself, and her quick, clever fingers, with their firm, cool touch, seemed to bring rest to the jangling nerves of the sick man. Whatever it was, whether the touch of her fingers or the relief of the cool water upon his fevered face and arm, by the time the bathing process was over, Jack was lying quietly, already rested and looking like sleep.

"I say, this is heavenly," he murmured. "Now a drink, if you please. I believe there is medicine about due too," he said. She gave him a drink, lifting up his head on her strong arm. "I could lift myself, you know," he said, looking up into her face with a little smile, "but I like this way so much better if you don't mind."

"Certainly not; I am your nurse, you know," replied Kathleen. "Now your medicine." She found the bottle under his direction and, again lifting his head, gave him his medicine.

"Oh, this is fine. I will take my medicine as often as you want me to, and I think another drink would be good." She brought him the glass. "I like to drink slowly," he said, looking up into her eyes. But she shook her head at him.

"No nonsense now," she warned him.

"Nonsense!" he said, sinking back with a sigh, "I want you to believe me, Kathleen, it is anything but nonsense. My God, it is religion!"

"Now then," said Kathleen, ignoring his words, "I shall just smooth out your pillows and straighten down your bed, tuck you in and make you comfortable for the night and then—"

"And then," he interrupted eagerly, "oh, Kathleen, all good children get it, you know."

A deep flush tinged her face. "Now you are not behaving properly."

"But, Kathleen," he cried, "why not? Listen to me. There's no use. I cannot let you go till I have this settled. I must know. No, don't pull away from me, Kathleen. You know I love you, with all my soul, with all I have, I love you. Oh, don't pull away from me. Ever since that day when I first saw you three months ago I have loved you. I have tried not to. God knows I have tried not to because I thought you were pledged to that—that German fellow. Tell me, Kathleen. Why you are shaking, darling! Am I frightening you? I would not frighten you. I would not take advantage of you. But do you care a little bit? Tell me. I have had ten days of sheer hell. For one brief minute I thought you loved me. You almost said you did. But then you never came to me and I have feared that you did not care. But to-night I must know. I must know now." He raised himself up to a sitting posture. "Tell me, Kathleen; I must know."

"Oh, Jack," she panted. "You are not yourself now. You are weak and just imagine things."

"Imagine things," he cried with a kind of fierce rage. "Imagine! Haven't I for these three months fought against this every day? Oh, Kathleen, if you only knew. Do you love me a little, even a little?"

Suddenly the girl ceased her struggling. "A little!" she cried. "No, Jack, not a little, but with all my heart I love you. I should not tell you to-night, and, oh, I meant to be so strong and not let you speak till you were well again, but I can't help it. But are you quite sure, Jack? Are you sure you won't regret this when you are well again?"

He put his strong arm round about her and drew her close.

"I can't half hold you, darling," he said in her ear. "This confounded arm of mine—but you do it for me. Put your arms around me, sweetheart, and tell me that you love me."

She wreathed her arms round about his neck and drew him close. "Oh, Jack," she said, "I may be wrong, but I am so happy, and I never thought to be happy again. I cannot believe it. Oh, what awful days these have been!" she said with a break in her voice and hiding her face upon his shoulder.

"Never mind, sweetheart, think of all the days before us."

"Are you sure, Jack?" she whispered to him, still hiding her face. "Are you very sure that you will not be ashamed of me? I felt so dreadful and I came in just to help you, and I was so sure of myself. But when I saw you lying there, Jack, I just could not help myself." Her voice broke.

He turned her face up a little toward him. "Look at me," he said. She opened her eyes and, looking steadily into his, held them there. "Say, 'Jack, I love you,'" he whispered to her.

A great flood of red blood rushed over her face, then faded, leaving her white, but still her eyes held his fast. "Jack," she whispered, "my Jack, I love you."

"Kathleen, dear heart," he said.

Closer he drew her lips toward his. Suddenly she closed her eyes, her whole body relaxed, and lay limp against him. As his lips met hers, her arms tightened about him and held him in a strong embrace. Then she opened her eyes, raised herself up, and gazed at him as if in surprise. "Oh, Jack," she cried, "I cannot think it is true. Are you sure? I could not bear it if you were mistaken."

There was the sound of a footstep on the stair. "Let me go, Jack; there's your sister coming. Quick! Lie down." Hurriedly, she began once more to bathe his face as Mrs. Waring-Gaunt came in.

"Is he resting?" she said. "Why, Jack, you seem quite feverish. Did you give him his medicine?"

"Yes, about an hour ago, I think."

"An hour! Why, before you came upstairs? How long have you been in?"

"Oh, no, immediately after I came down," said the girl in confusion. "I don't know how long ago. I didn't look at the time." She busied herself straightening the bed.

"Sybil, she doesn't know how long ago," said Jack. "She's been behaving as I never have heard of any properly trained nurse behaving. She's been kissing me."

"Oh, Jack," gasped Kathleen, flushing furiously.

"Kissing you!" exclaimed Mrs. Waring-Gaunt, looking from one to the other.

"Yes, and I have been kissing her," continued Jack shamelessly.

"Oh, Jack," again gasped Kathleen, looking at Mrs. Waring-Gaunt beseechingly.

"Yes," continued Jack in a voice of triumph, "and we are going to do it right along every day and all day long with suitable pauses for other duties and pleasures."

"Oh, you darling," exclaimed Mrs. Waring-Gaunt rushing at her. "I am so glad. Well, you are a 'wunner' as the Marchioness says. I had thought—but never mind. Jack, dear, I do congratulate you. I think you are in awful luck. Yes, and you too, Kathleen, for he is a fine boy. I will go and tell Tom this minute."

"Do," said Jack, "and please don't hurry. My nurse is perfectly competent to take care of me in the meantime."

CHAPTER XV

THE COMING OF JANE

At sixteen-forty-five the Waring-Gaunt car was standing at the Melville Station awaiting the arrival of the train which was to bring Jane and her father, but no train was in sight. Larry, after inquiry at the wicket, announced that she was an hour late. How much more the agent, after the exasperating habit of railroad officials, could not say, nor could he assign any reason for the delay.

"Let me talk to him," said Nora impatiently. "I know Mr. Field."

Apparently the official reserve in which Mr. Field had wrapped himself was not proof against the smile which Nora flung at him through the wicket.

"We really cannot say how late she will be, Miss Nora. I may tell you, but we are not saying anything about it, that there has been an accident."

"An accident!" exclaimed Nora. "Why, we are expecting—"

"No, there is no one hurt. A freight has been derailed, and torn up the track a bit. The passenger train is held up just beyond Fairfield. It will be a couple of hours, perhaps three, before she arrives." At this point the telegraph instrument clicked. "Just a minute, Miss Nora, there may be something on the wire." With his fingers on the key he executed some mysterious prestidigitations, wrote down some words, and came to the wicket again. "Funny," he said, "it is a wire for you, Miss Nora."

Nora took the yellow slip and read: "Delayed by derailed freight. Time of arrival uncertain. Very sorry, Jane."

"What do you think of this?" cried Nora, carrying the telegram out to the car. "Isn't it perfectly exasperating? That takes off one of their nights."

"Where is the accident?" inquired Mrs. Waring-Gaunt.

"Just above Fairfield."

"Fairfield! The poor things! Jump in and we will be there in no time. It is not much further to Wolf Willow from Fairfield than from here. Hurry up, we must make time."

"Now, Mrs. Waring-Gaunt, I know your driving. Just remember that I am an only son. I prefer using all four wheels on curves, please."

"Let her go," cried Nora.

And Mrs. Waring-Gaunt "let her go" at such speed that Larry declared he had time for only two perfectly deep breaths, one before they started, the other after they had pulled up beside the Pullman car at the scene of the wreck.

"Jane, Jane, Jane," yelled Larry, waving his hands wildly to a girl who was seen sitting beside a window reading.

The girl looked up, sprang from her seat, and in a moment or two appeared on the platform. "Come on," yelled Larry. He climbed over a wire fence, and up the steep grade of the railroad embankment. Down sprang the girl, met him half way up the embankment, and gave him both her hands. "Jane, Jane," exclaimed Larry. "You are looking splendidly. Do you know," he added in a low voice, "I should love to kiss you right here. May I? Look at all the people; they would enjoy it so much."

The girl jerked away her hands, the blood showing dully under her brown skin. "Stop it, you silly boy. Is that Nora? Yes, it is." She waved her hand wildly at Nora, who was struggling frantically with the barbed wire fence. "Wait, I am coming, Nora," cried Jane.

Down the embankment she scrambled and, over the wire, the two girls embraced each other to the delight of the whole body of the passengers gathered at windows and on platforms, and to the especial delight of a handsome young giant, resplendent in a new suit of striped flannels, negligee shirt, blue socks with tie to match, and wearing a straw hat adorned with a band in college colours. With a wide smile upon his face he stood gazing down upon the enthusiastic osculation of the young ladies.

"Mrs. Waring-Gaunt, this is Jane," cried Nora. "Mrs. Waring-Gaunt has come to meet you and take you home," she added to Jane. "You know we have no car of our own."

"How do you do," said Jane, smiling at Mrs. Waring-Gaunt. "I can't get at you very well just now. It was very kind of you to come for us."

"And she has left her brother very sick at home," said Nora in a low voice.

"We won't keep you waiting," said Jane, beginning to scramble up the bank again. "Come, Larry, I shall get father and you shall help with our things."

"Right you are," said Larry.

"Met your friends, I see, Miss Brown," said the handsome giant. "I know it is mean of me, but I am really disgusted. It is bad enough to be held up here for a night, but to lose your company too."

"Well, I am awfully glad," said Jane, giving him such a delighted smile that he shook his head disconsolately.

"No need telling me that. Say," he added in an undertone, "that's your friend Nora, ain't it? Stunning girl. Introduce me, won't you?"

"Yes, if you will help me with my things. I am in an awful hurry and don't want to keep them waiting. Larry, this is Mr. Dean Wakeham." The young man shook hands with cordial frankness, Larry with suspicion in his heart.

"Let me have your check, Jane, and I will go and get your trunk," said Larry.

"No, you come with me, Larry," said Jane decidedly. "The trunk is too big for you to handle. Mr. Wakeham, you will get it for me, won't you, please? I will send a porter to help."

"Gladly, Miss Brown. No, I mean with the deepest pain and regret," said Wakeham, going for the trunk while Larry accompanied her in quest of the minor impedimenta that constituted her own and her father's baggage.

"Jane, have you any idea how glad I am to see you?"

demanded Larry as they passed into the car.

Jane's radiant smile transformed her face. "Yes, I think so," she said simply. "But we must hurry. Oh, here is Papa."

Dr. Brown hailed Larry with acclaim. "This is very kind of you, my dear boy; you have saved us a tedious wait."

"We must hurry, Papa," said Jane, cutting him short. "Mrs. Waring-Gaunt, who has come for us in her car, has left her brother ill at home." She marshalled them promptly into the car and soon had them in line for the motor, bearing the hand baggage and wraps, the porter following with Jane's own bag. "Thank you, porter," said Jane, giving him a smile that reduced that functionary to the verge of grinning imbecility, and a tip which he received with an air of absent-minded indifference. "Good-bye, porter; you have made us very comfortable," said Jane, shaking hands with him.

"Thank you, Miss; it shuah is a pleasuah to wait on a young lady like you, Miss. It shuah is, Miss. Ah wish you a prospec jounay, Miss, Ah do."

"I wonder what is keeping Mr. Wakeham," said Jane. "I am very sorry to keep you waiting, Mrs. Waring-Gaunt. Larry, would you mind?"

"Certainly not," said Larry, hurrying off toward the baggage car. In a few minutes Mr. Wakeham appeared with the doleful news that the trunk was not in the car and must have been left behind.

"I am quite sure it is there," said Jane, setting off herself for the car, the crestfallen Mr. Wakeham and the porter following behind her.

At the door of the car the baggage man met her with regretful apologies. "The trunk must have been left behind."

He was brusquely informed by Jane that she had seen it put on board.

"Then it must have been put off by mistake at Calgary?" This suggestion was brushed aside as unworthy of consideration. The trunk was here in this car, she was sure. This the baggage man and Mr. Wakeham united in declaring quite impossible. "We have turned the blasted car upside down," said the latter.

"Impossible?" exclaimed Jane, who had been exploring the dark recesses of the car. "Why, here it is, I knew it was here."

"Hurrah," cried Larry, "we have got it anyway."

Mr. Wakeham and the baggage man went to work to extricate the trunk from the lowest tier of boxes. They were wise enough to attempt no excuse or explanation, and in Jane's presence they felt cribbed, cabined and confined in the use of such vocabulary as they were wont to consider appropriate to the circumstances, and in which they prided themselves as being adequately expert. A small triumphal procession convoyed the trunk to the motor, Jane leading as was fitting, Larry and Mr. Wakeham forming the rear guard. The main body consisted of the porter, together with the baggage man, who, under a flagellating sense of his incompetence, was so moved from his wonted attitude of haughty indifference as to the fate of a piece of baggage committed to his care when once he had contemptuously hurled it forth from the open door of his car as to personally aid in conducting by the unusual and humiliating process of actually handling this particular bit of baggage down a steep and gravelly bank and over a wire fence and into a motor car.

"Jane's a wonder," confided Larry to Mr. Wakeham.

"She sure is," said that young man. "You cannot slip anything past her, and she's got even that baggage man tamed and tied and ready to catch peanuts in his mouth. First time I have seen that done."

"You just wait till she smiles her farewell at him," said Larry, hugely enjoying the prospect.

Together they stood awaiting the occurrence of this phenomenon. "Gosh-a-mighty, look at him," murmured Mr. Wakeham. "Takes it like pie. He'd just love to carry that blasted trunk up the grade and back to the car, if she gave him the wink. Say, she ain't much to look at, but somehow she's got me handcuffed and chained to her chariot wheels. Say," he continued with a shyness not usual with him, "would you mind introducing me to the party?"

"Come along," said Larry.

The introduction, however, was performed by Jane, who apparently considered Mr. Wakeham as being under her protection. "Mrs. Waring-Gaunt, this is Mr. Wakeham. Mr. Wakeham is from Chicago, but," she hastened to add, "he knows some friends of ours in Winnipeg."

"So you see I am fairly respectable," said Mr. Wakeham, shaking hand with Mrs. Waring-Gaunt and Nora.

When the laughter had ceased, Mr. Wakeham said, "If your car were only a shade larger I should beg hospitality along with Dr. and Miss Brown."

"Room on the top," said Mrs. Waring-Gaunt with a smile, "but it seems the only place left. You are just passing through, Mr. Wakeham?"

"Yes, I am going on to Manor Mine."

"Oh, that's only twenty miles down the line."

"Then may I run up to see you?" eagerly asked Mr. Wakeham.

"Certainly, we shall be delighted to see you," said the lady.

"Count on me, then," said the delighted Mr. Wakeham, lifting his hat in farewell.

Dr. Brown took his place in the front seat beside Mrs. Waring-Gaunt, the three young people occupying the seat in the rear.

"Who is he?" asked Larry when they had finally got under way.

"A friend of the James Murrays in Winnipeg. You remember them, don't you? Ethel Murray was in your year. He is very nice indeed, don't you think so, Papa?" said Jane, appealing to her father.

"Fine young chap," said Dr. Brown with emphasis. "His father is in mines in rather a big way, I believe. Lives in Chicago, has large holdings in Alberta coal mines about here somewhere, I fancy. The young man is a recent graduate from Cornell and is going into his father's business. He strikes me as an exceptionally able young fellow." And for at least five miles of the way Dr. Brown discussed the antecedents, the character, the training, the prospects of the young American till Larry felt qualified to pass a reasonably stiff examination on that young man's history, character and career.

"Now tell me," said Larry to Jane at the first real opening that offered, "what does this talk about a three days' visit to us mean. The idea of coming a thousand miles on your first visit to your friends, some of whom you have not seen for eight years and staying three days!"

"You see Papa is on his way to Banff," explained Jane, "and then he goes to the coast and he only has a short time. So we could plan only for three days here."

"We can plan better than that," said Larry confidently, "but never mind just now. We shall settle that to-morrow."

The journey home was given to the careful recital of news of Winnipeg, of the 'Varsity, and of mutual friends. It was like listening to the reading of a diary to hear Jane bring up to date the doings and goings and happenings in the lives of their mutual friends for the past year. Gossip it was, but of such kindly nature as left no unpleasant taste in the mouth and gave no unpleasant picture of any living soul it touched.

"Oh, who do you think came to see me two weeks ago? An old friend of yours, Hazel Sleighter. Mrs. Phillips she is now. She has two lovely children. Mr. Phillips is in charge of a department in Eaton's store."

"You don't tell me," cried Larry. "How is dear Hazel? How I loved her once! I wonder where her father is and Tom and the little girl. What was her name?"

"Ethel May. Oh, she is married too, in your old home, to Ben—somebody."

"Ben, big Ben Hopper? Why, think of that kid married."

"She is just my age," said Jane soberly, glad of the dusk of the falling night. She would have hated to have Larry see the quick flush that came to her cheek. Why the reference to Ethel May's marriage should have made her blush she hardly knew, and that itself was enough to annoy her, for Jane always knew exactly why she did things.

"And Mr. and Mrs. Sleighter," said Jane, continuing her narrative, "have gone to Toronto. They have become quite wealthy, Hazel says, and Tom is with his father in some sort of financial business. What is it, Papa?"

Dr. Brown suddenly waked up. "What is what, my dear? You will have to forgive me. This wonderful scenery, these hills here and those mountains are absorbing my whole attention. So wonderful it all is that I hardly feel like apologising to Mrs. Waring-Gaunt for ignoring her."

"Don't think of it," said Mrs. Waring-Gaunt.

"Do you know, Jane," continued Dr. Brown, "that at this present moment you are passing through scenery of its kind unsurpassed possibly in the world?"

"I was talking to Larry, Papa," said Jane, and they all laughed at her.

"I was talking to Jane," said Larry.

"But look at this world about you," continued her father, "and look, do look at the moon coming up behind you away at the prairie rim." They all turned about except Mrs. Waring-Gaunt, whose eyes were glued to the two black ruts before her cutting through the grass. "Oh, wonderful, wonderful," breathed Dr. Brown. "Would it be possible to pause, Mrs. Waring-Gaunt, at the top of this rise?"

"No," said Mrs. Waring-Gaunt, "but at the top of the rise beyond, where you will get the full sweep of the country in both directions."

"Is that where we get your lake, Nora," inquired Jane, "and the valley beyond up to the mountains?"

"How do you know?" said Nora.

"I remember Larry told me once," she said.

"That's the spot," said Nora. "But don't look around now. Wait until you are told."

"Papa," said Jane in a quiet, matter-of-fact voice, "what is it that Tom is doing?" Larry shouted.

"Tom, what Tom? Jane, my dear," said Dr. Brown in a pained voice, "does Tom matter much or any one else in the midst of all this glory?"

"I think so, Papa," said Jane firmly. "You matter, don't you? Everybody matters. Besides, we were told not to look until we reached the top."

"Well, Jane, you are an incorrigible Philistine," said her father, "and I yield. Tom's father is a broker, and Tom is by way of being a broker too, though I doubt if he is broking very much. May I dismiss Tom for a few minutes now?" Again they all laughed.

"I don't see what you are all laughing at," said Jane, and lapsed into silence.

"Now then," cried Nora, "in three minutes."

At the top of the long, gently rising hill the motor pulled up, purring softly. They all stood up and gazed around about them. "Look back," commanded Nora. "It is fifty miles to that prairie rim there." From their feet the prairie spread itself in long softly undulating billows to the eastern horizon, the hollows in shadow, the crests tipped with the silver of the rising moon. Here and there wreaths of mist lay just above the shadow lines, giving a ghostly appearance to the hills. "Now look this way," said Nora, and they turned about. Away to the west in a flood of silvery light the prairie climbed by abrupt steps, mounting ever higher over broken rocky points and rocky ledges, over bluffs of poplar and dark masses of pine and spruce, up to the grey, bare sides of the mighty mountains, up to their snow peaks gleaming elusive, translucent, faintly discernible against the blue of the sky. In the valley immediately at their feet the waters of the little lake gleamed like a polished shield set in a frame of ebony. "That's our lake," said Nora, "with our house just behind it in the woods. And nearer in that little bluff is Mrs. Waring-Gaunts home."

"Papa," said Jane softly, "we must not keep Mrs. Waring-Gaunt."

"Thank you, Jane," said Mrs. Waring-Gaunt. "I fear I must go on."

"Don't you love it?" inquired Larry enthusiastically and with a touch of impatience in his voice.

"Oh, yes, it is lovely," said Jane.

"But, Jane, you will not get wild over it," said Larry.

"Get wild? I love it, really I do. But why should I get wild over it. Oh, I know you think, and Papa thinks, that I am awful. He says I have no poetry in me, and perhaps he is right."

In a few minutes the car stopped at the door of Mrs. Waring-Gaunt's house. "I shall just run in for a moment," said Mrs. Waring-Gaunt. "Kathleen will want to see you, and perhaps will go home with you. I shall send her out."

Out from the vine-shadowed porch into the white light came Kathleen, stood a moment searching the faces of the party, then moved toward Dr. Brown with her hands eagerly stretched out. "Oh, Dr. Brown," she cried, "it is so good to see you here."

"But my dear girl, my dear girl, how wonderful you look! Why, you have actually grown more beautiful than when we saw you last!"

"Oh, thank you, Dr. Brown. And there is Jane," cried Kathleen, running around to the other side of the car. "It is so lovely to see you and so good of you to come to us," she continued, putting her arms around Jane and kissing her.

"I wanted to come, you know," said Jane.

"Yes, it is Jane's fault entirely," said Dr. Brown. "I confess I hesitated to impose two people upon you this way, willy-nilly. But Jane would have it that you would be glad to have us."

"And as usual Jane was right," said Larry with emphasis.

"Yes," said Kathleen, "Jane was right. Jane is a dear to think that way about us. Dr. Brown," continued Kathleen with a note of anxiety in her voice, "Mrs. Waring-Gaunt wondered if you would mind coming in to see her brother. He was wounded with a gunshot in the arm about ten days ago. Dr. Hudson, who was one of your pupils, I believe, said he would like to have you see him when you came. I wonder if you would mind coming in now." Kathleen's face was flushed and her words flowed in a hurried stream.

"Not at all, not at all," answered the doctor, rising hastily from the motor and going in with Kathleen.

"Oh, Larry," breathed Jane in a rapture of delight, "isn't she lovely, isn't she lovely? I had no idea she was so perfectly lovely." Not the moon, nor the glory of the landscape with all its wonder of plain and valley and mountain peak had been able to awaken Jane to ecstasy, but the rare loveliness of this girl, her beauty, her sweet simplicity, had kindled Jane to enthusiasm.

"Well, Jane, you are funny," said Larry. "You rave and go wild over Kathleen, and yet you keep quite cool over that most wonderful view."

"View!" said Jane contemptuously. "No, wait, Larry, let me explain. I do think it all very wonderful, but I love people. People after all are better than mountains, and they are more wonderful too."

"Are they?" said Larry dubiously. "Not so lovely, sometimes."

"Some people," insisted Jane, "are more wonderful than all the Rocky Mountains together. Look at Kathleen," she cried triumphantly. "You could not love that old mountain

Ralph Connor

there, could you? But, Kathleen—"

"Don't know about that," said Larry. "Dear old thing."

"Tell me how Mr. Romayne was hurt," said Jane, changing the subject.

In graphic language Nora gave her the story of the accident with all the picturesque details, recounting Kathleen's part in it with appropriate emotional thrills. Jane listened with eyes growing wider with each horrifying elaboration.

"Do you think his arm will ever be all right?" she inquired anxiously.

"We do not know yet," said Nora sombrely.

"Nonsense," interrupted Larry sharply. "His arm will be perfectly all right. You people make me tired with your passion for horrors and possible horrors."

Nora was about to make a hot reply when Jane inquired quietly, "What does the doctor say? He ought to know."

"That's just it," said Nora. "He said yesterday he did not like the look of it at all. You know he did, Larry. Mrs. Waring-Gaunt told me so. They are quite anxious about it. But we will hear what Dr. Brown says and then we will know."

But Dr. Brown's report did not quite settle the matter, for after the approved manner of the profession he declined to commit himself to any definite statement except that it was a nasty wound, that it might easily have been worse, and he promised to look in with Dr. Hudson to-morrow. Meantime he expressed the profound hope that Mrs.

Waring-Gaunt might get them as speedily as was consistent with safety to their destination, and that supper might not be too long delayed.

"We can trust Mrs. Waring-Gaunt for the first," said Larry with confidence, "and mother for the second." In neither the one nor the other was Larry mistaken, for Mrs. Waring-Gaunt in a very few minutes discharged both passengers and freight at the Gwynnes' door, and supper was waiting.

"We greatly appreciate your kindness, Mrs. Waring-Gaunt," said Dr. Brown, bowing courteously over her hand. "I shall look in upon your brother to-morrow morning. I hardly think there is any great cause for anxiety."

"Oh, thank you, Dr. Brown, I am glad to hear you say that. It would be very good of you to look in to-morrow."

"Good-night," said Jane, her rare smile illuminating her dark face. "It was so good of you to come for us. It has been a delightful ride. I hope your brother will be better to-morrow."

"Thank you, my dear," said Mrs. Waring-Gaunt. "I should be glad to have you come over to us. I am sure my brother would be glad to know you."

"Do you think so," said Jane doubtfully. "You know I am not very clever. I am not like Kathleen or Nora." The deep blue eyes looked wistfully at her out of the plain little face.

"I am perfectly certain he would love to know you, Jane—if I may call you so," said Mrs. Waring-Gaunt, impulsively kissing her.

"Oh, you are so kind," said Jane. "I will come then to-morrow."

The welcome to the Gwynne home was without fuss or effusiveness but had the heart quality that needs no noisy demonstration.

"We are glad to have you with us at Lakeside Farm," said Mr. Gwynne heartily, as he ushered Dr. Brown and Jane into the big living room, where his wife stood waiting.

"You are welcome to us, Dr. Brown," said the little lady. And something in the voice and manner made Dr. Brown know that the years that had passed since his first meeting with her had only deepened the feeling of gratitude and affection in her heart toward him. "We have not forgotten nor shall we ever forget your kindness to us when we were strangers passing through Winnipeg, nor your goodness to Larry and Kathleen while in Winnipeg. They have often told us of your great kindness."

"And you may be quite sure, Mrs. Gwynne," said Dr. Brown heartily, "that Larry brought his welcome with him, and as for Kathleen, we regard her as one of our family."

"And this is Jane," said Mrs. Gwynne. "Dear child, you have grown. But you have not changed. Come away to your room."

Once behind the closed door she put her arms around the girl and kissed her. Then, holding her at arm's length, scrutinised her face with searching eyes. "No," she said again with a little sigh of relief, "you have not changed. You are the same dear, wise girl I learned to love in Winnipeg."

"Oh, I am glad you think I am not changed, Mrs. Gwynne," said Jane, with a glow of light in her dark blue eyes. "I do not like people to change and I would hate to have you think me changed. I know," she added shyly, "I feel just the same toward you and the others here. But oh, how lovely they are, both Kathleen and Nora."

"They are good girls," said Mrs. Gwynne quietly, "and they have proved good girls to me."

"I know, I know," said Jane, with impulsive fervour, "and through those winters and all. Oh, they were so splendid."

"Yes," said the mother, "they never failed, and Larry too."

"Yes, indeed," cried Jane with increasing ardour, her eyes shining, "with his teaching,—going there through the awful cold,—lighting the school fires,—and the way he stuck to his college work. Nora's letters told me all about it. How splendid that was! And you know, Mrs. Gwynne, in the 'Varsity he did so well. I mean besides his standing in the class lists, in the Societies and in all the college life. He was really awfully popular," added Jane with something of a sigh.

"You must tell me, dear, sometime all about it. But now you must be weary and hungry. Come away out if you are ready, and I hope you will feel as if you were just one of ourselves."

"Do you know, that is just the way I feel, Mrs. Gwynne," said Jane, putting the final touch to her toilet. "I seem to know the house, and everything and everybody about it. Nora is such a splendid correspondent, you see."

"Well, dear child, we hope the days you spend here will always be a very bright spot in your life," said Mrs.

Ralph Connor

Gwynne as they entered the living room.

The next few days saw the beginning of the realisation of that hope, for of all the bright spots in Jane's life none shone with a brighter and more certain lustre than the days of her visit to Lakeside Farm.

CHAPTER XVI

HOSPITALITY WITHOUT GRUDGING

By arrangement made the previous evening Jane was awake before the family was astir and in Nora's hands preparing for a morning ride with Larry, who was to give her her first lesson in equitation.

"Your habit will be too big for me, Nora, I am afraid," she said.

"Habit!" cried Nora. "My pants, you mean. You can pull them up, you know. There they are."

"Pants!" gasped Jane. "Pants! Nora, pants! Do you mean to say you wear these things where all the men will see you?" Even in the seclusion of her bedroom Jane's face at the thought went a fiery red. Nora laughed at her scornfully. "Oh, but I can't possibly go out in these before Larry. I won't ride at all. Haven't you a skirt, a regular riding habit?"

But Nora derided her scruples. "Why, Jane, we all wear them here."

"Does Kathleen?"

"Of course she does, and Mrs. Waring-Gaunt, and everybody."

"Oh, she might, but I am sure your mother would not."

Nora shouted joyfully. "Well, that is true, she never has, but then she has never ridden out here. Put them on, hurry up, your legs are straight enough, your knees don't knock."

"Oh, Nora, they are just terrible," said Jane, almost in tears. "I know I will just squat down if Larry looks at me."

"Why should he look at you? Don't you ever let on but that you have worn them often, and he will never think of looking at you."

In face of many protests Jane was at length arrayed in her riding apparel.

"Why, you look perfectly stunning," said Nora. "You have got just the shape for them. Pull them up a little. There, that is better. Now step out and let me see you."

Jane walked across the room and Nora rocked in laughter. "Oh, Nora, I will just take them off. You are as mean as you can be. I will pull them off."

"Not a bit," said Nora, still laughing, "only stretch your legs a bit when you walk. Don't mince along. Stride like a man. These men have had all the fun in the matter of clothes. I tell you it was one of the proudest moments of my life when I saw my own legs walking. Now step out and swing your arms. There, you are fine, a fine little chap, Jane, round as a barrel, and neat as a ballet dancer, although I never saw one except in magazines."

Trim and neat Jane looked, the riding suit showing off the beautiful lines of her round, shapely figure. Shrinking, blushing, and horribly conscious of her pants, Jane followed Nora from her bedroom. A swift glance she threw around the room. To her joy it was empty but for Mrs. Gwynne, who was ready with a big glass of rich milk and a slice of home-made bread and delicious butter.

"Good morning, my dear," said Mrs. Gwynne, kissing her. "You will need something before you ride. You will have breakfast after your return."

Jane went close to her and stood beside her, still blushing. "Oh, thank you," she cried, "I am really hungry already. I hope I won't get killed. I never was on a horse before, you know."

"Oh, never fear, Lawrence is very careful. If it were Nora now I would not be so sure about you, but Lawrence is quite safe."

At this point Larry came in. "Well, Jane, all ready? Good for you. I like a girl that is always on time."

"How do you like her pants, Larry?" said Nora, wickedly.

"Perfectly splendiferous," cried Larry.

"Oh, you mean thing, Nora," cried Jane, dropping hurriedly into a chair with scarlet face and indignant eyes.

"Come along, Jane, old chap, don't mind her. Those pants never looked so well before, I assure you. We are going to have a great time. I guarantee that in a few minutes you will be entirely oblivious of such trivial things as mere pants."

They all passed out into the front yard to see Jane mount and take her first lesson.

"This is Polly," said Larry. "She has taught us all to ride, and though she has lost her shape a bit, she has still 'pep' enough to decline to take a dare."

"What do I do?" said Jane, gazing fearfully at the fat and shapeless Polly.

"There is just one rule in learning to ride," said Larry, "step on and stick there. Polly will look after the rest."

"Step on—it is easy to say, but—"

"This way," said Nora. She seized hold of the horn of the saddle, put her foot into the stirrup and sprang upon Polly's back. "Oh, there's where the pants come in," she added as her dress caught on to the rear of the saddle. "Now up you go. Make up your mind you are going to DO it, not going to TRY."

A look of serious determination came into Jane's face, a look that her friends would have recognised as the precursor of a resolute and determined attempt to achieve the thing in hand. She seized the horn of the saddle, put her foot into the stirrup and "stepped on."

The riding lesson was an unqualified success, though for some reason, known only to herself, Polly signalised the event by promptly running away immediately her head was turned homeward, and coming back down the lane at a thundering gallop.

"Hello!" cried Nora, running out to meet them. "Why, Jane, you have been fooling us all along. You needn't tell me this is your first ride."

"My very first," said Jane, "but I hope not my last."

"But, my dear," said Mrs. Gwynne, who had also come out to see the return, "you are doing famously."

"Am I?" cried Jane, her face aglow and her eyes shining. "I think it is splendid. Shall we ride again to-day, Larry?"

"Right away after breakfast and all day long if you like. You are a born horsewoman, Jane."

"Weren't you afraid when Polly ran off with you like that?" inquired Nora.

"Afraid? I didn't know there was any danger. Was there any?" inquired Jane.

"Not a bit," said Nora, "so long as you kept your head."

"But there really was no danger, was there, Larry?" insisted Jane.

"None at all, Jane," said Nora, "I assure you. Larry got rattled when he saw you tear off in that wild fashion, but I knew you would be all right. Come in; breakfast is ready."

"And so am I," said Jane. "I haven't been so hungry I don't know when."

"Why, she's not plain-looking after all," said Nora to her mother as Jane strode manlike off to her room.

"Plain-looking?" exclaimed her mother. "I never thought her plain-looking. She has that beauty that shines from within, a beauty that never fades, but grows with every passing year."

A council of war was called by Nora immediately after breakfast, at which plans were discussed for the best employment of the three precious days during which the visitors were to be at the ranch. There were so many things to be done that unless some system were adopted valuable time would be wasted.

"It appears to me, Miss Nora," said Dr. Brown after a somewhat prolonged discussion, "that to accomplish all the things that you have suggested, and they all seem not only delightful but necessary, we shall require at least a month of diligent application."

"At the very least," cried Nora.

"So what are we going to do?" said the doctor.

It was finally decided that the Browns should extend their stay at Lakeside House for a week, after which the doctor should proceed to the coast and be met on his return at Banff by Jane, with Nora as her guest.

"Then that's all settled," said Larry. "Now what's for to-day?"

As if in answer to that question a honk of a motor car was heard outside. Nora rushed to the door, saying, "That's Mrs. Waring-Gaunt." But she returned hastily with heightened colour.

"Larry," she said, "it's that Mr. Wakeham."

"Wakeham," cried Larry. "What's got him up so early, I wonder?" with a swift look at Jane.

"I wonder," said Nora, giving Jane a little dig.

"I thought I would just run up and see if you had all got home safely last night," they heard his great voice booming outside to Larry.

"My, but he is anxious," said Nora.

"But who is he, Nora?" inquired her mother.

"A friend of Jane's, and apparently terribly concerned about her welfare."

"Stop, Nora," said Jane, flushing a fiery red. "Don't be silly. He is a young man whom we met on the train, Mrs. Gwynne, a friend of some of our Winnipeg friends."

"We shall be very glad to have him stay with us, my dear," said Mrs. Gwynne. "Go and bring him in."

"Go on, Jane," said Nora.

"Now, Nora, stop it," said Jane. "I will get really cross with you. Hush, there he is."

The young man seemed to fill up the door with his bulk. "Mr. Wakeham," said Larry, as the young fellow stood looking around on the group with a frank, expansive smile upon his handsome face. As his eye fell upon a little lady the young man seemed to come to attention. Insensibly he appeared to assume an attitude of greater respect as he bowed low over her hand.

"I hope you will pardon my coming here so early in the morning," he said with an embarrassed air. "I have the honour of knowing your guests."

"Any friend of our guests is very welcome here, Mr. Wakeham," said Mrs. Gwynne, smiling at him with gentle dignity.

"Good morning, Mr. Wakeham," said Jane, coming forward with outstretched hand. "You are very early in your calls. You could not have slept very much."

"No, indeed," replied Mr. Wakeham, "and that is one reason why I waked so early. My bed was not so terribly attractive."

"Oh," exclaimed Nora in a disappointed tone, as she shook hands with him, "we thought you were anxious to see us."

"Quite right," said the young man, holding her hand and looking boldly into her eyes. "I have come to see you."

Before his look Nora's saucy eyes fell and for some unaccountable reason her usually ready speech forsook her. Mr. Wakeham fell into easy conversation with Mr. Gwynne and Dr. Brown concerning mining matters, in which he was especially interested. He had spent an hour about the Manor Mine and there he had heard a good deal about Mr. Gwynne's mine and was anxious to see that if there were no objections. He wondered if he might drive Mr. Gwynne—and indeed, he had a large car and would be glad to fill it up with a party if any one cared to come. He looked at Mrs. Gwynne as he spoke.

"Yes, Mother, you go. It is such a lovely day," said Nora enthusiastically, "and Jane can go with you."

"Jane is going riding," said Larry firmly.

"I am going to Mrs. Waring-Gaunt's," said Jane. "I arranged with her last night."

While they were settling Mrs. Gwynne's protests, and covered by the noise of conversation, Mr. Wakeham managed to get close to Nora. "I want you to come," he said in a low voice. "That's what I came for."

Startled and confused by this extraordinary announcement, Nora could think of no answer.

"I think you were to show me the mine," he added. Then while Nora gasped at him, he said aloud, "My car is a seven passenger, so we can take quite a party."

"Why not Kathleen?" suggested Jane.

"Yes, indeed, Kathleen might like to go," said Mrs. Gwynne.

"Then let's all go," cried Nora.

"Thank you awfully," murmured Mr. Wakeham. "We shall only be two or three hours at most," continued Nora. "We shall be back in time for lunch."

"For that matter," said Mr. Gwynne, "we can lunch at the mine."

"Splendid," cried Nora. "Come along. We'll run up with you to the Waring-Gaunts' for Kathleen," she added to Mr. Wakeham.

At the Waring-Gaunts' they had some difficulty persuading Kathleen to join the party, but under the united influence of Jack and his sister, she agreed to go.

"Now then," said Mrs. Waring-Gaunt, "you have your full party, Mr. Wakeham—Mr. and Mrs. Gwynne, Dr. Brown, and the three girls."

"What about me?" said Larry dolefully.

"I shall stay with you," cried Nora, evading Mr. Wakeham's eyes.

"No, Nora," said Jane in a voice of quiet decision. "Last night Mrs. Waring-Gaunt and I arranged that I should visit her to-day."

There was a loud chorus of protests, each one making an alternative suggestion during which Jane went to Mrs. Waring-Gaunt's side and said quietly, "I want to stay with you to-day."

"All right, dear," said Mrs. Waring-Gaunt. "Stay you shall." And, then to the company announced, "We have it all arranged. Jane and I are to have a visit together. The rest of you go off."

"And what about me, Jane?" again said Larry.

"You are going with the others," said Jane calmly, "and in the afternoon we are to have our ride."

"And this is Jane," said Jack Romayne as Mrs. Waring-Gaunt ushered the girl into his room. "If half of what I have heard is true then I am a lucky man to-day. Kathleen has been telling me about you."

Jane's smile expressed her delight. "I think I could say the same of you, Mr. Romayne."

"What? Has Kathleen been talking about me?"

"No, I have not seen Kathleen since I came, but there are others, you know."

"Are there?" asked Jack. "I hadn't noticed. But I know all about you."

It was a hasty introduction for Jane. Kathleen was easily a subject for a day's conversation. How long she discoursed upon Kathleen neither of them knew. But when Mrs. Waring-Gaunt had finished up her morning household duties Jane was still busy dilating upon Kathleen's charms and graces and expatiating upon her triumphs and achievements during her stay in Winnipeg the previous winter.

"Still upon Kathleen?" inquired Mrs. Waring-Gaunt.

"Oh, I am learning a great deal and enjoying myself immensely," said Jack.

"You must be careful, Jane. Don't tell Jack everything about Kathleen. There are certain things we keep to ourselves, you know. I don't tell Tom everything."

Jane opened her eyes. "I have not told Jane yet, Sybil," said Jack quietly. "She doesn't know, though perhaps she has guessed how dear to me Kathleen is."

"Had you not heard?" inquired Mrs. Waring-Gaunt.

"No, I only came last night, you see." Then turning to Jack, she added, "And is—is Kathleen going to marry you?" Her astonishment was evident in her voice and eyes.

"I hope so," said Jack, "and you are no more astonished than I am myself. I only found it out night before last."

It was characteristic of Jane that she sat gazing at him in silence; her tongue had not learned the trick of easy compliment. She was trying to take in the full meaning of this surprising announcement.

"Well?" said Jack after he had waited for some moments.

"Oh, I beg your pardon," she said hurriedly. "I congratulate you. I think you are a very lucky man."

"I am, indeed," said Jack with emphasis. "And Kathleen? You are not so sure about her luck?"

"Well, I don't know you yet," said Jane gravely, "and Kathleen is a very lovely girl, the very loveliest girl I know."

"You are quite right," said Jack in a tone as grave as her own. "I am not good enough for her."

"Oh, I did not say that. Only I don't know you, and you see I know Kathleen. She is so lovely and so good. I love her." Jane's face was earnest and grave.

"And so do I, Jane, if I may call you so," said Jack, "and I am going to try to be worthy of her."

Jane's eyes rested quietly on his face. She made up her mind that it was an honest face and a face one could trust, but to Jane it seemed as if something portentous had befallen her friend and she could not bring herself immediately to accept this new situation with an outburst of joyous acclaim such as ordinarily greets an announcement of this kind. For a reason she could not explain her mind turned to the memory she cherished of her own mother and of the place she had held with her father. She wondered if this man could give to Kathleen a place so high and so secure in his heart. While her eyes were on his face Jack could see that her mind was far away. She was not thinking of him.

"What is it, Jane?" he said gently.

Jane started and the blood rushed to her face. She hesitated, then said quietly but with charming frankness, "I was thinking of my mother. She died when I was two years old. Father says I am like her. But I am not at all. She was very lovely. Kathleen makes me think of her, and father often tells me about her. He has never forgotten her. You see I think he loved her in quite a wonderful way, and he—" Jane paused abruptly.

Mrs. Waring-Gaunt rose quietly, came to her side. "Dear Jane, dear child," she said, kissing her. "That's the only way to love. I am sure your mother was a lovely woman, and a very happy woman, and you are like her."

But Jack kept his face turned away from them.

"Oh, Mrs. Waring-Gaunt," cried Jane, shaking her head emphatically, "I am not the least bit like her. That is one of the points on which I disagree with father. We do not agree upon everything, you know."

"No? What are some of the other points?"

"We agree splendidly about Kathleen," said Jane, laughing. "Just now we differ about Germany."

"Aha, how is that?" inquired Jack, immediately alert.

"Of course, I know very little about it, you understand, but last winter our minister, Mr. McPherson, who had just been on a visit to Germany the summer before, gave a lecture in which he said that Germany had made enormous preparations for war and was only waiting a favourable moment to strike. Papa says that is all nonsense."

"Oh, Jane, Jane," cried Mrs. Waring-Gaunt, "you have struck upon a very sore spot in this house. Jack will indorse all your minister said. He will doubtless go much further."

"What did he say, Jane?" inquired Jack.

"He was greatly in earnest and he urged preparation by Canada. He thinks we ought at the very least to begin getting our fleet ready right away."

"That's politics, of course," said Mrs. Waring-Gaunt, "and I do not know what you are."

"I am not sure that I do either," she replied, "but I believe too that Canada ought to get at her fleet without loss of time."

"But what did he say about Germany?" continued Jack.

"I can't tell you everything, of course, but he assured us that Germany had made the greatest possible preparation, that the cities, towns and villages were full of drilling men; that there were great stores of war material, guns and shells, everywhere throughout Germany; that they were preparing fleets of Zeppelins and submarines too; that they were ready to march at twenty-four hours' notice; that the whole railroad system of Germany was organised, was really built for war; that within the last few years the whole nation had come to believe that Germany must go to war in order to fulfil her great destiny. Father says that this is all foolish talk, and that all this war excitement is prompted chiefly by professional soldiers, like Lord Roberts and others, and by armament makers like the Armstrongs and the Krupps."

"What do you think about it all, Jane?" inquired Jack, looking at her curiously.

"Well, he had spent some months in Germany and had taken pains to inquire of all kinds of people, officers and professors and preachers and working people and politicians, and so I think he ought to know better than others who just read books and the newspapers, don't you think so?"

"I think you are entirely right, and I hope that minister of yours will deliver that lecture in many places throughout this country, for there are not many people, even in England, who believe in the reality of the German menace. But this is my hobby, my sister says, and I don't want to bore you."

"But I am really interested, Mr. Romayne. Papa laughs at me, and Larry too. He does not believe in the possibility of war. But I think that if there is a chance, even the slightest chance, of it being true, it is so terrible that we all ought to be making preparation to defend ourselves."

"Well, if it won't bore you," said Jack, "I shall tell you a few things."

"Then excuse me," said Mrs. Waring-Gaunt. "I have some matters to attend to. I have no doubt that you at least, Jack, will have a perfectly lovely time."

"I am sure I shall too," cried Jane enthusiastically. "I just want to hear about this."

"Will you please pass me that green book?" said Jack, after Mrs. Waring-Gaunt had left the room. "No, the next one. Yes. The first thing that it is almost impossible for us Britishers to get into our minds is this, that Germany, not simply the Kaiser and the governing classes, but the whole body of the German people, take themselves and their empire and their destiny with most amazing seriousness. Listen to this, for instance. This will give you, I say, the psychological condition out of which war may easily and naturally arise." He turned the leaves of the book and read:

"'To live and expand at the expense of other less meritorious peoples finds its justification in the conviction that we are of all people the most noble and the most pure, destined before others to work for the highest development of humanity.'"

"One of their poets—I haven't got him here—speaks of the 'German life curing all the evils of humanity by mere contact with it.' You see that row of books? These are only a few. Most of them are German. They are all by different authors and on different subjects, but they are quite unanimous in setting forth the German ideal, the governing principle of German World politics. They are filled with the most unbelievable glorification of Germany and the German people, and the most extraordinary prophecies as to her wonderful destiny as a World Power. Unhappily the German has no sense of humour. A Britisher talking in this way about his country would feel himself to be a fool. Not so the German. With a perfectly serious face he will attribute to himself and to his nation all the virtues in the calendar. For instance, listen to this:

"'Domination belongs to Germany because it is a superior nation, a noble race, and it is fitting that it should control its neighbours just as it is the right and duty of every individual endowed with superior intellect and force to control inferior individuals about him.'"

"Here's another choice bit:"

"'We are the superior race in the fields of science and of art. We are the best colonists, the best sailors, the best merchants.'"

"That's one thing. Then here's another. For many years after his accession I believe the Kaiser was genuinely anxious to preserve the peace of Europe and tried his best to do so, though I am bound to say that at times he adopted rather peculiar methods, a mingling of bullying and intrigue. But now since 1904—just hand me that thin book, please. Thank you—the Kaiser has changed his tone. For instance, listen to this:

"'God has called us to civilise the world. We are the missionaries of human progress.'"

"And again this:

"'The German people will be the block of granite on which our Lord will be able to elevate and achieve the civilisation of the world.'"

"But I need not weary you with quotations. The political literature of Germany for the last fifteen years is saturated with this spirit. The British people dismiss this with a good-natured smile of contempt. To them it is simply an indication of German bad breeding. If you care I shall have a number of these books sent you. They are somewhat difficult to get. Indeed, some of them cannot be had in English at all. But you read German, do you not? Kathleen told me about your German prize."

"I do, a little. But I confess I prefer the English," said Jane with a little laugh.

"The chief trouble, however, is that so few English-speaking people care to read them. But I assure you that the one all-absorbing topic of the German people is this one of Germany's manifest destiny to rule and elevate the world. And remember these two things go together. They have no idea of dominating the world intellectually or even commercially—but perhaps you are sick of this."

"Not at all. I am very greatly interested," said Jane.

"Then I shall just read you one thing more. The German has no idea that he can benefit a nation until he conquers it. Listen to this:

"'The dominion of German thought can only be extended under the aegis of political power, and unless we act in conformity to this idea we shall be untrue to out great duties toward the human race.'"

"I shall be very glad to get those books," said Jane, "and I wish you would mark some of these passages. And I promise you I shall do all I can to make all my friends read them. I shall begin with Papa and Larry. They are always making fun of me and my German scare."

"I can quite understand that," replied Jack. "That is a very common attitude with a great majority of the people of England to-day. But you see I have been close to these things for years, and I have personal knowledge of many of the plans and purposes in the minds of the German Kaiser and the political and military leaders of Germany, and unhappily I know too the spirit that dominates the whole body of the German people."

"You lived in Germany for some years?"

"Yes, for a number of years."

"And did you like the life there?"

"In many ways I did. I met some charming Germans, and then there is always their superb music."

And for an hour Jack Romayne gave his listener a series of vivid pictures of his life in Germany and in other lands for the past ten years, mingling with personal reminiscences incidents connected with international politics and personages. He talked well, not only because his subject was a part of himself, but also because Jane possessed that rare ability to listen with intelligence and sympathy. Never had she met with a man who had been in such intimate touch with the world's Great Affairs and who was possessed at the same time of such brilliant powers of description.

Before either of them was aware the party from the mine had returned.

"We have had a perfectly glorious time," cried Nora as she entered the room with her cheeks and eyes glowing.

"So have we, Miss Nora," said Jack. "In fact, I had not the slightest idea of the flight of time."

"You may say so," exclaimed Mrs. Waring-Gaunt. "These two have been so utterly absorbed in each other that my presence in the room or absence from it was a matter of perfect indifference. And how Jane managed it I don't know, but she got Jack to do for her what he has never done for me. He has actually been giving her the story of his life."

Jane stood by listening with a smile of frank delight on

her face.

"How did you do it, Jane?" asked Kathleen shyly. "He has never told me."

"Oh, I just listened," said Jane.

"That's a nasty jar for you others," said Nora.

"But he told me something else, Kathleen," said Jane with a bright blush, "and I am awfully glad." As she spoke she went around to Kathleen and, kissing her, said, "It is perfectly lovely for you both."

"Oh, you really mean that, do you?" said Jack. "You know she was exceedingly dubious of me this morning."

"Well, I am not now," said Jane. "I know you better, you see."

"Thank God," said Jack fervently. "The day has not been lost. You will be sure to come again to see me," he added as Jane said good-bye.

"Yes, indeed, you may be quite sure of that," replied Jane, smiling brightly back at him as she left the room with Nora.

"What a pity she is so plain," said Mrs. Waring-Gaunt when she had returned from seeing Jane on her way with Nora and Mr. Wakeham.

"My dear Sybil, you waste your pity," said her brother. "That young lady is so attractive that one forgets whether she is plain or not. I can't quite explain her fascination for me. There's perfect sincerity to begin with. She is never posing. And perfect simplicity. And besides that she is so intellectually keen, she keeps one alive."

"I just love her," said Kathleen. "She has such a good heart."

"You have said it," said Mrs. Waring-Gaunt, "and that is why Jane will never lose her charm."

CHAPTER XVII

THE TRAGEDIES OF LOVE

When the week had fled Dr. Brown could hardly persuade himself and his hosts at Lakeside Farm that the time had come for his departure to the coast. Not since he had settled down to the practice of his profession at Winnipeg more than twenty years ago had such a holiday been his. Alberta, its climate, its life of large spaces and far visions, its hospitable people, had got hold of him by so strong a grip that in parting he vowed that he would not await an opportunity but make one to repeat his visit to the ranch. And so he departed with the understanding that Jane should follow him to Banff ten days later with her friend Nora.

The ten days were to Jane as a radiant, swiftly moving dream. Yet with so much to gratify her, one wish had remained ungratified. Though from early morning until late night she had ridden the ranges now with one and now with another, but for the most part with Larry, Jane had never "done the mine."

"And I just know I shall go away without seeing that mine, and Winnipeg people will be sure to ask me about it, and what shall I say? And I have never seen that wonderful secretary, Mr. Switzer, either."

"To-morrow," said Larry solemnly, "no matter what happens we shall have you see that mine and the wonderful Mr. Switzer."

It was the seeing of Mr. Switzer that brought to Jane the only touch of tragedy to the perfect joy of her visit to Alberta. Upon arrival at the mine she was given over by Larry to Mr. Switzer's courteous and intelligent guidance, and with an enthusiasm that never wearied, her guide left nothing of the mine outside or in, to which with painstaking minuteness he failed to call her attention. It was with no small degree of pride that Mr. Switzer explained all that had been accomplished during the brief ten weeks during which the mine had been under his care. For although it was quite true that Mr. Steinberg was the manager, Switzer left no doubt in Jane's mind, as there was none in his own, that the mine owed its present state of development to his driving energy and to his organising ability. Jane readily forgave him his evident pride in himself as he exclaimed, sweeping his hand toward the little village that lay along the coolee,

"Ten weeks ago, Miss Brown, there was nothing here but a little black hole in the hillside over there. To-day look at it. We have a company organised, a village built and equipped with modern improvements, water, light, drainage, etc. We are actually digging and shipping coal. It is all very small as yet, but it is something to feel that a beginning has been made."

"I think it is really quite a remarkable achievement, Mr. Switzer. And I feel sure that I do not begin to know all that this means. They all say that you have accomplished great things in the short time you have been at work."

"We are only beginning," said Switzer again, "but I believe we shall have a great mine. It will be a good thing—for the Gwynnes, I mean—and that is worth while. Of course, my own money is invested here too and I am working for myself, but I assure you that I chiefly think of them. It is a joy, Miss Brown, to work for those you love."

"It is," replied Jane, slightly puzzled at this altruistic point of view; "The Gwynnes are dear people and I am glad for their sakes. I love them."

"Yes," continued Switzer, "this will be a great mine. They will be wealthy some day."

"That will be splendid," said Jane. "You see I have only got to know them well during this visit. Nine years ago I met them in Winnipeg when I was a little girl. Of course, Kathleen was with us a great deal last winter. I got to know her well then. She is so lovely, and she is lovelier now than ever. She is so happy, you know."

Switzer looked puzzled. "Happy? Because you are here?"

"No, no. Because of her engagement. Haven't you heard? I thought everybody knew."

Switzer stood still in his tracks. "Her engagement?" he said in a hushed voice. "Her engagement to—to that"—he could not apparently get the word out without a great effort—"that Englishman?"

Looking at his white face and listening to his tense voice, Jane felt as if she were standing at the edge of a mine that might explode at any moment.

"Yes, to Mr. Romayne," she said, and waited, almost holding her breath.

"It is not true!" he shouted. "It's a lie. Ha, Ha." Switzer's laugh was full of incredulous scorn. "Engaged? And how do YOU know?" He swung fiercely upon her, his eyes glaring out of a face ghastly white.

"I am sorry I said anything, Mr. Switzer. It was not my business to speak of it," said Jane quietly. "But I thought you knew."

Gradually the thing seemed to reach his mind. "Your business?" he said. "What difference whose business it is? It is not true. I say it is not true. How do you know? Tell me. Tell me. Tell me." He seized her by the arm, and at each "Tell me" shook her violently.

"You are hurting me, Mr. Switzer," said Jane.

He dropped her arm. "Then, my God, will you not tell me? How do you know?"

"Mr. Switzer, believe me it is true," said Jane, trying to speak quietly, though she was shaking with excitement and terror. "Mr. Romayne told me, they all told me, Kathleen told me. It is quite true, Mr. Switzer."

He stared at her as if trying to take in the meaning of her words, then glared around him like a hunted animal seeking escape from a ring of foes, then back at her again. There were workmen passing close to them on the path, but he saw nothing of them. Jane was looking at his ghastly face. She was stricken with pity for him.

"Shall we walk on this way?" she said, touching his arm.

He shook off her touch but followed her away from the busy track of the workers, along a quieter path among the trees. Sheltered from observation, she slowed her steps and turned towards him.

"She loves him?" he said in a low husky voice. "You say she loves him?"

"Yes, Mr. Switzer, she loves him," said Jane. "She cannot help herself. No one can help one's self. You must not blame her for that, Mr. Switzer."

"She does not love me," said Switzer as if stunned by the utterly inexplicable phenomenon. "But she did once," he cried. "She did before that schwein came." No words could describe the hate and contempt in his voice. He appeared to concentrate his passions struggling for expression, love, rage, hate, wounded pride, into one single stream of fury. Grinding his teeth, foaming, sputtering, he poured forth his words in an impetuous torrent.

"He stole her from me! this schwein of an Englishman! He came like a thief, like a dog and a dog's son and stole her! She was mine! She would have been mine! She loved me! She was learning to love me. I was too quick with her once, but she had forgiven me and was learning to love me. But this pig!" He gnashed his teeth upon the word.

"Stop, Mr. Switzer," said Jane, controlling her agitation and her terror. "You must not speak to me like that. You are forgetting yourself."

"Forgetting myself!" he raged, his face livid blue and white. "Forgetting myself! Yes, yes! I forget everything but one thing. That I shall not forget. I shall not forget him nor how he stole her from me. Gott in Himmel! Him I shall never forget. No, when these hairs are white," he struck his head with his clenched fist, "I shall still remember and curse him." Abruptly he stayed the rush of his words. Then more deliberately but with an added intensity of passion he continued, "But no, never shall he have her. Never. God hears me. Never. Him I will kill, destroy." He had wrought himself up into a paroxysm of uncontrollable fury, his breath came in jerking gasps, his features worked with convulsive twitchings, his jaws champed and snapped upon his words like a dog's worrying rats.

To Jane it seemed a horrible and repulsive sight, yet she could not stay her pity from him. She remembered it was love that had moved him to this pitch of madness. Love after all was a terrible thing. She could not despise him. She could only pity. Her very silence at length recalled him. For some moments he stood struggling to regain his composure. Gradually he became aware that her eyes were resting on his face. The pity in her eyes touched him, subdued him, quenched the heat of his rage.

"I have lost her," he said, his lips quivering. "She will never change."

"No, she will never change," replied Jane gently. "But you can always love her. And she will be happy."

"She will be happy?" he exclaimed, looking at her in astonishment. "But she will not be mine."

"No, she will not be yours," said Jane still very gently, "but she will be happy, and after all, that is what you most want. You are anxious chiefly that she shall be happy. You would give everything to make her happy."

"I would give my life. Oh, gladly, gladly, I would give my life, I would give my soul, I would give everything I have on earth and heaven too."

"Then don't grieve too much," said Jane, putting her hand on his arm. "She will be happy."

"But what of me?" he cried pitifully, his voice and lips trembling like those of a little child in distress. "Shall I be happy?"

"No, not now," replied Jane steadily, striving to keep back her tears, "perhaps some day. But you will think more of her happiness than of your own. Love, you know, seeks to make happy rather than to be happy."

For some moments the man stood as if trying to understand what she had said. Then with a new access of grief and rage, he cried, "But my God! My God! I want her. I cannot live without her. I could make her happy too."

"No, never," said Jane. "She loves him."

"Ach—so. Yes, she loves him, and I—hate him. He is the cause of this. Some day I will kill him. I will kill him."

"Then she would never be happy again," said Jane, and her face was full of pain and of pity.

"Go away," he said harshly. "Go away. You know not what you say. Some day I shall make him suffer as I suffer to-day. God hears me. Some day." He lifted his hands high above his head. Then with a despairing cry, "Oh, I have lost her, I have lost her," he turned from Jane and rushed into the woods.

Shaken, trembling and penetrated with pity for him, Jane made her way toward the office, near which she found Larry with the manager discussing an engineering problem which appeared to interest them both.

"Where's Ernest?" inquired Larry.

"He has just gone," said Jane, struggling to speak quietly. "I think we must hurry, Larry. Come, please. Good-bye, Mr. Steinberg." She hurried away toward the horses, leaving Larry to follow.

"What is it, Jane?" said Larry when they were on their way.

"Why didn't you tell me, Larry, that he was fond of Kathleen?" she cried indignantly. "I hurt him terribly, and, oh, it was awful to see a man like that."

"What do you say? Did he cut up rough?" said Larry.

Jane made no reply, but her face told its own story of shock and suffering.

"He need not have let out upon you, Jane, anyway," said Larry.

"Don't, Larry. You don't understand. He loves Kathleen. You don't know anything about it. How can you?"

"Oh, he will get over it in time," said Larry with a slight laugh.

Jane flashed on him a look of indignation. "Oh, how can you, Larry? It was just terrible to see him. But you do not know," she added with a touch of bitterness unusual with her.

"One thing I do know," said Larry. "I would not pour out my grief on some one else. I would try to keep it to myself."

Ralph Connor

But Jane refused to look at him or to speak again on the matter. Never in her sheltered life had there been anything suggesting tragedy. Never had she seen a strong man stricken to the heart as she knew this man to be stricken. The shadow of that tragedy stayed with her during all the remaining days of her visit. The sight of Kathleen's happy face never failed to recall the face of the man who loved her distorted with agony and that cry of despair, "I have lost her, I have lost her."

Not that her last days at the ranch were not happy days. She was far too healthy and wholesome, far too sane to allow herself to miss the gladness of those last few days with her friends where every moment offered its full measure of joy. Nora would have planned a grand picnic for the last day on which the two households, including Jack Romayne, who by this time was quite able to go about, were to pay a long-talked-of visit to a famous canyon in the mountains. The party would proceed to the canyon in the two cars, for Mr. Wakeham's car and Mr. Wakeham's person as driver had been constantly at the service of the Gwynnes and their guests during their stay at the farm.

"But that is our very last day, Nora," said Jane.

"Well, that's just why," replied Nora. "We shall wind up our festivities in one grand, glorious finale."

But the wise mother interposed. "It is a long ride, Nora, and you don't want to be too tired for your journey. I think the very last day we had better spend quietly at home."

Jane's eyes flashed upon her a grateful look. And so it came that the grand finale was set back to the day before the last, and proved to be a gloriously enjoyable if exhausting outing. The last day was spent by Nora in making preparations for her visit with Jane to Banff and in putting the final touches to such household tasks as might help to lessen somewhat the burden for those who would be left behind. Jane spent the morning in a farewell visit to the Waring-Gaunts', which she made in company with Kathleen.

"I hope, my dear Jane, you have enjoyed your stay with us here at Wolf Willow," said Mrs. Waring-Gaunt as Jane was saying good-bye.

"I have been very happy," said Jane. "Never in my life have I had such a happy time."

"Now it is good of you to say that," said Mrs. Waring-Gaunt. "You have made us all love you."

"Quite true," said her husband. "Repetition of the great Caesar's experience veni vidi vici, eh? What?"

"So say I," said Jack Romayne. "It has been a very real pleasure to know you, Jane. For my part, I shan't forget your visit to me, and the talks we have had together."

"You have all been good to me. I cannot tell you how I feel about it." Jane's voice was a little tremulous, but her smile was as bright as ever. "I don't believe I shall ever have such a perfectly happy visit again."

"What nonsense, my dear," said Mrs. Waring-Gaunt. "I predict many, many very happy days for you. You have that beautiful gift of bringing your joy with you."

Jack accompanied them on their way to the road. "Kathleen and I are hoping that perhaps you may be able to come to our wedding. It will be very soon—in a few weeks."

"Yes, could you, Jane, dear?" said Kathleen. "We should like it above everything else. I know it is a long, long journey, but if you could."

"When is it to be?" said Jane.

"Somewhere about the middle of October." But Jane shook her head disconsolately. By that time she knew she would be deep in her university work, and with Jane work ever came before play.

"I am afraid not," she said. "But, oh, I do wish you all the happiness in the world. Nothing has ever made me so glad. Oh, but you will be happy, I know. Both of you are so lovely." A sudden rush of tears filled the deep dark eyes as she shook hands with Jack in farewell. "But," she cried in sudden rapture, "why not come to us for a day on your wedding trip?"

"That's a splendid idea." For a moment or two Jack and Kathleen stood looking at each other.

"Jane, we shall surely come. You may count on us," said Jack.

In the afternoon Mrs. Gwynne sent Jane away for a ride with Larry.

"Just go quietly, Larry," said his mother. "Don't race and don't tire Jane."

"I will take care of her," said Larry, "but I won't promise that we won't race. Jane would not stand for that, you know. Besides she is riding Ginger, and Ginger is not exactly like old Polly. But never fear, we shall have a good ride, Mother," he added, waving his hand gaily as they rode away, taking the coolee trail to the timber lot.

Larry was in high spirits. He talked of his work for the winter. He was hoping great things from this his last year in college. For the first time in his university career he would be able to give the full term to study. He would be a couple of weeks late on account of Kathleen's marriage, but he would soon make that up. He had his work well in hand and this year he meant to do something worth while. "I should like to take that medal home to Mother," he said with a laugh. "I just fancy I see her face. She would try awfully hard not to seem proud, but she would just be running over with it." Jane gave, as ever, a sympathetic hearing but she had little to say, even less than was usual with her. Her smile, however, was as quick and as bright as ever, and Larry chattered on beside her apparently unaware of her silence. Up the coolee and through the woods and back by the dump their trail led them. On the way home they passed the Switzer house.

"Have you seen Mr. Switzer?" said Jane.

"No, by Jove, he hasn't been near us for a week, has he?" replied Larry.

"Poor man, I feel so sorry for him," said Jane.

"Oh, he will be all right. He is busy with his work. He is awfully keen about that mine of his, and once the thing is over—after Kathleen is married, I mean—it will be different."

Jane rode on in silence for some distance. Then she said,

"I wonder how much you know about it, Larry. I don't think you know the very least bit."

"Well, perhaps not," said Larry cheerfully, "but they always get over it."

Ralph Connor

"Oh, do they?" said Jane. "I wonder."

And again she rode on listening in silence to Larry's chatter.

"You will have a delightful visit at Banff, Jane. Do you know Wakeham is going to motor up? He is to meet his father there. He asked me to go with him," and as he spoke Larry glanced at her face.

"That would be splendid for you, Larry," she said, "but you couldn't leave them at home with all the work going on, could you?"

"No," said Larry gloomily, "I do not suppose I could. But I think you might have let me say that."

"But it is true, isn't it, Larry?" said Jane.

"Yes, it's true, and there's no use talking about it, and so I told him. But," he said, cheering up again, "I have been having a holiday these two weeks since you have been here."

"I know," said Jane remorsefully, "we must have cut into your work dreadfully."

"Yes, I have loafed a bit, but it was worth while. What a jolly time we have had! At least, I hope you have had, Jane."

"You don't need to ask me, do you, Larry?"

"I don't know. You are so dreadfully secretive as to your feelings, one never knows about you."

"Now, you are talking nonsense," replied Jane hotly.

"You know quite well that I have enjoyed every minute of my visit here."

They rode in silence for some time, then Larry said, "Jane, you are the best chum a fellow ever had. You never expect a chap to pay you special attention or make love to you. There is none of that sort of nonsense about you, is there?"

"No, Larry," said Jane simply, but she kept her face turned away from him.

CHAPTER XVIII

THE VOICE IN THE WILDERNESS

The results of the University examinations filled three sheets of the Winnipeg morning papers. With eager eyes and anxious hearts hundreds of the youth of Manitoba and the other western provinces scanned these lists. It was a veritable Day of Judgment, a day of glad surprises for the faithful in duty and the humble in heart, a day of Nemesis for the vainly self-confident slackers who had grounded their hopes upon eleventh hour cramming and lucky shots in exam papers. There were triumphs which won universal approval, others which received grudging praise.

Of the former, none of those, in the Junior year at least, gave more general satisfaction than did Jane Brown's in the winning of the German prize over Heinrich Kellerman, and for a number of reasons. In the first place Jane beat the German in his own language, at his own game, so to speak. Then, too, Jane, while a hard student, took her full share in college activities, and carried through these such a spirit of generosity and fidelity as made her liked and admired by the whole body of the students. Kellerman, on the other hand, was of that species of student known as a pot-hunter, who took no interest in college life, but devoted himself solely to the business of getting for himself everything that the college had to offer.

Perhaps Jane alone, of his fellow students, gave a single thought to the disappointment of the little Jew. She alone knew how keenly he had striven for the prize, and how surely he had counted upon winning it. She had the feeling, too, that somehow the class lists did not represent the relative scholarship of the Jew and herself. He knew more German than she. It was this feeling that prompted her to write him a note which brought an answer in formal and stilted English.

"Dear Miss Brown," the answer ran, "I thank you for your beautiful note, which is so much like yourself that in reading it I could see your smile, which so constantly characterises you to all your friends. I confess to disappointment, but the disappointment is largely mitigated by the knowledge that the prize which I failed to acquire went to one who is so worthy of it, and for whom I cherish the emotions of profound esteem and good will. Your devoted and disappointed rival, Heinrich Kellerman."

"Rather sporting of him, isn't it?" said Jane to her friend Ethel Murray, who had come to dinner.

"Sporting?" said Ethel. "It is the last thing I would have said about Kellerman."

"That is the worst of prizes," said Jane, "some one has to lose."

"Just the way I feel about Mr. MacLean," said Ethel. "He ought to have had the medal and not I. He knows more philosophy in a minute than I in a week."

"Oh, I wouldn't say that," said Jane judicially. "And though I am awfully glad you got it, Ethel, I am sorry for Mr. MacLean. You know he is working his way through college, and has to keep up a mission through the term. He is a good man."

"Yes, he is good, a little too good," said Ethel, making a little face. "Isn't it splendid about Larry Gwynne getting the Proficiency, and the first in Engineering? Now he is what I call a sport. Of course he doesn't go in for games much, but he's into everything, the Lit., the Dramatic Society, and Scuddy says he helped him tremendously with the Senior class in the Y. M. C. A. work."

"Yes," said Jane, "and the Register told Papa that the University had never graduated such a brilliant student. And Ramsay Dunn told me that he just ran the Athletic Association and was really responsible for the winning of the track team."

"What a pity about Ramsay Dunn," said Ethel. "He just managed to scrape through. Do you know, the boys say he kept himself up mostly on whiskey-and-sodas through the exams. He must be awfully clever, and he is so good-looking."

"Poor Ramsay," said Jane, "he has not had a very good chance. I mean, he has too much money. He is coming to dinner to-night, Ethel, and Frank Smart, too."

"Oh, Frank Smart! They say he is doing awfully well. Father says he is one of the coming men in his profession. He is a great friend of yours, isn't he, Jane?" said Ethel, with a meaning smile.

"We have known him a long time," said Jane, ignoring the smile. "We think a great deal of him."

"When have you seen Larry?" enquired Ethel. "He comes here a lot, doesn't he?"

"Yes. He says this is his Winnipeg home. I haven't seen him all to-day."

"You don't mean to tell me!" exclaimed Ethel.

"I mean I haven't seen him to congratulate him on his medal. His mother will be so glad."

"You know his people, don't you? Tell me about them. You see, I may as well confess to you that I have a fearful crush on Larry."

"I know," said Jane sympathetically.

"But," continued Ethel, "he is awfully difficult. His people are ranching, aren't they? And poor, I understand."

"Yes, they are ranching," said Jane, "and Larry has had quite a hard time getting through. I had a lovely visit last fall with them."

"Oh, tell me about it!" exclaimed Ethel. "I heard a little, you know, from Larry."

For half an hour Jane dilated on her western visit to the Lakeside Farm.

"Oh, you lucky girl!" cried Ethel. "What a chance you had! To think of it! Three weeks, lonely rides, moonlight, and not a soul to butt in! Oh, Jane! I only wish I had had such a chance! Did nothing happen, Jane? Oh, come on now, you are too awfully oysteresque. Didn't he come across at all?"

Jane's face glowed a dull red, but she made no pretence of failing to understand Ethel's meaning. "Oh, there is no nonsense of that kind with Larry," she said. "We are just good friends."

"Good friends!" exclaimed Ethel indignantly. "That's just where he is so awfully maddening. I can't understand him. He has lots of red blood, and he is a sport, too. But somehow he never knows a girl from her brother. He treats me just the way he treats Bruce and Leslie. I often wonder what he would do if I kissed him. I've tried squeezing his hand."

"Have you?" said Jane, with a delighted laugh. "What did he do?"

"Why, he never knew it. I could have killed him," said Ethel in disgust.

"He is going away to Chicago," said Jane abruptly, "to your friends, the Wakehams. Mr. Wakeham is in mines, as you know. Larry is to get two thousand dollars to begin with. It is a good position, and I am glad for him. Oh, there I see Mr. MacLean and Frank Smart coming in."

When the party had settled down they discussed the Class lists and prize winners till Dr. Brown appeared.

"Shall we have dinner soon, Jane?" he said as she welcomed him. "I wish to get through with my work early so as to take in the big political meeting this evening. Mr. Allen is to speak and there is sure to be a crowd."

"I shall have it served at once, Papa. Larry is coming, but we won't wait for him."

They were half through dinner before Larry appeared. He

came in looking worn, pale and thinner even than usual. But there was a gleam in his eye and an energy in his movements that indicated sound and vigorous health.

"You are not late, Larry," said Jane; "we are early. Papa is going to the political meeting."

"Good!" cried Larry. "So am I. You are going, Frank, and you, MacLean?"

"I don't know yet," said MacLean.

"We are all due at Mrs. Allen's, Larry, you remember. It is a party for the Graduating Class, too," said Jane.

"So we are. But we can take in the political meeting first, eh, Mac?"

But MacLean glanced doubtfully at Ethel.

"I have just had a go with Holtzman," said Larry, "the German Socialist, you know. He was ramping and raging like a wild man down in front of the post office. I know him quite well. He is going to heckle Mr. Allen to-night."

The girls were keen to take in the political meeting, but Larry objected.

"There will be a rough time, likely. It will be no place for ladies. We will take you to the party, then join you again after the meeting."

The girls were indignant and appealed to Dr. Brown.

"I think," said he, "perhaps you had better not go. The young gentlemen can join you later, you know, at Allens' party."

"Oh, we don't want them then," said Ethel, "and, indeed, we can go by ourselves to the party."

"Now, Ethel, don't be naughty," said Larry.

"I shall be very glad to take you to the party, Miss Murray," said MacLean. "I don't care so much for the meeting."

"That will be fine, Mac!" exclaimed Larry enthusiastically. "In this way neither they nor we will need to hurry."

"Disgustingly selfish creature," said Ethel, making a face at him across the table.

Jane said nothing, but her face fell into firmer lines and her cheeks took on a little colour. The dinner was cut short in order to allow Dr. Brown to get through with his list of waiting patients.

"We have a few minutes, Ethel," said Larry. "Won't you give us a little Chopin, a nocturne or two, or a bit of Grieg?"

"Do, Ethel," said Jane, "although you don't deserve it, Larry. Not a bit," she added.

"Why, what have I done?" said Larry.

"For one thing," said Jane, in a low, hurried voice, moving close to him, "you have not given me a chance to congratulate you on your medal. Where have you been all day?"

The reproach in her eyes and voice stirred Larry to quick defence. "I have been awfully busy, Jane," he said, "getting ready to go off to-morrow. I got a telegram calling me to Chicago."

"To Chicago? To-morrow?" said Jane, her eyes wide open with surprise. "And you never came to tell me—to tell us? Why, we may never see you again at all. But you don't care a bit, Larry," she added.

The bitterness in her voice was so unusual with Jane that Larry in his astonishment found himself without reply.

"Excuse me, Ethel," she said, "I must see Ann a minute."

As she hurried from the room Larry thought he caught a glint of tears in her eyes. He was immediately conscience-stricken and acutely aware that he had not treated Jane with the consideration that their long and unique friendship demanded. True, he had been busy, but he could have found time for a few minutes with her. Jane was no ordinary friend. He had not considered her and this had deeply wounded her. And to-morrow he was going away, and going away not to return. He was surprised at the quick stab of pain that came with the thought that his days in Winnipeg were over. In all likelihood his life's work would take him to Alberta. This meant that when he left Winnipeg tomorrow there would be an end to all that delightful comradeship with Jane which during the years of his long and broken college course had formed so large a part of his life, and which during the past winter had been closer and dearer than ever. Their lives would necessarily drift apart. Other friends would come in and preoccupy her mind and heart. Jane had the art of making friends and of "binding her friends to her with hooks of steel." He had been indulging the opinion that of all her friends he stood first with her. Even if he were right, he could not expect that this would continue. And now on their last evening together, through

Ralph Connor

his selfish stupidity, he had hurt her as never in all the years they had been friends together. But Jane was a sensible girl. He would make that right at once. She was the one girl he knew that he could treat with perfect frankness. Most girls were afraid, either that you were about to fall in love with them, or that you would not. Neither one fear nor the other disturbed the serenity of Jane's soul.

As Jane re-entered the room, Larry sprang to meet her. "Jane," he said in a low, eager tone, "I am going to take you to the party."

But Jane was her own serene self again, and made answer, "There is no need, Larry. Mr. MacLean will see us safely there, and after the meeting you will come. We must go now, Ethel." There was no bitterness in her voice. Instead, there was about her an air of gentle self-mastery, remote alike from pain and passion, that gave Larry the feeling that the comfort he had thought to bring was so completely unnecessary as to seem an impertinence. Jane walked across to where Frank Smart was standing and engaged him in an animated conversation.

As Larry watched her, it gave him a quick sharp pang to remember that Frank Smart was a friend of older standing than he, that Smart was a rising young lawyer with a brilliant future before him. He was a constant visitor at this house. Why was it? Like a flash the thing stood revealed to him. Without a doubt Smart was in love with Jane. His own heart went cold at the thought. But why? he impatiently asked himself. He was not in love with Jane. Of that he was quite certain. Why, then, this dog-in-the-manger feeling? A satisfactory answer to this was beyond him. One thing only stood out before his mind with startling clarity, if Jane should give herself to Frank Smart, or, indeed, to any other, then for him life would be emptied of one of its greatest joys. He threw down the music book whose leaves he had been idly turning and, looking at his watch, called out, "Do you know it is after eight o'clock, people?"

"Come, Ethel," said Jane, "we must go. And you boys will have to hurry. Larry, don't wait for Papa. He will likely have a seat on the platform. Good night for the present. You can find your way out, can't you? And, Mr. MacLean, you will find something to do until we come down?"

Smiling over her shoulder, Jane took Ethel off with her upstairs.

"Come, Smart, let's get a move on," said Larry, abruptly seizing his hat and making for the door. "We will have to fight to get in now."

The theatre was packed, pit to gods. Larry and his friend with considerable difficulty made their way to the front row of those standing, where they found a group of University men, who gave them enthusiastic welcome to a place in their company. The Chairman had made his opening remarks, and the first speaker, the Honourable B. B. Bomberton, was well on into his oration by the time they arrived. He was at the moment engaged in dilating upon the peril through which the country had recently passed, and thanking God that Canada had loyally stood by the Empire and had refused to sell her heritage for a mess of pottage.

"Rot!" cried a voice from the first gallery, followed by cheers and counter cheers.

The Honourable gentleman, however, was an old campaigner and not easily thrown out of his stride. He fiercely turned upon his interrupter and impaled him upon the spear point of his scornful sarcasm, waving the while with redoubled vigour, "the grand old flag that for a thousand years had led the embattled hosts of freedom in their fight for human rights."

"Rot!" cried the same voice again. "Can the flag stuff. Get busy and say something." (Cheers, counter cheers, yells of "Throw him out," followed by disturbance in the gallery.)

Once more the speaker resumed his oration. He repeated his statement that the country had been delivered from a great peril. The strain upon the people's loyalty had been severe, but the bonds that bound them to the Empire had held fast, and please God would ever hold fast. (Enthusiastic demonstration from all the audience, indicating intense loyalty to the Empire.) They had been invited to enter into a treaty for reciprocal trade with the Republic south of us. He would yield to none in admiration, even affection, for their American neigh-bours. He knew them well; many of his warmest friends were citizens of that great Republic. But great as was his esteem for that Republic he was not prepared to hand over his country to any other people, even his American neighbours, to be exploited and finally to be led into financial bondage. He proceeded further to elaborate and illustrate the financial calamity that would overtake the Dominion of Canada as a result of the establishment of Reciprocity between the Dominion and the Republic. But there was more than that. They all knew that ancient political maxim "Trade follows the flag." But like most proverbs it was only half a truth. The other half was equally true that "The flag followed trade." There was an example of that within their own Empire. No nation in the world had a prouder record for loyalty than Scotland. Yet in 1706 Scotland was induced to surrender her independence as a nation and to enter into union with

England. Why? Chiefly for the sake of trade advantages.

"Ye're a dom leear," shouted an excited Scot, rising to his feet in the back of the hall. "It was no Scotland that surrendered. Didna Scotland's king sit on England's throne. Speak the truth, mon." (Cheers, uproarious laughter and cries, "Go to it, Scotty; down wi' the Sassenach. Scotland forever!")

When peace had once more fallen the Honourable B. B. Bomberton went on. He wished to say that his Scottish friend had misunderstood him. He was not a Scot himself—

"Ye needna tell us that," said the Scot. (Renewed cheers and laughter.)

But he would say that the best three-quarters of him was Scotch in that he had a Scotch woman for a wife, and nothing that he had said or could say could be interpreted as casting a slur upon that great and proud and noble race than whom none had taken a larger and more honourable part in the building and the maintaining of the Empire. But to resume. The country was asked for the sake of the alleged economic advantage to enter into a treaty with the neighbouring state which he was convinced would perhaps not at first but certainly eventually imperil the Imperial bond. The country rejected the proposal. The farmers were offered the double lure of high prices for their produce and a lower price for machinery. Never was he so proud of the farmers of his country as when they resisted the lure, they refused the bait, they could not be bought, they declined to barter either their independence or their imperial allegiance for gain. (Cheers, groans, general uproar.)

Upon the subsidence of the uproar Frank Smart who, with

Larry, had worked his way forward among a body of students standing in the first row immediately behind the seats, raised his hand and called out in a clear, distinct and courteous voice, "Mr. Chairman, a question if you will permit me." The chairman granted permission. "Did I understand the speaker to say that those Canadians who approved of the policy of Reciprocity were ready to barter their independence or their imperial allegiance for gain? If so, in the name of one half of the Canadian people I want to brand the statement as an infamous and slanderous falsehood."

Instantly a thousand people were on their feet cheering, yelling, on the one part shouting, "Put him out," and on the other demanding, "Withdraw." A half dozen fights started up in different parts of the theatre. In Smart's immediate vicinity a huge, pugilistic individual rushed toward him and reached for him with a swinging blow, which would undoubtedly have ended for him the meeting then and there had not Larry, who was at his side, caught the swinging arm with an upward cut so that it missed its mark. Before the blow could be repeated Scudamore, the centre rush of the University football team, had flung himself upon the pugilist, seized him by the throat and thrust him back and back through the crowd, supported by a wedge of his fellow students, striking, scragging, fighting and all yelling the while with cheerful vociferousness. By the efforts of mutual friends the two parties were torn asunder just as a policeman thrust himself through the crowd and demanded to know the cause of the uproar.

"Here," he cried, seizing Larry by the shoulder, "what does this mean?"

"Don't ask me," said Larry, smiling pleasantly at him. "Ask that fighting man over there."

"You were fighting. I saw you," insisted the policeman.

"Did you?" said Larry. "I am rather pleased to hear you say it, but I knew nothing of it."

"Look here, Sergeant," shouted Smart above the uproar. "Oh, it's you, Mac. You know me. You've got the wrong man. There's the man that started this thing. He deliberately attacked me. Arrest him."

Immediately there were clamorous counter charges and demands for arrest of Smart and his student crew.

"Come now," said Sergeant Mac, "keep quiet, or I'll be takin' ye all into the coop."

Order once more being restored, the speaker resumed by repudiating indignantly the accusation of his young friend. Far be it from him to impugn the loyalty of the great Liberal party, but he was bound to say that while the Liberals might be themselves loyal both to the Dominion and to the Empire, their policy was disastrous. They were sound enough in their hearts but their heads were weak. After some further remarks upon the fiscal issues between the two great political parties and after a final wave of the imperial flag, the speaker declared that he now proposed to leave the rest of the time to their distinguished fellow citizen, the Honourable J. J. Allen.

Mr. Allen found himself facing an audience highly inflamed with passion and alert for trouble. In a courteous and pleasing introduction he strove to allay their excited feelings and to win for himself a hearing. The matter which he proposed to bring to their attention was one of the very greatest importance, and one which called for calm and deliberate consideration. He only asked a hearing for some facts which every Canadian ought to know and for some arguments based thereupon which they might receive or reject according as they appealed to them or not.

"You are all right, Jim; go to it," cried an enthusiastic admirer.

With a smile Mr. Allen thanked his friend for the invitation and assured him that without loss of time he would accept it. He begged to announce his theme: "The Imperative and Pressing Duty of Canada to Prepare to do Her Part in Defence of the Empire." He was prepared frankly and without hesitation to make the assertion that war was very near the world and very near our Empire and for the reason that the great military power of Europe, the greatest military power the world had ever seen—Germany—purposed to make war, was ready for war, and was waiting only a favourable opportunity to begin.

"Oh, r-r-rats-s," exclaimed a harsh voice.

"That's Holtzman," said Larry to Smart.

(Cries of "Shut up!—Go on.")

"I beg the gentleman who has so courteously interrupted me," continued Mr. Allen, "simply to wait for my facts." ("Hear! Hear!" from many parts of the building.) The sources of his information were three: first, his own observation during a three months' tour in Germany; second, his conversations with representative men in Great Britain, France and Germany; and third, the experience of a young and brilliant attache of the British Embassy at Berlin now living in Canada, with whom he had been brought into touch by a young University student at present in this city. From this latter source he had also obtained possession of literature accessible only to a few. He spoke with a full sense of responsibility and with a full appreciation of the value of words.

The contrast between the Honourable Mr. Allen and the speaker that preceded him was such that the audience was not only willing but eager to hear the facts and arguments which the speaker claimed to be in a position to offer. Under the first head he gave in detail the story of his visit to Germany and piled up an amazing accumulation of facts illustrative of Germany's military and naval preparations in the way of land and sea forces, munitions and munition factories, railroad construction, food supplies and financial arrangements in the way of gold reserves and loans. The preparations for war which, in the world's history, had been made by Great Powers threatening the world's freedom, were as child's play to these preparations now made by Germany, and these which he had given were but a few illustrations of Germany's war preparations, for the more important of these were kept hidden by her from the rest of the world. "My argument is that preparation by a nation whose commercial and economic instincts are so strong as those of the German people can only reasonably be interpreted to mean a Purpose to War. That that purpose exists and that that purpose determines Germany's world's politics, I have learned from many prominent Germans, military and naval officers, professors, bankers, preachers. And more than that this same purpose can be discovered in the works of many distinguished German writers during the last twenty-five years. You see this pile of books beside me? They are filled, with open and avowed declarations of this purpose. The raison d'etre of the great Pan-German League, of the powerful Navy League with one million and a half members, and of the other great German organisations is war. Bear with me while I read to you extracts from some of these writings. I respectfully ask a patient hearing. I would not did I not feel it to be important that from representative Germans themselves you should learn the dominating purpose that has directed and determined the course of German activity in every department of its national life for the last quarter of a century."

For almost half an hour the speaker read extracts from the pile of books on the table beside him. "I think I may now fairly claim to have established first the fact of vast preparations by Germany for war and the further fact that Germany cherishes in her heart a settled Purpose of War." It was interesting to know how this purpose had come to be so firmly established in the heart of a people whom we had always considered to be devoted to the cultivation of the gentler arts of peace. The history of the rise and the development of this Purpose to War would be found in the history of Germany itself. He then briefly touched upon the outstanding features in the history of the German Empire from the days of the great Elector of Brandenburg to the present time. During these last three hundred years, while the English people were steadily fighting for and winning their rights to freedom and self-government from tyrant kings, in Prussia two powers were being steadily built up, namely autocracy and militarism, till under Bismarck and after the War of 1870 these two powers were firmly established in the very fibre of the new modern German Empire. Since the days of Bismarck the autocrat of Germany had claimed the hegemony of Europe and had dreamed of winning for himself and his Empire a supreme place among the nations of the world. And this dream he had taught his people to share with him, for to them it meant not simply greater national glory, which had become a mania with them, but expansion of trade and larger commercial returns. And for the realisation of this dream, the German Kaiser and his people with him were ready and were waiting the opportunity to plunge the world into the bloodiest war of all time.

At some length the speaker proceeded to develop the idea of the necessary connection between autocracy and militarism, and the relation of autocratic and military power to wars of conquest. "The German Kaiser," he continued, "is ready for war as no would-be world conqueror in the world's history has ever been ready. The German Kaiser cherishes the purpose to make war, and this purpose is shared in and approved by the whole body of the German people." These facts he challenged any one to controvert. If these things were so, what should Canada do? Manifestly one thing only—she should prepare to do her duty in defending herself and the great Empire. "So far," he continued, "I have raised no controversial points. I have purposely abstained from dealing with questions that may be regarded from a partisan point of view. I beg now to refer to a subject which unhappily has become a matter of controversy in Canada—the subject, namely, of the construction of a Canadian Navy. [Disturbance in various parts of the building.] You have been patient. I earnestly ask you to be patient for a few moments longer. Both political parties fortunately are agreed upon two points; first, that Canada must do its share and is willing to do its share in the defence of the Empire. On this point all Canadians are at one, all Canadians are fully deter- mined to do their full duty to the Empire which has protected Canada during its whole history, and with which it is every loyal Canadian's earnest desire to maintain political connection. Second, Canada must have a Navy. Unfortunately, while we agree upon these two points, there are two points upon which we differ. First, we differ upon the method to be adopted in constructing our Navy and, second, upon the question of Navy control in war. In regard to the second point, I would only say that I should be content to leave the settlement of that question to the event. When war comes that question will speedily be settled, and settled, I am convinced, in a way consistent with what we all desire to preserve, Canadian

Ralph Connor

autonomy. In regard to the first, I would be willing to accept any method of construction that promised efficiency and speed, and with all my power I oppose any method that necessitates delay. Considerations of such questions as location of dockyards, the type of ship, the size of ship, I contend, are altogether secondary. The main consideration is speed. I leave these facts and arguments with you, and speaking not as a party politician but simply as a loyal Canadian and as a loyal son of the Empire, I would say, 'In God's name, for our country's honour and for the sake of our Empire's existence, let us with our whole energy and with all haste prepare for war.'"

The silence that greeted the conclusion of this address gave eloquent proof of the profound impression produced.

As the chairman rose to close the meeting the audience received a shock. The raucous voice of Holtzman was heard again demanding the privilege of asking two questions.

"The first question I would ask, Mr. Chairman, is this: Is not this immense war preparation of Germany explicable on the theory of the purpose of defence? Mr. Allen knows well that both on the eastern and southern frontiers Germany is threatened by the aggression of the Pan-Slavic movement, and to protect herself from this Pan-Slavic movement, together with a possible French alliance, the war preparations of Germany are none too vast. Besides, I would ask Mr. Allen, What about Britain's vast navy?"

"The answer to this question," said Mr. Allen, "is quite simple. What nation has threatened Germany for the past forty years? On the contrary, every one knows that since 1875 five separate times has Germany threatened war against France and twice against Russia. Furthermore military experts assure us that in defensive war an army equipped with modern weapons can hold off from four to eight times its own strength. It is absurd to say that Germany's military preparations are purely defensive. As for Britain's navy, the answer is equally simple. Britain's Empire is like no other Empire in the world in that it lies spread out upon the seven seas. It is essential to her very life that she be able to keep these waterways open to her ships. Otherwise she exists solely upon the sufferance of any nation that can wrest from her the supremacy of the sea. At her will Germany has the right to close against all the world the highways of her empire; the highways of Britain's empire are the open seas which she shares with the other nations of the world and which she cannot close. Therefore, these highways she must be able to make safe."

"If Mr. Allen imagines that this answer of his will satisfy any but the most bigoted Britain, I am content. Another question I would ask. Does not Mr. Allen think that if the capitalistic classes, who leave their burdens to be borne by the unhappy proletariat, were abolished wars would immediately cease? Does he not know that recently it was proved in Germany that the Krupps were found to be promoting war scares in France in the interests of their own infernal trade? And lastly does not history prove that Britain is the great robber nation of the world? And does he not think that it is time she was driven from her high place by a nation which is her superior, commercially, socially, intellectually and every other way?"

As if by a preconcerted signal it seemed as if the whole top gallery broke into a pandemonium of approving yells, while through other parts of the house arose fierce shouts, "Throw him out." Mr. Allen rose and stood quietly waiting till the tumult had ceased.

"If the gentleman wishes to engage me in a discussion on socialism, my answer is that this is not the time nor place for such a discussion. The question which I have been considering is one much too grave to be mixed up with an academic discussion of any socialistic theories."

"Aha! Aha!" laughed Holtzman scornfully.

"As for Britain's history, that stands for all the world to read. All the nations have been guilty of crimes; but let me say that any one who knows the history of Germany for the last three hundred years is aware that in unscrupulous aggression upon weaker neighbours, in treachery to friend and foe, Germany is the equal of any nation in the world. But if you consider her history since 1864 Germany stands in shameless and solitary pre-eminence above any nation that has ever been for unscrupulous greed, for brutal, ruthless oppression of smaller peoples, and for cynical disregard of treaty covenants, as witness Poland, Austria, Denmark, Holland and France. As to the treachery of the Krupps, I believe the gentleman is quite right, but I would remind him that the Kaiser has no better friend to-day than Bertha Krupp, and she is a German."

From every part of the theatre rose one mighty yell of delight and derision, during which Holtzman stood wildly gesticulating and shouting till a hand was seen to reach his collar and he disappeared from view. Once more order was restored and the chairman on the point of closing the meeting, when Larry said to his friend Smart:

"I should dearly love to take a hand in this."

"Jump in," said Smart, and Larry "jumped in."

"Mr. Chairman," he said quietly, "may I ask Mr. Allen

a question?"

"No," said the chairman in curt reply. "The hour is late and I think further discussion at present is unprofitable."

But here Mr. Allen interposed. "I hope, Mr. Chairman," he said, "you will allow my young friend, Mr. Gwynne, of whose brilliant achievements in our University we are all so proud, to ask his question."

"Very well," said the chairman in no good will.

"Allow me to thank Mr. Allen for his courtesy," said Larry. "Further I wish to say that though by birth, by training, and by conviction I am a pacifist and totally opposed to war, yet to-night I have been profoundly impressed by the imposing array of facts presented by the speaker and by the arguments built upon these facts, and especially by the fine patriotic appeal with which Mr. Allen closed his address. But I am not satisfied, and my question is this—"

"Will not Mr. Gwynne come to the platform?" said Mr. Allen.

"Thank you," said Larry, "I prefer to stay where I am, I am much too shy."

Cries of "Platform! Platform!" however, rose on every side, to which Larry finally yielded, and encouraged by the cheers of his fellow students and of his other friends in the audience, he climbed upon the platform. His slight, graceful form, the look of intellectual strength upon his pale face, his modest bearing, his humorous smile won sympathy even from those who were impatient at the prolonging of the meeting.

"Mr. Chairman," he began with an exaggerated look of fear upon his face, "I confess I am terrified by the position in which I find myself, and were it not that I feel deeply the immense importance of this question and the gravity of the appeal with which the speaker closed his address, I would not have ventured to say a word. My first question is this: Does not Mr. Allen greatly exaggerate the danger of war with Germany? And my reasons for this question are these. Every one knows that the relations between Great Britain and Germany have been steadily improving during the last two or three years. I note in this connection a statement made only a few months ago by the First Lord of the Admiralty, Mr. Winston Churchill. It reads as follows:

"'The Germans are a nation with robust minds and a high sense of honour and fair play. They look at affairs in a practical military spirit. They like to have facts put squarely before them. They do not want them wrapped up lest they should be shocked by them, and relations between the two countries have steadily improved during the past year. They have steadily improved side by side with every evidence of our determination to maintain our naval supremacy.'"

"These words spoken in the British House of Commons give us Mr. Winston Churchill's deliberate judgment as to the relations between Germany and Great Britain. Further Mr. Allen knows that during the past two years various peace delegations composed of people of the highest standing in each country have exchanged visits. I understand from private correspondence from those who have promoted these delegations that the last British delegation was received in Germany with the utmost enthusiasm by men of all ranks and professions, generals, admirals, burgomasters, professors and by the Kaiser himself, all professing devotion to the cause of peace and all wishing the delegation Godspeed. Surely these are indications that the danger of war is passing away. You, Sir, have made an appeal for war preparation tonight, a great and solemn appeal and a moving appeal for war—merciful God, for war! I have been reading about war during the past three months, I have been reading again Zola's Debacle—a great appeal for preparedness, you would say. Yes, but a terrific picture of the woes of war."

Larry paused. A great silence had fallen upon the people. There flashed across his mind as he spoke a vision of war's red, reeking way across the fair land of France. In a low but far-penetrating voice, thrilling with the agonies which were spread out before him in vision, he pictured the battlefield with its mad blood lust, the fury of men against men with whom they had no quarrel, the mangled ruins of human remains in dressing station and hospital, the white-faced, wild-eyed women waiting at home, and back of all, safe, snug and cynical, the selfish, ambitious promoters of war. Steady as a marching column without pause or falter, in a tone monotonous yet thrilling with a certain subdued passion, he gave forth his indictment of war. He was on familiar ground for this had been the theme of his prize essay last winter. But to-night the thing to him was vital, terrifying, horrible. He was delivering no set address, but with all the power of his soul he was pleading for comrades and friends, for wives and sweethearts, for little babes and for white-haired mothers, "and in the face of all this, you are asking us to prepare that we Canadians, peaceful and peace-loving, should do our share to perpetrate this unspeakable outrage upon our fellow men, this insolent affront against Almighty God. Tell me, if Canada, if Britain, were to expend one-tenth, one-hundredth part of the energy, skill, wealth, in promoting peace which they spend on war, do you not think we might have a surer hope of warding off from our Canadian homes this unspeakable horror?" With white

Ralph Connor

face and flaming eyes, his form tense and quivering, he stood facing the advocate of war. For some moments, during which men seemed scarcely to breathe, the two faced each other. Then in a voice that rang throughout the theatre as it had not in all his previous speech, but vibrant with sad and passionate conviction, Mr. Allen made reply.

"It is to ward off from our people and from our Canadian homes this calamity that you have so vividly pictured for us that I have made my appeal to-night. Your enemy who seeks your destruction will be more likely to halt in his spring if you cover him with your gun than if you appeal to him with empty hands. For this reason, it is that once more I appeal to my fellow Canadians in God's name, in the name of all that we hold dear, let us with all our power and with all speed prepare for war."

"God Save the King," said the Chairman. And not since the thrilling days of Mafeking had Winnipeg people sung that quaint archaic, but moving anthem as they sang it that night.

CHAPTER XIX

THE CLOSING OF THE DOOR

From the remarks of his friends even as they thronged him, offering congratulations, Mr. Allen could easily gather that however impressive his speech had been, few of his audience had taken his warning seriously.

"You queered my speech, Larry," he said, "but I forgive you."

"Not at all, Sir," replied Larry. "You certainly got me."

"I fear," replied Mr. Allen, "that I am 'the voice crying in the wilderness.'"

At the Allens' party Larry was overwhelmed with congratulations on his speech, the report of which had been carried before him by his friends.

"They tell me your speech was quite thrilling," said Mrs. Allen as she greeted Larry.

"Your husband is responsible for everything," replied Larry.

"No," said Mr. Allen, "Miss Jane here is finally

Ralph Connor

responsible. Hers were the big shells I fired."

"Not mine," replied Jane. "I got them from Mr. Romayne, your brother-in-law, Larry."

"Well, I'm blowed!" said Larry. "That's where the stuff came from! But it was mighty effective, and certainly you put it to us, Mr. Allen. You made us all feel like fighting. Even Scuddy, there, ran amuck for a while."

"What?" said Mr. Allen, "you don't really mean to say that Scudamore, our genial Y. M. C. A. Secretary, was in that scrap? That cheers me greatly."

"Was he!" said Ramsay Dunn, whose flushed face and preternaturally grave demeanour sufficiently explained his failure to appear at Dr. Brown's dinner. "While Mr. Smart's life was saved by the timely upper-cut of our distinguished pacifist, Mr. Gwynne, without a doubt Mr. Scudamore—hold him there, Scallons, while I adequately depict his achievement—" Immediately Scallons and Ted Tuttle, Scudamore's right and left supports on the scrimmage line, seized him and held him fast. "As I was saying," continued Dunn, "great as were the services rendered to the cause by our distinguished pacifist, Mr. Gwynne, the supreme glory must linger round the head of our centre scrim and Y. M. C. A. Secretary, Mr. Scudamore, to whose effective intervention both Mr. Smart and Mr. Gwynne owe the soundness of their physical condition which we see them enjoying at the present moment."

In the midst of his flowing periods Dunn paused abruptly and turned away. He had caught sight of Jane's face, grieved and shocked, in the group about him. Later he approached her with every appearance of profound humiliation. "Miss Brown," he said, "I must apologise for not appearing at dinner this evening."

"Oh, Mr. Dunn," said Jane, "why will you do it? Why break the hearts of all your friends?"

"Why? Because I am a fool," he said bitterly. "If I had more friends like you, Miss Brown," he paused abruptly, then burst forth, "Jane, you always make me feel like a beast." But Larry's approach cut short any further conversation.

"Jane, I want to talk to you," said Larry impetuously. "Let us get away somewhere."

In the library they found a quiet spot, where they sat down.

"I want to tell you," said Larry, "that I feel that I treated you shabbily to-day. I have only a poor excuse to offer, but I should like to explain."

"Don't, Larry," said Jane, her words coming with hurried impetuosity. "I was very silly. I had quite forgotten it. You know we have always told each other things, and I expected that you would come in this morning just to talk over your medal, and I did want a chance to say how glad I was for you, and how glad and how proud I knew your mother would be; and to tell the truth really," she added with a shy little laugh, "I wanted to have you congratulate me on my prize too. But, Larry, I understand how you forgot."

"Forgot!" said Larry. "No, Jane, I did not forget, but this telegram from Chicago came last night, and I was busy with my packing all morning and then in the afternoon I thought I would hurry through a few calls—they always take longer than one thinks—and before I knew it I was late for dinner. I had not forgotten; I was thinking of you all day, Jane."

"Were you, Larry?" said Jane, a gentle tenderness in her smile. "I am glad."

Then a silence fell between them for some moments. They were both thinking of the change that was coming to their lives. Larry was wondering how he would ever do without this true-hearted friend whose place in his life he was only discovering now to be so large. He glanced at her. Her eyes were glowing with a soft radiance that seemed to overflow from some inner spring.

"Jane," he cried with a sudden impulse, "you are lovely, you are perfectly lovely."

A shy, startled, eager look leaped into her eyes. Then her face grew pale. She waited, expectant, tremulous. But at that instant a noisy group passed into the library.

"Larry," whispered Jane, turning swiftly to him and laying her hand upon his arm, "you will take me home to-night."

"All right, Jane, of course," said Larry.

As they passed out from the library Helen Brookes met them. "Larry, come here," she said in a voice of suppressed excitement. "Larry, don't you want to do something for me? Scuddy wants to take me home tonight, and I don't want him to."

"But why not, Helen? You ought to be good to Scuddy, poor chap. He's a splendid fellow, and I won't have him abused."

"Not to-night, Larry; I can't have him to-night. You will

take me home, won't you? I am going very soon."

"You are, eh? Well, if you can go within ten minutes, I shall be ready."

"Say fifteen," said Helen, turning to meet Lloyd Rushbrook, the Beau Brummel of the college, who came claiming a dance.

Larry at once went in search of Jane to tell her of his engagement with Helen Brookes, but could find her nowhere, and after some time spent in a vain search, he left a message for her with his hostess. At the head of the stairs he found Helen waiting.

"Oh, hurry, Larry," she cried in a fever of excitement. "Let's get away quickly."

"Two minutes will do me," said Larry, rushing into the dressing room.

There he found Scudamore pacing up and down in fierce, gloomy silence.

"You are taking her home, Larry?" he said.

"Who?" said Larry. Then glancing at his face, he added, "Yes, Scuddy, I am taking Helen home. She is apparently in a great hurry."

"She need not be; I shall not bother her any more," said Scuddy bitterly, "and you can tell her that for me, if you like."

"No, I won't tell her that, Scuddy," said Larry, "and, Scuddy," he added, imparting a bit of worldly wisdom, "campaigns are not won in a single battle, and, Scuddy, remember too that the whistling fisherman catches the fish. So cheer up, old boy." But Scuddy only glowered at him.

Larry found Helen awaiting him, and quietly they slipped out together. "This is splendid of you, Larry," she said, taking his arm and giving him a little squeeze.

"I don't know about that, Helen. I left Scuddy raging upstairs there. You girls are the very devil for cruelty sometimes. You get men serious with you, then you flirt and flutter about till the unhappy wretches don't know where they are at. Here's our car."

"Car!" exclaimed Helen. "With this moonlight, Larry? And you going away to-morrow? Not if I know it."

"It is fearfully unromantic, Helen, I know. But I must hurry. I have to take Jane home."

"Oh, Jane! It's always Jane, Jane!"

"Well, why not?" said Larry. "For years Jane has been my greatest pal, my best friend."

"Nothing more?" said Helen earnestly. "Cross your heart, Larry."

"Nothing more, cross my heart and all the rest of it," replied Larry. "Why! here's another car, Helen."

"Oh, Larry, you are horrid, perfectly heartless! We may never walk together again. Here I am throwing myself at you and you only think of getting away back." Under her chaffing words there sounded a deeper note.

"So I see," said Larry, laughing and refusing to hear the

deeper undertone. "But I see something else as well."

"What?" challenged Helen.

"I see Scuddy leading out from Trinity some day the loveliest girl in Winnipeg."

"Oh, I won't talk about Scuddy," said Helen impatiently. "I want to talk about you. Tell me about this Chicago business."

For the rest of the way home she led Larry to talk of his plans for the future. At her door Helen held out her hand. "You won't come in, Larry, I know, so we will say good-bye here." Her voice was gentle and earnest. The gay, proud, saucy air which she had ever worn and which had been one of her chief charms, was gone. The moonlight revealed a lovely wistful face from which misty eyes looked into his. "This is the end of our good times together, Larry. And we have had good times. You are going to be a great man some day. I wish you all the best in life."

"Thank you, Helen," said Larry, touched by the tones of her voice and the look in her eyes. "We have been good friends. We shall never be anything else. With my heart I wish you—oh, just everything that is good, Helen dear. Good-bye," he said, leaning toward her. "How lovely you are!" he murmured.

"Good-bye, dear Larry," she whispered, lifting up her face.

"Good-bye, you dear girl," he said, and kissed her.

"Now go," she said, pushing him away from her.

"Be good to Scuddy," he replied as he turned from her and hurried away.

He broke into a run, fearing to be late, and by the time he arrived at the Allens' door he had forgotten all about Helen Brookes and was thinking only of Jane and of what he wanted to say to her. At the inner door he met Macleod and Ethel coming out.

"Jane's gone," said Ethel, "some time ago."

"Gone?" said Larry.

"Yes, Scuddy took her home."

"Are they all gone?" inquired Larry.

"Yes, for the most part."

"Oh, all right then; I think I shall not go in. Good-night," he said, turned abruptly about and set off for Dr. Brown's. He looked again at his watch. He was surprised to find it was not so very late. Why had Jane not waited for him? Had he hurt her again? He was sorely disappointed. Surely she had no reason to be offended, and this was his last night. As he thought the matter over he came to the conclusion that now it was he that had a grievance. Arrived at Dr. Brown's house the only light to be seen was in Jane's room upstairs. Should he go in or should he go home and wait till to-morrow. He was too miserable to think of going home without seeing her. He determined that he must see her at all cost to-night. He took a pebble and flung it up against her window, and another and another. The window opened and Jane appeared.

"Oh, Larry," she whispered. "Is it you? Wait, I shall be down."

She opened the door for him and stood waiting for him to speak. "Why didn't you wait?" he asked, passing into the hall. "I was not very long."

"Why should I wait, Larry?" she said quietly. "Scuddy told me you had gone home with Helen."

"But didn't I promise that I would take you home?"

"You did, and then went away."

"Well, all I have to say, Jane, is that this is not a bit like you. I am sorry I brought you down, and I won't keep you any longer. Good-night. I shall see you tomorrow."

But Jane got between him and the door and stood with her back to it. "No, Larry, you are not going away like that. Go into the study." Larry looked at her in astonishment. This was indeed a new Jane to him. Wrathful, imperious, she stood waving him toward the study door. In spite of his irritation he was conscious of a new admiration for her. Feeling a little like a boy about to receive his punishment, he passed into the study.

"Didn't Mrs. Allen give you my message?" he said.

"Your message, Larry?" cried Jane, a light breaking upon her face. "Did you leave a message for me?"

"I did. I told Mrs. Allen to tell you where I had gone— Helen was so anxious to go—and that I would be right back." Larry's voice was full of reproach.

"Oh, Larry, I am so glad," said Jane, her tone indicating the greatness of her relief. "I knew it was all right—that something had prevented. I am so glad you came in. You must have thought me queer."

"No," said Larry, appeased, "I knew all the time there must be some explanation, only I was feeling so miserable."

"And I was miserable, too, Larry," she said gently. "It seemed a pity that this should happen on our last night." All her wrath was gone. She was once more the Jane that Larry had always known, gentle, sweet, straightforward, and on her face the old transfiguring smile. Before this change of mood all his irritation vanished. Humbled, penitent, and with a rush of warm affection filling his heart, he said,

"I should have known you were not to blame, but you are always right. Never once in all these years have you failed me. You always understand a fellow. Do you know I am wondering how I shall ever do without you? Have you thought, Jane, that to-morrow this old life of ours together will end?"

"Yes, Larry." Her voice was low, almost a whisper, and in her eyes an eager light shone.

"It just breaks my heart, Jane. We have been—we are such good friends. If we had only fallen in love with each other.—But that would have spoiled it all. We are not like other people; we have been such chums, Jane."

"Yes, Larry," she said again, but the eager light had faded from her eyes.

"Let's sit a bit, Larry," she said. "I am tired, and you are tired, too," she added quickly, "after your hard day."

For a little time they sat in silence together, both shrinking from the parting that they knew was so near. Larry gazed at her, wondering to himself that he had ever thought her plain. Tonight she seemed beautiful and very dear to him. Next to his mother, was her place in his heart. Was this that he felt for her what they called love? With all his soul he wished he could take her in his arms and say, "Jane, I love you." But still he knew that his words would not ring true. More than that, Jane would know it too. Besides, might not her feeling for him be of the same quality? What could he say in this hour which he recognised to be a crisis in their lives? Sick at heart and oppressed with his feeling of loneliness and impotence, he could only look at her in speechless misery. Then he thought she, too, was suffering, the same misery was filling her heart. She looked utterly spent and weary.

"Jane," he said desperately. She started. She, too, had been thinking. "Scuddy is in love with Helen, Macleod is in love with Ethel. I wish to God I had fallen in love with you and you with me. Then we would have something to look forward to. Do you know, Jane, I am like a boy leaving home? We are going to drift apart. Others will come between us."

"No, Larry," cried Jane with quick vehemence. "Not that. You won't let that come."

"Can we help it, Jane?" Then her weariness appealed to him. "It is a shame to keep you up. I have given you a hard day, Jane." She shook her head. "And there is no use waiting. We can only say good-bye." He rose from his chair. Should he kiss her, he asked himself. He had had no hesitation in kissing Helen an hour ago. That seemed a light thing to him, but somehow he shrank from offering to kiss Jane. If he could only say sincerely, "Jane, I love you," then he could kiss her, but this he could not say truly. Anything but perfect sincerity he knew she would detect; and she would be outraged by it. Yet as he stood looking down upon her pale face, her wavering smile, her

Ralph Connor

quivering lips, he was conscious of a rush of pity and of tenderness almost uncontrollable.

"Good-bye, Jane; God keep you always, dear, dear Jane." He held her hands, looking into the deep blue eyes that looked back at him so bravely. He felt that he was fast losing his grip upon himself, and he must hurry away.

"Good-bye, Larry," she said simply.

"Good-bye," he said again in a husky voice. Abruptly he turned and left her and passed out through the door.

Sore, sick at heart, he stumbled down the steps. "My God," he cried, "what a fool I am! Why didn't I kiss her? I might have done that at least."

He stood looking at the closed door, struggling against an almost irresistible impulse to return and take her in his arms. Did he not love her? What other was this that filled his heart? Could he honestly say, "Jane, I want you for my wife"? He could not. Miserable and cursing himself he went his way.

CHAPTER XX

THE GERMAN TYPE OF CITIZENSHIP

Mr. Dean Wakeham was always glad to have a decent excuse to run up to the Lakeside Farm. His duties at the Manor Mine were not so pressing that he could not on occasion take leave of absence, but to impose himself upon the Lakeside household as frequently as he desired made it necessary for him to utilise all possible excuses. In the letter which he held in his hand and which he had just read he fancied he had found a perfectly good excuse for a call. The letter was from his sister Rowena and was dated May 15th, 1914. It was upon his sister's letters that he depended for information regarding the family life generally and about herself in particular. His mother's letters were intimate and personal, reflecting, however, various phases of her ailments, her anxieties for each member of the family, but especially for her only son now so far from her in that wild and uncivilised country, but ever overflowing with tender affection. Dean always put down his mother's letters with a smile of gentle pity on his face. "Poor, dear Mater," he would say. "She is at rest about me only when she has me safely tucked up in my little bed." His father's letters kept him in touch with the office and, by an illuminating phrase or two, with the questions of Big Business. But when he had finished Rowena's letters he always felt as if he had been paying a

Ralph Connor

visit to his home. Through her letters his sister had the rare gift of transmitting atmosphere. There were certain passages in his letter just received which he felt he should at the earliest moment share with the Lakeside Farm people, in other words, with Nora.

His car conveyed him with all speed to Lakeside Farm in good time for the evening meal. To the assembled family Dean proceeded to read passages which he considered of interest to them. "'Well, your Canadian has really settled down into his place in the office and into his own rooms. It was all we could do to hold him with us for a month, he is so fearfully independent. Are all Canadians like that? The Mater would have been glad to have had him remain a month longer. But would he stay? He has a way with him. He has struck up a terrific friendship with Hugo Raeder. You remember the Yale man who has come to Benedick, Frame and Company, father's financial people? Quite a presentable young man he is of the best Yale type, which is saying something. Larry and he have tied up to each other in quite a touching way. In the office, too, Larry has found his place. He captured old Scread the very first day by working out some calculations that had been allowed to accumulate, using some method of his own which quite paralysed the old chap. Oh, he has a way with him, that Canadian boy! Father, too, has fallen for him. To hear him talk you would imagine that he fully intended handing over ere long the business to Larry's care. The Mater has adopted him as well, but with reservations. Of course, what is troubling her is her dread of a Canadian invasion of her household, especially—'um um—" At this point Mr. Dean Wakeham read a portion of the letter to himself with slightly heightened colour. "'While as for Elfie, he has captured her, baggage and bones. The little monkey apparently lives only for him. While as for Larry, you would think that the office and the family were the merest side issues in comparison with the kid. All the same it is very beautiful to see them together. At times you would think they were the same age and both children. At other times she regards him with worshipful eyes and drinks in his words as if he were some superior being and she his equal in age and experience. She has taken possession of him, and never hesitates to carry him off to her own quarters, apparently to his delight. Oh, he has a way with him, that Canadian boy! The latest is that he has invited Elfie to stay a month with him in Alberta when he gets his first holiday. He has raved to her over Polly. Elfie, I believe, has accepted his invitation regardless of the wishes of either family. The poor little soul is really better, I believe, for his companionship. She is not so fretful and she actually takes her medicine without a fight and goes to bed at decent hours upon the merest hint of his Lordship's desire in the matter. In short, he has the family quite prostrate before him. I alone have been able to stand upright and maintain my own individuality.'"

"I am really awfully glad about the kid," said Dean. "After all she really has rather a hard time. She is so delicate and needs extra care and attention, and that, I am afraid, has spoiled her a bit."

"Why shouldn't the little girl spend a few weeks with us here this summer, Mr. Wakeham?" said Mrs. Gwynne. "Will you not say to your mother that we should take good care of her?"

"Oh, Mrs. Gwynne, that is awfully good of you, but I am a little afraid you would find her quite a handful. As I have said, she is a spoiled little monkey and not easy to do with. She would give you all a lot of trouble," added Dean, looking at Nora.

"Trouble? Not at all," said Nora. "She could do just as she

likes here. We would give her Polly and let her roam. And on the farm she would find a number of things to interest her."

"It would be an awfully good thing for her, I know," said Dean, vainly trying to suppress the eagerness in his tone, "and if you are really sure that it would not be too much of a burden I might write."

"No burden at all, Mr. Wakeham," said Mrs. Gwynne. "If you will write and ask Mrs. Wakeham, and bring her with you when you return, we shall do what we can to make her visit a happy one, and indeed, it may do the dear child a great deal of good."

Thus it came about that the little city child, delicate, fretted, spoiled, was installed in the household at Lakeside Farm for a visit which lengthened out far beyond its original limits. The days spent upon the farm were full of bliss to her, the only drawback to the perfect happiness of the little girl being the separation from her beloved fidus Achates, with whom she maintained an epistolary activity extraordinarily intimate and vivid. Upon this correspondence the Wakeham family came chiefly to depend for enlightenment as to the young lady's activities and state of health, and it came to be recognised as part of Larry's duty throughout the summer to carry a weekly bulletin regarding Elfie's health and manners to the Lake Shore summer home, where the Wakehams sought relief from the prostrating heat of the great city. These week ends at the Lake Shore home were to Larry his sole and altogether delightful relief from the relentless drive of business that even throughout the hottest summer weather knew neither let nor pause.

It became custom that every Saturday forenoon Rowena's big car would call at the Rookery Building and carry off her father, if he chanced to be in town, and Larry to the Lake Shore home. An hour's swift run over the perfect macadam of the Lake Shore road that wound through park and boulevard, past splendid summer residences of Chicago financial magnates, through quiet little villages and by country farms, always with gleams of Michigan's blue-grey waters, and always with Michigan's exhilarating breezes in their faces, would bring them to the cool depths of Birchwood's shades and silences, where for a time the hustle and heat and roar of the big city would be as completely forgotten as if a thousand miles away. It was early on a breathless afternoon late in July when from pavement and wall the quivering air smote the face as if blown from an opened furnace that Rowena drove her car down La Salle Street and pulled up at the Rookery Building resolved to carry off with her as a special treat "her men" for an evening at Birchwood.

"Come along, Larry, it is too hot to live in town today," she said as she passed through the outer office where the young man had his desk. "I am just going in to get father, so don't keep me waiting."

"Miss Wakeham, why will you add to the burdens of the day by breezing thus in upon us and making us discontented with our lot. I cannot possibly accept your invitation this afternoon."

"What? Not to-day, with the thermometer at ninety-four? Nonsense!" said the young lady brusquely. "You look fit to drop."

"It is quite useless," said Larry with a sigh. "You see we have a man in all the way from Colorado to get plans of a mine which is in process of reconstruction. These plans will take hours to finish. The work is pressing, in short must be done to-day."

"Now, look here, young man. All work in this office is pressing but none so pressing that it cannot pause at my command."

"But this man is due to leave to-morrow."

"Oh, I decline to talk about it; it is much too hot. Just close up your desk," said the young lady, as she swept on to her father's office.

In a short time she returned, bearing that gentleman in triumph with her. "Not ready?" she said. "Really you are most exasperating, Larry."

"You may as well throw up your hands, Larry. You'd better knock off for the day," said Mr. Wakeham. "It is really too hot to do anything else than surrender."

"You see, it is like this, sir," said Larry. "It is that Colorado mine reconstruction business. Their manager, Dimock, is here. He must leave, he says, tomorrow morning. Mr. Scread thinks he should get these off as soon as possible. So it is necessary that I stick to it till we get it done."

"How long will it take?" said Mr. Wakeham.

"I expect to finish to-night some time. I have already had a couple of hours with Dimock to-day. He has left me the data."

"Well, I am very sorry, indeed," said Mr. Wakeham. "It is a great pity you cannot come with us, and you look rather fagged. Dimock could not delay, eh?"

"He says he has an appointment at Kansas City which he must keep."

"Oh, it is perfect rubbish," exclaimed Rowena impatiently, "and we have a party on to-night. Your friend, Mr. Hugh Raeder, is to be out, and Professor Schaefer and a friend of his, and some perfectly charming girls."

"But why tell me these things now, Miss Wakeham," said Larry, "when you know it is impossible for me to come?"

"You won't come?"

"I can't come."

"Come along then, father," she said, and with a stiff little bow she left Larry at his desk.

Before the car moved off Larry came hurrying out.

"Here is Elfie's letter," he said. "Perhaps Mrs. Wakeham would like to see it." Miss Wakeham was busy at the wheel and gave no sign of having heard or seen. So her father reached over and took the letter from him.

"Do you know," said Larry gravely, "I do not think it is quite so hot as it was. I almost fancy I feel a chill."

"A chill?" said Mr. Wakeham anxiously. "What do you mean?"

Miss Wakeham bit her lip, broke into a smile and then into a laugh. "Oh, he's a clever thing, he is," she said. "I hope you may have a real good roast this afternoon."

"I hope you will call next Saturday," said Larry earnestly. "It is sure to be hot."

"You don't deserve it or anything else that is good."

"Except your pity. Think what I am missing."

"Get in out of the heat," she cried as the car slipped away.

For some blocks Miss Wakeham was busy getting her car through the crush of the traffic, but as she swung into the Park Road she remarked, "That young man takes himself too seriously. You would think the business belonged to him."

"I wish to God I had more men in my office," said her father, "who thought the same thing. Do you know, young lady, why it is that so many greyheads are holding clerk's jobs? Because clerks do not feel that the business is their own. The careless among them are working for five o'clock, and the keen among them are out for number one. Do you know if that boy keeps on thinking that the business is his he will own a big slice of it or something better before he quits. I confess I was greatly pleased that you failed to move him."

"All the same, he is awfully stubborn," said his daughter.

"You can't bully him as you do your old dad, eh?"

"I had counted on him for our dinner party to-night. I particularly want to have him meet Professor Schaefer, and now we will have a girl too many. It just throws things out."

They rolled on in silence for some time through the park when suddenly her father said, "He may be finished by six o'clock, and Michael could run in for him."

At six o'clock Miss Wakeham called Larry on the 'phone. "Are you still at it?" she enquired. "And when will you be finished?"

"An hour, I think, will see me through," he replied.

"Then," said Miss Wakeham, "a little before seven o'clock the car will be waiting at your office door."

"Hooray!" cried Larry. "You are an angel. I will be through."

At a quarter of seven Larry was standing on the pavement, which was still radiating heat, and so absorbed in watching for the Wakehams' big car that he failed to notice a little Mercer approaching till it drew up at his side.

"What, you, Miss Rowena?" he cried. "Your own self? How very lovely of you, and through all this heat!"

"Me," replied the girl, "only me. I thought it might still be hot and a little cool breeze would be acceptable. But jump in."

"Cool breeze, I should say so!" exclaimed Larry. "A lovely, cool, sweet spring breeze over crocuses and violets! But, I say, I must go to my room for my clothes."

"No evening clothes to-night," exclaimed Rowena.

"Ah, but I have a new, lovely, cool suit that I have been hoping to display at Birchwood. These old things would hardly do at your dinner table."

"We'll go around for it. Do get in. Do you know, I left my party to come for you, partly because I was rather nasty this afternoon?"

"You were indeed," said Larry. "You almost broke my heart, but this wipes all out; my heart is singing again.

That awfully jolly letter of Elfie's this week made me quite homesick for the open and for the breezes of the Alberta foothills."

"Tell me what she said," said Rowena, not because she wanted so much to hear Elfie's news but because she loved to hear him talk, and upon no subject could Larry wax so eloquent as upon the foothill country of Alberta. Long after they had secured Larry's new suit and gone on their way through park and boulevard, Larry continued to expatiate upon the glories of Alberta hills and valleys, upon its cool breezes, its flowing rivers and limpid lakes, and always the western rampart of the eternal snow-clad peaks.

"And how is the mine doing?" inquired Rowena, for Larry had fallen silent.

"The mine? Oh, there's trouble there, I am afraid. Switzer —you have heard of Switzer?"

"Oh, yes, I know all about him and his tragic disappointment. He's the manager, isn't he?"

"The manager? No, he's the secretary, but in this case it means the same thing, for he runs the mine. Well, Switzer wants to sell his stock. He and his father hold about twenty-five thousand dollars between them. He means to resign. And to make matters worse, the manager left last week. They are both pulling out, and it makes it all the worse, for they had just gone in for rather important extensions. I am anxious a bit. You see they are rather hard up for money, and father raised all he could on his ranch and on his mining stock."

"How much is involved?" inquired Rowena.

"Oh, not so much money as you people count it, but for us it is all we have. He raised some fifty thousand dollars. While the mine goes on and pays it is safe enough, but if the mine quits then it is all up with us. There is no reason for anxiety at present as far as the mine is concerned, however. It is doing splendidly and promises better every day. But Switzer's going will embarrass them terribly. He was a perfect marvel for work and he could handle the miners as no one else could. Most of them, you know, are his own people."

"I see you are worrying," said Rowena, glancing at his face, which she thought unusually pale.

"Not a bit. At least, not very much. Jack is a levelheaded chap—Jack Romayne, I mean—my brother-in-law. By the way, I had a wire to say that young Jack had safely arrived."

"Young Jack? Oh, I understand. Then you are Uncle Larry."

"I am. How ancient I feel! And what a lot of responsibility it lays upon me!"

"I hope your sister is quite well."

"Everything fine, so I am informed. But what was I saying? Oh, yes, Jack is a level-headed chap and his brother-in-law, Waring-Gaunt, who is treasurer of the company, is very solid. So I think there's no doubt but that they will be able to make all necessary arrangements."

"Well, don't worry to-night," said Rowena. "I want you to have a good time. I am particularly anxious that you should meet and like Professor Schaefer."

"A German, eh?" said Larry.

"Yes—that is, a German-American. He is a metallurgist, quite wonderful, I believe. He does a lot of work for father, and you will doubtless have a good deal to do with him yourself. And he spoke so highly of Canada and of Canadians that I felt sure you would be glad to meet him. He is really a very charming man, musical and all that, but chiefly he is a man of high intelligence and quite at the top of his profession. He asked to bring a friend of his with him, a Mr. Meyer, whom I do not know at all; but he is sure to be interesting if he is a friend of Professor Schaefer's. We have some nice girls, too, so we hope to have an interesting evening."

The company was sufficiently varied to forbid monotony, and sufficiently intellectual to be stimulating, and there was always the background of Big Business. Larry was conscious that he was moving amid large ideas and far-reaching interests, and that though he himself was a small element, he was playing a part not altogether insignificant, with a promise of bigger things in the future. Professor Schaefer became easily the centre of interest in the party. He turned out to be a man of the world. He knew great cities and great men. He was a connoisseur in art and something more than an amateur in music. His piano playing, indeed, was far beyond that of the amateur. But above everything he was a man of his work. He knew metals and their qualities as perhaps few men in America, and he was enthusiastic in his devotion to his profession. After dinner, with apologies to the ladies, he discoursed from full and accurate knowledge of the problems to be met within his daily work and their solutions. He was frequently highly technical, but to everything he touched he lent a charm that captivated his audience. To Larry he was especially gracious. He was interested in Canada. He apparently had a minute knowledge of its mineral history, its great deposits in metals, in coal, and oil, which he declared to be among the richest in the world. The mining operations, however, carried out in Canada, he dismissed as being unworthy of consideration. He deplored the lack of scientific knowledge and the absence of organisation.

"We should do that better in our country. Ah, if only our Government would take hold of these deposits," he exclaimed, "the whole world should hear of them." The nickel mining industry alone in the Sudbury district he considered worthy of respect. Here he became enthusiastic. "If only my country had such a magnificent bit of ore!" he cried. "But such bungling, such childish trifling with one of the greatest, if not the very greatest, mining industries in the world! To think that the Government of Canada actually allows the refining of that ore to be done outside of its own country! Folly, folly, criminal folly! But it is all the same in this country, too. The mining work in America is unscientific, slovenly, unorganised, wasteful. I am sorry to say," he continued, turning suddenly upon Larry, "in your western coal fields you waste more in the smoke of your coke ovens than you make out of your coal mines. Ah, if only those wonderful, wonderful coal fields were under the organised and scientific direction of my country! Then you would see— ah, what would you not see!"

"Your country?" said Hugo Raeder, smiling. "I understood you were an American, Professor Schaefer."

"An American? Surely! I have been eighteen years in this country."

"You are a citizen, I presume?" said Mr. Wakeham.

"A citizen? Yes. I neglected that matter till recently; but I love my Fatherland."

"Speaking of citizenship, I have always wanted to know about the Delbruck Law, Professor Schaefer, in regard to citizenship," said Larry.

The professor hesitated, "The Delbruck Law?"

"Yes," said Larry. "How does it affect, for instance, your American citizenship?"

"Not at all, I should say. Not in the very least," replied Professor Schaefer curtly and as if dismissing the subject.

"I am not so sure of that, Professor Schaefer," said Hugo Raeder. "I was in Germany when that law was passed. It aroused a great deal of interest. I have not looked into it myself, but on the face of it I should say it possesses certain rather objectionable features."

"Not at all, not at all, I assure you," exclaimed Professor Schaefer. "It is simply a concession to the intense, but very natural affection for the Fatherland in every German heart, while at the same time it facilitates citizenship in a foreign country. For instance, there are millions of Germans living in America who like myself shrank from taking the oath which breaks the bond with the Fatherland. We love America, we are Americans, we live in America, we work in America; but naturally our hearts turn to Germany, and we cannot forget our childhood's home. That is good, that is worthy, that is noble—hence the Delbruck Law."

"But what does it provide exactly?" enquired Mr. Wakeham. "I confess I never heard of it."

"It permits a German to become an American citizen, and at the same time allows him to retain his connection, his heart connection, with the Fatherland. It is a beautiful law."

"A beautiful law," echoed his friend, Mr. Meyer.

"Just what is the connection?" insisted Hugo Raeder.

"Dear friend, let me explain to you. It permits him to retain his place, his relations with his own old country people. You can surely see the advantage of that. For instance: When I return to Germany I find myself in full possession of all my accustomed privileges. I am no stranger. Ah, it is beautiful! And you see further how it establishes a new bond between the two countries. Every German-American will become a bond of unity between these two great nations, the two great coming nations of the world."

"Beautiful, beautiful, glorious!" echoed Meyer.

"But I do not understand," said Larry. "Are you still a citizen of Germany?"

"I am an American citizen, and proud of it," exclaimed Professor Schaefer, dramatically.

"Ach, so, geviss," said Meyer. "Sure! an American citizen!"

"But you are also a citizen of Germany?" enquired Hugo Raeder.

"If I return to Germany I resume the rights of my German citizenship, of course."

"Beautiful, beautiful!" exclaimed Meyer.

"Look here, Schaefer. Be frank about this. Which are you to-day, a citizen of Germany or of America?"

"Both, I tell you," exclaimed Schaefer proudly. "That is the beauty of the arrangement."

"Ah, a beautiful arrangement!" said Meyer.

"What? You are a citizen of another country while you claim American citizenship?" said Raeder. "You can no more be a citizen of two countries at the same time than the husband of two wives at the same time."

"Well, why not?" laughed Schaefer. "An American wife for America, and a German wife for Germany. You will excuse me," he added, bowing toward Mrs. Wakeham.

"Don't be disgusting," said Hugo Raeder. "Apart from the legal difficulty the chief difficulty about that scheme would be that whatever the German wife might have to say to such an arrangement, no American wife would tolerate it for an instant."

"I was merely joking, of course," said Schaefer.

"But, Professor Schaefer, suppose war should come between Germany and America," said Larry.

"War between Germany and America—the thing is preposterous nonsense, not to be considered among the possibilities!"

"But as a mere hypothesis for the sake of argument, what would your position be?" persisted Larry.

Professor Schaefer was visibly annoyed. "I say the hypothesis is nonsense and unthinkable," he cried.

"Come on, Schaefer, you can't escape it like that, you know," said Hugo Raeder. "By that law of yours, where would your allegiance be should war arise? I am asking what actually would be your standing. Would you be a German citizen or an American citizen?"

"The possibility does not exist," said Professor Schaefer.

"Quite impossible," exclaimed Meyer.

"Well, what of other countries then?" said Hugo, pursuing the subject with a wicked delight. His sturdy Americanism resented this bigamous citizenship. "What of France or Britain?"

"Ah," said Professor Schaefer with a sharpening of his tone. "That is quite easy."

"You would be a German, eh?" said Raeder.

"You ask me," exclaimed Professor Schaefer, "you ask me as between Germany and France, or between Germany and Britain? I reply," he exclaimed with a dramatic flourish of his hand, "I am a worshipper of the life-giving sun, not of the dead moon; I follow the dawn, not the dying day."

But this was too much for Larry. "Without discussing which is the sun and which is the moon, about which we might naturally differ, Professor Schaefer, I want to be quite clear upon one point. Do I understand you to say that if you were, say a naturalised citizen of Canada, having sworn allegiance to our Government, enjoying the full rights and privileges of our citizenship, you at the same time would be free to consider yourself a citizen of Germany, and in case of war with Britain, you would feel in duty bound to support Germany? And is it that which the Delbruck Law is deliberately drawn, to permit you to do?"

"Well put, Larry!" exclaimed Hugo Raeder, to whom the German's attitude was detestable.

Professor Schaefer's lips curled in an unpleasant smile. "Canada, Canadian citizenship! My dear young man, pardon! Allow me to ask you a question. If Britain were at war with Germany, do you think it at all likely that Canada would allow herself to become involved in a European war? Canada is a proud, young, virile nation. Would she be likely to link her fortunes with those of a decadent power? Excuse me a moment," checking Larry's impetuous reply with his hand. "Believe me, we know something about these things. We make it our business to know. You acknowledge that we know something about your mines; let me assure you that there is nothing about your country that we do not know. Nothing. Nothing. We know the feeling in Canada. Where would Canada be in such a war? Not with Germany, I would not say that. But would she stand with England?"

Larry sprang to his feet. "Where would Canada be? Let me tell you, Professor Schaefer," shaking his finger in the professor's face. "To her last man and her last dollar Canada would be with the Empire."

"Hear, hear!" shouted Hugo Raeder.

The professor looked incredulous. "And yet," he said with a sneer, "one-half of your people voted for Reciprocity with the United States."

"Reciprocity! And yet you say you know Canada," exclaimed Larry in a tone of disgust. "Do you know, sir, what defeated Reciprocity with this country? Not hostility to the United States; there is nothing but the kindliest feeling among Canadians for Americans. But I will tell you what defeated Reciprocity. It was what we might call the ultra loyal spirit of the Canadian people toward the Empire. The Canadians were Empire mad. The bare suggestion of the possibility of any peril to the Empire bond made them throw out Sir Wilfrid Laurier and the Liberal Party. That, of course, with other subordinate causes."

"I fancy our Mr. Taft helped a bit," said Hugo Raeder.

"Undoubtedly Mr. Taft's unfortunate remarks were worked to the limit by the Conservative Party. But all I say is that any suggestion, I will not say of disloyalty, but even of indifference, to the Empire of Canada is simply nonsense."

At this point a servant brought in a telegram and handed it to Mr. Wakeham. "Excuse me, my dear," he said to his wife, opened the wire, read it, and passed it to Hugo Raeder. "From your chief, Hugo."

"Much in that, do you think, sir?" inquired Hugo, passing the telegram back to him.

"Oh, a little flurry in the market possibly," said Mr. Wakeham. "What do you think about that, Schaefer?" Mr. Wakeham continued, handing him the wire.

Professor Schaefer glanced at the telegram. "My God!" he exclaimed, springing to his feet. "It is come, it is come at last!" He spoke hurriedly in German to his friend, Meyer, and handed him the telegram.

Meyer read it. "God in heaven!" he cried. "It is here!" In intense excitement he poured forth a torrent of interrogations in German, receiving animated replies from Professor Schaefer. Then grasping the professor's hand in both of his, he shook it with wild enthusiasm.

"At last!" he cried. "At last! Thank God, our day has come!"

Completely ignoring the rest of the company, the two Germans carried on a rapid and passionate conversation in their own tongue with excited gesticulations, which the professor concluded by turning to his hostess and saying, "Mrs. Wakeham, you will excuse us. Mr. Wakeham, you can send us to town at once?"

By this time the whole company were upon their feet gazing with amazement upon the two excited Germans.

"But what is it?" cried Mrs. Wakeham. "What has happened? Is there anything wrong? What is it, Professor Schaefer? What is your wire about, Garrison?"

"Oh, nothing at all, my dear, to get excited about. My financial agent wires me that the Press will announce to-morrow that Austria has presented an ultimatum to Servia demanding an answer within forty-eight hours."

"Oh, is that all," she said in a tone of vast relief. "What a start you all gave me. An ultimatum to Servia? What is it all about?"

"Why, you remember, my dear, the murder of the Archduke Ferdinand about three weeks ago?"

"Oh, yes, I remember. I had quite forgotten it. Poor thing, how terrible it was! Didn't they get the murderer? It seems to me they caught him."

"You will excuse us, Mrs. Wakeham," said Professor Schaefer, approaching her. "We deeply regret leaving this pleasant party and your hospitable home, but it is imperative that we go."

"But, my dear Professor Schaefer, to-night?" exclaimed Mrs. Wakeham.

"Why, Schaefer, what's the rush? Are you caught in the market?" said Wakeham with a little laugh. "You cannot do anything to-night at any rate, you know. We will have you in early to-morrow morning."

"No, no, to-night, now, immediately!" shouted Meyer in uncontrollable excitement.

"But why all the excitement, Schaefer?" said Hugo Raeder, smiling at him. "Austria has presented an ultimatum to Servia—what about it?"

"What about it? Oh, you Americans; you are so provincial. Did you read the ultimatum? Do you know what it means? It means war!"

"War!" cried Meyer. "War at last! Thank God! Tonight must we in New York become."

Shaking hands hurriedly with Mrs. Wakeham, and with a curt bow to the rest of the company, Meyer hurriedly left the room, followed by Professor Schaefer and Mr. Wakeham.

"Aren't they funny!" said Rowena. "They get so excited about nothing."

"Well, it is hardly nothing," said Hugo Raeder. "Any European war is full of all sorts of possibilities. You cannot throw matches about in a powder magazine without some degree of danger."

"May I read the ultimatum?" said Larry to Mrs. Wakeham, who held the telegram in her hand.

"Pretty stiff ultimatum," said Hugo Raeder. "Read it out, Larry."

"Servia will have to eat dirt," said Larry when he had finished. "Listen to this: She must 'accept the collaboration in Servia of representatives of the Austro-Hungarian Government for the consideration of the subversive movements directed against the Territorial integrity of the Monarchy.' 'Accept collaboration' of the representatives of the Austro-hungarian Government in this purely internal business, mind you. And listen to this: 'Delegates of the Austro-Hungarian Government will take part in the investigation relating thereto.' Austrian lawyers and probably judges investigating Servian subjects in Servia? Why, the thing is impossible."

"It is quite evident," said Hugo Raeder, "that Austria means war."

"Poor little Servia, she will soon be eaten up," said Rowena. "She must be bankrupt from her last war."

"But why all this excitement on the part of our German friends?" inquired Mrs. Wakeham. "What has Germany to do with Austria and Servia?"

At this point Professor Schaefer and his friend re-entered the room ready for their departure.

"I was just inquiring," said Mrs. Wakeham, "how this

ultimatum of Austria's to Servia can affect Germany particularly."

"Affect Germany?" cried Professor Schaefer.

"Yes," said Hugo Raeder, "what has Germany to do with the scrap unless she wants to butt in?"

"Ha! ha! My dear man, have you read no history of the last twenty years? But you Americans know nothing about history, nothing about anything except your own big, overgrown country."

"I thought you were an American citizen, Schaefer?" inquired Hugo.

"An American," exclaimed Schaefer, "an American, ah, yes, certainly; but in Europe and in European politics, a German, always a German."

"But why should Germany butt in?" continued Hugo.

"Butt in, Germany butt in? Things cannot be settled in Europe without Germany. Besides, there is Russia longing for the opportunity to attack."

"To attack Germany?"

"To attack Austria first, Germany's ally and friend, and then Germany. The trouble is you Americans do not live in the world. You are living on your own continent here removed from the big world, ignorant of all world movements, the most provincial people in all the world. Else you would not ask me such foolish questions. This ultimatum means war. First, Austria against Servia; Russia will help Servia; France will help Russia; Germany will help Austria. There you have the beginning of a great European war. How far this conflagration will spread, only God knows."

The car being announced, the Germans made a hurried exit, in their overpowering excitement omitting the courtesy of farewells to household and guests.

"They seem to be terribly excited, those Germans," said Miss Rowena.

"They are," said Hugo; "I am glad I am not a German. To a German war is so much the biggest thing in life."

"It is really too bad," said Mrs. Wakeham; "we shall not have the pleasure of Professor Schaefer's music. He plays quite exquisitely. You would all have greatly enjoyed it. Rowena, you might play something. Well, for my part," continued Mrs. Wakeham, settling herself placidly in her comfortable chair, "I am glad I am an American. Those European countries, it seems to me, are always in some trouble or other."

"I am glad I am a Canadian," said Larry. "We are much too busy to think of anything so foolish and useless as war."

CHAPTER XXI

WAR

"Come, Jane, we have just time to take a look at the lake from the top of the hill before we get ready for church," said Ethel Murray. "It will be worth seeing to-day."

"Me too, me too," shrieked two wee girls in bare legs and sandals, clutching Jane about the legs.

"All right, Isabel; all right, Helen. I'll take you with me," said Jane. "But you must let me go, you know."

They all raced around the house and began to climb the sheer, rocky hill that rose straight up from the rear.

"Here, Jim, help me with these kiddies," said Jane to a lank lad of fifteen, whom she ran into at the corner of the house just where the climb began.

Jim swung the younger, little Helen, upon his shoulder and together they raced to the top, scrambling, slipping, falling, but finally arriving there, breathless and triumphant. Before them lay a bit of Canada's loveliest lake, the Lake of the Woods, so-called from its myriad, heavily wooded islands, that make of its vast expanse a maze of channels, rivers and waterways. Calm, without a ripple,

Ralph Connor

lay the glassy, sunlit surface, each island, rock and tree meeting its reflected image at the water line, the sky above flecked with floating clouds, making with the mirrored sky below one perfect whole.

"Oh, Ethel, I had forgotten just how beautiful this is," breathed Jane, while the rest stood silent looking down upon the mirrored rocks and islands, trees and sky.

Even the two little girls stood perfectly still, for they had been taught to take the first views from the top in silence.

"Look at the Big Rock," said Helen. "They are two rocks kissing each other."

"Oh, you little sweetheart," said Jane, kissing her. "That is just what they are doing. It is not often that you get it so perfectly still as this, is it, Jim?"

"Not so very often. Sometimes just at sunrise you get it this way."

"At sunrise! Do you very often see it then?"

"Yes, he gets up to catch fishes," said wee Helen.

"Do you?"

Jim nodded. "Are you game to come along to-morrow morning?"

"At what hour?"

"Five o'clock."

"Don't do it, Jane," said Ethel. "It tires you for the day."

"I will come, Jim; I would love to come," said Jane.

For some time they stood gazing down upon the scene below them. Then turning to the children abruptly, Ethel said, "Now, then, children, you run down and get ready; that is, if you are going to church. Take them down, Jim."

"All right, Ethel," said Jim. "See there, Jane," he continued, "that neck of land across the traverse—that's where the old Hudson Bay trail used to run that goes from the Big Lakes to Winnipeg. It's the old war trail of the Crees too. Wouldn't you like to have seen them in the old days?"

"I would run and hide," said Isabel, "so they could not see me."

"I would not be afraid," said Helen, straightening up to her full height of six years. "I would shoot them dead."

"Poor things," said Jane, in a pitiful voice. "And then their little babies at home would cry and cry."

Helen looked distressed. "I would not shoot the ones that had babies."

"But then," said Jane, "the poor wives would sit on the ground and wail and wail, like the Indians we heard the other night. Oh, it sounded very sad."

"I would not shoot the ones with wives or babies or anything," said Helen, determined to escape from her painful dilemma.

"Oh, only the boys and young men?" said Jane. "And then the poor old mothers would cry and cry and tear their hair for the boys who would never come back."

Ralph Connor

Helen stood in perplexed silence. Then she said shyly, "I wouldn't shoot any of them unless they tried to shoot me or Mother or Daddy."

"Or me," said Jane, throwing her arms around the little girl.

"Yes," said Helen, "or you, or anybody in our house."

"That seems a perfectly safe place to leave it, Helen," said Ethel. "I think even the most pronounced pacifist would accept that as a justification of war. I fancy that is why poor little Servia is fighting big bullying Austria to-day. But run down now; hurry, hurry; the launch will be ready in a few minutes, and if you are not ready you know Daddy won't wait."

But they were ready and with the round dozen, which with the visitors constituted the Murray household at their island home, they filled the launch, Jim at the wheel. It was a glorious Sunday morning and the whole world breathed peace. Through the mazes of the channels among the wooded islands the launch made its way, across open traverse, down long waterways like rivers between high, wooded banks, through cuts and gaps, where the waters boiled and foamed, they ran, for the most part drinking in silently the exquisite and varied beauty of lake and sky and woods. Silent they were but for the quiet talk and cheery laughter of the younger portion of the company, until they neared the little town, when the silence that hung over the lake and woods was invaded by other launches outbound and in. The Kenora docks were crowded with rowboats, sailboats, canoes and launches of all sorts and sizes, so that it took some steering skill on Jim's part to land them at the dock without bumping either themselves or any one else.

"Oh, look!" exclaimed Isabel, whose sharp eyes were darting everywhere. "There's the Rushbrooke's lovely new launch. Isn't it beautiful!"

"Huh!" shouted Helen. "It is not half as pretty as ours."

"Oh, hush, Helen," said the scandalised Isabel. "It is lovely, isnt it, Jane? And there is Lloyd Rushbrooke. I think he's lovely, too. And who is that with him, Jane—that pretty girl? Oh, isn't she pretty?"

"That's Helen Brookes," said Jane in a low voice.

"Oh, isn't she lovely!" exclaimed Isabel.

"Lovely bunch, Isabel," said Jim with a grin.

"I don't care, they are," insisted Isabel. "And there is Mr. McPherson, Jane," she added, her sharp eyes catching sight of their Winnipeg minister through the crowd. "He's coming this way. What are the people all waiting for, Jane?"

The Reverend Andrew McPherson was a tall, slight, dark man, straight but for the student's stoop of his shoulders, and with a strikingly Highland Scotch cast of countenance, high cheek bones, keen blue eyes set deep below a wide forehead, long jaw that clamped firm lips together. He came straight to where Mr. Murray and Dr. Brown were standing.

"I have just received from a friend in Winnipeg the most terrible news," he said in a low voice. "Germany has declared war on Russia and France."

"War! War! Germany!" exclaimed the men in awed, hushed voices, a startled look upon their grave faces.

"What is it, James?" said Mrs. Murray.

Mr. Murray repeated the news to her.

"Germany at war?" she said. "I thought it was Austria and Servia. Isn't it?"

"Yes, my dear," said Mr. Murray hastily, as if anxious to cover up his wife's display of ignorance of the European situation. "Austria has been at war with Servia for some days, but now Germany has declared war apparently upon France and Russia."

"But what has Germany to do with it, or Russia either, or France?"

They moved off together from the docks toward the church, discussing the ominous news.

"Oh, look, Jane," said Isabel once more. "There's Ramsay Dunn. Isn't he looking funny?"

"Pickled, I guess," said Jim, with a glance at the young man who with puffed and sodden face was gazing with dull and stupid eyes across the lake. On catching sight of the approaching party Ramsay Dunn turned his back sharply upon them and became intensely absorbed in the launch at his side. But Jane would not have it thus.

"Ask him to come over this afternoon," she said to Ethel. "His mother would like it."

"Good morning, Ramsay," said Ethel as they passed him.

Ramsay turned sharply, stood stiff and straight, then saluted with an elaborate bow. "Good morning, Ethel. Why, good morning, Jane. You down here? Delighted to see you."

"Ramsay, could you come over this afternoon to our island?" said Ethel. "Jane is going back this week."

"Sure thing, Ethel. Nothing but scarlet fever, small-pox, or other contectious or infagious, confagious or intexious —eh, disease will prevent me. The afternoon or the evening?" he added with what he meant to be a most ingratiating smile. "The late afternoon or the early evening?"

The little girls, who had been staring at him with wide, wondering eyes, began to giggle.

"I'll be there," continued Ramsay. "I'll be there, I'll be there, when the early evening cometh, I'll be there." He bowed deeply to the young ladies and winked solemnly at Isabel, who by this time was finding it quite impossible to control her giggles.

"Isn't he awfully funny?" she said as they moved off. "I think he is awfully funny."

"Funny!" said Ethel. "Disgusting, I think."

"Oh, Ethel, isn't it terribly sad?" said Jane. "Poor Mrs. Dunn, she feels so awfully about it. They say he is going on these days in a perfectly dreadful way."

The little brick church was comfortably filled with the townsfolk and with such of the summer visitors as had not "left their religion behind them in Winnipeg," as Jane said. The preacher was a little man whose speech betrayed his birth, and the theology and delivery of whose sermon bore the unmistakable marks of his Edinburgh training. He discoursed in somewhat formal but in finished style upon the blessings of rest, with obvious application to the special circumstances of the greater part of his audience who had come to this most beautiful of all Canada's beautiful spots seeking these blessings. To further emphasise the value of their privileges, he contrasted with their lot the condition of unhappy Servia now suffering from the horrors of war and threatened with extinction by its tyrannical neighbour, Austria. The war could end only in one way. In spite of her gallant and heroic fight Servia was doomed to defeat. But a day of reckoning would surely come, for this was not the first time that Austria had exercised its superior power in an act of unrighteous tyranny over smaller states. The God of righteousness was still ruling in his world, and righteousness would be done.

At the close of the service, while they were singing the final hymn, Mr. McPherson, after a whispered colloquy with Mr. Murray, made his way to the pulpit, where he held an earnest conversation with the minister. Instead of pronouncing the benediction and dismissing the congregation when the final "Amen" had been sung, the minister invited the people to resume their seats, when Mr. McPherson rose and said,

"Friends, we have just learned that a great and terrible evil has fallen upon the world. Five days ago the world was shocked by the announcement that Austria had declared war upon Servia. Through these days the powers of Europe, or at least some of them, and chief among them Great Britain, have been labouring to localise the war and to prevent its extension. To-day the sad, the terrible announcement is made that Germany has declared war upon both Russia and France. What an hour may bring forth, we know not. But not in our day, or in our fathers' day, have we faced so great a peril as we face to-day. For we cannot forget that our Empire is held by close and vital ties to the Republic of France in the entente cordiale.

Let us beseech Almighty God to grant a speedy end to war and especially to guide the King's counsellors that they may lead this Empire in the way that is wise and right and honourable."

In the brief prayer that followed there fell upon the people an overpowering sense of the futility of man's wisdom, and of the need of the might and wisdom that are not man's but God's.

Two days later Mr. Murray and the children accompanied Dr. Brown and Jane to Kenora on their way back to the city. As they were proceeding to the railway station they were arrested by a group that stood in front of the bulletin board upon which since the war began the local newspaper was wont to affix the latest despatches. The group was standing in awed silence staring at the bulletin board before them. Dr. Brown pushed his way through, read the despatch, looked around upon the faces beside him, read the words once more, came back to where his party were standing and stood silent.

"What is it?" inquired Mr. Murray.

"War," said Dr. Brown in a husky whisper. Then clearing his throat, "War—Britain and Germany."

War! For the first time in the memory of living man that word was spoken in a voice that stopped dead still the Empire in the daily routine of its life. War! That word whispered in the secret silent chamber of the man whose chief glory had been his title as Supreme War Lord of Europe, swift as the lightning's flash circled the globe, arresting multitudes of men busy with their peaceful tasks, piercing the hearts of countless women with a new and nameless terror, paralysing the activities of nations engaged in the arts of peace, transforming into bitter

Ralph Connor

enemies those living in the bonds of brotherhood, and loosing upon the world the fiends of hell.

Mr. Murray turned to his boy. "Jim," he said, "I must go to Winnipeg. Take the children home and tell their mother. I shall wire you to-morrow when to meet me." Awed, solemnised and in silence they took their ways.

Arrived at the railway station, Mr. Murray changed his mind. He was a man clear in thought and swift in action. His first thought had been of his business as being immediately affected by this new and mighty fact of war. Then he thought of other and wider interests.

"Let us go back, Dr. Brown," he said. "A large number of our business men are at the Lake. I suppose half of our Board of Trade are down here. We can reach them more easily here than any place else, and it is important that we should immediately get them together. Excuse me while I wire to my architect. I must stop that block of mine."

They returned together to the launch. On their way back to their island they called to see Mr. McPherson. "You were right," was Mr. Murray's greeting to him. "It has come; Britain has declared war."

Mr. McPherson stood gazing at him in solemn silence. "War," he said at length. "We are really in."

"Yes, you were right, Mr. McPherson," said Dr. Brown. "I could not believe it; I cannot believe it yet. Why we should have gone into this particular quarrel, for the life of me I cannot understand."

"I was afraid from the very first," said McPherson, "and when once Russia and France were in I knew that Britain could not honourably escape."

As they were talking together a launch went swiftly by. "That's the Rushbrooke's launch," said Jim.

Mr. Murray rushed out upon the pier and, waving his hand, brought it to a halt and finally to the dock. "Have you heard the news?" he said to the lady who sat near the stern. "Britain has declared war."

"Oh," replied Mrs. Rushbrooke, "why on earth has she done that? It is perfectly terrible."

"Terrible, indeed," said Mr. McPherson. "But we must face it. It changes everything in life—business, society, home, everything will immediately feel the effect of this thing."

"Oh, Mr. McPherson," exclaimed Mrs. Rushbrooke, "I can hardly see how it will quite change everything for us here in Canada. For instance," she added with a gay laugh, "I do not see that it will change our bonfire tonight. By the way, I see you are not gone, Dr. Brown. You and Jane will surely come over; and, Mr. Murray, you will bring your young people and Mrs. Murray; and, Mr. McPherson, I hope you will be able to come. It is going to be a charming evening and you will see a great many of your friends. I think a bonfire on one of the islands makes a very pretty sight."

"I am not sure whether I can take the time, Mrs. Rushbrooke," said Mr. Murray. "I had thought of seeing a number of our business men who are down here at the Lake."

"Oh, can't you leave business even while you are here? You really ought to forget business during your holidays, Mr. Murray."

Ralph Connor

"I mean in relation to the war," said Mr. Murray.

"Good gracious, what can they possibly do about the war down here? But if you want to see them they will all be with us to-night. So you had better come along. But we shall have to hurry, Lloyd; I have a lot of things to do and a lot of people to feed. We have got to live, haven't we?" she added as the launch got under way.

"Got to live," said Mr. McPherson after they had gone. "Ah, even that necessity has been changed. The necessity for living, which I am afraid most of us have considered to be of first importance, has suddenly given place to another necessity."

"And that?" said Mr. Murray.

"The necessity not to live, but to do our duty. Life has become all at once a very simple thing."

"Well, we have got to keep going in the meantime at any rate," said Mr. Murray.

"Going, yes; but going where?" said Mr. McPherson. "All roads now, for us, lead to one spot."

"And that spot?" said Mr. Murray.

"The battlefield."

"Why, Mr. McPherson, we must not lose our heads; we must keep sane and reasonable. Eh, Doctor?"

"I confess that this thing has completely stunned me," said Dr. Brown. "You see I could not believe, I would not believe that war was possible in our day. I would not believe you, Mr. McPherson. I thought you had gone mad on this German scare. But you were right. My God, I can't get my bearings yet; we are really at war!"

"God grant that Canada may see its duty clearly," said Mr. McPherson. "God make us strong to bear His will."

They hurried back to their island, each busy with his thoughts, seeking to readjust life to this new and horrible environment.

Mrs. Murray met them at the dock. "You are back, Dr. Brown," she cried. "Did you forget something? We are glad to see you at any rate." Then noticing the men's faces, she said, "What is the matter, James? Is there anything wrong?"

"We bring terrible news, Mother," he said. "We are at war."

Mrs. Murray's' mind, like her husband's, moved swiftly. She was a life partner in the fullest sense. In business as in the home she shared his plans and purposes. "What about the block, James?" she asked.

"I wired Eastwood," he replied, "to stop that."

"What is it, Mother?" inquired Isabel, who stood upon the dock clinging to her mother's dress, and who saw in the grave, faces about her signs of disaster.

"Hush, dear," said her mother. "Nothing that you can understand." She would keep from her children this horror as long as she could.

At lunch in the midst of the most animated conversation the talk would die out, and all would be busy fitting their lives to war. Like waves ever deepening in volume and

Ralph Connor

increasing in force, the appalling thought of war beat upon their minds. After lunch they sat together in the screened veranda talking quietly together of the issues, the consequences to them and to their community, to their country, and to the world at large, of this thing that had befallen them. They made the amazing discovery that they were almost entirely ignorant of everything that had to do with war, even the relative military strength of the belligerent nations. One thing like a solid back wall of rock gave them a sense of security—the British Navy was still supreme.

"Let's see, did they cut down the Navy estimates during the last Parliament? I know they were always talking of reduction," inquired Mr. Murray.

"I am afraid I know nothing about it," said Dr. Brown. "Last week I would have told you 'I hope so'; to-day I profoundly hope not. Jane, you ought to know about this. Jane is the war champion in our family," he added with a smile.

"No, there has been no reduction; Winston Churchill has carried on his programme. He wanted to halt the building programme, you remember, but the Germans would not agree. So I think the Navy is quite up to the mark. But, of course," she added, "the German Navy is very strong too."

"Ah, I believe you are right, Jane," said Dr. Brown. "How completely we were all hoodwinked. I cannot believe that we are actually at war. Our friend Romayne was right. By the way, what about Romayne, Jane?"

"Who is he?" inquired Mr. Murray.

"Romayne?" said Dr. Brown. "Oh, he's a great friend of ours in the West. He married a sister of young Gwynne, you know. He was an attache of the British Embassy in Berlin, and was, as we thought, quite mad on the subject of preparation for war. He and Jane hit it off tremendously last autumn when we were visiting the Gwynnes. Was he not an officer in the Guards or something, Jane?"

"Yes," replied Jane, fear leaping into her eyes. "Oh, Papa, do you think he will have to go? Surely he would not."

"What? Go back to England?" said Dr. Brown. "I hardly think so. I do not know, but perhaps he may."

"Oh, Papa!" exclaimed Jane, the quick tears in her eyes. "Think of his wife and little baby!"

"My God!" exclaimed Dr. Brown. "It is war that is upon us."

A fresh wave of horror deeper than any before swept their souls. "Surely he won't need to go," he said after a pause.

"But his regiment will be going," said Jane, whose face had become very pale and whose eyes were wide with horror. "His regiment will be going and," she added, "he will go too." The tears were quietly running down her face. She knew Jack Romayne and she had the courage to accept the truth which as yet her father put from his mind.

Dumb they sat, unschooled in language fitted to deal with the tides of emotion that surged round this new and overwhelming fact of war. Where next would this dread thing strike?

"Canada will doubtless send some troops," said Dr. Brown. "We sent to South Africa, let me see, was it five thousand?"

"More, I think, Papa," said Jane.

"We will send twice or three times that number this time," said Mr. Murray.

And again silence fell upon them. They were each busy with the question who would go. Swiftly their minds ran over the homes of their friends and acquaintances.

"Well, Doctor," said Mr. Murray, with a great effort at a laugh, "you can't send your boy at any rate."

"No," said Dr. Brown. "But if my girl had been a boy, I fear I could not hold her. Eh, Jane?" But Jane only smiled a very doubtful smile in answer.

"We may all have to go, Doctor," said Mr. Murray. "If the war lasts long enough."

"Nonsense, James," said his wife with a quick glance at her two little girls. Her boy was fifteen. Thank God, she would not have to face the question of his duty in regard to war. "They would not be taking old men like you, James," she added.

Mr. Murray laughed at her. "Well, hardly, I suppose, my dear," he replied. "I rather guess we won't be allowed to share the glory this time, Doctor."

Dr. Brown sat silent for a few moments, then said quietly, "The young fellows, of course, will get the first chance."

"Oh, let's not talk about it," said Ethel. "Come, Jane, let's go exploring."

Jane rose.

"And me, too," cried Isabel.

"And me," cried Helen.

Ethel hesitated. "Let them come, Ethel," said Jane. "We shall go slowly."

An exploration of the island was always a thing of unmixed and varied delight. There were something over twenty-five acres of wooded hills running up to bare rocks, ravines deep in shrub and ferns, and lower levels thick with underbrush and heavy timber. Every step of the way new treasures disclosed themselves, ferns and grasses, shrubs and vines, and everywhere the wood flowers, shy and sweet. Everywhere, too, on fallen logs, on the grey rocks, and on the lower ground where the aromatic balsams and pines stood silent and thick, were mosses, mosses of all hues and depths. In the sunlit open spaces gorgeous butterflies and gleaming dragon flies fluttered and darted, bees hummed, and birds sang and twittered. There the children's voices were mingled in cheery shouts and laughter with the other happy sounds that filled the glades. But when they came to the dark pines, solemn and silent except when the wind moved in their tasselled tops with mysterious, mournful whispering, the children hushed their voices and walked softly upon the deep moss.

"It is like being in church," said Helen, her little soul exquisitely sensitive to the mystic, fragrant silences and glooms that haunted the pine grove.

On a sloping hillside under the pines they lay upon the mossy bed, the children listening for the things that lived in these shadowy depths.

"They are all looking at us," said Isabel in a voice of awed

Ralph Connor

mystery. "Lots and lots of eyes are just looking, looking, and looking."

"Why, Isabel, you give me the creeps," laughed Jane. "Whisht! They'll hear you," said Isabel, darting swift glances among the trees.

"The dear things," said Jane. "They would love to play with you if they only knew how." This was quite a new idea to the children. Hitherto the shy things had been more associated with fear than with play. "They would love to play tag with you," continued Jane, "round these trees, if you could only coax them out. They are so shy."

Stealthily the children began to move among the bushes, alert for the watching eyes and the shy faces of the wild things that made their homes in these dark dwellings. The girls sat silent, looking out through the interlacing boughs upon the gleam of the lake below. They dearly loved this spot. It was a favourite haunt with them, the very spot for confidence, and many a happy hour had they spent together here. To-day they sat without speech; there was nothing that they cared to talk about. It was only yesterday in this same place they had talked over all things under the sun. They had exchanged with each other their stores of kindly gossip about all their friends and their friends' friends. Only yesterday it was that Ethel for the twentieth time had gone over with Jane all the intricately perplexing and delightful details in regard to her coming-out party next winter. All the boys and girls were to be invited, and Jane was to help with the serving. It was only yesterday that in a moment of quite unusual frankness Ethel had read snatches of a letter which had come from Macleod, who was out in a mission field in Saskatchewan. How they had laughed together, all in a kindly way, over the solemn, formal phrases of the young Scotch Canadian missionary, Ethel making sport of his solemnity and Jane warmly defending him. How they had talked over the boys' affairs, as girls will talk, and of their various loves and how they fared, and of the cruelties practised upon them. And last of all Ethel had talked of Larry, Jane listening warily the while and offering an occasional bit of information to keep the talk going. And all of this only yesterday; not ten years ago, or a year ago, but yesterday! And to-day not a word seemed possible. The world had changed over night. How different from that unshaded, sunny world of yesterday! How sunny it was but yesterday! Life now was a thing of different values. Ah, that was it. The values were all altered. Things big yesterday had shrunk almost to the point of disappearance to-day. Things that yesterday seemed remote and vague, to-day filled their horizon, for some of them dark enough. Determined to ignore that gaunt Spectre standing there, in the shadow silent and grim, they would begin to talk on themes good yesterday for an hour's engrossing conversation, but before they were aware they had forgotten the subject of their talk and found themselves sitting together dumb and looking out upon the gleam of the waters, thinking, thinking and ever thinking, while nearer and ever more terrible moved the Spectre of War. It was like the falling of night upon their world. From the landscape things familiar and dear were blotted out, and in their place moved upon them strange shapes unreal and horrible.

At length they gave it up, called the children and went back to the others. At the dock they found a launch filled with visitors bringing news—great news and glorious. A big naval battle had been fought in the North Sea! Ten British battleships had been sunk, but the whole German fleet had been destroyed! For the first time war took on some colour. Crimson and purple and gold began to shoot through the sombre black and grey. A completely new set of emotions filled their hearts, a new sense of exultation, a new pride in that great British Navy which hitherto had been a mere word in a history book, or in a song. The children who, after their manner, were quickest to catch and to carry on to their utmost limits the emotions of the moment, were jubilantly triumphant. Some of them were carrying little Union Jacks in their hands. For the first time in their lives that flag became a thing of pride and power, a thing to shout for. It stood for something invisible but very real. Even their elders were not insensible to that something. Hitherto they had taken that flag for granted. They had hung it out of their windows on Empire Day or on Dominion Day as a patriotic symbol, but few of them would have confessed, except in a half-shamed, apologetic way, to any thrill at the flapping of that bit of bunting. They had shrunk from a display of patriotic emotion. They were not like their American cousins, who were ever ready to rave over Old Glory. That sort of emotional display was un-Canadian, un-British. But to-day somehow the flag had changed. The flag had changed because it fluttered in a new world, a new light fell upon it, the light of battle. It was a war flag to-day. Men were fighting under it, were fighting for all it represented, were dying under its folds, and proudly and gladly.

"And all the men will go to fight, your father and my father, and all the big boys," Ethel heard a little friend confide to Isabel.

"Hush, Mabel," said Ethel sharply. "Don't be silly."

But the word had been spoken and as a seed it fell upon fertile soil. The launch went off with the children waving their flags and cheering. And again upon those left upon the dock the shadow settled heavier than before. That was the way with that shadow. It was always heavier, thicker, more ominous after each interlude of relief.

It was the same at the bonfire in the evening at the Rushbrookes'. The island was a fairy picture of mingling lights and shadows. As the flaming west grew grey, the pale silver of the moon, riding high and serene, fell upon the crowding, gaily decked launches that thronged the docks and moored to the shore; upon the dark balsams and silver birches hung with parti-coloured gaudy Chinese lanterns; upon the groups of girls, fair and sweet in their white summer camping frocks, and young men in flannels, their bare necks and arms showing brown and strong; upon little clusters of their fathers and mothers gravely talking together. From the veranda above, mingling with the laughing, chattering voices, the alluring strains of the orchestra invited to waltz, or fox trot. As the flame died from the western sky and the shadows crept down from the trees, the bonfire was set alight. As the flame leaped high the soft strains of the orchestra died away. Then suddenly, clear, full and strong, a chord sounded forth, another, and then another. A hush fell upon the chattering, laughing crowd. Then as they caught the strain men lolling upon the ground sprang to their feet; lads stood at attention.

"Send him victorious,"

some one sang timidly, giving words to the music. In one instant a hundred throats were wide open singing the words:

"Happy and glorious,
Long to reign over us,
God save our King."

Again the chords sounded and at once the verse from the first was sung again.

"God save our gracious King,

Ralph Connor

Long live our noble King,
God save our King,
Send him victorious,
Happy and glorious,
Long to reign over us,
God save our King."

As the last note died Ramsay Dunn leaped upon a huge boulder, threw up his hand and began,

"In days of yore, from Britain's shore."

A yell greeted him, sudden, fierce, triumphant, drowned his voice, then ceased! And again from a hundred throats of men and women, boys and girls, the words rang out,

"There may it wave, our boast and pride,
And joined in love together,
The thistle, shamrock, rose entwine,
The Maple Leaf forever."

Again and again and once again they followed Ramsay in the quick, shrill Canadian cheer that was to be heard in after days in places widely different and far remote from that gay, moonlit, lantern-decked, boat-thronged, water-lapped island in that far northern Canadian lake. Following the cheers there came stillness. Men looked sheepishly at each other as if caught in some silly prank. Then once more the Spectre drew near. But this time they declined not to look, but with steady, grave, appraising eyes they faced The Thing, resolute to know the worst, and in quiet undertones they talked together of War.

The bonfire roared gloriously up through the dark night, throwing far gleams out upon the moonlit waters in front and upon the dark woods behind. The people gathered about the fire and disposed themselves in groups upon the sloping, grassy sward under the trees, upon the shelving rocks and upon the sandy shore.

But Mr. Murray had business on hand. In company with Dr. Brown and the minister, Mr. McPherson, he sought his host. "Would it be possible, Mr. Rushbrooke," he said, "to gather a number of business men here together?"

"What for?" inquired Rushbrooke.

"Well, I may be all wrong," said Mr. Murray apologetically, "but I have the feeling that we ought without delay to discuss what preliminary steps should be taken to meet with the critical conditions brought on by the war."

"But, Mr. Murray," cried Mrs. Rushbrooke, who was standing by her husband's side, "they are all so happy it would seem a great pity to introduce this horrible thing at such a time."

"Do you really think it necessary, Murray?" said Mr. Rushbrooke, who was an older man than Mr. Murray, and who was unwilling to accede to him any position of dominance in the business world of Winnipeg. "There's really nothing we can do. It seems to me that we must keep our heads and as far as possible prevent undue excitement and guard against panic."

"Perhaps you are right, Mr. Rushbrooke. The thought in my mind was that we ought to get a meeting together in Winnipeg soon. But everybody is away. A great many are here at the Lake; it seemed a good opportunity to make some preliminary arrangement."

"My dear Mr. Murray," said Mrs. Rushbrooke, "I cannot help feeling that you take this too seriously, besides there can hardly be need for such precipitate action. Of course, we are at war, and Canada will do her part, but to introduce such a horrible theme in a company of young people seems to me to be somehow out of place."

"Very well, Mrs. Rushbrooke, if you say so. I have no desire to intrude," said Mr. Murray.

"But, Mr. Rushbrooke, the thing has to be faced," interposed Mr. McPherson. "We cannot shut our eyes to the fact of war, and this is the supreme fact in our national life to-day. Everything else is secondary."

"Oh, I do not agree with you, Mr. McPherson," said Mrs. Rushbrooke, taking the word out of her husband's mouth. "Of course war is terrible and all that, but men must do their work. The Doctor here must continue to look after his sick, Mr. Murray has his business, you must care for your congregation."

"I do not know about that, Mrs. Rushbrooke," said the minister. "I do not know about that at all."

"Why, Mr. McPherson, you surprise me! Must not my husband attend to his business, must not the Doctor look after his patients?"

A number of men had gathered about during the course of the conversation. "No," said Mr. McPherson, his voice ringing out in decided tones. "There is only one 'must' for us now, and that is War. For the Empire, for every man, woman, and child in Canada, the first thing, and by comparison the only thing, is War."

That dread word rang out sharp, insistent, penetrating through the quiet hum of voices rising from the groups about the fire. By this time a very considerable number of men present had joined themselves to the group about the speakers.

"Well, Mr. Murray," said Mr. Rushbrooke, with a laugh, "it seems to me that we cannot help it very well. If you wish to discourse upon the war, you have your audience and you have my permission."

"It is not my intention to discourse upon the war, Mr. Rushbrooke, but with your permission I will just tell our friends here how my mind has worked since learning this terrible news this morning. My first impulse was to take the first train to Winnipeg, for I know that it will be necessary for me to readjust my business to the new conditions created by war. My second thought was that there were others like me; that, in fact, the whole business public of Winnipeg would be similarly affected. I felt the need of counsel so that I should make no mistake that would imperil the interests of others. I accepted Mrs. Rushbrooke's invitation to come to-night in the hope of meeting with a number of the business men of Winnipeg. The more I think of it the more terrible this thing becomes. The ordinary conditions of business are gone. We shall all need to readjust ourselves in every department of life. It seems to me that we must stand together and meet this calamity as best we can, wisely, fairly and fearlessly. The main point to be considered is, should we not have a general meeting of the business men of Winnipeg, and if so, when?"

Mr. Murray's words were received in deep silence, and for a time no one made reply. Then Mr. Rushbrooke made answer.

"We all feel the importance of what Mr. Murray has said. Personally, though, I am of the opinion that we should avoid all unnecessary excitement and everything approaching panic. The war will doubtless be a short one.

Germany, after long preparation, has decided to challenge Great Britain's power. Still, Britain is ready for her. She has accepted the challenge; and though her army is not great, she is yet not unprepared. Between the enemy and Britain's shores there lies that mighty, invisible and invincible line of defence, the British navy. With the French armies on the one side and the Russian on the other, Germany can not last. In these days, with the terrible engines of destruction that science has produced, wars will be short and sharp. Germany will get her medicine and I hope it will do her good."

If Mr. Rushbrooke expected his somewhat flamboyant speech to awaken enthusiastic approval, he must have been disappointed. His words were received in grave silence. The fact of war was far too unfamiliar and too overwhelming to make it easy for them to compass it in their thoughts or to deal in any adequate way with its possible issues.

After some moments of silence the minister spoke. "I wish I could agree with Mr. Rushbrooke," he said. "But I cannot. My study of this question has impressed me with the overwhelming might of Germany's military power. The war may be short and sharp, and that is what Germany is counting upon. But if it be short and sharp, the issue will be a German victory. The French army is not fully prepared, I understand. Russia is an untrained and unwieldy mass. There is, of course, the British navy, and with all my heart I thank God that our fleet appears to be fit for service. But with regard even to our navy we ought to remember that it is as yet untried in modern warfare. I confess I cannot share Mr. Rushbrooke's optimistic views as to the war. But whether he be right or I, one thing stands out clear in my mind—that we should prepare ourselves to do our duty. At whatever cost to our country or to ourselves, as individuals, this duty is laid upon us. It is the first, the immediate, the all-absorbing duty of every man, woman and child in Canada to make war. God help us not to shrink."

"How many in this company will be in Winnipeg this week, say to-morrow?" inquired Mr. Murray. The hand of every business man in the company went up. "Then suppose we call a meeting at my office immediately upon the arrival of the train." And to this they agreed.

The Rushbrooke bonfire was an annual event and ever the most notable of all its kind during the holiday season at the Lake. This year the preparations for the festive gathering had exceeded those of previous years, and Mrs. Rushbrooke's expectations of a brilliantly successful function were proportionately high. But she had not counted upon War. And so it came that ever as the applause following song or story died down, the Spectre drew near, and upon even the most light-hearted of the company a strange quiet would fall, and they would find themselves staring into the fire forgetful of all about them, thinking of what might be. They would have broken up early but Mrs. Rushbrooke strenuously resisted any such attempt. But the sense of the impending horror chilled the gaiety of the evening and halted the rush of the fun till the hostess gave up in despair and no longer opposed the departure of her guests.

"Mr. McPherson," she said, as that gentleman came to bid her good-night, "I am quite cross with you. You made us all feel so blue and serious that you quite spoiled our bonfire."

"I wish it were only I that had spoiled it, Mrs. Rushbrooke," said Mr. McPherson gravely. "But even your graceful hospitality to-night, which has never been excelled even by yourself at the Lake of the Woods, could not make us forget, and God forgive us if we do forget."

"Oh, Mr. McPherson," persisted Mrs. Rushbrooke, in a voice that strove to be gaily reproachful, "we must not become pessimistic. We must be cheerful even if we are at war."

"Thank you for that word," said the minister solemnly. "It is a true word and a right word, and it is a word we shall need to remember more and more."

"The man would drive me mad," said Mrs. Rushbrooke to Mr. Murray as they watched the boats away. "I am more than thankful that he is not my clergyman."

"Yes, indeed," said her husband, who stood near her and shared her feelings of disappointment. "It seems to me he takes things far too seriously."

"I wonder," said Dr. Brown, who stood with Mr. Murray preparatory to taking his departure. "I wonder if we know just how serious this thing is. I frankly confess, Mr. Rushbrooke, that my mind has been in an appalling condition of chaos this afternoon; and every hour the thing grows more terrible as I think of it. But as you say, we must cheer up."

"Surely we must," replied Rushbrooke impatiently. "I am convinced this war will soon be over. In three months the British navy together with the armies of their allies will wind this thing up."

Through a wonder world of moonlit waterways and dark, mysterious channels, around peninsulas and between islands, across an open traverse and down a little bay, they took their course until Jim had them safely landed at their own dock again. The magic beauty of the white light upon wooded island and gleaming lake held them in its spell for some minutes after they had landed till Mrs. Murray came down from the bungalow to meet them.

"Safe back again," she cried with an all too evident effort to be cheery. "How lovely the night is, and how peaceful! James," she said in a low voice, turning to her husband, "I wish you would go to Isabel. I cannot get her to sleep. She says she must see you."

"Why, what's up?"

"I think she has got a little fright," said his wife. "She has been sobbing pitifully."

Mr. Murray found the little thing wide awake, her breath coming in the deep sobs of exhaustion that follows tempestuous tears. "What's the trouble, Sweetheart?"

"Oh, Daddy," cried the child, flinging herself upon him and bursting anew into an ecstasy of weeping, "she—said—you would—have—to—go. But—you won't—will you—Daddy?"

"Why, Isabel, what do you mean, dear? Go where?"

"To the—war—Daddy—they said—you would—have—to go—to the war."

"Who said?"

"Mabel. But—you—won't, will you, Daddy?"

"Mabel is a silly little goose," said Mr. Murray angrily. "No, never fear, my Sweetheart, they won't expect me to go. I am far too old, you know. Now, then, off you go to sleep. Do you know, the moon is shining so bright outside that the little birds can't sleep. I just heard a little bird as we were coming home cheeping away just like, you. I believe she could not go to sleep."

But the child could not forget that terrible word which had rooted itself in her heart. "But you will not go; promise me, Daddy, you will not go."

"Why, Sweetheart, listen to me."

"But promise me, Daddy, promise me." The little thing clung to him in a paroxysm of grief and terror.

"Listen, Isabel dear," said her father quietly. "You know I always tell you the truth. Now listen to me. I promise you I won't go until you send me yourself. Will that do?"

"Yes, Daddy," she said, and drew a long breath. "Now I am so tired, Daddy." Even as she spoke the little form relaxed in his arms and in a moment she was fast asleep.

As her father held her there the Spectre drew near again, but for the moment his courage failed him and he dared not look.

CHAPTER XXII

THE TUCK OF DRUM

In the midst of her busy summer work in field and factory, on lake and river, in mine and forest, on an August day of 1914, Canada was stricken to the heart. Out of a blue summer sky a bolt as of death smote her, dazed and dumb, gasping to God her horror and amaze. Without word of warning, without thought of preparation, without sense of desert, War, brutal, bloody, devilish War, was thrust into her life by that power whose business in the world, whose confidence and glory, was war.

For some days, stunned by the unexpectedness of the blow, as much as by its weight, Canada stood striving to regain her poise. Then with little outcry, and with less complaint, she gathered herself for her spring. A week, and then another, she stood breathless and following with eyes astrain the figure of her ally, little Belgium, gallant and heroic, which had moved out upon the world arena, the first to offer battle to the armour-weighted, monstrous war lord of Europe, on his way to sate his soul long thirsty for blood—men's if he could, women's and little children's by preference, being less costly. And as she stood and strained her eyes across the sea by this and other sights moved to her soul's depths, she made choice, not by compulsion but of her own free will, of war, and

Ralph Connor

having made her choice, she set herself to the business of getting ready. From Pacific to Atlantic, from Vancouver to Halifax, reverberated the beat of the drum calling for men willing to go out and stand with the Empire's sons in their fight for life and faith and freedom. Twenty-five thousand Canada asked for. In less than a month a hundred thousand men were battering at the recruiting offices demanding enlistment in the First Canadian Expeditionary Force. From all parts of Canada this demand was heard, but nowhere with louder insistence than in that part which lies beyond the Great Lakes. In Winnipeg, the Gateway City of the West, every regiment of militia at once volunteered in its full strength for active service. Every class in the community, every department of activity, gave an immediate response to the country's call. The Board of Trade; the Canadian Club, that free forum of national public opinion; the great courts of the various religious bodies; the great fraternal societies and whatsoever organisation had a voice, all pledged unqualified, unlimited, unhesitating support to the Government in its resolve to make war.

Early in the first week of war wild rumours flew of victory and disaster, but the heart of Winnipeg as of the nation was chiefly involved in the tragic and glorious struggle of little Belgium. And when two weeks had gone and Belgium, bruised, crushed, but unconquered, lay trampled in the bloody dust beneath the brutal boots of the advancing German hordes, Canada with the rest of the world had come to measure more adequately the nature and the immensity of the work in hand. By her two weeks of glorious conflict Belgium had uncovered to the world's astonished gaze two portentous and significant facts: one, stark and horrible, that the German military power knew neither ruth nor right; the other, gloriously conspicuous, that Germany's much-vaunted men-of-war were not invincible.

On the first Sunday of the war the churches of Winnipeg were full to the doors. Men, whose attendance was more or less desultory and to a certain extent dependent upon the weather, were conscious of an impulse to go to church. War had shaken the foundations of their world, and men were thinking their deepest thoughts and facing realities too often neglected or minimised. "I have been thinking of God these days," said a man to Mr. Murray as they walked home from business on Saturday, and there were many like him in Canada in those first days of August. Without being able definitely to define it there was in the hearts of men a sense of need of some clear word of guiding, and in this crisis of Canadian history the churches of Canada were not found wanting. The same Spirit that in ancient days sent forth the Hebrew Isaiah with a message of warning and counsel for the people of his day and which in the great crises of nations has found utterance through the lips of men of humble and believing hearts once more became a source of guidance and of courage.

The message varied with the character and training of the messenger. In the church of which Reverend Andrew McPherson was the minister the people were called to repentance and faith and courage.

"Listen to the Word of God," cried the minister, "spoken indeed to men of another race and another time, but spoken as truly for the men of this day and of this nation. 'Thus saith Jehovah, thy Redeemer, the Holy One of Israel; I am Jehovah thy God, which teacheth thee to profit, which leadeth thee by the way that thou shouldst go. Oh, that thou wouldst hearken to my commandments! then would thy peace be as a river, and thy righteousness as the waves of the sea. . . . There is no peace, saith Jehovah, to the wicked.' Echoing down through the centuries, these great words have verified themselves in every age and may in our day verify themselves anew. Peace and righteousness are necessarily and eternally bound together." He refused to discuss with them to-day the causes of this calamity that had fallen upon them and upon the world. But in the name of that same Almighty, Holy God, he summoned the people to repentance and to righteousness, for without righteousness there could be no peace.

In the Cathedral there rang out over the assembled people the Call to Sacrifice. "He that saveth his life shall lose it; and he that loseth his life for My sake shall find it." The instinct to save life was fundamental and universal. There were times when man must resist that instinct and choose to surrender life. Such was the present time. Dear as life was, there were things infinitely more precious to mankind, and these things were in peril. For the preserving of these things to the world our Empire had resolved upon war, and throughout the Empire the call had sounded forth for men willing to sacrifice their lives. To this call Canada would make response, and only thus could Canada save her life. For faith, for righteousness, for humanity, our Empire had accepted war. And now, as ever, the pathway to immortality for men and for nations was the pathway of sacrifice.

In St. Mary's the priest, an Irishman of warm heart and of fiery fighting spirit, summoned the faithful to faith and duty. To faith in the God of their fathers who through his church had ever led his people along the stern pathway of duty. The duty of the hour was that of united and whole-hearted devotion to the cause of Freedom, for which Great Britain had girded on her sword. The heart of the Empire had been thrilled by the noble words of the leader of the Irish Party in the House of Commons at Home, in which he pledged the Irish people to the cause of the world's Freedom. In this great struggle all loyal Sons of Canada of all races and creeds would be found united in the defence of this sacred cause.

The newspaper press published full reports of many of the sermons preached. These sermons all struck the same note—repentance, sacrifice, service. On Monday morning men walked with surer tread because the light was falling clearer upon the path they must take.

In the evening, when Jane and her friend, Ethel Murray, were on their way downtown, they heard the beat of a drum. Was it fancy, or was there in that beat something they had never heard in a drum beat before, something more insistent, more compelling? They hurried to Portage Avenue and there saw Winnipeg's famous historic regiment, the Ninetieth Rifles, march with quick, brisk step to the drum beat of their bugle band.

"Look," cried Ethel, "there's Pat Scallons, and Ted Tuttle, and Fred Sharp, too. I did not know that he belonged to the Ninetieth." And as they passed, rank on rank, Ethel continued to name the friends whom she recognised.

But Jane stood uttering no word. The sight of these lads stepping to the drum beat so proudly had sent a chill to her heart and tears to her eyes. "Oh, Ethel," she cried, touching her friend's arm, "isn't it terrible?"

"Why, what's the matter?" cried Ethel, glancing at her. "Think of what they are marching to!"

"Oh, I can't bear it," said Jane.

But Ethel was more engaged with the appearance of the battalion, from the ranks of which she continued to pick out the faces of her friends. "Look," she cried, "that surely is not Kellerman! It is! It is! Look, Jane, there's that little

Jew. Is it possible?"

"Kellerman?" cried Jane. "No, it can't be he. There are no Jews in the Ninetieth."

"But it is," cried Ethel. "It is Kellerman. Let us go up to Broadway and we shall meet them again."

They turned up a cross street and were in time to secure a position from which they could get a good look at the faces of the lads as they passed. The battalion was marching at attention, and so rigid was the discipline that not a face was turned toward the two young ladies standing at the street corner. A glance of the eye and a smile they received from their friends as they passed, but no man turned his head.

"There he is," said Jane. "It is Kellerman—in the second row, see?"

"Sure enough, it is Kellerman," said Ethel. "Well, what has come to Winnipeg?"

"War," said Jane solemnly. "And a good many more of the boys will be going too, if they are any good."

As Kellerman came stepping along he caught sight of the girls standing there, but no sign of recognition did he make. He was too anxious to be considered a soldier for that. Steadiness was one of the primary principles knocked into the minds of recruits by the Sergeant Major.

The girls moved along after the column had passed at a sufficient distance to escape the rabble. At the drill hall they found the street blocked by a crowd of men, women and children.

"What is all this, I wonder?" said Ethel. "Let us wait here awhile. Perhaps we may come across some one we know."

It was a strange crowd that gathered about the entrance to the drill hall, not the usual assemblage of noisy, idly curious folk of the lighter weight that are wont to follow a marching battalion or gather to the sound of a band. It was composed of substantial and solid people, serious in face and quiet in demeanour. They were there on business, a business of the gravest character. As the girls stood waiting they heard far down Broadway the throbbing of drums.

"Listen, Ethel," cried Jane. "The Pipes!"

"The Pipes!" echoed Ethel in great excitement. "The Kilties!"

Above the roll and rattle of the drums they caught those high, heart-thrilling sounds which for nearly two hundred years have been heard on every famous British battlefield, and which have ever led Scotland's sons down the path of blood and death to imperishable glory.

A young Ninetieth officer, intent on seeing that the way was kept clear for the soldiers, came striding out of the armoury.

"Oh, there's Frank Smart," said Ethel. "I wish he would see us."

As if in answer to her wish, Smart turned about and saw them in the crowd. Immediately he came to them.

"I didn't know you were a soldier, Frank," said Jane, greeting him with a radiant smile.

"I had almost forgotten it myself," said Frank. "But I was at church yesterday and I went home and looked up my uniform and here I am."

"You are not going across, Frank, are you?" said Ethel.

"If I can. There is very strong competition between both officers and men. I have been paying little attention to soldiering for a year or so; I have been much too busy. But now things are different. If I can make it, I guess I will go."

"Oh, Frank, YOU don't need to go, said Ethel. I mean there are heaps of men all over Canada wanting to go. Why should YOU go?"

"The question a fellow must ask himself is rather why should he stay," replied the young officer. "Don't you think so, Jane?"

"Yes," said Jane, drawing in her breath sharply but smiling at him.

"Do you want to go in?" asked Frank.

"Oh, do let's go in," said Ethel.

But Jane shrank back. "I don't like to go through all those men," she said, "though I should like greatly to see Kellerman," she added. "I wonder if I could see him."

"Kellerman?"

"Yes, he's Jane's special, you know," said Ethel. "They ran close together for the German prize, you remember. You don't know him? A little Jew chap."

"No, I don't know him," said Smart. "But you can certainly see him if you wish. Just come with me; I will get you in. But first I have got to see that this way is kept clear for the Highlanders."

"Oh, let's wait to see them come up," said Ethel.

"Well, then, stand here," said Frank. "There may be a crush, but if you don't mind that we will follow right after them. Here they come. Great lads, aren't they?"

"And they have their big feather bonnets on, too," said Ethel.

Down the street the Highlanders came in column of fours, the pipe band leading.

"Aren't they gorgeous?" said Smart with generous praise for a rival battalion. "Chesty-looking devils, eh?" he added as they drew near. "You would think that Pipe Major owned at least half of Winnipeg."

"And the big drummer the other half," added Ethel. "Look at his sticks. He's got a classy twirl, hasn't he?"

Gorgeous they were, their white spats flashing in time with their step, their kilts swaying free over their tartan hose and naked knees, their white tunics gleaming through the dusk of the evening, and over all the tossing plumes of their great feather bonnets nodding rhythmically with their swinging stride.

"Mighty glad we have not to fight those boys," said Frank as the column swung past into the armoury.

The crowd which on other occasions would have broken into enthusiastic cheers to-night stood in silence while the

Highlanders in all their gorgeous splendour went past. That grave silence was characteristic of the Winnipeg crowds those first days of war. Later they found voice.

"Now we can go in. Come right along," said Smart. "Stand clear there, boys. You can't go in unless you have an order."

"We ar-r-e wantin' tae join," said a Scotch voice.

"You are, eh? Come along then. Fall into line there." The men immediately dropped into line. "Ah, you have been there before, I see," said Smart.

"Aye, ye'er-r-r right ther-r-re, sir-r-r," answered the voice.

"You will be for the Kilties, boys?" said Frank.

"Aye. What else?" asked the same man in surprise.

"There is only one regiment for the Scotchman apparently," said Frank, leading the way to the door. "Just hold these men here until I see what's doing, will you?" he said to the sentry as he passed in. "Now, then, young ladies, step to your right and await me in that corner. I must see what's to be done with these recruits. Then I shall find Kellerman for you."

But he had no need to look for Kellerman, for before he returned the little Jew had caught sight of the young ladies and had made his way to them.

"Why, how splendid you look, Mr. Kellerman," said Ethel. "I did not know you were in the Ninetieth."

"I wasn't until Friday."

"Do you mean to say you joined up to go away?" inquired Ethel.

"That's what," said Kellerman.

"But you are—I mean—I do not see—" Ethel stopped in confusion.

"What you mean, Miss Murray, is that you are surprised at a Jew joining a military organisation," said Kellerman with a quiet dignity quite new to him. Formerly his normal condition was one of half defiant, half cringing nervousness in the presence of ladies. To-night he carried himself with an easy self-possession, and it was due to more than the uniform.

"I am afraid you are right. It is horrid of me and I am awfully sorry," said Ethel, impulsively offering him her hand.

"Why did you join, Mr. Kellerman?" said Jane in her quiet voice.

"Why, I hardly know if I can tell you. I will, though," he added with a sudden impulse, "if you care to hear."

"Oh, do tell us," said Ethel. But Kellerman looked at Jane.

"If you care to tell, Mr. Kellerman," she said.

The little Jew stood silent a few minutes, leaning upon his rifle and looking down upon the ground. Then in a low, soft voice he began: "I was born in Poland—German Poland. The first thing I remember is seeing my mother kneeling, weeping and wringing her hands beside my father's dead body outside the door of our little house in our village. He was a student, a scholar, and a patriot."

Kellerman's voice took on a deeper and firmer tone. "He stood for the Polish language in the schools. There was a riot in our village. A German officer struck my father down and killed him on the ground. My mother wiped the blood off his white face—I can see that white face now—with her apron. She kept that apron; she has it yet. We got somehow to London soon after that. The English people were good to us. The German people are tyrants. They have no use for free peoples." The little Jew's words snapped through his teeth. "When war came a week ago I could not sleep for two nights. On Friday I joined the Ninetieth. That night I slept ten hours." As he finished his story the lad stood staring straight before him into the moving crowd. He had forgotten the girls who with horror-stricken faces had been listening to him. He was still seeing that white face smeared with blood.

"And your mother?" said Jane gently as she laid her hand upon his arm.

The boy started. "My mother? Oh, my mother, she went with me to the recruiting office and saw me take the oath. She is satisfied now."

For some moments the girls stood silent, unable to find their voices. Then Jane said, her eyes glowing with a deep inner light, "Mr. Kellerman, I am proud of you."

"Thank you, Miss Brown; it does me good to hear you say that. But you have always been good to me."

"And I want you to come and see me before you go," said Jane as she gave him her hand. "Now will you take us out through the crowd? We must get along."

"Certainly, Miss Brown. Just come with me." With a fine, soldierly tread the young Jew led them through the crowd and put them on their way. He did not shake hands with them as he said good-bye, but gave them instead a military salute, of which he was apparently distinctly proud.

"Tell me, Jane," said Ethel, as they set off down the street, "am I awake? Is that little Kellerman, the greasy little Jew whom we used to think such a beast?"

"Isn't he splendid?" said Jane. "Poor little Kellerman! You know, Ethel, he had not one girl friend in college? I am sorry now we were not better to him."

The streets were full of people walking hurriedly or gathered here and there in groups, all with grave, solemn faces. In front of The Times office a huge concourse stood before the bulletin boards reading the latest despatches. These were ominous enough: "The Germans Still Battering Liege Forts—Kaiser's Army Nearing Brussels—Four Millions of Men Marching on France—Russia Hastening Her Mobilisation—Kitchener Calls for One Hundred Thousand Men—Canada Will Send Expeditionary Force of Twenty-five Thousand Men—Camp at Valcartier Nearly Ready—Parliament Assembles Thursday." Men read the bulletins and talked quietly to each other. They had not yet reached clearness in their thinking as to how this dread thing had fallen upon their country so far from the storm centre, so remote in all vital relations. There was no cheering—the cheering days came later—no ebullient emotion, but the tightening of lip and jaw in their stern, set faces was a sufficient index of the tensity of feeling. Canadians were thinking things out, thinking keenly and swiftly, for in the atmosphere and actuality of war mental processes are carried on at high pressure.

As the girls stood at the corner of Portage Avenue and

Main waiting for a crossing, an auto held up in the traffic drew close to their side.

"Hello, Ethel! Won't you get in?" said a voice at their ear.

"Hello, Lloyd! Hello, Helen!" cried Ethel. "We will, most certainly. Are you joying, or what?"

"Both," said Lloyd Rushbrooke, who was at the wheel. "Helen wanted to see the soldiers. She is interested in the Ninetieth but he wasn't there and I am just taking her about."

"We saw the Ninetieth and the Kilties too," said Ethel. "Oh, they are fine! Oh, Helen, whom do you think we saw in the Ninetieth? You will never guess—Heinrich Kellerman."

"Good Lord! That greasy little Sheeney?" exclaimed Rushbrooke.

"Look out, Lloyd. He's Jane's friend," said Ethel.

Lloyd laughed uproariously at the joke. "And you say the little Yid was in the Ninetieth? Well, what is the Ninetieth coming to?"

"Lloyd, you mustn't say a word against Mr. Kellerman," said Jane. "I think he is a real man."

"Oh, come, Jane. That little Hebrew Shyster? Why, he does not wash more than once a year!"

"I don't care if he never washes at all. I won't have you speak of him that way," said Jane. "I mean it. He is a friend of mine."

"And of mine, too," said Ethel, "since to-night. Why, he gave me thrills up in the armoury as he told us why he joined up."

"One ten per, eh?" said Lloyd.

"Shall I tell him?" said Ethel.

"No, you will not," said Jane decidedly. "Lloyd would not understand."

"Oh, I say, Jane, don't spike a fellow like that. I am just joking."

"I won't have you joke in that way about Mr. Kellerman, at least, not to me." Few of her college mates had ever seen Jane angry. They all considered her the personification of even-tempered serenity.

"If you take it that way, of course I apologise," said Lloyd.

"Now listen to me, Lloyd," said Jane. "I am going to tell you why he joined up." And in tones thrilling with the intensity of her emotion and finally breaking, she recounted Kellerman's story. "And that is why he is going to the war, and I am proud of him," she added.

"Splendid!" cried Helen Brookes. "You are in the Ninetieth, too, Lloyd, aren't you?"

"Yes," said Lloyd. "At least, I was. I have not gone much lately. I have not had time for the military stuff, so I canned it."

"And we saw Pat Scallons and Ted Tuttle in the Ninetieth, too, and Ramsay Dunn—oh, he did look fine in his uniform—and Frank Smart—he is going if he can," said Ethel. "I wonder what his mother will do. He is the only son, you know."

"Well, if you ask me, I think that is rot. It is not right for Smart. There are lots of fellows who can go," said Lloyd in quite an angry tone. "Why, they say they have nearly got the twenty-five thousand already."

"My, I would like to be in the first twenty-five thousand if I were a man," said Ethel. "There is something fine in that. Wouldn't you, Jane?"

"I am not a man," said Jane shortly.

"Why the first twenty-five thousand?" said Lloyd. "Oh, that is just sentimental rot. If a man was really needed, he would go; but if not, why should he? There's no use getting rattled over this thing. Besides, somebody's got to keep things going here. I think that is a fine British motto that they have adopted in England, 'Business as usual.'"

"'Business as usual!'" exclaimed Jane in a tone of unutterable contempt. "I think I must be going home, Lloyd," she added. "Can you take me?"

"What's the rush, Jane? It is early yet. Let's take a turn out to the Park."

But Jane insisted on going home. Never before in all her life had she found herself in a mood in which she could with difficulty control her speech. She could not understand how it was that Lloyd Rushbrooke, whom she had always greatly liked, should have become at once distasteful to her. She could hardly bear the look upon his handsome face. His clever, quick-witted fun, which she had formerly enjoyed, now grated horribly. Of all the college boys in her particular set, none was more popular, none better liked, than Lloyd Rushbrooke. Now she was mainly conscious of a desire to escape from his company. This feeling distressed her. She wanted to be alone that she might think it out. That was Jane's way. She always knew her own mind, could always account for her emotions, because she was intellectually honest and had sufficient fortitude to look facts in the face. At the door she did not ask even her friend, Ethel, to come in with her. Nor did she make excuse for omitting this courtesy. That, too, was Jane's way. She was honest with her friends as with herself. She employed none of the little fibbing subterfuges which polite manners approve and which are employed to escape awkward situations, but which, of course, deceive no one. She was simple, sincere, direct in her mental and moral processes, and possessed a courage of the finest quality. Under ordinary circumstances she would have cleared up her thinking and worked her soul through the mist and stress of the rough weather by talking it over with her father or by writing a letter to Larry. But during the days of the past terrible week she had discovered that her father, too, was tempest-tossed to an even greater degree than she was herself; and somehow she had no heart to write to Larry. Indeed, she knew not what to say. Her whole world was in confusion.

And in Winnipeg there were many like her. In every home, while faces carried bold fronts, there was heart searching of the ultimate depths and there was purging of souls. In every office, in every shop, men went about their work resolute to keep minds sane, faces calm, and voices steady, but haunted by a secret something which they refused to call fear—which was not fear—but which as yet they were unwilling to acknowledge and which they were unable to name. With every bulletin from across the sea the uncertainty deepened. Every hour they waited for news of a great victory for the fleet. The second day of the war a rumour of such a victory had come across the wires and had raised hopes for a day which next day were dashed to despair. One ray of light, thin but marvellously bright, came from Belgium. For these six breathless days that gallant little people had barred the way against the onrushing multitudes of Germany's military hosts. The story of the defence of Liege was to the Allies like a big drink of wine to a fainting man. But Belgium could not last. And what of France? What France would do no man could say. It was exceedingly doubtful whether there was in the French soul that enduring quality, whether in the army or in the nation, that would be steadfast in the face of disaster. The British navy was fit, thank God! But as to the army, months must elapse before a British army of any size could be on the fighting line.

Another agonising week passed and still there was no sure word of hope from the Front. In Canada one strong, heartening note had been sounded. The Canadian Parliament had met and with splendid unhesitating unanimity had approved all the steps the Government had taken, had voted large sums for the prosecution of the war, and had pledged Canada to the Empire to the limit of her power. That fearless challenge flung out into the cloud wrapped field of war was like a clear bugle call in the night. It rallied and steadied the young nation, touched her pride, and breathed serene resolve into the Canadian heart. Canadians of all classes drew a long, deep breath of relief as they heard of the action of their Parliament. Doubts, uncertainties vanished like morning mists blown by the prairie breeze. They knew not as yet the magnitude of the task that lay before them, but they knew that whatever it might be, they would not go back from it.

At the end of the second week the last fort in Liege had fallen; Brussels, too, was gone; Antwerp threatened. Belgium was lost. From Belgian villages and towns were beginning to come those tales of unbelievable atrocities that were to shock the world into horrified amazement. These tales read in the Canadian papers clutched men's throats and gripped men's hearts as with cruel fingers of steel. Canadians were beginning to see red. The blood of Belgium's murdered victims was indeed to prove throughout Canada and throughout the world the seed of mighty armies.

At the end of the second week Jane could refrain no longer. She wrote to Larry.

CHAPTER XXIII

A NEUTRAL NATION

The first days of the war were for Larry days of dazed
bewilderment and of ever-deepening misery. The thing
which he had believed impossible had come. That great
people upon whose generous ideals and liberal Christian
culture he had grounded a sure hope of permanent peace
had flung to the winds all the wisdom, and all justice, and
all the humanity which the centuries had garnered for
them, and, following the primal instincts of the brute, had
hurled forth upon the world ruthless war. Even the great
political party of the Social Democrats upon which he had
relied to make war impossible had without protest or
division proclaimed enthusiastic allegiance to the war
programme of the Kaiser. The universities and the
churches, with their preachers and professors, had led the
people in mad acclaim of war. His whole thinking on the
subject had been proved wrong. Passionately he had
hoped against hope that Britain would not allow herself to
enter the war, but apparently her struggle for peace had
been in vain. His first feeling was one of bitter disappointment and of indignation with the great leaders of the
British people who had allowed themselves to become
involved in a Mid-European quarrel. Sir Edward Grey's
calm, moderate—sub-moderate, indeed—exposition of
the causes which had forced Britain into war did much to

cool his indignation, and Bethmann-Hollweg's cynical explanation of the violation of Belgium's neutrality went far to justify Britain's action consequent upon that outraging of treaty faith. The deliberate initiation of the policy of "frightfulness" which had heaped such unspeakable horrors upon the Belgian people tore the veil from the face of German militarism and revealed in its sheer brutality the ruthlessness and lawlessness of that monstrous system.

From the day of Austria's ultimatum to Servia Larry began to read everything he could find dealing with modern European history, and especially German history. Day and night he studied with feverish intensity the diplomacy and policies of the great powers of Europe till at length he came to a somewhat clear understanding of the modern theory and world policy of the German state which had made war inevitable. But, though his study made it possible for him to relieve his country from the charge of guilt in this war, his anxiety and his misery remained. For one thing, he was oppressed with an overwhelming loneliness. He began to feel that he was dwelling among an alien people. He had made many and close friends during the months of his stay in Chicago. But while they were quick to offer him sympathy in his anxiety and misery, he could not fail to observe on every hand the obvious and necessary indications of the neutral spirit. He could expect nothing else. In this conflict America had decided that she was not immediately concerned and she was resolute to remain unconcerned. A leading representative of the Chicago press urged Americans to be careful not to "rock the boat." The President of the United States counselled his people "to keep calm" and to observe the strictest neutrality. Larry discovered, too, an unconfessed, almost unconscious desire in the heart of many an American, a relic of Revolutionary days, to see England not destroyed or even seriously disabled, but, say, "well trimmed." It would do her good. There was, beside, a large element in the city distinctly and definitely pro-German and intensely hostile to Great Britain. On his way to the office one afternoon Larry found himself held up by a long procession of young German reservists singing with the utmost vigour and with an unmistakable note of triumph the German national air, "Die Wacht Am Rhein," and that newer song which embodied German faith and German ambition, "Deutschland Uber Alles." When he arrived at the office that afternoon he was surprised to find that he was unable to go on with his work for the trembling of his hands. In the office he was utterly alone, for, however his friends there might take pains to show extra kindness, he was conscious of complete isolation from their life. Unconcerned, indifferent, coolly critical of the great conflict in which his people were pouring out blood like water, they were like spectators at a football match on the side lines willing to cheer good play on either side and ready to acclaim the winner.

The Wakehams, though extremely careful to avoid a word or act that might give him pain, naturally shared the general feeling of their people. For them the war was only another of those constantly recurring European scraps which were the inevitable result of the forms of government which these nations insisted upon retaining. If peoples were determined to have kings and emperors, what other could they expect but wars. France, of course, was quite another thing. The sympathy of America with France was deep, warm and sincere. America could not forget the gallant Lafayette. Besides, France was the one European republic. As for Britain, the people of Chicago were content to maintain a profoundly neutral calm, and to a certain extent the Wakehams shared this feeling.

In Larry's immediate circle, however, there were two

exceptions. One, within the Wakeham family, was Elfie. Quick to note the signs of wretchedness in him and quick to feel the attitude of neutrality assumed by her family toward the war, the child, without stint and without thought, gave him a love and a sympathy so warm, so passionate, that it was to his heart like balm to an open wound. There was no neutrality about Elfie. She was openly, furiously pro-Ally. The rights and wrongs of the great world conflict were at first nothing to her. With Canada and the Canadians she was madly in love, they were Larry's people and for Larry she would have gladly given her life. Another exception to the general state of feeling was that of Hugo Raeder. From the first Raeder was an intense and confessed advocate of the cause of the Allies. From personal observation he knew Germany well, and from wide reading he had come to understand and appreciate the significance of her world policy. He recognised in German autocracy and in German militarism and in German ambition a menace to the liberties of Europe. He represented a large and intellectually influential class of men in the city and throughout the country generally. Graduates of the great universities, men high in the leadership of the financial world, the editors of the great newspapers almost to a man, magazine editors and magazine writers untinged by racial or personal affinity with Germany, these were represented by Raeder, and were strongly and enthusiastically in sympathy with the aims of the Allies, and as the war advanced became increasingly eager to have their country assume a definite stand on the side of those nations whom they believed to be fighting for the liberties and rights of humanity. But though these exceptions were a source of unspeakable comfort to him, Larry carried day by day a growing sense of isolation and an increasing burden of anxiety.

Then, too, there was the question of his duty. He had no clear conviction as to what his duty was. With all his hatred and loathing of war, he had come to the conviction that should he see it to be the right thing for him, he would take his place in the fighting line. There appeared, however, to be no great need for men in Canada just now. In response to the call for twenty-five thousand men for the First Expeditionary Force, nearly one hundred thousand had offered. And yet his country was at war; his friends whether enlisted for the fighting line or in the civilian ranks were under the burden. Should he not return to Canada and find some way to help in the great cause? But again, on the other hand, his work here was important, he had been treated with great consideration and kindness, he had made a place for himself where he seemed to be needed. The lack of clear vision of his duty added greatly to his distress.

A wire had informed him in the first days of the war that his brother-in-law had gone to rejoin his old regiment in the Coldstream Guards. A letter from Nora did not help much. "Jack has gone," she wrote. "We all felt he could do nothing else. Even poor, dear Mother agreed that nothing else was possible. Kathleen amazes us all. The very day after the awful news came, without a word from Jack, I found her getting his things together. 'Are you going to let him go?' I asked her, perfectly amazed at her coolness. 'Let me go?' said Jack, who was muddling about her. 'Let me go? She would not let me stay. Would you, Kathleen?' 'No,' she said, 'I do not think I would like you to stay, Jack.' And this is our pacifist, Kathleen, mind you! How she came to see through this thing so rapidly I don't know. But sooner than any of us Kathleen saw what the war was about and that we must get in. She goes about her work quietly, cheerfully. She has no illusions, and there is no bravado. Oh, Larry dear, I do not believe I could do it. When she smiles at the dear wee man in her arms I have to run away or I should howl. I must tell you about Duckworth. You know what a dear he is. We have seen a good deal of him this year. He has quite captivated Mother. Well, he had a letter from his father saying, 'I am just about rejoining my regiment; your brother has enlisted; your sister has gone to the Red Cross. We have given our house to the Government for a hospital. Come home and join up.' What a man he must be! The dear boy came to see us and, Larry, he wanted me. Oh, I wish I could have said yes, but somehow I couldn't. Dear boy, I could only kiss him and weep over him till he forgot himself in trying to comfort me. He went with the Calgary boys. Hec Ross is off, too; and Angus Fraser is up and down the country with kilt and pipes driving Scotchmen mad to be at the war. He's going, too, although what his old mother will do without him I do not know. But she will hear of nothing less. Only four weeks of this war and it seems like a year. Switzer has gone, you know, the wicked devil. If it had not been for Sam, who had been working around the mine, the whole thing would have been blown up with dynamite. Sam discovered the thing in time. The Germans have all quit work. Thank God for that. So the mine is not doing much. Mother is worried about the war, I can see, thinking things through."

A letter from Jane helped him some. It was very unlike Jane and evidently written under the stress of strong emotion. She gave him full notes of the Reverend Andrew McPherson's sermons, which she appeared to set great store by. The rapid progress of recruiting filled her with delight. It grieved her to think that her friends were going to the war, but that grief was as nothing compared to the grief and indignation against those who seemed to treat the war lightly. She gave a page of enthusiastic appreciation to Kellerman. Another page she devoted to an unsuccessful attempt to repress her furious contempt for Lloyd Rushbrooke, who talked largely and coolly about the need of keeping sane. The ranks of the first contingent were all filled up. She knew there were two million

Canadians in the United States who if they were needed would flock back home. They were not needed yet, and so it would be very foolish for them to leave good positions in the meantime.

Larry read the last sentence with a smile. "Dear old Jane," he said to himself. "She wants to help me out; and, by George, she does." Somehow Jane's letter brought healing to his lacerated nerves and heart, and steadied him to bear the disastrous reports of the steady drive of the enemy towards Paris that were released by the censor during the last days of that dreadful August. With each day of that appalling retreat Larry's agony deepened. The reports were vague, but one thing was clear—the drive was going relentlessly forward, and the French and the British armies alike were powerless to stay the overwhelming torrent. The check at the Marne lifted the gloom a bit. But the reports of that great fight were meagre and as yet no one had been able to estimate the full significance of that mighty victory for the Allied armies, nor the part played therein by the gallant and glorious little army that constituted the British Expeditionary Force.

Blacker days came in late September, when the news arrived of the disaster to the Aboukir and her sister ships, and a month later of the destruction of the Good Hope and the Monmouth in the South Pacific sea fight. On that dreadful morning on his way downtown he purchased a paper. After the first glance he crushed the paper together till he reached his office, where he sat with the paper spread out before him on his desk, staring at the head-lines, unable to see, unable to think, able only to suffer. In the midst of his misery Professor Schaefer passed through the office on his way to consult with Mr. Wakeham and threw him a smile of cheery triumph. It was a way Schaefer had these days. The very sight of him was enough to stir Larry to a kind of frenzied madness. This morning the German's smile was the filling up of his cup of misery. He stuffed the paper into his desk, took up his pen and began to make figures on his pad, gnawing his lips the while.

An hour later Hugo Raeder came in with a message for him. Raeder after one look at his face took Larry away with him, sick with rage and fear, in his car, and for an hour and a half drove through the Park at a rate that defied the traffic regulations, talking the while in quiet, hopeful tones of the prospects of the Allies, of the marvellous recovery of the French and British armies on the Marne and of the splendid Russian victories. He touched lightly upon the recent naval disaster, which was entirely due to the longer range of the enemy's guns and to a few extraordinarily lucky shots. The clear, crisp air, the swift motion, the bright sun, above all the deep, kindly sympathy of this strong, clear-thinking man beside him, brought back to Larry his courage if not his cheer. As they were nearly back to the office again, he ventured his first observation, for throughout the drive he had confined his speech to monosyllabic answers to Raeder's stream of talk.

"In spite of it all, I believe the navy is all right," he said, with savage emphasis.

"My dear chap," exclaimed Raeder, "did you ever doubt it? Did you read the account of the fight?"

"No," said Larry, "only the headlines."

"Then you did not see that the British ships were distinctly outclassed in guns both as to range and as to weight. Nothing can prevent disaster in such a case. It was a bit of British stupidity to send those old cruisers on such an expedition. The British navy is all right. If not, then

God help America."

"Say, old chap," said Larry as they stepped out of the car, "you have done me a mighty good turn this morning, and I will not forget it."

"Oh, that is all right," said Raeder. "We have got to stand together in this thing, you know."

"Stand together?" said Larry.

"Yes, stand together. Don't you forget it. We are with you in this. Deep down in the heart America is utterly sound; she knows that the cause of the Allies is the cause of justice and humanity. America has no use for either brutal tyranny or slimy treachery. The real American heart is with you now, and her fighting army will yet be at your side."

These sentiments were so unusual in his environment that Larry gazed at him in amazement.

"That is God's truth," said Raeder. "Take a vote of the college men to-day, of the big business men, of the big newspaper men—these control the thinking and the acting of America—and you will find, ninety per cent. of these pro-Ally. Just be patient and give the rest of us time. Americans will not stand for the bully," added Raeder, putting his hand on Larry's shoulder. "You hear me, my boy. Now I am going in to see the boss. He thinks the same way, too, but he does not say much out loud."

New hope and courage came into Larry's heart as he listened to the pronouncement of this clear-headed, virile young American. Oh, if America would only say out loud what Raeder had been saying, how it would tone up the spirit of the Allies! A moral vindication of their cause from America would be worth many an army corps.

The morning brought him another and unexpected breeze of cheer in the person of Dean Wakeham straight from Alberta and the Lakeside Farm. A little before lunch he walked in upon Larry, who was driving himself to his work that he might forget. It was a veritable breath from home for Larry, for Dean was one who carried not only news but atmosphere as well. He was a great, warm-hearted boy, packed with human energies of body, heart and soul.

"Wait till I say good-morning to father," he said after he had shaken hands warmly with Larry. "I will be back then in a minute or two."

But in a few minutes Mr. Wakeham appeared and called Larry to him. "Come in, boy, and hear the news," he said.

Larry went in and found Dean in the full tide of a torrential outpouring of passionate and enthusiastic, at times incoherent, tales of the Canadians, of their spirit, of their sacrifice and devotion in their hour of tragedy.

"Go on, Dean," said Raeder, who was listening with face and eyes aglow.

"Go on? I cannot stop. Never have I come up against anything like what is going on over there in Canada. Not in one spot, either, but everywhere; not in one home, but in every home; not in one class, but in every class. In Calgary during the recruiting I saw a mob of men in from the ranches, from the C. P. R. shops, from the mines, from the offices, fighting mad to get their names down. My God! I had to go away or I would have had mine in too. The women, too, are all the same. No man is getting under his wife's skirts. You know old Mrs. Ross, Larry, an old Scotch woman up there with four sons. Well, her eldest son could not wait for the Canadian contingent, but went off with Jack Romayne and joined the Black Watch. He was in that Le Cateau fight. Oh, why don't these stupid British tell the people something about that great fighting retreat from Mons to the Marne? Well, at Le Cateau poor Hec Ross in a glorious charge got his. His Colonel wrote the old lady about it. I never saw such a letter; there never was one like it. I motored Mrs. Gwynne, your mother, Larry, over to see her. Say, men, to see those two women and to hear them! There were no tears, but a kind of exaltation. Your mother, Larry, is as bad, as good, I mean, as any of them now. I heard that old Scotch woman say to your mother in that Scotch voice of hers, 'Misthress Gwynne, I dinna grudge my boy. I wouldna hae him back.' Her youngest son is off with the Canadians. As she said good-bye to us I heard her say to your mother, 'I hae gi'en twa sons, Misthress Gwynne, an' if they're wanted, there's twa mair.' My God! I found myself blubbering like a child. It sounds all mad and furious, but believe me, there is not much noise, no hurrahing. They know they are up against a deadly serious business, and that is getting clearer every minute. Did you see that the Government had offered one hundred and fifty thousand men now, and more if wanted? And all classes are the same. That little Welch preacher at Wolf Willow—Rhye, his name is, isn't it? By George, you should hear him flaming in the pulpit. He's the limit. There won't be a man in that parish will dare hold back. He will just have to go to war or quit the church. And it is the same all over. The churches are a mighty force in Canada, you know, even a political force. I have been going to church every Sunday, Father, this last year. Believe me, God is some real Person to those people, and I want to tell you He has become real to me too." As Dean said this he glanced half defiantly at his father as if expecting a challenge.

But his father only cleared his throat and said, "All right, my boy. We won't do anything but gladly agree with you there. And God may come to be more real to us all before we are through with this thing. Go on."

"Let's see, what was I talking about?"

"Churches."

"Yes, in Calgary, on my way down this time, the Archdeacon preached a sermon that simply sent thrills down my spine. In Winnipeg I went with the Murrays to church and heard a clergyman, McPherson, preach. The soldiers were there. Great Caesar! No wonder Winnipeg is sending out thousands of her best men. He was like an ancient Hebrew prophet, Peter the Hermit and Billy Sunday all rolled into one. Yet there was no noisy drum pounding and no silly flag flapping. Say, let me tell you something. I said there was a battalion of soldiers in church that day. The congregation were going to take Holy Communion. You know the Scotch way. They all sit in their pews and you know they are fearfully strict about their Communion, have rules and regulations and so on about it. Well, that old boy McPherson just leaned over his pulpit and told the boys what the thing stood for, that it was just like swearing in, and he told them that he would just throw the rules aside and man to man would ask them to join up with God. Say, that old chap got my goat. The boys just naturally stayed to Communion and I stayed too. I was not fit, I know, but I do not think it did me any harm." At this point the boy's voice broke up and there was silence for some moments in the office. Larry had his face covered with his hands to hide the tears that were streaming down. Dean's father was openly wiping his eyes, Raeder looking stern and straight in front of him.

"Father," said Dean suddenly, "I want to give you

warning right now. If it ever comes that Canada is in need of men, I am not going to hold back. I could not do it and stay in the country. I am an American, heart, body and soul, but I would count myself meaner than a polecat if I declined to line up with that bunch of Canadians."

"Think well, my boy," said his father. "Think well. I have only one son, but I will never stand between you and your duty or your honour. Now we go to lunch. Where shall we go?"

"With me, at the University Club, all of you," said Raeder.

"No, with me," said Mr. Wakeham. "I will put up the fatted calf, for this my son is home again. Eh, my boy?"

During the lunch hour try as they would they could not get away from the war. Dean was so completely obsessed with the subject that he could not divert his mind to anything else for any length of time.

"I cannot help it," he said at length. "All my switches run the same way."

They had almost finished when Professor Schaefer came into the dining hall, spied them and hastened over to them.

"Here's this German beast," said Dean.

"Steady, Dean. We do business with him," said his father.

"All right, Father," replied the boy.

The Professor drew in a chair and sat down. He only wanted a light lunch and if they would allow him he would break in just where they were. He was full of excitement over the German successes on sea and on land.

"On land?" said Raeder. "Well, I should not radiate too freely about their land successes. What about the Marne?"

"The Marne!" said Schaefer in hot contempt. "The Marne—strategy—strategy, my dear sir. But wait. Wait a few days. If we could only get that boasted British navy to venture out from their holes, then the war would be over. Mark what happens in the Pacific. Scientific gunnery, three salvos, two hundred minutes from the first gun. It is all over. Two British ships sunk to the bottom. That is the German way. They would force war upon Germany. Now they have it. In spite of all the Kaiser's peace efforts, they drove Germany into the war."

"The Kaiser!" exclaimed Larry, unable any longer to contain his fury. "The Kaiser's peace efforts! The only efforts that the Kaiser has made for the last few years are efforts to bully Europe into submission to his will. The great peace-maker of Europe of this and of the last century was not the Kaiser, but King Edward VII. All the world knows that."

"King Edward VII!" sputtered Schaefer in a fury of contempt. "King Edward VII a peacemaker! A—!" calling him a vile name. "And his son is like him!"

The foul word was like a flame to powder with Larry. His hand closed upon his glass of water. "You are a liar," he said, leaning over and thrusting his face close up to the German. "You are a slanderous liar." He flung his glass of water full into Schaefer's face, sprang quickly to his feet, and as the German rose, swung with his open hand and struck hard upon the German's face, first on one cheek and then on the other.

Ralph Connor

With a roar Schaefer flung himself at him, but Larry in a cold fury was waiting for him. With a stiff, full-armed blow, which carried the whole weight of his body, he caught him on the chin. The professor was lifted clear over his chair. Crashing back upon the floor, he lay there still.

"Good boy, Larry," shouted Dean. "Great God! You did something that time."

Silent, white, cold, rigid, Larry stood waiting. More than any of them he was amazed at what he had done. Some friends of the Professor rushed toward them.

"Stand clear, gentlemen," said Raeder. "We are perfectly able to handle this. This man offered my friend a deadly insult. My friend simply anticipated what I myself would gladly have done. Let me say this to you, gentlemen, for some time he and those of his kind have made themselves offensive. Every man is entitled to his opinion, but I have made up my mind that if any German insults my friends the Allies in my presence, I shall treat him as this man has been treated."

There was no more of it. Schaefer's friends after reviving him led him off. As they passed out of the dining hall Larry and his friends were held up by a score or more of men who crowded around him with warm thanks and congratulations. The affair was kept out of the press, but the news of it spread to the limits of clubland. The following day Raeder thought it best that they should lunch again together at the University Club. The great dining-room was full. As Raeder and his company entered there was first a silence, then a quick hum of voices, and finally applause, which grew in volume till it broke into a ringing cheer. There was no longer any doubt as to where the sympathy of the men of the University Club, at least, lay in this world conflict.

Two days later a telegram was placed upon Larry's desk. Opening it, he read, "Word just received Jack Romayne killed in action." Larry carried the telegram quietly into the inner office and laid it upon his chief's desk.

"I can stand this no longer, sir," he said in a quiet voice. "I wish you to release me. I must return to Canada. I am going to the war."

"Very well, my boy," said Mr. Wakeham. "I know you have thought it over. I feel you could not do otherwise. I, too, have been thinking, and I wish to say that your place will await you here and your salary will go on so long as you are at the war. No! not a word! There is not much we Americans can do as yet, but I shall count it a privilege as an American sympathising with the Allies in their great cause to do this much at least. And you need not worry about that coal mine. Dean has been telling me about it. We will see it through."

Ralph Connor

CHAPTER XXIV

THE MAJOR AND THE MAJOR'S WIFE

When Larry went to take farewell of the Wakehams he found Rowena with Hugo Raeder in the drawing-room.

"You are glad to leave us," said Rowena, in a tone of reproach.

"No," said Larry, "sorry. You have been too good to me."

"You are glad to go to war?"

"No; I hate the war. I am not a soldier, but, thank God, I see my duty, and I am going to have a go at it."

"Right you are," said Hugo. "What else could any man do when his country is at war?"

"But I hate to go," said Larry, "and I hate this business of saying good-bye. You have all been so good to me."

"It was easy," said Rowena. "Do you know I was on the way to fall in love with you? Hugo here and Jane saved me. Oh, I mean it," she added, flushing as she laughed.

"Jane!" exclaimed Larry.

"Yes, Jane. Oh, you men are so stupid," said Rowena. "And Hugo helped me out, too," she added, with a shy glance at him.

Larry looked from one to the other, then rushed to Hugo. "Oh, you lucky beggar! You two lucky beggars! Oh, joy, glory, triumph! Could anything be finer in the wide world?" cried Larry, giving a hand to each.

"And, Larry, don't be a fool," said Rowena. "Try to under- stand your dear, foolish heart, and don't break your own or any one's else."

Larry gazed at her in astonishment and then at Hugo, who nodded wisely at him.

"She is quite right, Larry. I want to see that young lady Jane. She must be quite unique. I owe her something."

"Good-bye, then," said Larry. "I have already seen your mother. Good-bye, you dear things. God give you every- thing good. He has already given you almost the best."

"Good-bye, you dear boy," said Rowena. "I have wanted to kiss you many a time, but didn't dare. But now—you are going to the war"—there was a little break in her voice—"where men die. Good-bye, Larry, dear boy, good-bye." She put her arms about him. "And don't keep Jane waiting," she whispered in his ear.

"If I were a German, Larry," said Hugo, giving him both hands, "I would kiss you too, old boy, but being plain American, I can only say good luck. God bless you."

"You will find Elfie in her room," said Rowena. "She refuses to say good-bye where any one can see her. She is not going to weep. Soldiers' women do not weep, she says. Poor kid!"

Larry found Elfie in her room, with high lights as of fever on her cheeks and eyes glittering.

"I am not going to cry," she said between her teeth. "You need not be afraid, Larry. I am going to be like the Canadian women."

Larry took the child in his arms, every muscle and every nerve in her slight body taut as a fiddle-string. He smoothed her hair gently and began to talk quietly with her.

"What good times we have had!" he said. "I remember well the very first night I saw you. Do you?"

"Oh," she breathed, "don't speak of it, or I can't hold in."

"Elfie," said Larry, "our Canadian women when they are seeing their men off at the station do not cry; they smile and wave their hands. That is, many of them do. But in their own rooms, like this, they cry as much as they like."

"Oh, Larry, Larry," cried the child, flinging herself upon him. "Let me cry, then. I can't hold in any longer."

"Neither can I, little girl. See, Elfie, there is no use trying not to, and I am not ashamed of it, either," said Larry.

The pent-up emotion broke forth in a storm of sobbing and tears that shook the slight body as the tempest shakes the sapling. Larry, holding her in his arms, talked to her about the good days they had had together.

"And isn't it fine to think that we have those forever, and, whenever we want to, we can bring them back again?

And I want you to remember, Elfie, that when I was very lonely and homesick here you were the one that helped me most."

"And you, Larry, oh, what you did for me!" said the child. "I was so sick and miserable and bad and cross and hateful."

"That was just because you were not fit," said Larry. "But now you are fit and fine and strong and patient, and you will always be so. Remember it is a soldier's duty to keep fit." Elfie nodded. "And I want you to send me socks and a lot of things when I get over there. I shall write you all about it, and you will write me. Won't you?" Again Elfie nodded.

"I am glad you let me cry," she said. "I was so hot and sore here," and she laid her hands upon her throat. "And I am glad you cried too, Larry; and I won't cry before people, you know."

"That is right. There are going to be too many sad people about for us to go crying and making them feel worse," said Larry.

"But I will say good-bye here, Larry. I could go to the train, but then I might not quite smile."

But when the train pulled out that night the last face that Larry saw of all his warm-hearted American friends was that of the little girl, who stood alone at the end of the platform, waving both her hands wildly over her head, her pale face effulgent with a glorious smile, through which the tears ran unheeded down her cheeks like rain on a sunny day. And on Larry's face, as he turned away, there was the same gleam of sunshine and of rain.

"This farewell business is something too fierce," he said to himself savagely, thinking with a sinking heart of the little group at Wolf Willow in the West to whom he must say farewell, and of the one he must leave behind in Winnipeg. "How do these women send their husbands off and their sons? God knows, it is beyond me."

Throughout the train journey to Calgary his mind was chiefly occupied with the thought of the parting that awaited him. But when he reached his destination he found himself so overwhelmed with the rush of preparation and with the strenuous daily grind of training that he had no time nor energy left for anything but his work. A change, too, was coming swiftly over the heart of Canada and over his own heart. The tales of Belgian atrocities, at first rejected as impossible, but afterwards confirmed by the Bryce Commission and by many private letters, kindled in Canadian hearts a passion of furious longing to wipe from the face of the earth a system that produced such horrors. Women who, with instincts native of their kind, had at the first sought how they might with honour keep back their men from the perils of war, now in their compassion for women thus relentlessly outraged and for their tender babes pitilessly mangled, consulted chiefly how they might best fit their men for the high and holy mission of justice for the wronged and protection for the helpless. It was this that wrought in Larry a fury of devotion to his duty. Night and day he gave himself to his training with his concentrated powers of body, mind and soul, till he stood head and shoulders above the members of the Officers' Training Corps at Calgary.

After six weeks of strenuous grind Larry was ordered to report to his battalion at Wolf Willow. A new world awaited him there, a world recreated by the mysterious alchemy of war, a world in which men and women moved amid high ideals and lofty purposes, a world where the dominant note was sacrifice and the regnant motive duty.

Nora met him at the station in her own car, which, in view of her activity in connection with the mine where her father was now manager, the directors had placed at her disposal.

"How big and fine you look, Larry! You must be pounds heavier," she cried, viewing him from afar.

"Twenty pounds, and hard as hickory. Never so fit in my life," replied her brother, who was indeed a picture of splendid and vigorous health.

"You are perfectly astonishing. But everything is astonishing these days. Why, even father, till he broke his leg—"

"Broke his leg?"

"There was no use worrying you about it. A week ago, while he was pottering about the mine, he slipped down a ladder and broke his leg. He will probably stay where he belongs now—in the office. But father is as splendid as any one could well be. He has gripped that mine business hard, and even Switzer in his palmiest days could not get better results. He has quite an extraordinary way with the men, and that is something these days, when men are almost impossible to get."

"And mother?" enquired Larry.

"Mother is equally surprising. But you will see for yourself. And dear old Kathleen. She is at it day and night. They made her President of the Women's War Association, and she is—Well, it is quite beyond words. I can't talk about it, that's all." Nora's voice grew unsteady and she took refuge in silence. After a few moments she went on: "And she has had the most beautiful letter from Jack's colonel. It was on the Big Retreat from Mons that he was killed at the great fight at Landrecies. You know about that, Larry?"

"No, never heard anything; I know really nothing of that retreat," said Larry.

"Well, we have had letters about it. It must have been great. Oh, it will be a glorious tale some day. They began the fight, only seventy-five thousand of the British—think of it! with two hundred guns against four hundred thousand Germans with six hundred guns. They began the fight on a Saturday. The French on both their flanks gave way. One army on each flank trying to hem them in and an army in front pounding the life out of them. They fought all Saturday. They began the retreat on Saturday night, fought again Sunday, marched Sunday night, they fought Monday and marched Monday night, fought Tuesday, and marched Tuesday night. The letter said they staggered down the roads like drunken men. Wednesday, dead beat, they fought again—and against ever fresh masses of men, remember. Wednesday night one corps came to Landrecies. At half-past nine they were all asleep in billets. At ten o'clock a perfectly fresh army of the enemy, field guns backing them up behind, machine guns in front, bore down the streets into the village. But those wonderful Coldstreams and Grenadiers and Highlanders just filled the streets and every man for himself poured in rifle fire, and every machine gun fired into the enemy masses, smashed the attack and then they went at them with the bayonet and flung them back. Again and again throughout the night this thing was repeated until the Germans drew off, leaving five hundred dead before the village and in its streets. It was in the last bayonet charge, when leading his men, that Jack was killed."

"My God!" cried Larry. "What a great death!"

"And so Kathleen goes about with her head high and Sybil, too,—Mrs. Waring-Gaunt, you know," continued Nora, "she is just like the others. She never thinks of herself and her two little kids who are going to be left behind but she is busy getting her husband ready and helping to outfit his men, as all the women are, with socks and mits and all the rest of it. Before Tom made up his mind to raise the battalion they were both wretched, but now they are both cheery as crickets with a kind of exalted cheeriness that makes one feel like hugging the dear things. And, Larry, there won't be a man left in this whole country if the war keeps on except old McTavish, who is furious because they won't take him and who declares he is going on his own. Poor Mr. Rhye is feeling so badly. He was rejected—heart trouble, though I think he is more likely to injure himself here preaching as he does than at the war."

"And yourself, Nora? Carrying the whole load, I suppose,—ranch, and now this mine. You are getting thin, I see."

"No fear," said Nora. "Joe is really doing awfully well on the ranch. He practically takes charge. By the way, Sam has enlisted. He says he is going to stick to you. He is going to be your batman. And as for the mine, since father's accident Mr. Wakeham has been very kind. If he were not an American he would have enlisted before this."

"Oh! he would, eh?"

"He would, or he would not be coming about Lakeside Farm."

Ralph Connor

"Then he does come about?"

"Oh, yes," said Nora with an exaggerated air of indifference. "He would be rather a nuisance if he were not so awfully useful and so jolly. After all, I do not see what we should have done without him."

"Ah, a good man is Dean."

"I had a letter from Jane this week," continued Nora, changing the subject abruptly.

"I have not heard for two weeks," said Larry.

"Then you have not heard about Scuddy. Poor Scuddy! But why say 'poor' Scuddy? He was doing his duty. It was a patrol party. He was scouting and ran into an enemy patrol and was instantly killed. The poor girl, Helen Brookes, I think it is."

"Helen Brookes!" exclaimed Larry.

"Yes, Jane says you knew her. She was engaged to Scuddy. And Scallons is gone too."

"Scallons!"

"And Smart, Frank Smart."

"Frank Smart! Oh! his poor mother! My God, this war is awful and grows more awful every day."

"Jane says Mrs. Smart is at every meeting of the Women's Association, quiet and steady, just like our Kathleen. Oh, Larry, how can they do it? If my husband—if I had one—were killed I could not, I just could not, bear it."

"I fancy, little girl, you would measure up like the others. This is a damnable business, but we never knew our women till now. But the sooner that cursed race is wiped off the face of the earth the better."

"Why, Larry, is that you? I cannot believe my ears."

"Yes, it is me. I have come to see that there is no possibility of peace or sanity for the world till that race of mad militarists is destroyed. I am still a pacifist, but, thank God, no longer a fool. Is there no other news from Jane?"

"Did you hear about Ramsay Dunn? Oh, he did splendidly. He was wounded; got a cross or something."

"Did you know that Mr. Murray had organised a battalion and is Lieutenant-Colonel and that Doctor Brown is organising a Field Ambulance unit and going out in command?"

"Oh, that is settled, is it? Jane told me it was possible."

"Yes, and perhaps Jane and Ethel Murray will go with the Ambulance Unit. Oh, Larry, is there any way I might go? I could do so much—drive a car, an ambulance, wash, scrub, carry despatches, anything."

"By Jove, you would be a good one!" exclaimed her brother. "I would like to have you in my company."

"Couldn't it be worked in any possible way?" cried Nora.

But Larry made no reply. He knew well that no reply was needed. What was her duty this splendid girl would do, whether in Flanders or in Alberta.

Ralph Connor

At the door of their home the mother met them. As her eyes fell upon her son in his khaki uniform she gave a little cry and ran to him with arms uplifted.

"Come right in here," she whispered, and took him to the inner room. There she drew him to the bedside and down upon his knees. With their arms about each other they knelt, mingling tears and sobs together till their strength was done. Then through the sobs the boy heard her voice. "You gave him to me," he heard her whisper, not in her ordinary manner of reverent formal prayer, but as if remonstrating with a friend. "You know you gave him to me and I gave him back.—I know he is not mine.—But won't you let me have him for a little while?—It will not be so very long.—Yes, yes, I know.—I am not holding him back.—No, no, I could not, I would not do that.—Oh, I would not.—What am I better than the others?—But you will give him back to me again.—There are so many never coming back, and I have only one boy.—You will let him come back.—He is my baby boy.—It is his mother asking."

Larry could bear it no longer. "Oh, mother, mother, mother," he cried. "You are breaking my heart. You are breaking my heart." His sobs were shaking the bed on which he leaned.

His mother lifted her head. "What is it, Lawrence, my boy?" she asked in surprise. "What is it?" Her voice was calm and steady. "We must be steadfast, my boy. We must not grudge our offering. No, with willing hearts we must bring our sacrifice." She passed into prayer. "Thou, who didst give Thy Son, Thine only Son, to save Thy world, aid me to give mine to save our world to-day. Let the vision of the Cross make us both strong. Thou Cross-bearer, help us to bear our cross." With a voice that never faltered, she poured forth her prayer of sacrifice, of thanksgiving, of supplication, till serene, steady, triumphant, they arose from their knees. She was heard "in that she feared," in her surrender she found victory, in her cross, peace. And that serene calm of hers remained undisturbed to the very last.

There were tears again at the parting, but the tears fell gently, and through them shone ever her smile.

A few short days Larry spent at his home moving about among those that were dearer to him than his own life, wondering the while at their courage and patience and power to sacrifice. In his father he seemed to discover a new man, so concentrated was he in his devotion to business, and so wise, his only regret being that he could not don the king's uniform. With Kathleen he spent many hours. Not once throughout all these days did she falter in her steady, calm endurance, and in her patient devotion to duty. Without tears, without a word of repining against her cruel fate, with hardly a suggestion, indeed, of her irreparable loss, she talked to him of her husband and of his glorious death.

After two months an unexpected order called the battalion on twenty-four hours' notice for immediate service over seas, and amid the cheers of hundreds of their friends and fellow citizens, although women being in the majority, the cheering was not of the best, they steamed out of Melville Station. There were tears and faces white with heartache, but these only after the last cheer had been flung upon the empty siding out of which the cars of the troop-train had passed. The tears and the white faces are for that immortal and glorious Army of the Base, whose finer courage and more heroic endurance make victory possible to the army of the Fighting First Line.

At Winnipeg the train was halted for a day and a night,

Ralph Connor

where the battalion ENJOYED the hospitality of the city which never tires of welcoming and speeding on the various contingents of citizen soldiers of the West en route for the Front. There was a dinner and entertainment for the men. For Larry, because he was Acting Adjutant, there was no respite from duty through all the afternoon until the men had been safely disposed in the care of those who were to act as their hosts at dinner. Then the Colonel took him off to Jane and her father, who were waiting with their car to take them home.

"My! but you do look fine in your uniform," said Jane, "and so strong, and so big; you have actually grown taller, I believe." Her eyes were fairly standing out with pride and joy.

"Not much difference north and south," said Larry, "but east and west, considerable. And you, Jane, you are looking better than ever. Whatever has happened to you?"

"Hard work," said Jane.

"I hear you are in the Big Business up to your neck," said Larry. "There is so much to do, I can well believe it. And so your father is going? How splendid of him!"

"Oh, every one is doing what he can do best. Father will do the ambulance well."

"And I hear you are going too."

"I do not know about that," said Jane. "Isn't it awfully hard to tell just what to do? I should love to go, but that is the very reason I wonder whether I should. There is so much to do here, and there will be more and more as we go on, so many families to look after, so much work to keep going; work for soldiers, you know, and for their wives and children, and collecting money. And it is all so easy to do, for every one is eager to do what he can. I never knew people could be so splendid, Larry, and especially those who have lost some one. There is Mrs. Smart, for instance, and poor Scallan's mother, and Scuddy's."

"Jane," said Larry abruptly, "I must see Helen. Can we go at once when we take the others home?"

"I will take you," said Jane. "I am glad you can go. Oh, she is lovely, and so sweet, and so brave."

Leaving the Colonel in Dr. Brown's care, they drove to the home of Helen Brookes.

"I dread seeing her," said Larry, as they approached the house.

"Well, you need not dread that," said Jane.

And after one look at Helen's face Larry knew that Jane was right. The bright colour in the face, the proud carriage of the head, the saucy look in the eye, once so characteristic of the "beauty queen" of the 'Varsity, were all gone. But the face was no less beautiful, the head carried no less proudly, the eye no less bright. There was no shrinking in her conversation from the tragic fact of her lover's death. She spoke quite freely of Scuddy's work in the battalion, of his place with the men and of how they loved him, and all with a fine, high pride in him.

"The officers, from the Colonel down, have been so good to me," she said. "They have told me so many things about Harry. And the Sergeants and the Corporals, every one in his company, have written me. They are beautiful letters. They make me laugh and cry, but I love them.

Dear boys, how I love them, and how I love to work for them!" She showed Larry a thick bundle of letters. "And they all say he was so jolly. I like that, for you know, being a Y. M. C. A. man in college and always keen about that sort of thing—I am afraid I did not help him much in that way—he was not so fearfully jolly. But now I am glad he was that kind of a man, a good man, I mean, in the best way, and that he was always jolly. One boy says, 'He always bucked me up to do my best,' and another, a Sergeant, says, 'He put the fear of God into the slackers,' and the Colonel says, 'He was a moral tonic in the mess,' and his chum officer said, 'He kept us all jolly and clean.' I love that. So you see I simply have to buck up and be jolly too."

"Helen, you are wonderful," said Larry, who was openly wiping away his tears. "Scuddy was a big man, a better man I never knew, and you are worthy of him."

They were passing out of the room when Helen pulled Larry back again. "Larry," she said, her words coming with breathless haste, "don't wait, oh, don't wait. Marry Jane before you go. That is my great regret to-day. Harry wanted to be married and I did too. But father and mother did not think it wise. They did not know. How could they? Oh! Larry," she suddenly wrung her hands, "he wished it so. Now I know it would have been best. Don't make my mistake, don't, Larry. Don't make my mistake. Thank you for coming to see me. Good-bye, Larry, dear. You were his best friend. He loved you so." She put her arms around his neck and kissed him, hastily wiped her eyes, and passed out to Jane with a smiling face.

They hurried away, for the hours in Winnipeg were short and there was much to do and much to say.

"Let her go, Jane," said Larry. "I am in a deuce of

a hurry."

"Why, Larry, what is the rush about just now?" said Jane in a slightly grieved voice.

"I have something I must attend to at once," said Larry. "So let her go." And Jane drove hard, for the most part in silence, till they reached home.

Larry could hardly wait till she had given her car into the chauffeur's charge. They found Dr. Brown and the Colonel in the study smoking.

"Dr. Brown," said Larry, in a quick, almost peremptory voice, "may I see you for a moment or two in your office?"

"Why, what's up? Not feeling well?" said Dr. Brown, while the others looked anxiously at him.

"Oh, I am fit enough," said Larry impatiently, "but I must see you."

"I am sure there is something wrong," said Jane, "he has been acting so queer this evening. He is so abrupt. Is that the military manner?"

"Perhaps so," said the Colonel. "Nice chap, Larry—hard worker—good soldier—awfully keen in his work—making good too—best officer I've got. Tell you a secret, Jane—expect promotion for him any time now."

Meantime Larry was facing Dr. Brown in his office. "Doctor," he said, "I want to marry Jane."

"Good heavens, when did this strike you?"

"This evening. I want to marry her right away."

"Right away? When?"

"Right away, before I go. To-night, to-morrow."

"Are you mad? You cannot do things like that, you know. Marry Jane! Do you know what you are asking?"

"Yes, Doctor, I know. But I have just seen Helen Brookes. She is perfectly amazing, perfectly fine in her courage and all that, and she told me about Scuddy's death without a tear. But, Doctor, there was a point at which she broke all up. Do you know when? When she told me of her chief regret, and that was that she and Scuddy had not been married. They both wanted to be married, but her parents were unwilling. Now she regrets it and she will always regret it. Doctor, I see it very clearly. I believe it is better that we should be married. Who knows what will come? So many of the chaps do not come back. You are going out too, I am going out. Doctor, I feel that it is best that we should be married."

"And what does Jane think about it?" enquired the Doctor, gazing at Larry in a bewildered manner.

"Jane! Good Lord! I don't know. I never asked her!" Larry stood gaping at the Doctor.

"Well, upon my word, you are a cool one!"

"I never thought of it, Doctor," said Larry.

"Never thought of it? Are you playing with me, boy?" said the Doctor sternly.

"I will go and see her," said Larry, and he dashed from the

room. But as he entered the study, dinner was announced, and Larry's question perforce must wait.

Never was a meal so long-drawn-out and so tedious. The Colonel and Jane were full of conversation. They discussed the news from the West, the mine and its prospects, the Lakeside Farm and its people, the Colonel's own family, the boys who had enlisted and those who were left behind, the war spirit of Canada, its women and their work and their heroism (here the Colonel talked softly), the war and its prospects. The Colonel was a brilliant conversationalist when he exerted himself, and he told of the way of the war in England, of the awakening of the British people, of the rush to the recruiting offices, of the women's response. He had tales, too, of the British Expeditionary Force which he had received in private letters, of its glorious work in the Great Retreat and afterwards. Jane had to tell of her father's new Unit, now almost complete, of Mr. Murray's new battalion, now in barracks, of the Patriotic Fund and how splendidly it was mounting up into the hundreds of thousands, and of the Women's War Association, of which she was Secretary, and of the Young Women's War Organisation, of which she was President; and all with such animation, with such radiant smiles, with such flashing eyes, such keen swift play of thought and wit that Larry could hardly believe his eyes and ears, so immense was the change that had taken place in Jane during these ten months. He could hardly believe, as he glanced across the table at her vivid face, that this brilliant, quick-witted, radiant girl was the quiet, demure Jane of his college days, his good comrade, his chum, whom he had been inclined to patronise. What was this that had come to her? What had released those powers of mind and soul which he could now recognise as being her own, but which he had never seen in action. As in a flash it came to him that this mighty change was due to the terribly energising touch of War. The development which in normal times would have required years to accomplish, under the quickening impulse of this mighty force which in a day was brought to bear upon the life of Canada, this development became a thing of weeks and months only. War had poured its potent energies through her soul and her soul had responded in a new and marvellous efflorescence. Almost over night as it were the flower of an exquisite womanhood, strong, tender, sweet, beautiful, had burst into bloom. Her very face was changed. The activities with which her days and nights were filled had quickened all her vital forces so that the very texture and colour of her skin radiated the bloom of vigorous mental and physical health. Yet withal there remained the same quick, wise sympathy, quicker, wiser than before war's poignant sorrows had disciplined her heart; the same far-seeing vision that anticipated problems and planned for their solution; the same proud sense of honour that scorned things mean and gave quick approval to things high. As he listened Larry felt himself small and poor in comparison with her. More than that he had the sense of being excluded from her life. The war and its activities, its stern claims, its catastrophic events had taken possession of the girl's whole soul. Was there a place for him in this new, grand scheme of life? A new and terrible master had come into the lordship of her heart. Had love yielded its high place? To that question Larry was determined to have an answer to-night. To-morrow he was off to the Front. The growing fury of the war, its appalling losses, made it increasingly doubtful that he should ever see her face again. What her answer would be he could not surely say. But to-night he would have it from her. If "yes" there was time to-morrow to be married; if "no" then the more gladly he would go to the war.

After dinner the Doctor and the Colonel took their way to the study to smoke and talk over matters connected with military organisation, in regard to which the Doctor confessed himself to be woefully ignorant. Jane led Larry into the library, where a bright fire was burning.

"Awfully jolly, this fire. We'll do without the lights," said Larry, touching the switch and drawing their chairs forward to the fire, wondering the while how he should get himself to the point of courage necessary to his purpose. Had it been a few months ago how easy it would have been. He could see himself with easy camaraderie put his arm about Jane with never a quiver of voice or shiver of soul, and say to her, "Jane, you dear, dear thing, won't you marry me?" But at that time he had neither desire nor purpose. Now by some damnable perversity of things, when heart and soul were sick with the longing for her, and his purpose set to have her, he found himself nerveless and shaking like a silly girl. He pushed his chair back so that, unaware to her, his eyes could rest upon her face, and planned his approach. He would begin by speaking of Helen, of her courage, of her great loss, then of her supreme regret, at which point he would make his plea. But Jane would give him no help at all. Silent she sat looking into the fire, all the vivacity and brilliance of the past hour gone, and in its place a gentle, pensive sadness. The firelight fell on her face, so changed from what it had been in those pre-war days, now so long ago, yet so familiar and so dear. To-morrow at this hour he would be far down the line with his battalion, off for the war. What lay beyond that who could say? If she should refuse—"God help me then," he groaned aloud, unthinking.

"What is it, Larry?" she said, turning her face quickly toward him.

"I was just thinking, Jane, that to-morrow I—that is—" He paused abruptly.

"Oh, Larry, I know, I know." Her hands went quickly to her breast. In her eyes he saw a look of pain so acute, so pitiful, that he forgot all his plan of approach.

"Jane," he cried in a voice sharp with the intensity of his feeling.

In an instant they were both on their feet and facing each other.

"Jane, dear, dear Jane, I love you so, and I want you so." He stretched out his arms to take her.

Startled, her face gone deadly pale, she put out her hands against his breast, pushing him away from her.

"Larry!" she said. "Larry, what are you saying?"

"Oh, Jane, I am saying I love you; with all my heart and soul, I love you and I want you, Jane. Don't you love me a bit, even a little bit?"

Slowly her arms dropped to her side. "You love me, Larry?" she whispered. Her eyes began to glow like stars in a pool of water, deep and lustrous, her lips to quiver. "You love me, Larry, and you want me to—to—"

"Yes, Jane, I want you to be my wife."

"Your wife, Larry?" she whispered, coming a little closer to him. "Oh, Larry," she laid her hands upon his breast, "I love you so, and I have loved you so long." The lustrous eyes were misty, but they looked steadily into his.

"Dear heart, dear love," he said, drawing her close to him and still gazing into her eyes.

She wound her arms about his neck and with lips slightly parted lifted her face to his.

"Jane, Jane, you wonderful girl," he said, and kissed the parted lips, while about them heaven opened and took them to its bosom.

When they had come back to earth Larry suddenly recalled his conversation with her father. "Jane," he said, "when shall we be married? I must tell your father."

"Married?" said Jane in a voice of despair. "Not till you return, Larry." Then she clung to him trembling. "Oh, why were you so slow, Larry? Why did you delay so long?"

"Slow?" cried Larry. "Well, we can make up for it now." He looked at his watch. "It's nine o'clock, Jane. We can be married to-night."

"Nonsense, you silly boy!"

"Then to-morrow we shall be married, I swear. We won't make Helen's mistake." And he told her of Helen Brookes's supreme regret. "We won't make that mistake, Jane. To-morrow! To-morrow! To-morrow it will be!"

"But, Larry, listen. Papa—"

"Your father will agree."

"And my clothes?"

"Clothes? You don't need any. What you have on will do."

"This old thing?"

"Perfectly lovely, perfectly splendid. Never will you wear

anything so lovely as this."

"And then, Larry, what should I do? Where would I go? You are going off."

"And you will come with me."

But Jane's wise head was thinking swiftly. "I might come across with Papa," she said. "We were thinking—"

"No," cried Larry. "You come with me. He will follow and pick you up in London. Hurry, come along and tell him."

"But, Larry, this is awful."

"Splendid, glorious, come along. We'll settle all that later."

He dragged her, laughing, blushing, almost weeping, to the study. "She says she will do it to-morrow, sir," he announced as he pushed open the door.

"What do you say?" said the Doctor, gazing open-mouthed at him.

"She says she will marry me to-morrow," he proclaimed as if announcing a stupendous victory.

"She does!" said the Doctor, still aghast.

"Good heavens!" exclaimed the Colonel. "To-morrow? We are off to-morrow!"

Larry swung upon him eagerly. "Before we go, sir. There is lots of time. You see we do not pull out until after three. We have all the morning, if you could spare me an hour or so. We could get married, and she would just come along with us, sir."

Jane gasped. "With all those men?"

"Good Lord!" exclaimed the Colonel. "The boy is mad."

"We might perhaps take the later train," suggested Jane demurely. "But, of course, Papa, I have never agreed at all," she added quickly, turning to her father.

"That settles it, I believe," said Dr. Brown. "Colonel, what do you say? Can it be done?"

"Done?" shouted the Colonel. "Of course, it can be done. Military wedding, guard of honour, band, and all that sort of thing. Proper style, first in the regiment, eh, what?"

"But nothing is ready," said Jane, appalled at the rush of events. "Not a dress, not a bridesmaid, nothing."

"You have got a 'phone," cried Larry, gloriously oblivious of difficulties. "Tell everybody. Oh, sir," he said, turning to Dr. Brown with hand outstretched, "I hope you will let her come. I promise you I will be good to her."

Dr. Brown looked at the young man gravely, almost sadly, then at his daughter. With a quick pang he noted the new look in her eyes. He put out his hand to her and drew her toward him.

"Dear child," he said, and his voice sounded hoarse and strained, "how like you are to your mother to-night." Her arms went quickly about his neck. He held her close to him for a few moments; then loosing her arms, he pushed her gently toward Larry, saying, "Boy, I give her to you. As you deal with her, so may God deal with you."

Ralph Connor

"Amen," said Larry solemnly, taking her hand in his.

Never was such a wedding in Winnipeg! Nothing was lacking to make it perfectly, gloriously, triumphantly complete. There was a wedding dress, and a bridal veil with orange blossoms. There were wedding gifts, for somehow, no one ever knew how, the morning Times had got the news. There was a church crowded with friends to wish them well, and the regimental band with a guard of honour, under whose arched swords the bride and groom went forth. Never had the Reverend Andrew McPherson been so happy in his marriage service. Never was such a wedding breakfast with toasts and telegrams from absent friends, from Chicago, and from the Lakeside Farm in response to Larry's announcements by wire. Two of these excited wild enthusiasm. One read, "Happy days. Nora and I following your good example. See you later in France. Signed, Dean." The other, from the Minister of Militia at Ottawa to Lieutenant-Colonel Waring-Gaunt. "Your suggestion approved. Captain Gwynne gazetted to-morrow as Major. Signed, Sam Hughes."

"Ladies and Gentlemen," cried the Colonel, beaming upon the company, "allow me to propose long life and many happy days for the Major and the Major's wife." And as they drank with tumultuous acclaim, Larry turned and, looking upon the radiant face at his side, whispered:

"Jane, did you hear what he said?"

"Yes," whispered Jane. "He said 'the Major.'"

"That's nothing," said Larry, "but he said 'the Major's wife!'"

And so together they went to the war.

Choose from Thousands of 1stWorldLibrary Classics By

A. M. Barnard
Ada Leverson
Adolphus William Ward
Aesop
Agatha Christie
Alexander Aaronsohn
Alexander Kielland
Alexandre Dumas
Alfred Gatty
Alfred Ollivant
Alice Duer Miller
Alice Turner Curtis
Alice Dunbar
Allen Chapman
Alleyne Ireland
Ambrose Bierce
Amelia E. Barr
Amory H. Bradford
Andrew Lang
Andrew McFarland Davis
Andy Adams
Angela Brazil
Anna Alice Chapin
Anna Sewell
Annie Besant
Annie Hamilton Donnell
Annie Payson Call
Annie Roe Carr
Annonaymous
Anton Chekhov
Archibald Lee Fletcher
Arnold Bennett
Arthur C. Benson
Arthur Conan Doyle
Arthur M. Winfield
Arthur Ransome
Arthur Schnitzler
Arthur Train
Atticus
B.H. Baden-Powell
B. M. Bower
B. C. Chatterjee
Baroness Emmuska Orczy
Baroness Orczy
Basil King
Bayard Taylor
Ben Macomber
Bertha Muzzy Bower
Bjornstjerne Bjornson

Booth Tarkington
Boyd Cable
Bram Stoker
C. Collodi
C. E. Orr
C. M. Ingleby
Carolyn Wells
Catherine Parr Traill
Charles A. Eastman
Charles Amory Beach
Charles Dickens
Charles Dudley Warner
Charles Farrar Browne
Charles Ives
Charles Kingsley
Charles Klein
Charles Hanson Towne
Charles Lathrop Pack
Charles Romyn Dake
Charles Whibley
Charles Willing Beale
Charlotte M. Braeme
Charlotte M. Yonge
Charlotte Perkins Stetson
Clair W. Hayes
Clarence Day Jr.
Clarence E. Mulford
Clemence Housman
Confucius
Coningsby Dawson
Cornelis DeWitt Wilcox
Cyril Burleigh
D. H. Lawrence
Daniel Defoe
David Garnett
Dinah Craik
Don Carlos Janes
Donald Keyhoe
Dorothy Kilner
Dougan Clark
Douglas Fairbanks
E. Nesbit
E. P. Roe
E. Phillips Oppenheim
E. S. Brooks
Earl Barnes
Edgar Rice Burroughs
Edith Van Dyne
Edith Wharton

Edward Everett Hale
Edward J. O'Biren
Edward S. Ellis
Edwin L. Arnold
Eleanor Atkins
Eleanor Hallowell Abbott
Eliot Gregory
Elizabeth Gaskell
Elizabeth McCracken
Elizabeth Von Arnim
Ellem Key
Emerson Hough
Emilie F. Carlen
Emily Bronte
Emily Dickinson
Enid Bagnold
Enilor Macartney Lane
Erasmus W. Jones
Ernie Howard Pie
Ethel May Dell
Ethel Turner
Ethel Watts Mumford
Eugene Sue
Eugenie Foa
Eugene Wood
Eustace Hale Ball
Evelyn Everett-green
Everard Cotes
F. H. Cheley
F. J. Cross
F. Marion Crawford
Fannie E. Newberry
Federick Austin Ogg
Ferdinand Ossendowski
Fergus Hume
Florence A. Kilpatrick
Fremont B. Deering
Francis Bacon
Francis Darwin
Frances Hodgson Burnett
Frances Parkinson Keyes
Frank Gee Patchin
Frank Harris
Frank Jewett Mather
Frank L. Packard
Frank V. Webster
Frederic Stewart Isham
Frederick Trevor Hill
Frederick Winslow Taylor

Friedrich Kerst
Friedrich Nietzsche
Fyodor Dostoyevsky
G.A. Henty
G.K. Chesterton
Gabrielle E. Jackson
Garrett P. Serviss
Gaston Leroux
George A. Warren
George Ade
Geroge Bernard Shaw
George Cary Eggleston
George Durston
George Ebers
George Eliot
George Gissing
George MacDonald
George Meredith
George Orwell
George Sylvester Viereck
George Tucker
George W. Cable
George Wharton James
Gertrude Atherton
Gordon Casserly
Grace E. King
Grace Gallatin
Grace Greenwood
Grant Allen
Guillermo A. Sherwell
Gulielma Zollinger
Gustav Flaubert
H. A. Cody
H. B. Irving
H.C. Bailey
H. G. Wells
H. H. Munro
H. Irving Hancock
H. R. Naylor
H. Rider Haggard
H. W. C. Davis
Haldeman Julius
Hall Caine
Hamilton Wright Mabie
Hans Christian Andersen
Harold Avery
Harold McGrath
Harriet Beecher Stowe
Harry Castlemon
Harry Coghill
Harry Houidini

Hayden Carruth
Helent Hunt Jackson
Helen Nicolay
Hendrik Conscience
Hendy David Thoreau
Henri Barbusse
Henrik Ibsen
Henry Adams
Henry Ford
Henry Frost
Henry James
Henry Jones Ford
Henry Seton Merriman
Henry W Longfellow
Herbert A. Giles
Herbert Carter
Herbert N. Casson
Herman Hesse
Hildegard G. Frey
Homer
Honore De Balzac
Horace B. Day
Horace Walpole
Horatio Alger Jr.
Howard Pyle
Howard R. Garis
Hugh Lofting
Hugh Walpole
Humphry Ward
Ian Maclaren
Inez Haynes Gillmore
Irving Bacheller
Isabel Cecilia Williams
Isabel Hornibrook
Israel Abrahams
Ivan Turgenev
J.G.Austin
J. Henri Fabre
J. M. Barrie
J. M. Walsh
J. Macdonald Oxley
J. R. Miller
J. S. Fletcher
J. S. Knowles
J. Storer Clouston
J. W. Duffield
Jack London
Jacob Abbott
James Allen
James Andrews
James Baldwin

James Branch Cabell
James DeMille
James Joyce
James Lane Allen
James Lane Allen
James Oliver Curwood
James Oppenheim
James Otis
James R. Driscoll
Jane Abbott
Jane Austen
Jane L. Stewart
Janet Aldridge
Jens Peter Jacobsen
Jerome K. Jerome
Jessie Graham Flower
John Buchan
John Burroughs
John Cournos
John F. Kennedy
John Gay
John Glasworthy
John Habberton
John Joy Bell
John Kendrick Bangs
John Milton
John Philip Sousa
John Taintor Foote
Jonas Lauritz Idemil Lie
Jonathan Swift
Joseph A. Altsheler
Joseph Carey
Joseph Conrad
Joseph E. Badger Jr
Joseph Hergesheimer
Joseph Jacobs
Jules Vernes
Julian Hawthrone
Julie A Lippmann
Justin Huntly McCarthy
Kakuzo Okakura
Karle Wilson Baker
Kate Chopin
Kenneth Grahame
Kenneth McGaffey
Kate Langley Bosher
Kate Langley Bosher
Katherine Cecil Thurston
Katherine Stokes
L. A. Abbot
L. T. Meade

L. Frank Baum
Latta Griswold
Laura Dent Crane
Laura Lee Hope
Laurence Housman
Lawrence Beasley
Leo Tolstoy
Leonid Andreyev
Lewis Carroll
Lewis Sperry Chafer
Lilian Bell
Lloyd Osbourne
Louis Hughes
Louis Joseph Vance
Louis Tracy
Louisa May Alcott
Lucy Fitch Perkins
Lucy Maud Montgomery
Luther Benson
Lydia Miller Middleton
Lyndon Orr
M. Corvus
M. H. Adams
Margaret E. Sangster
Margret Howth
Margaret Vandercook
Margaret W. Hungerford
Margret Penrose
Maria Edgeworth
Maria Thompson Daviess
Mariano Azuela
Marion Polk Angellotti
Mark Overton
Mark Twain
Mary Austin
Mary Catherine Crowley
Mary Cole
Mary Hastings Bradley
Mary Roberts Rinehart
Mary Rowlandson
M. Wollstonecraft Shelley
Maud Lindsay
Max Beerbohm
Myra Kelly
Nathaniel Hawthrone
Nicolo Machiavelli
O. F. Walton
Oscar Wilde

Owen Johnson
P.G. Wodehouse
Paul and Mabel Thorne
Paul G. Tomlinson
Paul Severing
Percy Brebner
Percy Keese Fitzhugh
Peter B. Kyne
Plato
Quincy Allen
R. Derby Holmes
R. L. Stevenson
R. S. Ball
Rabindranath Tagore
Rahul Alvares
Ralph Bonehill
Ralph Henry Barbour
Ralph Victor
Ralph Waldo Emmerson
Rene Descartes
Ray Cummings
Rex Beach
Rex E. Beach
Richard Harding Davis
Richard Jefferies
Richard Le Gallienne
Robert Barr
Robert Frost
Robert Gordon Anderson
Robert L. Drake
Robert Lansing
Robert Lynd
Robert Michael Ballantyne
Robert W. Chambers
Rosa Nouchette Carey
Rudyard Kipling
Saint Augustine
Samuel B. Allison
Samuel Hopkins Adams
Sarah Bernhardt
Sarah C. Hallowell
Selma Lagerlof
Sherwood Anderson
Sigmund Freud
Standish O'Grady
Stanley Weyman
Stella Benson
Stella M. Francis

Stephen Crane
Stewart Edward White
Stijn Streuvels
Swami Abhedananda
Swami Parmananda
T. S. Ackland
T. S. Arthur
The Princess Der Ling
Thomas A. Janvier
Thomas A Kempis
Thomas Anderton
Thomas Bailey Aldrich
Thomas Bulfinch
Thomas De Quincey
Thomas Dixon
Thomas H. Huxley
Thomas Hardy
Thomas More
Thornton W. Burgess
U. S. Grant
Upton Sinclair
Valentine Williams
Various Authors
Vaughan Kester
Victor Appleton
Victor G. Durham
Victoria Cross
Virginia Woolf
Wadsworth Camp
Walter Camp
Walter Scott
Washington Irving
Wilbur Lawton
Wilkie Collins
Willa Cather
Willard F. Baker
William Dean Howells
William le Queux
W. Makepeace Thackeray
William W. Walter
William Shakespeare
Winston Churchill
Yei Theodora Ozaki
Yogi Ramacharaka
Young E. Allison
Zane Grey

www.ingramcontent.com/pod-product-compliance
Lightning Source LLC
Chambersburg PA
CBHW020827030726
47496CB00001B/131